THE
LAST
LUMENIAN

S.G. BLAISE

Second paperback edition June 2021

Book design by Dissect Designs
Edited by Julie Tibbott and William Drennan
Map illustrated by Clifton Chandler

Paperback ISBN: 978-1-7347605-0-7
E-Book ISBN: 978-1-7347605-6-9

www.thelastlumenian.com

To Alex who read every version without cringing.

To Gabe who put aside his dislike of reading for ten days (that's how long it took to finish reading this story.)

To my Mom: It's done now.

To all of you, dear readers, who took a chance without realizing the dangers of how addictive this story will be. Good news: there will be more to come.

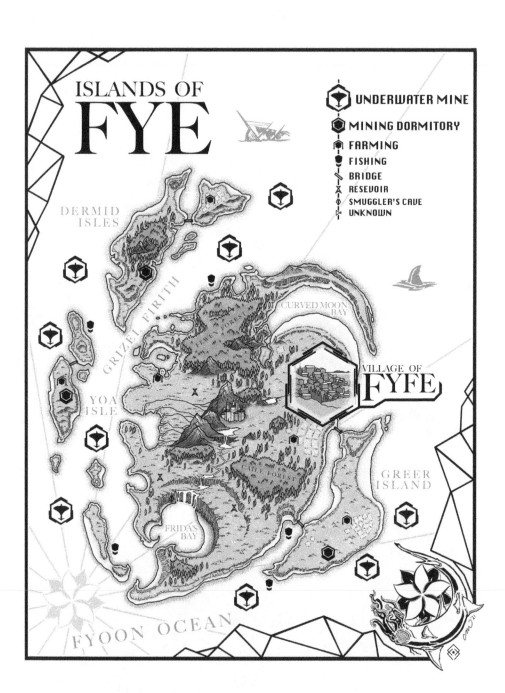

CHAPTER 1

"I can't breathe," I say through clenched teeth. Panic cascades down my spine like waves of a crushing tide. Panic so familiar yet so alien. My constant companion for the past fourteen years, since I was five.

My skin burns hot-and-cold-and-hot-again. Black spots bleed into my vision until it narrows into a pinpoint. I can no longer see the control compartment of our beat-up space vessel.

My seat swallows me up. I buck against its constraints, tearing against the tight harness. "I have to get out of here!"

I can't slow my breathing. The icy air burns against my throat with each inhalation. I am drowning without being in water.

"Lilla, listen to my voice," Arrov, the pilot of our ship, says. "I am here. You're not alone."

He brushes my hands to the side, off the stubborn harness buckles. With a click, the restraints cutting into me disappear.

I spring to my feet. The urge to flee! to run! pumps my blood, drowning out the hum of the ship.

A gentle hand touches mine.

Still blind to my surroundings, I grasp it before it can retreat. My lifeline out of the madness.

"You're fine. You'll be all right now."

Arrov's voice conjures his image—his almost seven-foot height, his athletic build, his angular face with pale-blue skin framed by short dark-blue hair, his straight nose and always smiling lips. I've heard him called "stunningly handsome" behind his back, followed by heaving sighs. I must admit they're right. Of course I would never say that out loud in his presence!

His thumb rubs a circle in my palm, a mesmerizing motion. I focus on his touch. For the first time since setting foot on this godsforsaken ship, I can take a deep breath.

Inhale through the nose, exhale through the mouth.

Again.

1

Minutes, or hours, drag by before the hot-and-cold-and-hot-again vanish. I look up, right into blue eyes that are so dark they're almost black.

"Better?"

I nod.

Arrov flashes white, even teeth. His smile makes him appear younger than I am, though he is in his midtwenties.

I look at our hands, embarrassed that he had to witness one of my "episodes," and I pull my hand away. Arrov is the only person in the rebellion who doesn't judge me. Or hold who I am against me. Will that change from now on? I shudder.

"Here, this should help." Arrov takes off his jacket and drapes it over my shoulders.

"I was getting hot anyway," he says, cutting off any argument. "I don't think the temp controls work on this junk."

"Thank you." I burrow into his warm jacket.

A dark blue blush appears on Arrov's cheeks. He is the perfect image of his home planet, A'ice. One of the richer worlds in the nineteen-planet-strong Pax Septum Coalition, where winter rules three quarters of the year.

My gaze flickers to the control panel, outdated with its manual levers. "We should check for incoming messages . . ." my voice trails off when I notice a fast blinking light, signaling incoming messages. How long has it been blinking like that?

Arrov sees it too, and a flash of concern crosses his expression.

My stomach drops. We had three tasks: wait for the message from the rebellion's patron; respond with the code to receive coordinates; and meet with their caravan to load supplies. Simple.

Arrov runs his fingers over the controls to retrieve the message. "We missed our chance. They sent the message more than ten minutes ago."

Ten minutes! By making the caravan wait, we indicated "mission compromised."

"But I'll send our code anyway." Arrov taps a few controls. "Maybe they waited for us."

And maybe I'd turn into a believer of the Archgoddess of the Eternal Light and Order and start praying for Her help. As if.

We stare at the light, waiting for it to blink again. Without getting the coordinates, we have no hope of completing our mission.

"Anything?" I sit back before I start pacing. I buckle my harness, but this time I don't make it as tight. Better not to trigger the panic that hovers at the edge of my consciousness, waiting to pounce. Never fully gone.

Arrov glances at me. "Nothing."

"Xor will be furious!" I blew the mission. My first mission. One that I volunteered for, and only got because Arrov offered to pilot the craft. It seems that bad luck *is* contagious.

"Don't beat yourself up, Lilla. There will be other chances."

I am not so sure about that. I proved Xor's right-hand man, Belthair, right. I failed the mission as he predicted.

Something appears on our view screen.

Arrov, oblivious, says, "Listen, I know how you must feel—"

"But—" I point toward the view screen.

Arrov grabs my flailing hand in both of his. "I know there is a lot of pressure on you right now."

"You don't understand—"

"You're right." He pats my hand. "I can't understand, but I can imagine how you must worry. But you cannot overreact—"

"Stop!" I shout.

"No need to be so harsh, I was just trying to—"

"Asteroids!"

CHAPTER 2

"There shouldn't be asteroids here," Arrov curses, but it gets lost in the blaring tocsins.

Debris clang, bouncing off the hull of our vessel. The flickering overhead light shuts off, only to come back flashing red and yellow.

My vision fills with a porous light-gray asteroid, the size of a small mountain, tumbling toward us, in the midst of other giant orbs.

"Get us out of here!" Where did they come from? A second ago this quadrant was empty except for the blinking stars.

"I'm trying!" Arrov shouts. "If only this stupid junk would work!"

Is this ancient spacecraft with its faded green paint and rusting metal going to be our tomb?

Dents appear everywhere, and the craft jars and jerks. The screeching noise shrieks louder than the alarms.

The sensory overload is too much. My brain can't process so much danger.

"We have to evacuate!" Arrov shouts.

"Evacuate? Where?"

Before Arrov can respond, the whole stern of the ship tears clean off. Wires and jagged metal hang. Billowing smoke obscures our view.

Time ceases to exist.

Then space rushes in.

CHAPTER 3

Six Months Earlier

My life should replay in my mind right before my death. Instead, it gets stuck on that horrible day.

The day of The Wedding.

All my troubles started then.

"Forgive me, Mom," I whisper into the silence of the resting gardens. There is no one to overhear my words. Yet it feels sacrilegious to disturb the quiet of the gardens, where those no longer with us rest. Embraced by Lume and guarded by the Archgoddess of the Eternal Light and Order.

Long ash-white branches of weeping willows sweep over small rock piles, tied together with silk ribbons. They are the markers of each ancestor. Cold and crisp wind rushes through, rustling the long wispy strands, fluttering the ribbons. Purple flowers lift off the branches, drifting on the currents, perfuming the air in a silent prayer only nature can conjure.

I close my eyes. "We are made of Lume. When we die, we return to Lume." The traditional invocation to The Lady echoes in my mind. It brings no comfort. Only a sad reminder of that rainy day. When life without Mom started and childhood ended.

I lean back on my elbows, not caring how the long blades of grass stain my dress. The rhythmic sounds of water lapping on the rocks below mingle with the chirping of birds above. The last flock to leave as fall pushes summer out of its way on Fye Island. A perfect day for a wedding.

That fog-cursed wedding! What would Mom do in my place?

Goose bumps run down my arms. Even the light of two suns can't seem to bring any warmth today.

Footsteps grind on the pebbled path.

I sit up, hugging my knees. I am not ready.

"It's hard to believe that it has been fourteen years," Glenna, my best friend, says from behind me.

I wipe a tear from the corner of my eye. "There isn't a single day when I don't miss her. I wish she could be here." Then this dreadful event wouldn't be happening.

Glenna tucks a few locks of her crimson hair that escaped from her elegant bun behind her ear. Her dark crimson eyes glint in compassion. "If my healer's oath wouldn't hold me, I would—"

A throat cleared interrupts her.

Both of us turn to face six guards. Metal helmets cover their faces, blending into half of a chest plate and a black leather tunic—a style that's more ornamental now than it was seven hundred years ago. A nod to our pirate past, along with the serrated cutlass swords that hang from their belts.

Glenna helps me up. "It's time."

"She sent guards to escort me," I say, as the guards position themselves around us, like a living cage. What a grotesque procession we make.

"Of course she did," Glenna says as we follow after them. "You played right into *her* hands."

Glenna is right. I should have known better.

For the rest of the short trip, I stay silent. We march down the hill, toward the white sands of the beach, the scene of the big celebration.

The whole court is here. The guards cut a path through the elegant silk forest of the ma'hars and ma'haras—lords and ladies.

As we pass, they bow. Their mutterings are as vicious as their smiles are polite.

"The ma'hana had to make a scene."

Just surviving another day at court.

"The ma'hana never fit in. Now what will she do?"

Who would want to fit in here? All they care about is what to wear, or how to stay young forever.

"The ma'hana deserves to be put in her place."

They can try.

Suddenly the crowd surges toward me, shoving the guards too close.

Panic rises and my throat locks, constricting air.

No! Not now! I hold my breath until black spots dance in my vision. Fainting is better than having an episode in front of everyone.

Something ice cold lands in my hand. It's a small hydro-gel pack. "Just breathe," Glenna whispers.

I grip the cold pack, hiding it against my dress. Allowing the cold to distract me.

The guards push back the courtiers, and I force a deep breath into my struggling lungs.

A cool ocean breeze rustles my gown and chills the sweat on my forehead. I don't dare raise my hand to wipe it off. It might still shake.

Glenna stops and takes the gel pack back. She cannot follow me from this point. She has to go to the servants' side, all the way in the back. Behind the high society members. Behind the low society members. Behind the few selected esteemed civilians who earned their respected status by working well into their old age.

The guards step aside to reveal a hovering wooden platform infused with A'ris—air magic, the third of the six light elements.

Since mages infused our technology with elemental magic hundreds of years ago, Uhna entered a golden age. Technological marvels sprouted. Uhna's economy boomed. Until we were the wealthiest planet in the Pax Septum Coalition. By the time the other planets joined the magical technology wave, we were miles ahead of them in progress.

I'm sure the mages never intended the technology they infused to be applied this way. For pomp. For a stupid wedding. A wedding so cliché it's pathetic.

A white gauzy canopy held in place by A'ris magic hovers over a hexagonal wooden platform. Around the canopy, a flock of colorful birds flutters in place, tamed by A'nima, the fifth light element. Around the platform, a multitude of palm trees waves. Their crowns of frond leaves sparkle with millions of crystal diamond specks, painted on like artificial snow. In the middle of the platform, a shimmering wall of water arches down, suspended by A'qua, the first light element. It symbolizes the all-powerful Fyoon Ocean, from which all titles originate.

I climb the seven wooden steps to the platform and take my place behind my half brother Nic. He could be a replica of my father with his fit build, black hair and dark brown eyes.

7

Behind are the fourteen advisers, grouped in sevens on each side of Father. Their disapproving gazes weigh on me, judging. Only High Adviser Ellar smiles at me. He tried to console me yesterday, but I found no comfort in his wise words. Both of us knew this wedding was not fair.

Behind my father, the ma'ha and king of Uhna. He stands tall in his formal white uniform—a long jacket with a red sash across it, and sharp pants. He looks in control. Happy. As if this is something he truly wants.

My father glances back at me, smiling in a peace offering. I glare until his expression sobers. Until he has to look back. Toward *her*.

Nic hands me a small bouquet of white starflowers, the national symbol, representing innocence. "I thought you'd never show. They wouldn't start the ceremony without you, sis."

"How lucky I am." I grip the flowers, clenching them hard. Poor things. It's not their fault. It's *hers*.

Beathag. Father's bride-to-be, who is barely older than I am, and a third of my father's sixty-five. Someone I used to know well and thought I'd never see again.

As if she knows I am thinking about her, Beathag turns toward me. She looks over her slender shoulder, left bare by the body-hugging red lace dress. Her long blond hair falls down on her back with starflowers woven into the hair.

I meet her hazel eyes head on. Daring her to blink first. Daring her to read my mind and see how much she is not welcome here.

Her eyes flicker behind me, where the guards still wait, as if anticipating my escape. She dismisses me with a sniff.

Nic pokes an elbow in my side. "Stop prodding the hag, sis."

"She started it." I am forced to witness this wedding because of her.

A stranger steps in front of the couple with confidence that borders on arrogance. Loud murmurs sweep through the crowd.

He stands tall, his long silver hair flying over his shoulders in the breeze. He wears a black robe, with all six light elements embroidered in a circle over his heart.

He introduces himself as Royal Elementalist Mage Ragnald, causing another wave of outraged mutterings. No mages have been in the royal court in my lifetime. It seems this wedding has an underlying political current.

No one has forgotten the Magical Cleansing War twenty-five years ago that ravaged the Pax Septum Coalition and took its toll on the people. Millions were killed, while hundreds of thousands ended up with terrible injuries from the battle mages' magic. Incurable by our healers. Ironically, the coalition won the war by the superior power of the elemental magic-in-fused weapons. Weapons that the mages created, but out of pride refused to use.

For more than two decades, we hadn't seen a single mage. They were banned from entering any coalition worlds. Yet here he is, the first one allowed to set foot on Uhna. And he is officiating Father's marriage as if the mages are all forgiven.

Is he the first mage in *all* the Pax Septum Coalition to leave Raghild, the mages' home world?

"And let those who have anything to say," Royal Elementalist Ragnald declares, "say it now without repercussion. Hence we can all judge this wedding and the direction in which it may proceed."

My heart jumps into my throat. Sweat breaks out on my palms. My skin burns hot-and-cold-and-hot-again. I open my mouth.

"Don't do it, sis. Just don't—"

"It's not right!" I say with a ringing voice.

CHAPTER 4

"Then what happened?" Eita asks.

It's dawn, but the wedding celebration is still going on at the beach. I escaped to the kitchen. Hiding from my family and the drunken court. Drowning my humiliation in boomberry tarts Eita served me.

At first I was hesitant to talk to Eita, and not just because of her age— sixteen, but so tiny she looks more like ten. Before, I always confided in Deidre, but her advanced age forced her to rely on others more lately. Like on Deidre's apprentice Eita. Nothing I told the young girl made it back to me as gossip, cementing my trust in her.

I offer her a tart, and after a moment of hesitation she takes it.

"The whole court got quiet." I shudder. "Father and Beathag looked at me as if I'd morphed into a deepwater shark. I thought they'd throw me into the ocean and feed me to one for my insolence." It is, after all, the traditional punishment for treason.

Eita gasps, the bite she took almost falling from her mouth. "They wouldn't do that to you, Your um . . . would they?" After all this time, she still falls back to the habit of calling me Your Highness, a title all servants must use in court. But we are not at court. Besides, my father and my brother are called that. Every time I hear it, I look over my shoulder, expecting Father to appear and tell me how I disappointed him. Again.

"Ask my Uncle Louis. Oh, wait, you can't. Because he got executed precisely like that for colluding with civilians." Poor Uncle. He had high notions about democracy and voting. The saddest part, besides getting executed? He hated seafood. What a horrible way to die.

"Then what happened?"

I pick up another warm tart and devour it in one bite. Its sweet and tangy taste a delightful comfort.

"Before Father and Beathag could react, the mage came to my rescue. He acted unfazed and continued the ceremony without making a big deal out of it."

"That's great." Eita picks up the empty plate. With quick and efficient moves, she clears the countertop. "I mean, how horrible it must have been for you."

I nod and get to my feet. Stretching, I stifle a yawn. I itch to get out of this horrible dress, which represents everything that's wrong with the court—it's flashy, superficial, and stifling.

"I don't know what got into me." My feet throb, and I kick my high-heeled sandals off. "I hoped Father would change his mind. That he would remember Mom and wouldn't replace her with someone so wrong."

Tears spring into my eyes, I pick up my shoes to hide them. "I humiliated myself in front of the court. Yet again. Not that it matters."

Eita nods with understanding shining in her eyes. "You should get some rest and—"

"Do not presume to tell the ma'hana what to do!" a cold male voice snaps.

Both of us turn to see a man stepping out of the shadows and into the small circle of light coming from above Eita's work counter. "I should have you, an impetuous sh'all, whipped right here for daring to address Her Royal Highness without using her proper title!"

The man, dressed in a tight silk pantsuit, glares at Eita.

Sh'all? Who uses that archaic term for servant? Its origins go back to the pirate times, when the lowest-ranking mates were called "shells that cover the hull, or sh'alls." It's not only a derogatory term, but one my great-great-many-great grandfather eliminated from the court. Or so I thought.

I face the man. "Who are you?"

He has the bearing of a high society ma'har, someone who's used to ordering others around and expecting instant obedience. "Show me your crystal," I demand, knowing full well what a slap it is. Low society members, civilians, and servants are the ones required to identify themselves.

The man stiffens. On his cheeks purple patches appear, a sharp contrast with his alabaster skin. He swipes a fake blond strand out of his face and shows me the transparent crystalline pendant at the end of his necklace chain.

Crystalline, or crystal for short, is a personal computing and communication device and a language translator as well as a proclaimer of social rank. Everyone on Uhna carries one. The color of the chain and the shape of the pendants are the status identifiers. Mine is a platinum chain, for high society, with a hexagonally shaped crystal for the ruling house. His crystal is on a platinum chain, but it is diamond-shaped to represent a major house.

I turn his crystal over to check its back. Starflowers are etched on it to distinguish his house, and how far back his house's line goes. "Ma'har Irvine, heir to the Major House of Swinestones." It seems he is the last surviving heir of his house.

He bows just enough to be polite.

"That doesn't explain what you're doing here," I say and release the crystal.

Pursing his narrow lips, he murmurs, "Camp Seven, as I suspected," then snaps his fingers. Five guards rush into the kitchen and line up by the smirking lord.

"What is this?"

Ma'har Irvine glances at a pale Eita. A pair of guards grab her.

"Let her go this instant!" But the guards don't obey my order.

"I'm afraid that's not possible," the ma'har says, and nods toward the exit. The guards escort Eita out.

I try to follow her, but Irvine steps in front of me. "Let me introduce myself. I am the newly appointed Overseer of Refugee Affairs. It is with pleasure I express my gratitude for Your Highness's aid in the apprehension of another illegal refugee."

"My help?" Illegal refugee?

"Had you not reminded me, I never would have checked her necklace. She may have managed to disguise herself as a sh'all, but she couldn't hide that her crystal was a stolen one."

"But—"

"Caste lines are there for a reason, so everyone knows their correct place. When these lines are crossed, people get hurt."

CHAPTER 5

"I hope we're not too late," I murmur into my gloves, my breath coming out like a thick cloud of fog.

Next to me, Glenna yawns. I dragged her out of bed early this morning because I needed her help.

Harsh Fla'mma-infused floodlights shine an unforgiving glow over the sign WELCOME TO REFUGEE CAMP NUMBER SEVEN positioned above the black metal gates. But there is nothing welcoming about the camp. Barbed wire curls inward on top of the ten-foot-high cement walls surrounding the camp. Like a prison.

Glenna narrows her eyes at the unmoving line. "This is taking much longer than usual."

"It's that new Overseer Irvine," I say and drag my boot out of the muddy trail with a squelching sound.

The Old Capital City is just visible through the receding marine layer painted amber by the two suns' light. Cold wind carries various scents of the waking city. Its towering cloudscrapers loom over the camp, like silent glass giants.

"He is busy establishing his lines."

"What lines?" Glenna asks.

"The overseer believes in clear lines between societal ranks."

"He should be busy taking care of the camps, if you ask my opinion."

She is right. Nothing changed about the camp since it opened more than a hundred years ago. Refugees came to us from all over the Seven Galaxies. Many escaping their home worlds due to constant marauding or interstellar fighting. They came to Galaxy Five, to the Pax Septum Coalition worlds, to Uhna, for safe haven. What they've found was less than ideal.

Glenna pulls the hood of my blue healer's cloak lower over my head. "Remember, don't say a word. I'll take care of this." She turns smiling to the stocky guard in his syn-booth and lifts her bronze chain necklace to show the crescent-shaped crystalline pendant representing servants.

The guard glances at it and takes some notes on a digi-scroll, a hand-size frosted device of crystalline that can roll up on itself. Finished tapping on it, the guard grunts, pointing at me. "I need to see credentials for the other healer too."

Oh, no! If he realizes I'm from the palace, masquerading as a healer, Glenna will be arrested, or worse.

Glenna huffs. "Why are you wasting my time? Overseer Irvine ordered me here to take care of an urgent matter. Do you want to be responsible for disobeying the overseer? Can't imagine you'll find another cushy job like this, once fired." With a frustrated exhale, she extends a hand as if asking me to show my necklace.

The guard clutches the digi-scroll in his meaty hand. "No need for that, uh, ma'am," he says and waves us through the gates.

Inside the camp, I stop Glenna. "I don't know where Eita could be."

Men and women dressed in handwoven clothing mill around us on the mud-covered "main road." The colorful geometric patterns of their clothing are the only cheer in the grimy and overcrowded camp. Though the thin material that leaves parts of feathers, scales, or stone-patch skin visible will not protect them from the seven months of winter.

"She could be in any one of those billets," I say.

Long ramshackle containers, piled on top of each other without much logic, line the wide road. Small alleys between the five-to-seven-stories-high structures branch off from the main road, twisting deeper into the camp, like a rusted metal forest. There are no windows, only ragged curtains as doors. They look ready to tumble down from the harsh wind at any moment.

"This is pointless," I say, imagining the worst.

"Or you have to know where to look," Glenna says, watching a large group of refugees scuttle past us in a hurry. "Come on!"

We follow the group until a large gathering blocks our way.

Dozens of camp guards, armed with Fla'mma-infused machine guns, hold the surging throng back. Their riot gear—smoke-tinted helmets, with hovering and rotating energy fields circling their bodies—is a sharp contrast against the weaponless refugees.

Meaty noises sound like flesh being hit hard.

Glenna elbows people out of our way.

Six thin girls, bruised and bloody, and ranging in age from eight to fifteen, lie on the sullied floor of the lowest container. Eita, with tears streaming from her blackened, swollen eyes, hangs limp between two stout guards. The other guards beat a semiconscious man, her father, without care.

When one of the guards lifts his T'erra-infused baton, Glenna rushes in and grabs his arm.

Gasps ripple through the crowd as two dozen guards aim their machine guns on her with an audible whirring—the last sound you'll ever hear before the flaming bullets tear through you.

"That's enough!" Glenna shouts, her expression unfazed.

The camp guard lowers his baton to threaten her. "This is the business of the overseer. Step aside or you will be punished too."

She shakes her head. "I can't heal the dead."

"We're done here," the guard says. "Do what you must, healer, but finish in an hour. Understood?"

Glenna heads to the unconscious elderly man.

The guards shoulder their way past the crowd, dragging the sobbing Eita away.

Glenna runs after the departing guards. "Where are you taking her? I need care for her injuries too!"

One of the burly guards turns and slams his hand into Glenna's chest. The force of the blow sends her to the ground. "This refugee won't need healing where she's going. No one survives long in the crystal mines."

Wincing in pain, Glenna gets to her feet and returns to the beaten family.

I stare after the retreating guards. How is this equal punishment for whatever crime Eita committed? All she ever did was talk to me. And because of that she got caught.

"Lia!" Glenna shouts, using the shortened version of my name. "Get in here!"

When I enter the trashed container, the curious mob surges in. They fill up the small space in seconds. They surround us, pressing me into the rusted metal wall.

Panic clamors in my head. Burning heat makes me break into a sweat, then cold chills run goose bumps on my skin. Hot-and-cold-and-hot-again. Blood rushes in my ears, and I can't hear Glenna anymore. The container spins sideways.

"I can't!" I shout and stumble out.

"Lia, stop!"

CHAPTER 6

My heart thunders, matching the frantic rhythm of my running steps. I don't know where I am or how to get back. I have taken too many twisting alleyways.

I squint at a patch of sky, visible between the stacks of containers. Black clouds roll in—a storm must be close behind. As if to confirm, the wind picks up, plastering the blue cloak to my body and scattering loose debris in circles.

I don't know how much time has passed. I don't dare pull out my crystal to check, for fear of getting caught. It's not just my hide at risk—it's Glenna's, too.

I shouldn't have run away like that. Like a coward.

I reach a dead end with a small gathering.

The refugees, mostly women and children, focus on a bald-headed green man whose face is obscured by a large leather tome. Before I could leave, a third eye on his forehead pops open, staring at me.

His voice rings out, "And the children had nothing to fear in the land of Ha'art, their new home. They were free to roam as they wished, and—"

A small boy, no older than four, lifts his feathered arm. "What is 'free'?"

Women look away; the few men present scowl at their feet. The child's mother pulls the boy under her winglike arm. "Forgive my son's interruption, Xor. He meant no offense; he was always too inquisitive for his own good."

Xor marks his place in the leather tome before closing it. "Nothing to apologize for, Gallina. You should be proud of him. He asked an important question." He turns to the little boy. "Tell me, Cornix, were you born in the camp?"

The little boy pulls away from his mother's wing. "Yes. How did you know?"

Out of nowhere, two pairs of hands grasp my forearms. Something presses in the small of my back. Something that feels very much like a pistol's muzzle.

"I am a healer—"

The pressure increases. "Be quiet."

17

"Free is when you can go wherever you want," Xor says, "eat whatever you want, and do whatever you want. Free is when nobody is telling you where to live. With the exception of your parents or guardians, of course."

Ringing laughter comes from the adults as if on cue, while the children groan in response.

A young girl's hand shoots into the air, with skin the texture of sun-cracked rocks. "You mean there are no fences, and no camp guards, and no rules?"

The kids whisper among themselves, as if the idea is impossible to comprehend. Another boy adds, "No beatings? No overseer?"

Xor flows to his feet in a smooth motion, like a soldier, and hands the tome to an elderly woman with a brown veil over her eyes. He rubs the boy's hair. "Not a single camp guard."

The kids cheer as he says, "Not if I can help it."

Then he strides past me. "Bring her."

CHAPTER 7

"We don't have time for the lost palace healer," a young male voice says. "The Teryn warriors are savaging my home world as we speak! We have to fight back! It's not too late to save the rest of my people!"

Someone pulls the blindfold off my eyes. Blinking against the sharp light of torch fire—no magic-infused lamps here—I look around. Not that there is much to see in the circular, windowless room that's made out of packed dirt, with cracked planks supporting its low ceiling.

A cacophony of angry shouts rises from the thirty people gathered. Xor perches on the only piece of furniture in the room, a rickety metal table, observing the crowd with all three of his eyes open. Next to him stands a muscled woman, her brown hair streaked with scarlet strands, framing a beautiful face with cooled-lava-toned skin. She reminds me of someone.

"Are you insane?" a bearded man asks. "Nobody in their right mind would go and fight the Brutes of the Seven Galaxies! We can't even get free from that Uhna tyrant or escape this camp! With what imaginary battalion would you have us go against their superior armada?"

Murmurs of "crazy" and "pure suicide" rise from the crowd.

The young man's face turns red. "I am not insane! I've seen those nightmarish things, and my family was among the disappeared. Then those brutes showed up. We have to do something!"

"What nightmarish things?" a tall woman asks. "Peterre, were you seeing them at the bottom of your bottles?" She mimics drinking with her hand. The crowd bursts into laughter.

The young man pushes forward, into the center of the room. "I am sober and have been for a while now. I am telling you," he says, looking around, but no one meets his pleading eyes, "those monsters—those were the children of the Archgod of Chaos and Destruction. When the Teryns came, we all knew our world was lost. They weren't there to save us. They were there to eliminate all threats. Even if it meant killing millions of innocents."

A red-haired man shakes his head. "Peterre, hold your ships. That would mean the Era War started."

Era War? I always thought it was something the mages made up to scare children and keep monarchs in line. Not a real one that spawned "nightmarish creatures."

Peterre nods. "We have to go now! We have to chase the Teryns away before it's too late!"

The red-haired man places a hand on Peterre's thin shoulder. "I hate to tell you this, friend, but there is nothing anyone can do. It's already too late for your world."

Peterre pales, with eyes shining. The tall woman pulls him into a hug. "It's not like we could have won against those warriors anyway."

"We won't be fighting the Teryn Praelium," the woman standing by Xor says. She doesn't raise her voice yet commands the attention of everyone. "We can't fight them. They have numbers, resources, and technological advantages over us."

Many nod their heads.

"If the Era War has started—and that is a big *if*, mind you—it's not our concern," she says. "We have more immediate problems, such as how to get the refugees free from the camps. That is where we focus."

Her voice is so familiar. I know I've met her. But where?

Clapping, feet drumming on the ground, and whistles are her answers. She smiles and her eyes, the color of lava, twinkle. Just like Captain Murtagh.

"Jorha," I shout over the racket, "does your father know you are here, instead of backpacking the Pax Septum Coalition?!"

Jorha laughs and dismisses the crowd.

"I wondered how long it would take for you to recognize me," Jorha says. "It took me a second when I saw you in the square. The real question is, does *your* father know you're Ma'hana Lilla?"

"What are you going to do with me?"

Jorha cocks her head. "We could ransom her."

"We wouldn't live long enough to spend the credits."

"There is that." Jorha clucks her tongue. "We could kill her."

Xor grimaces. "It wouldn't take long before they track her into this camp. She didn't come alone."

"Don't you get Glenna involved in this!" I take a step toward Xor, but Jorha bodychecks me.

"It's fine," Xor says. "She is not a threat. I admire your loyalty and fearlessness to protect your healer friend. You are very much like your mother."

"You knew my mom? I mean, how did you know her?" I don't recall seeing him when Mom and I visited the camp in secret.

"She was compassionate to our cause and wanted to join us," Xor says. "She wanted to do more for the refugees."

I blink. I had no idea that Mom knew about the rebellion and wanted to be a rebel.

Jorha scoffs. "We cannot let the ma'hana go back to the palace now that she knows where the rebel center is—"

"I have no idea where I am."

"—and I wouldn't take her word not to betray us."

"That doesn't leave us with many choices," Xor says. There is no jest in his voice. Only finality.

I won't have it! My skin burns hot-and-cold-and-hot-again.

"Let me join your ranks," I say, the words tumbling upon each other. "You knew my mom. You must know that I've been doing everything I can. I've been visiting the camp with Glenna to help out for many years. Let me fight for you—make me swear the blood oath if you don't believe me." Here's hoping the rumor that circulated in the camp is true.

Jorha snorts. "We don't need 'healers.'"

"I don't waste my blood on everyone," Xor says. "Why should I for you?"

"Because what I said is true." Because of the promise I made to my mom.

Xor pulls a dagger out of its sheath. He pricks his thumb, drawing a green drop of blood. "If I cut your hand, will your blood boil from touching mine, betraying your lie? Or will it lay calm in truth?"

He flips the dagger, while Jorha grabs my hand, palm up. "One way to find out," he says, and cuts the middle of my hand. Then he smears the red with his blood.

We stare at my palm. But the mixed blood remains unaffected.

"What do you know?" Jorha laughs under her breath. She slaps my back, making me stumble from the force of it. "Welcome to the rebellion, kid!"

CHAPTER 8

"It's been six months, kid," Jorha says next to me. She leans over to tie her bootlace. "It sure went by fast."

"Didn't feel that fast to me." I zip up my brown overalls, the rebellion "uniform." Everyone wears these overalls to protect our clothes and to help us blend in the myriad of camp maintenance crews. Who happen to have similar clothing.

"I told you it's not going to be easy to get accepted by the rebels. If they knew who you really are . . . Let's just say, it's a good thing only a few are aware. Give it time." She drops next to me and bumps her shoulder into mine, nearly toppling me off the bench. "If I can learn to like you, they can too. You'll see."

Each day I am here, I hide my hair in a tight knot, under a cap, and wear colored lenses. I look nothing like the ma'hana Father allows out into the public eye—all fancied up and plastered with layers of makeup. Shoved in the back, behind Father, Nic and a long line of advisers.

"All I've been allowed to do is trivial tasks," I complain. "I feel everyone thinks I am guilty of some crime, because I'm not pulling my weight. I know I am ready to do more! To show Xor and the others that I am capable." I might as well be back in the palace, haunting the library or the kitchen for all the good I am doing here. Ironically, it's the only reason Father isn't missing me—he thinks I am sulking around the palace.

Jorha jumps to her feet. "Enough with the self-pity. You want things to change? Do something about it. Complaining will get you nowhere." As she pulls me up, she adds, "Not that it's not entertaining. You crack me up, kid."

"I'm glad my problems are funny to you," I grumble and wipe the seat of my overalls to get rid of the dirt that covers everything here in thick layers. It permeates the air with a stuffy heaviness. I had to fight my panic in those first few weeks, but I was so anxious to fit in that the panic had no room left. "Besides, I asked you to stop calling me 'kid.'"

Jorha slaps my shoulder, propelling me through the curtained doorway of the dressing area. "When you stop acting like a child, I'll stop calling you 'kid.'"

I glare at her.

"See what I mean?" She laughs. You're hilarious, kid!"

I halt at the outskirts of the meeting room. Jorha moves to the front to wait for Xor. I can't wait to "help" in the canteen. *Again.*

"Hey," Arrov says. He is a new rebel, like me, but he is much more liked. Unlike me. "Maybe this time he'll call for you." He flashes an encouraging smile.

"Maybe." For these past few months, since I've known Arrov, he has been nothing but nice to me. One night, when we were stuck washing greasy pots in the canteen, he told me that never in his life had he done chores like this. A perk of being the seventh son of Queen Amra, ruler of A'ice. I confessed to him who I was, and why I was there, but he never treated me any different after that or betrayed my secret.

Arrov's arm brushes against mine. "Cheer up, Lia. Today might be the day."

"I'm sure Xor wouldn't want to ruin the running bet the rebels have—"

Someone shoves me, and I stumble forward.

"What the fog is she doing here?" an outraged male voice asks. He pushes me again and I fall into others, causing a tumult.

"Hey!" I say and turn. "What's your . . ." My voice trails off when my gaze lands on the man who stands in a wide stance before me.

It takes me a second to find my voice. "Belthair?" I whisper. "You're alive!"

"No thanks to you." He shoves his hair out of his eyes with one of his six hands.

He hasn't changed much since I last saw him. Two years ago. On that terrible night. It's hard to believe that the man who glares at me with so much hatred is the man I used to know so well. There is nothing warm in his dark gray eyes that flash at me. His handsome face twists in anger. His light gray skin feverish with dark gray patches. My mind cannot comprehend all his hate, even if it's justified.

"I didn't know . . . I would have . . ."

Belthair leans down from his six-foot height. "Spare me your useless excuses." He grabs me with his top right hand and drags me after him.

Most of the rebels are unaware of the scene that just happened in the back. They congratulate him, saying, "Welcome back, Major Belthair!" or "Great run, Major!" while he marches toward Xor and Jorha.

Then he propels me forward. Jorha catches me before I head-butt Xor.

"It's a bit much, don't you think, Major?" Jorha says, her gaze running between us. Then the light of realization sparks in the depth of her lava-colored eyes. "Since when do you bring your issues with your loveygulls to the rebel briefing?"

"I am not his . . . I mean it was a long time ago . . ."

"She is not my *loveygull*! She doesn't even deserve to—"

"Enough," Xor says, and the whole room comes to attention.

"What is she doing here?" Belthair demands. "You have no idea who she really is!"

How dare he ruin six months of hard work? Trample what little trust I managed to earn? I lunge at Belthair, but Arrov catches me across my waist and pulls back.

"I said enough!" Xor barks.

The rebels look stunned, or suspicious, already condemning me. I should be used to it by now, but it hurts more coming from the rebels than it did coming from the court.

Reading from a digi-scroll, Jorha tallies the rebels in the room.

I disengage from Arrov. "Thank you for helping me out. There is more to this than what you just saw . . ." I sound pathetic even to my own ears.

"I didn't know you cared what I thought."

Heat creeps into my face. I didn't know either.

"Due to an increase of missing rebels," Jorha says, "we now have a new policy: those who desert the rebellion will be shot on the spot when found. And mark my words, they will be found."

Ripples of shock go through the crowd at her announcement.

"Xor gives you this last chance to leave without consequence."

Belthair, with his eyes locked on me, nods toward the exit. I raise my chin, ignoring him.

Jorha quietly confers with Xor. A low hum sparks up as everyone talks among themselves.

"This is unusual," Arrov says.

"What do you mean?" I ask.

"They must have lost a great number of rebels to implement such drastic measures," he says as he glances around the room. "These rebels are volunteers, and the rebellion can't be picky—most refugees consist of the elderly, and women with children. We joined for the cause, and we stay of our own volition. Not because of fear. Something is not right."

No; this doesn't sound right.

Xor clears his throat. "I see no one has left. Good. Next up is a simple mission that I need volunteers to—"

I step forward. "I'll do it."

Xor sighs. "You don't even know what the mission is."

Arrov joins me. "We'll do it, sir."

Belthair smirks. "Let them do it and fail."

CHAPTER 9

Back to Now

"Wake up," a distant male voice says, full of urgency. It breaks into the darkness, at the edge of my consciousness.

I manage to lift one swollen eyelid, not much wider than a crack. Bright light blurs my vision, and sharp pain flashes through my head. Ow.

A hoarse groan escapes my chapped lips. Warm air, permeated by smells of metal, oil, and desert sand, tickles my nose when I inhale. Why am I in so much pain?

"Wake up," the man repeats, like an order.

I tilt my head in his direction, trying to tell him that I need a moment. But my throat clicks with a dry sound. It feels raw, as if I had screamed for hours. Had I? I can't remember.

Unconsciousness threatens again. My body drifts farther away from me. Drifting toward Lume. *We are made of light, and we will return to Lume at the end of our time. We are made of light . . .*

"Come back to me," he urges. Something sharp jabs into my neck. Liquid rushes into my vein, shattering the inviting light. Healing.

My back bows and my heart beats, *bam, bam, bam*. Its rhythm frantic at first, then gradually slowing. The unbearable pain recedes to mere discomfort levels, freeing me from its clutches.

"I thought I lost you there," he says.

Blinking a few times, I open my eyes. I glimpse space vessels around me.

I must be in a shuttlebay, judging by the sheer size of it, on an enormous spaceship. Metal arches with lines of light illuminate the cavernous room. The black spaceships look like aggressive stars with their three pairs of pointed wings. A visible array of weaponry glints on them. Fighter ships. Each ship has a red or yellow runic marking. I don't recognize the symbol, nor can I read the lines of writing on the walls.

The brightness is too much, and I rest my eyes for a moment. I should feel scared, but my instincts tell me I'm safe.

"Take your time." He lifts me up, bracing my back with a muscular arm.

When I open my eyes again, my gaze lands on a tanned, handsome-in-a-rough-way man, about twenty-five years old. He projects an air of authority. Short black hair frames an intriguing face with prominent cheekbones. A thin scar runs from his jagged eyebrow to his strong jawline. A straight nose perches above lips that are not too thin or fleshy. Intelligence flashes in his clear blue gaze. How would he look if he smiled?

A lopsided grin appears at the corner of his mouth, as if summoned by my wish. His face transforms to attractive.

I can't look away. I stare at him with burning cheeks.

His inquisitive gaze travels over my face, studying me. He wears a black military uniform. The jacket has lapels turned to the side, showing dark gray lining in a V. Colorful triangular buttons line up on it. His black pants are tight enough to show the muscular shape of his thighs. Knee-high black boots complete his outfit.

"I must be dead," I mutter. How else can I explain the fact that I ogled him as if I've never seen a man before? I had, of course. Just not many worthy of a second look.

"You're very much alive. I made sure of that."

Was I in an accident? Did he save me?

He shifts his hold on my back and flows to his feet without much effort, as if he isn't holding a person of a healthy weight.

The shuttlebay tilts, and I rest my head on his chest, fighting nausea. "Not so fast, please."

He stops moving, his muscles taut under my cheek. "Deep breaths. I'll take you to medical as soon as—"

"No!" I'm surprised at the vehemence in my tone. Something makes me believe that I am not an easy case when it comes to healing. I can almost remember . . . the memory is right there, before it slips away the next second.

"Thank you, but I am fine. I just need a bit more time." Maybe it's the gravitational pull that feels heavier on this ship than what I am used to.

Motion catches my eye. There are dozens of people—men and women in the hangar, blending in with their black overalls. They work around the ships, pretending hard not to watch us.

"Maybe you should put me down."

He doesn't respond, just strides out of the shuttlebay. We pass under an indigo blue arch to a corridor where the ceiling is much lower. Under his feet, a black grate covers wide, transparent tubes with green liquid swishing through them.

Something blue swims past in the green liquid. It's long with glimmering scales, reminding me of an Amnag lizard with its beady eyes. But I've never seen one with eight legs, an elongated head, and hair-thin teeth. "What on Uhna is that thing?"

"That's a beaked salamander. He, and many like him, keep our fuel clean from space particles and rare parasites that like the warmth of the fuel."

He glances down as if to see if I'm impressed. "That, um, must be helpful." The technology seems more advanced than I am familiar with. Which begs the questions—Where am I? How did I get here?

As if he can sense the shift in my thoughts, his arms tighten around me, and his smile falters. The time is now when reality has to return to break this illusion between us.

"Who are you?"

He seems to change under my gaze, transforming into someone else. "My name is Callum a'ruun, Second War General of the Teryn Praelium."

Teryn Praelium. I know that name.

I place a hand over my eyes, as if to block the recollection. But it bombards my mind; the barrages of thoughts are unstoppable. I've heard about them. More than I cared. Their empire, bent on conquering the Seven Galaxies, put more refugees into the camps than any other nation.

"The Brutes of the Seven Galaxies."

Hazy images of my first mission flicker in my mind. I know why I am wearing a blue healer's cloak under a white jacket. I remember having a panic attack on the ship. I remember the asteroids. And there was someone else there, too. The owner of the jacket. Arrov.

"Put. Me. Down."

CHAPTER 10

I should have known something wasn't right! Of all the places, I had to end up on the Teryns' doorstep. Or their spaceship's shuttlebay, to be exact.

The general lowers me to my feet with a deep sigh.

Swaying a bit, I ignore his outstretched hand and lean against one of the indigo blue columns for support. I jerk away when I touch material that feels like an animal hide. It feels warm to the touch, as if still alive. What the heck kind of ship is this?

"I see you've heard of us."

"Your violence, I mean. Your reputation precedes you."

A reddish-yellow light flashes in General Callum's eyes, blocking the blue of his iris for a split second. Then it's gone, making me wonder if I imagined it. "You have no idea what you're talking about."

"The fact that you're here, in Galaxy Five, is enough," I say. "Where is Arrov? What have you done with my pilot?" He took such a chance volunteering with me, and this is how I repay his kindness. By letting him fall into enemy hands. And forgetting all about him.

Another reddish-yellow light flashes again in his eyes. I knew I didn't imagine it!

"Your pilot is fine." He looks to the left with anticipation.

"Why are you avoiding my questions?"

"I'm not." He grabs me by the elbow and pulls me to the side.

"Let me go." I pull my arm out of his grasp. The wall next to me opens with a quiet swoosh.

Seven men march through, led by one whose black hair has streaks of scarlet, white, and blond. He keeps it longer than the others, past his shoulders. It frames his tanned, angular face. He is tall and wide-shouldered, like the men behind him. They wear uniforms similar to the general's, but the triangular buttons vary in color and quantity on each man. The man with the streaks in his hair has the most among them. Over each man's right shoulder, a sword's hilt pokes through.

"Do you need backup to deal with me?"

A cough that's a lot like laughter sounds from the man with streaked hair. The general growls, saying something in a foreign language my translator cannot decipher.

Two men holding a black rectangular board separate from the pack. With a few clicks, they turn it into a hovering stretcher. The general nods at the stretcher as the two men, medics, approach me.

I back away. "Don't even think about it."

"Why are you still refusing medical help? You can barely stand on your feet." He grasps the lapel of the white jacket.

I spin out of the jacket with a quick turn. "I am fine and can walk on my own." Pointing at the ruined jacket hanging in his hand, I add, "You can keep that."

"Fine." He throws it to the side. "If that's what you wish, no medical help for you."

"I hate to interrupt," the man with the streaks in his hair says, "but you look ready to keel over any second. You really should reconsider."

There is no filter with this man, is there? "I can assure you—"

"Colonel Teague, at your service," he says and winks at me.

"I can assure you, Colonel Teague, that I won't 'keel over,' and if I do, I'll give plenty of notice beforehand."

"Don't bother, Teague," the general says, "she's made up her mind." I have a feeling he isn't only referring about my health.

Colonel Teague shakes his head. "She looks half dead. At least. Maybe more."

"I'm not dead, half or otherwise." Yet. My stomach knots, and I rub it to ease the pressure. "If you could put me on the next spacecraft—" I swallow a sudden burst of saliva in my mouth. Going home sounds like a good idea right about now.

Colonel Teague pats my shoulder, making my knees buckle. "I can't see why not." He looks at the general. "Why is she still here and not on a ship heading to Uhna?"

General Callum crosses his arms. "I want to know the answer to that question too. The Uhnans guaranteed clear landing for us. Yet I found her right in a collision course with us. Explain that to me."

Colonel Teague tilts his head. "Could be coincidence."

"My pilot and I were on a, uh, healing mission," I stammer. "We were heading to Evander. Here are the documents to prove it." I pull out the crescent-shaped necklace on a bronze chain with the appropriate holo-papers the rebellion provided. "See? There's the royal crest of approval. Now can my pilot and I go home? Since you ruined our day already?"

Both the colonel and the general lean close to study the holo-papers projected above the crystal. These fake documents should pass muster with even the greatest detectors. The best hackers in the whole of Seven Galaxies, Isa and Bella, made them.

Colonel Teague takes out a small, transparent screen. Lines of language, similar to the markings on the wall, flash on it.

Long moments pass and sweat pebbles on my upper lip. Finally the colonel nods and puts the small screen away. "All is well, Healer Lia."

"Thank you, Colonel. Now—"

General Callum points at me. "She works in the royal palace. That's another coincidence?"

Colonel Teague spreads his arms. "Coincidences are not that rare."

"What are you implying?" I snap with as much indignation in my voice as all my years in the palace taught me.

"I believe you were there, in the path of our ship, on purpose," General Callum says. "You got there just in time to be rescued. By me. How convenient!"

Oh, the arrogance! And I thought him handsome mere minutes ago!

"Who in their right mind would risk their life just to meet you? That's ridiculous! If you ask these nice medics, I'm sure they'll give you something to help your ego deflate."

General Callum leans down until our noses almost touch. "That's exactly what a spy would say. And you even look like the perfect spy." His narrowed gaze travels from my eyes to my lips, over my body, then all the way back. "Petite and pretty, despite that horrible cloak. With the most amazing violet-colored hair. Paired with passionate violet-colored eyes that even now flash with such 'indignation.' As I said, the perfect spy." He turns away from me. "You give me no choice but to interrogate you and that pilot of yours."

Colonel Teague lifts a hand. "Wait a minute now. This is un—"

What do I have to do to get off this godsforsaken ship?!

I grab the general's arm and turn him to face me. I get close to him and poke his chest. "I didn't know you were coming." I poke him again. "I don't know who you are, but I don't care." Another poke. "How dare you accuse me of being a spy? I am nothing but a healer." A lie, but he doesn't need to know that. I poke him again for good measure. "Get it through your thick head!"

Swaying on my feet, I stumble back, pressing a hand into my aching belly.

"Excuses," General Callum says in a cold voice. "Where is your proof? You think that holo-paper will convince me of anything? Why should I believe you? I can smell you are hiding something!"

Smell? What is wrong with him?

I grasp the lapels of his jacket with both of my hands and stand on my tiptoes to glare into his eyes. "I am not a spy! Do you hear me? Not. A. Spy. If you don't believe me, then kill me! Otherwise let me go!"

He grasps my hands. "Now, you listen—"

But the pressure bursts in my stomach, rolling up in my throat.

Bending down, I throw up all over his shiny boots.

CHAPTER 11

Loch Ramor

Loch Ramor struggles to keep his breath under the canvas sack.

His mind races. *They know! My secret's been found out! They're going to get rid of me!*

Cold and disgusting panic rises. A feeling he isn't used to. For a second, he is transported forty years into the past. Into the frightened and traumatized child he once was. Powerless. But he isn't a child anymore.

He takes a breath, inhaling the putrid odor of old blood, dirt, and the pungent scent of excrement.

I have to stay calm. He goes through his routine of relaxing every one of his muscles. From head to toe, slowing his breathing.

This must be connected to the disappearances he was looking into. Disappearances of ma'hars and ma'haras from both high society and low society. Sh'alls as well. He must have been on the right track, because someone went to considerable effort to get him. Though how his kidnapping happened didn't make much sense.

Six men with rotting skin and blank stares entered his bedroom just before dawn. They dragged him out of his bed and shoved the revolting burlap sack over his head. A sack that reaches almost to his knees, secured around his body with tight ropes. They've been taking him deeper. Into the underbelly of the castle ever since.

They shouldn't have such complex knowledge of the palace. Other than himself, few are aware of the existence of these sublevels. The pirates used them for smuggling a long time ago. Now these creatures are smuggling him.

Any other man would have done either of two things by now: they would have tried to run, or they would have begged for mercy.

But Loch isn't just *any* man. He ceased to be one after he killed to get himself a better life. A life that he worked meticulously to build for more than forty years. *I won't let anyone take it from me!*

They push Loch when he slows, forcing him to keep moving. Stumbling, his bare feet slip in his own blood on the freezing cobblestones, broken and jagged from disuse. He counts each step to keep his mind off them.

It can't be long before we reach our destination. But he isn't worried. He has at least five different plans ready. He has money. He has influence. In no time he'll be back in his room.

His feet slide on a smooth surface. His kidnappers tear the sack off his head, taking a few strands of his well-conditioned hair with it.

Blinking against bright light, he looks around. His gaze takes in the polished white marble room with no windows or doors. The walls and floors blend into each other, creating an illusion of endless space.

This place shouldn't exist. He knows every corner of the palace and Fye Island, and he has never stumbled upon this room.

There has to be a way out. Loch turns. But there is no door. He runs his manicured fingers over the wall's smooth surface, searching for any seams. He can't detect any indication that there was a doorway there before. Impossible!

Loch turns back. A man stands across from him, holding a dripping paintbrush. An unfinished, artistic, and colorful landscape hovers in mid-air by the man, the paint still wet on the stretched canvas. A masterpiece.

Loch takes on a bored expression, careful not to let his surprise show. He wipes the sleeve of his pajamas, removing the stray strands the sack left behind.

When Loch looks up, he finds the man right in front of him sans paintbrush and canvas.

The man's face, unmarred and with striking features, borders on beautiful. Thick black hair reaches wide shoulders, shining as if it's made out of the purest silk. An aura of ascendancy envelops him, like pure power. Yet he wears a simple gray shirt tucked into matching pants.

Loch's primal instincts scream *danger!* and the hair on the back of his neck stands up. "Let me go this instant, or you'll regret it. I am too important to go missing." He stares into the man's emotionless eyes, showing dominance. He's ready for the other man to cower in front of him. *They always do in the end.*

Unimaginable white-hot agony stabs into his mind. *Pain shouldn't have a color,* he thinks before all thoughts are gone. Replaced by pure, unfiltered, nerve-flaying, burning-up-every-inch-of-his-body torment.

When Loch Ramor comes to, he kneels on the white floor. Wetness covers his face. With hands that never shook but now do, he wipes his cheeks. He stares for a long moment before he understands that the redness he sees, covering his fingers, is blood.

You are tougher than the others! booms the voice of the other man in Loch's mind. Proof that he isn't dealing with a mere man. No. He is dealing with a god.

Which means this man is either a guardian god, though Loch never heard of any who strayed from their assigned territory, the world they oversee. Or he is one of the archgods. No one else left on the divine hierarchy. Based on the terror he felt, this must be the Archgod of Chaos and Destruction.

Loch gets to his feet. "Let me go and I'll pretend this never happened."

The archgod shoves his hand into Loch's chest.

Loch stares at the arm disappearing elbow deep into his torso. Claws curl around his frantically beating heart.

Then the pain hits, intensifying. He shrieks until he cannot take a breath.

The archgod's fingers relent, and the piercing pressure ceases around Loch's heart. He leans intimately close to Loch, with face void of emotion.

This was just a test! Loch realizes. He gasps for blessed air, fighting to stay alive. His pajamas are soaked through with sweat, and urine to his shame, sticking to his shaking body.

The archgod cocks his head to the side. The motion reminds Loch of the A'ice wolves he hunts off-world. *Now I am the prey.*

"Loch Ramor. That is your true name, isn't it? You are clever. Your body is sturdier than it looks, despite its age. Maybe it will survive the transition when the others didn't. It's been days and I need a mortal body," the god shivers as if disgusted, "to hide from Her. Yours will do just fine."

This must be why all those people were disappearing! Loch thinks.

The archgod turns into a thick black column of smoke, heading toward Loch.

"Wait! I can serve you better alive. I am influential in the court. I can go places where you won't be able to. Use me! You won't regret it!"

For a long moment, nothing happens. *I failed. I should have—*

Then crushing pressure bears down on his mind. The archgod rummages through Loch's thoughts on the surface, digging deeper until nothing is left hidden. Only the truth.

Loch blinks, and it is over.

"You are not lying now, unlike you do about your name. I've seen what you are capable of. Maybe I can use you. I will know in time."

So cold, and so without compassion or empathy. So much like me.

The archgod paces away. A wall opens up by him to show part of the Seven Galaxies with its twinkling stars and gem-like planets. "I've broken many rules to get here and to set my plan in motion."

The archgod surveys the stars with his hands clasped behind his back. "I despise these rules, imposed on me, in the name of balance. She doesn't abide by them. She was always jealous of me, though I shared the Seven Galaxies with her. Now She wants all the control for herself. But I won't let that happen. I will win this Era War. . . . The prophecy foretells it so. *There will be a new beginning. There will be a new liberation.* Mine."

Loch stares at the archgod's back. He hates him for making him feel so weak.

The archgod swipes with his hand and the wall turns back to white marble. "Everything depends on my success here, on this small backwater world, at the farthest corner of the Seven Galaxies. She doesn't know where I am, or that I disappeared. I have the element of surprise. But not for long."

The archgod turns back to Loch. He has just enough presence of the mind to avert his eyes from the archgod's direct gaze, staring at his chin instead.

"Any other time, I would have taken pleasure wreaking chaos on this spoiled little world, watching it rot with each passing year. The soil is so ripe, so full of corrupt and morally twisted people. Fertile ground for my children." The archgod inhales, falling silent for a long moment, as if fighting temptation.

Loch swallows his outburst. Uhna is not a backwater world.

"But I don't have years to wait," the archgod says. "I've begun the Era War again."

Loch hides his surprise. Era War?

The legendary era wars, six altogether, had peppered the history of the Seven Galaxies. They burned through the galaxies, destroying worlds and cultures. The previous Era War had been more than a millennium ago. The mages thought that was the last one.

Now it seems like Loch has an insider's knowledge of the Era War. And if he's smart, he'll use this to his advantage.

The archgod extends his hand.

Loch drops to his knees, pressing his forehead to the ground.

"First things first. I command you to bring me a suitable body."

"As you wish, master."

CHAPTER 12

Lilla

"Let me go," I demand. We disembark the Teryn's fighter ship, stepping onto the gray marble floor of the palace docking hangar. General Callum tightens his hold on my arm in response.

After I threw up, I received medical attention for my concussion. Although I don't remember much of it. I was semiconscious the whole time. I came to, right before landing. I've been dozing on the general's shoulder, drooling on his uniform. He seemed to get a kick out of that.

"Stop dragging me around!" I pull against his hold, but the general keeps striding toward the double doors.

"At some point you have to let our dear guests go," Colonel Teague says next to us, and winks. "Before we create a scene that could cause a diplomatic nightmare. They are Uhnan citizens after all."

In the vast royal hangar, hundreds of elegant spacecraft are lined up in order of value, one more ostentatious than the next. Uhnan workers in purple overalls clean and polish the mirror-like surfaces with eyes averted from us. The two guards present are doing their best to look like statues, standing still and quiet, staring at the opposite wall.

"Yes," General Callum says. "I can see the signs of 'unwanted interest' all over."

I sigh. Usually any arrival at the royal hangar warrants a parade of welcomers. The higher the visitors' esteem and importance, the bigger the parade and kowtowing. But there is no one here to greet the Teryn warriors. Not a single soul. The general has no idea of the insult my father delivered. Which makes me wonder, again, why they are here.

"This is ridiculous," I say. "We have to get back to the Healing Center, right, Arrov?" I glance back at him for confirmation.

Arrov hangs between two robust warriors. His light blue face bears dark bruises around his temple and forehead. He took the brunt of the crash, and it shows.

"I won't let these two go," General Callum says. "One is barely alive, and the other might faint. Or worse, throw up again."

I groan. That happened only once.

We march through the metal sliding exit doors, arriving at a bank of T'erra-infused elevators. Thanks to the magic, the elevators are nothing more than hovering platforms housed in tubular enclosures. They are ready for anyone—anyone with a crystal, that is—to use.

Which explains why, when the general approaches the first elevator with me in tow, nothing happens. The frosted glass door stays shut. He curses and studies the smooth surface and then slaps his palm on the glass with a loud bang. A large crack forms in the middle of the glass.

"If I were you, *Your Generalness*," I say, "I would stop vandalizing the palace. The ma'ha might frown upon that."

Colonel Teague stifles a laugh. "I agree. I would also like to add that marching through a foreign palace might look presumptuous. Especially dragging along two of their residents. We should wait for someone to show up and *properly* escort us."

"Don't tell me what I should or shouldn't do," the general says with a snarl. "This is a waste of my time." He looks at me, expecting me to do something about the elevator.

I smile up at him as if I have no clue what he wants.

A reddish-yellow light flashes across his blue irises. "Show me," he growls.

"What was that?" I ask.

"Show me how it works," he repeats. The impatience is clear in his voice. He still won't let my arm go.

"It must be frustrating for you to not know something, isn't it?" I ask.

Colonel Teague snorts, then steadies his expression.

The sound of a swoosh interrupts us. The elevator door slides open. Revealing Beathag.

She wobbles to us, her pink body-hugging dress limiting her steps. It is see-through with strategically placed floral appliqués and a neckline that stops just above her navel, leaving little to the imagination.

I pull the hood of the healer's cloak over my head. Why is she here?

Her calculating gaze searches our group, slipping past me and locking on the general with certainty. "Let me be the first to welcome you, esteemed guests, to Uhna's Crystal Palace."

She is the welcoming parade Father sent? Does Father know she's doing her best to seduce the general? Not that I care, but he married her after all.

Beathag flicks her long blond hair out of her face. She runs her gaze over the general from head to toe, biting on her red lip.

Both the general and the colonel eye her, mildly curious.

Beathag's smile falters. She extends her hand, arching her long fingers, waiting for the appropriate gesture etiquette dictates.

And waits.

And waits.

General Callum and Colonel Teague regard her outstretched hand unimpressed. If I wouldn't risk a chance of discovery, I would laugh at Beathag's crestfallen expression. I bet she never had to endure such humiliation. An escape plan formulates in my mind.

I lean toward the general and whisper, "She wants you to take her hand and kiss it."

"Why?"

Colonel Teague mutters, "Kiss it? What for?"

"It's customary," I say.

The general's expression darkens as he thinks this through. Instead of giving in and bowing over Beathag's hand, he grasps it. With his left. Then shakes it, hard, jiggling the flesh on her upper arm.

Beathag's eyes widen, but she doesn't give up. She is used to getting what she wants, and I'm counting on it.

Smiling, she steps to the general. Looking up from under her long lashes, she says, "On Uhna, we have many customs and traditions you may not be familiar with."

Transparent coral-colored ribbons float around her head. Like some kind of magic.

The ribbons wrap around the general, but he doesn't seem to notice. Beathag steps even closer, until she is almost standing on his boots. She reaches out a hand as if to steady herself, placing it on the general's chest.

"I would be happy to teach you. All of it."

Reddish-yellow light flashes in General Callum's eyes. He grabs her hand, letting go of my arm.

I jump back and kick his shin.

The general hisses out in pain, but my kick doesn't slow him down. He shoves Beathag aside and leaps after me. Colonel Teague restrains him long enough for me to make it to the hovering platform in the open elevator tube.

Arrov comes to life, shaking off the warriors, following after me. "Not so dead, am I?"

General Callum, furious, pulls the colonel with him. Two more warriors rush to help restrain the general.

Arrov snaps a command at the elevator. I wave as the glass doors close, grinning wide when the general's eyes flash again.

"This is not over!" he shouts.

"Don't mind him." Arrov rests his chin on top of my head. "There is nothing he can do."

CHAPTER 13

"Father's going to kill me," I mutter. I kick off my shoes and pick them up along with the long skirt of my silver dress while running to the reception hall.

When I got back to my room after escaping that Teryn general, I took a nice long A'ris-infused dry shower, letting the hot magic-infused air clean my skin and soothe my sore muscles. That relaxed feeling lasted ten seconds, until my gaze landed on my necklace crystal—the royal one. An urgent message from Father waited for me, demanding my attendance at the reception hall right away.

Picking up my pace, I grip a decorative column and use it to make the turn faster, letting the force of it propel me forward. My body protests against the speed I exert. If it were up to me, I'd be sleeping. But it's not up to me.

I halt in front of wooden carved doors, leading to the reception hall. They are closed. Not a good sign. I am late. Not just fashionably late, but what-on-Uhna-were-you-doing? late. I can't just burst in now.

Sneaking in is my only chance. I walk back down the corridor until I find a small wooden door—the servants' entrance. Looking left and right to make sure no one sees me, I open it.

The busy servants glance up when I enter the narrow passage, but they are used to me showing up here and go back to work without a comment. The servants' corridor runs the perimeter of the reception hall, with little entrances to allow the servants to appear out of nowhere and disappear the same way.

Servants rush by me laden with trays of mouthwatering appetizers. I snatch a buttery confection and pop it into my mouth. Spicy and tart flavors burst on my tongue, so hot I have to huff a few breaths openmouthed to get it cool enough to swallow.

I count the doors as I pass, heading to the one that would let me out at the right spot, by the royal family. When I reach it, I hesitate. I don't want to go in.

Sounds of violin strings and a loud hum of conversation draw me in. I peek through a long crack between two boards of the door.

Low-hanging crystal chandeliers sparkle in the Fla'mma-infused oil lamps. Gold and brown marble tiles line the floor and run up the wall. Colorful mosaic murals depict pirate scenes that Father dislikes and would love to remove but can't. Not without damaging the marble around them. Red Evander spider-silk curtains frame floor-to-ceiling windows that gape into the dark night outside. High society members crowd the circular hall, with Father overlooking them.

Maybe he didn't notice I'm not there. Slipping my high-heeled sandals back on, I take a deep breath. Best to get it over with.

I push against the door. The hinges resist, as if they need oiling. It takes a lot of force to get it open wide enough. I slide through, struggling to hold the heavy door with my greasy fingers. The door slips from my grasp.

It slams shut.

Right when the violins stop playing.

All eyes turn to me. Including Father's.

With face flaming hot, I shuffle past the ma'hars and ma'haras, and the group of advisers surrounding Father.

Beathag smirks as I take my place behind everyone. She looks composed and stunning in a blue dress, flowing and with no back this time.

"You're in trouble, my daughter," Father says and turns away with a disappointed sigh.

"Oh, sis." Nic bumps his shoulder into mine. "When will you learn?"

It's easy for Nic to judge. He never had to ask Father's permission to do anything. He can go anywhere he wants, date anyone he wants, and chose any career he wants—well, except for being a pilot in the coalition's armada. Thanks to the accident.The music starts up again. Father engages someone in polite conversation, his attention focused elsewhere.

"You have one obligation—to be a good daughter," Beathag says, "and yet you fail every single time."

"You should know about failure," I say.

Beathag sniffs and threads her arm into Father's. He smiles at her, his expression full of bliss.

43

There was a time when he would have smiled with so much happiness only at me.

Father clears his throat to get my attention. He pulls me forward. "May I introduce you to my daughter, Ma'hana Lilla of the ruling House of Serrain of Uhna. You may address her as Ma'hana Lilla."

Plastering a fake smile on my lips, I lift my head to greet another tedious dignitary. Only to look into clear blue eyes.

The court seems to fall away. Until he and I are the only ones in the room.

Recognition shines in the depth of his gaze.

Father, oblivious, places my hand on General Callum's, as our custom dictates. He turns my hand; his skin is warm and dry. His grip is gentle, as if he is holding something fragile.

Oh, fishguts! My fate is literally in his hands.

General Callum's lips curl into a smile. He enjoys this too much. Then he lifts my hand as he leans down. He brushes his lips on the back of my hand with a gentle kiss, his breath hot on my skin.

Glancing up, with my hand still held close to his lips, he says, "I was told it is customary to kiss a lady's hand."

I manage an awkward nod. My brain is useless to come up with any plan to salvage the situation. Beathag studies us with a bitter expression.

The general releases my hand. "Ma'hana Lilla, I feel as if I've met you before."

I lower my eyes as blood drains from my face. "I uh . . ." I have no idea what to do!

Colonel Teague rubs his chin. "She does seem familiar." He winks. "I wonder why."

Father shakes his head as he looks between the Teryn warriors in disbelief. "No one has ever said that before. In fact, the opposite is true. My daughter is considered unique in the Pax Septum Coalition, if not the whole Seven Galaxies. No one else has hair and eyes with such colors as hers."

I implore the general with my eyes. *Please don't betray me.*

General Callum's gaze follows my long hair, reaching past my bare shoulders. "Yes, you're right. I have never seen hair the color of hers." His gaze lingers on my lips for a moment before he looks back into my eyes.

"Nor have I ever seen eyes like hers. I know I would never forget meeting someone like you, Ma'hana Lilla. My mistake."

Father claps his hands. "Well then. Let us continue to the royal dining hall." He gestures to the adjoining glass doors.

Father lets the Teryn warriors move past him. Before following after them, he turns back to me. "It seems that the general is fascinated with you. You'll sit at their table tonight."

CHAPTER 14

The low hum of conversation fills the royal dining hall. A twin of the reception hall, it boasts the same gold and brown marble tiles and red curtains. Dozens of oval tables with white and red silk tablecloths and enormous white starflower centerpieces pepper the hall, arranged in a spiral pattern.

I glance at General Callum. "Thank you." I may be stubborn, but not ungrateful.

General Callum nods. He scans the elegant room with a pained expression. He has no idea that this torture, spelled d-i-n-n-e-r, will last four more hours. We have at least that much in common: neither of us wants to be here any longer than necessary.

Father stands up, with his back toward our table—another slight against the Teryns. Holding a crystal glass filled with red boomberry wine, he proceeds to deliver one of his speeches reserved for visitors from outside the coalition. It is full of metaphors of friendship, and sharing riches, and blah, blah, blah.

"This is not over," General Callum says, eyeing the numerous trays packed with mountains of food that flood into the dining room. I wonder if he sees this affair as wasteful and extravagant, or is he used to such luxury?

He looks at me, expecting an answer.

"Yes, it *is* over." I fall silent when servants appear at our table to serve our dinner.

When I notice that my plate is full of tiny crawling crabs, I try to hand my plate back to the confused-looking servant girl. "This must be a mistake." I know Deidre would never make me eat these living crabs. But the servant backs away from me, making her escape. Then I catch Beathag's satisfied glance. This must be part of my punishment.

"Is something wrong?" the general asks.

"Why would anything be wrong?" I snap. Coin-size white crabs scuttle in all directions on the square plate in front of me. One of them bravely clenches the piercer I'm holding, a long, needlelike utensil. When I pull the piercer back, it doesn't let go, maintaining its grip. The crab dangles from the end, its small legs running in place. I sigh.

"Don't you like your food?" The general picks up a small crab and smells it.

"It's not that . . . Fine! I don't like seafood, okay?" Even the smell of it makes me queasy. I shudder.

General Callum bursts into laughter. "You live on an island, surrounded by ocean, and you don't like seafood?"

"Yes, the irony is not lost on me." I drop the piercer, and the crab with it, back on the plate. The crab happily scurries away, dragging the utensil after him like a war prize.

"You owe me," the general says, changing topic.

"Just what do you think I owe you, Your Generalness? Why—"

Colonel Teague bumps his elbow into mine. "Love, do tell what these things are."

"They're called sand crabs, a delicacy of Uhna. They are native to Fye Island. Only the royal family and their guests have the exclusive privilege to enjoy them. You're supposed to—"

A tap on my right shoulder interrupts me.

"I saved your life, and that of your incompetent pilot," General Callum says, counting off his fingers. "I kept your secret."

Just stay calm. Don't let him rile you up. "I am well aware of everything you've done for me. I did thank you, as you recall. What more—"

A bump on my left elbow interrupts me. Again.

Colonel Teague, his face in a grimace, says, "They are kind of hard to eat." Red juice drips from the corner of his mouth. He wipes the juice off with the back of his hand.

"You aren't supposed to chew them. Their shell shatters into tiny pieces, making them a choking hazard. Just swallow them whole," I advise him, while I try hard not to gag. If it were up to me, I'd dump the whole platter back into the ocean where they came from.

The colonel nods and picks out a claw from the back of his teeth. "Yes, that makes sense." With the claw, he points at my full plate. "Are you going to eat them?" I shiver. "Have at it."

The colonel picks up my plate. "Good! I'm absolutely famished."

When I feel a tap on my right shoulder, I am glad for the excuse to turn away from the shellfish massacre.

"Ma'hana Lilla," General Callum says in a low voice, "or should I call you my little spy?"

I resist wiping the smug look off his face. Slapping foreign dignitaries is usually frowned upon.

"I don't know why you were in disguise," he continues, "or why you're keeping our meeting secret from your father. But I'll find out soon enough. Until then, you owe me three favors."

CHAPTER 15

I try to sneak away after the long dinner, but Father stops me with a hand on my arm. "Not so fast, my daughter." He escorts me from the royal dining room to his antechamber next to it.

I never liked this long, rectangular room, where gold dominates. Plush gold carpet covers dark hardwood floors. Gold-colored curtains hug windows that stretch all the way to the gold-coffered ceiling. Gold-colored sofas and tall-backed chairs pepper the room, arranged in groups. An enormous gold desk with a glass top waits in front of a tall white and gold fireplace. The desk, Father's "throne" from which he metes out all my punishments.

High Adviser Ellar and Overseer Irvine get to their feet when we enter. They wait for Father to settle behind his desk before sitting back onto gold chairs.

To my surprise, Beathag glides into the room and drops at the end of a gold sofa. What is *she* doing here?

"Father, it's late. Maybe I should come back tomorrow—"

"You're not going anywhere." Father clasps his hands on the glass desktop. "You'll wait your turn."

I'm not surprised. After Mom died, Father buried himself in a never-ending parade of political matters. They always take precedence over his daughter.

There was a time when I would have done anything to be in my father's company, even if it meant getting reprimanded. Any attention was better than nothing after Mom died. But now that I am older, I would do anything to get out of these prolonged preaching sessions that only drive a bigger chasm between us.

High Adviser Ellar glances at me. "Ma'hana Lilla, I apologize for the inconvenience. Unfortunately, these state troubles cannot wait."

I shrug. It's always the adviser who apologizes in Father's stead.

Father raps his knuckles on the glass top, demanding attention.

"Your Highness," High Adviser Ellar says, "there was another flood in our second- largest crystal diamond mine. At last count, the death toll was one hundred, but the numbers are still rising—"

Father waves his hand. "Was it sabotage?"

"Yes, Your Highness," Overseer Irvine says. "I'm afraid it was. I caught the saboteur and personally interrogated the culprit—a rebel who pretended to be a miner. He used one of the Fla'mma-infused mine explosives, taking out a support wall. It was meant to be a warning, but the charge went off at the wrong time—in the beginning of the shift, and not after. I've instructed my guards to run a surprise 'visit' in all the refugee camps. That will show them we're not preys."

My face pales just as Beathag says, "Very good, Overseer. The monarchy cannot look weak in the public eye."Father nods. "What about production? When will it resume?"High Adviser Ellar glares at the overseer, his expression disapproving. "The rescue and rebuild teams are working hard, Your Highness. I fully expect the production to resume by the end of the week."

This is a devastating blow to Father. Crystal diamonds are the main commodity of the ruling house, and the most important export of Uhna. These valuable gems earned their name because they hold a small amount of Fla'mma magic inside them, making them sparkle with an inner light on their own. There are five underwater mines, not far from Fye Island. The working conditions are dangerous. There is no cure for the crystal lung disease that suffocates miners.

If those mines had not been found in our territory by my ancestor, maybe this tragedy wouldn't have happened. But it was sheer luck that when the first king, my great-great-many-*many*-great grandfather divided the islands of Uhna among the houses, that those diamonds happened to fall into my family's possession. These sparkling gems bought my family authority, creating the monarchy, and paving the way to power in the Pax Septum Coalition, where votes can be bought, and bribes speak louder than democracy. Now it is my father who is the coalition's leader, and Uhna has been the coalition's capital for more than thirty years in a row—even though the other coalition worlds are not afraid to voice their disagreement with that. But I suspect that as long as Father keeps up the flow of crystal diamonds to pay them off, nothing will change.

"End of the week? Unacceptable," Father says. "How much are we losing?"

High Adviser Ellar fidgets in his chair, looking uncomfortable. "Two million credits per day, Your Highness."

Father narrows his eyes.

"All our able-bodied citizens under the ruling house's control are working overtime in the other mines." The high adviser drags a hand through his well-kept black hair, a rare show of nerves. "Other than the elderly and underage, we have no one else left to employ. I took the initiative and sent requests to all the major houses for employees. No one has offered any of their citizens."

"What about the minor houses?" Beathag asks.

The high adviser shakes his head. "The minor houses are already burdened beyond their limit maintaining our infrastructure. They cannot spare anyone."

That is where the true conundrum lies. It's not only that the mines are losing profit, but Father is running out of people to employ.

"I could veto the territorial governance laws"—laws that allow each house full authority over their own territories, and citizens who live there.

"Your Highness, I would caution against such a rash decision," the high adviser says. "That would be cause for a civil war. We cannot afford to fight on multiple fronts while fighting the rebellion as well. A rebellion Overseer Irvine assured us to solve and has yet to deliver any results."

Irvine's face turns purple. "I am *actively* dealing with the rebellion. I am setting up traps, following every thread. I can assure you, Your Highness, I am getting close to catching their leader."

Father leans back in his chair. "Is that all?"

"There is more, Your Highness," Overseer Irvine says. "The Coalition Assembly is introducing a new refugee regulation. This regulation will give the coalition power to investigate the state of the refugee camps on every planet, including all seven on Uhna."

"How is it that this passed without my knowledge or approval?" Father asks, drumming his fingers on the polished glass surface of his desk.

"Administrative regulations such as these are open for voting with simple majority of the Assembly. They do not require the presence of the coalition leader," explains High Adviser Ellar.

This is how the Coalition Assembly, the parliament and governing system of the Pax Septum Coalition, garners any control from Father, its unwanted leader.

"What does this 'regulation' mean to us?"

"Your Highness, it limits the number of refugees to a maximum of twenty thousand per camp," Overseer Irvine says. "If that number is bigger, then it requires dismantling the camp to create smaller ones instead. Failure to comply results in severe fines."

"How severe?" Father asks.

"Double what we're losing in the mines," High Adviser Ellar says. "Four billion credits, Your Highness, per day, with interest."

Father cannot afford to pay the fines with one of his mines out of commission. He also cannot afford to dismantle the refugee camps. There is no more land left available for expansion.

The coalition might cite humanitarian reasons for this regulation, but this will only hurt the people it is supposed to help. It won't elevate the refugees' poor living conditions. Refugees who are forgotten. Worldless, with no rights. Nowhere to go, and no place to call home. No one wants them, and no one cares about them. They are invisible.

Overseer Irvine scoffs. "Your Highness, these refugees are expensive and useless for Uhna. We should find a way to remove them from our world altogether." That would eliminate his job, but I doubt the ma'har even realizes it. He is either too stupid, or this role is nothing but a stepping-stone for him.

"The overseer has a point," Beathag says, smiling at Irvine. "Why not relocate the overflow of refugees onto other coalition worlds?"

High Adviser Ellar glances at her. "Ma'hara Beathag, I am afraid that's not as easy as you suggest. Other coalition worlds have the same problems with their teeming camps. The flood of refugees has tripled over the years, not just for Uhna, but for everyone else too. They'll have to establish smaller camps first before they can even consider helping us."

"I thought I asked you, High Adviser, to address me as Ma'hata. Or am I not the queen?"

"Marriage to the king does *not* automatically warrant the title of Ma'hata,"

I snap. "One has to be crowned by the ma'ha, and that hasn't happened in a hundred years."

At least I *am* married to the ma'ha." Beathag smirks. "Unlike your mother, the concubine."

CHAPTER 16

I take a step toward Beathag. "How dare you! I'll—"

"Enough, daughter!"

I look away from Father, to hide the hurt his lack of respect to Mom caused. He never explained to my why he didn't marry Mom. And now he let Beathag think it is all right to shame her because of that.

"I am getting tired of hearing what I cannot do," Father says.

"Your Highness," the overseer says, "there is one solution that could take care of both the crystal mine and the refugee camp problems."

High Adviser Ellar raises a hand. "I fervently disagree—"

"I would like to hear more before I decide."

"It's simple." Overseer Irvine hands a digi-scroll to Father. "Your Highness, by signing this order, you could send the refugees to the crystal mines."

"Are you suggesting that I give them a choice to work in the mines?" Father asks and takes the digi-scroll. He places it on his desk. "Or something else?"

"It is entirely up to you, Your Highness, how to proceed," Overseer Irvine says. "There are advantages to both. But there is no question that one outweighs the other, saving you labor costs, so to speak."

"Father, you cannot consider this insanity!" I say. "The refugees are free people."

"It is not your job, my daughter, to educate me on politics that you know nothing about. These are serious matters, and the solutions must be serious, too."

"I cannot believe you're considering this. What would Mom think of you?"

Father dismisses the two ma'hars.

Once they've left the room, he gets up from his desk. "I told you, my daughter, do not judge me on matters you know nothing about. My duty is to my people, *all* of my people. There are no easy decisions here. My hand has been forced by the coalition. I have to be responsible for the whole of

Uhna. You cannot even do the one responsibility I ask of you—to be at dinner. On time. As per our agreement."

The agreement High Adviser Ellar helped broker between Father and me after the Belthair fiasco. As long as I am where Father demands, he will not assign guards to me.

"On top of that, I know you left the palace without permission," Father says. "That's why you were late. You ignore everything I ask of you. You go back on your given word. I don't know what to do with you anymore, Lilla."

The blood drains from my face. "You don't have to 'do' anything with me. I've never asked anything from you. You lock me inside this palace as if I am your prisoner. I've had enough of it!"

"As long as I am ma'ha, you obey me."

I cross my arms. "Make me."

Father's face turns red. Beathag glides to him and threads her arm into his, pulling him away from me. She saved us from escalating this fight, but I doubt she did it for me.

Father leans on the edge of his desk, hugging Beathag to him. She picks up one of his hands, massaging it, as if they're alone in the room. Transparent coral-colored ribbons coalesce from her and snake around Father.

"My husband, there is no question we are in a crisis. We cannot look weak in the eyes of the major houses, or they'll wrest control from us." Father nods along with Beathag's words, his attention rapt, oblivious to how the ribbons tighten around him. "You have to think about the future of your children. Is this a problem you want your son to inherit? No monarchy to rule? We need the crystal diamonds to survive. I know you'll do what's best for us. What's best for Uhna."

"You're right, my dear wife." He picks up the digi-scroll from his desk and signs it with a flourish. "It is what's best for Uhna."

He lifts Beathag's hand to his mouth and kisses it.

"Stop that," I snap.

Father looks at me, confused. As if he'd forgotten I'm still in the room. "What are you talking about, my daughter? Stop what?"

Could he truly not feel Beathag influencing him with magic? I doubt he would listen to my warning. Besides, Beathag would simply deny my accusation.

Exhaustion spreads through my body. "It's late, Father." Or more pre-cisely, it's early—they managed to talk well into morning. "I think we should continue this at another time."

"You are right." He seems to shake the haze off of him. "You should go."

I turn to leave, relieved that for once he forgot about my punishment, but Beathag's words stop me in my tracks. "Not before we tell her our good news."

Good news? "Gods, please tell me you're not pregnant."

"Yesterday, my daughter, I realized something. You are too old to stay on Uhna any longer. You cannot help but feel restless and make mistakes."

Beathag's grin widens. I don't like where this is going.

"It is time for you to fulfill your royal obligations, my daughter. It's time for you to enter into a marriage contract."

CHAPTER 17

Servants of all ages hustle around the vast space of the kitchen, pots clanking and steam rising from their stations as breakfast is prepared for the masses. Dodging around them, I make my way to the back. I need Deidre.

Deidre, a portly woman in her late eighties, kneads dough as she listens to a stout man with cooled-lava skin and scarlet streaks in his gray hair.

Leaning against the warm wall of the fireplace, I stay out of view so I don't interrupt them.

"It ca'nna be so bad," Deidre says.

"You are right, it is worse," Captain Murtagh says in a grave tone. "This morning I found that more than a dozen ma'hars and ma'haras, all from minor houses, are missing from their rooms. Add those to the twenty servants you said never showed up for morning duty, and we have more than thirty people unaccounted for."

"Yo' al'ways hada such dramatics." Deidre makes a tsk sound. "Those minor houses al'ways bicker and fight 'mong themselves. And as to the missin' cooks, well, it coulda be just them scared off by those scary men, whatcha call th'm?" She gestures, scattering tiny pieces of dough.

"The Teryns," I say, stepping around the wide column of the fireplace.

Deirdre puts a flour-covered hand to her throat. "Stop a'scaring me so, g'rl. At my age me heart ca'nna take such fright!"

I hug her shoulders and plant a kiss on her face. "You are too young to have a heart attack."

Captain Murtagh bows in respect. I salute him like one of his soldiers— two fingers to the temple and then to the forehead. "Didn't mean to scare you, but I overheard your conversation. You said there are people missing from the palace?"

I glance at the captain. I know he'll tell me the truth. He's always given me straight answers, even when it hurt to hear—like when I tried to join Nic in his self-defense training at age seven, only to be told it's not for girls. He did train me, in secret, once he realized how much I wanted to learn.

Or when I refused to get back on the saddle after the first time Fearghas, my battle horse, threw me off at age eight, and I was too scared to ever ride again. Captain Murtagh convinced me to never give up.

"Thirty-five people just today," he says. "Ma'hars, ma'haras, and servants, all gone. They didn't even pack their belongings. And you know how these folks get with their expensive clothes. I've heard reports of hundreds of missing citizens from all over Uhna. There must be a pattern, but I cannot figure it out. It's too random."

That is strange. "Have you talked with Father about the disappearances?"

"I never made it to the ma'ha." He grimaces. "Overseer Irvine intercepted me, and I reported it to him. He assured me he would look into it."

As if. "That lord is too busy being self-important to be useful."

"Lass, I couldn't have said it better myself." He picks up his white hat. "If you'll excuse me, duty waits."

Deidre gazes in admiration after the captain, with a slight blush on her cheeks. "If I'd be ten years young'r . . ." She clears her throat and turns back to the dough. "Whatcha brings yo' to me kitchen this morning, sweetling?" She points to the left. "Th're be some boomberry tarts for yo' in the oven."

I head over and pop a sweet tart into my mouth. "You should ask him out. He always talks about you." After washing my hands, I strap on a red apron.

Standing next to her at the long wooden table, I reach for the dough and knead it, as I've done many times before.

Deidre wipes her cheek with the back of her hand, leaving behind a streak of flour. "He's a wid'w, like me self, with a gr'wn child. This woman's too old to court 'gain or marry 'gain."

She smiles fondly, as if reminiscing about her late husband. I never met him—he died at sea when I was small. I'm glad she had happiness, however brief it was, in her life. Will I ever find mine?

"Yo' too quiet. Had 'nother spat with yo'r da', haven'tcha?"

I shrug. She reads me like an open digi-scroll. She's been doing that ever since Mom died.

"It ca'nna be healthy to fight so much. Whatcha this time?"

"Marriage contract."

"Oh, sweetling!" She hugs me to her ample bosom. "Now don't yo' worry. Yo' strong like yo'r mo'mma. Yo'll figure it. I just know'a it. And long before yo' know, it's over, and yo'll be back here with me." She wipes at the corners of her eyes.

I hug her back. "Enough with the sadness. This dough won't knead itself." She laughs. "Yo're right, my sweetling."

As long as I have Deidre, I know I can handle anything.

"He is late," I grumble into the quiet of my living quarters. I don't want to upset Xor any more than necessary.

I pick a holo-picture of my mom from the fireplace mantel. In it she is smiling as she hugs my younger self. We didn't know that was the last happy moment we would ever have.

Familiar zapping and crackling sounds.

A seven-foot-tall oval-shaped gateway appears in the middle of my room. The gateway, made out of swirling shadows, is an ancient method of travel called umbrae travel. The clamoring sounds and typical scents of the refugee camp drift into my room when Arrov steps through. "Sorry I'm late."

He taps on the worn leather gauntlet with two metal plates in the middle to close the gateway. Xor smuggled a few of these gauntlets with him and allowed the most trusted of his people, such as Arrov, to use them for short-distance travel. But not me.

"It's not like I have to be anywhere," I say. "At least not for a while."

"What do you mean?"

I tell him about the marriage contract. I tell him how I knew of the possibility but never thought it would happen.

Arrov leans on the mantel by me and crosses his feet at the ankles. "I would run away before I let my mother trick me into a marriage contract. I am a free spirit, living for adventure. I love my life the way it is."

That must be nice.

"What are you going to do?" he asks.

"Nothing. My focus is on the refugees, especially now."

Arrov raises an eyebrow in question.

"Xor has to hear this first. It's bad."

59

CHAPTER 18

We step out of the swirling shadows onto the dirt floor of the rebel meeting room.

Xor strides past us to the rickety metal table. Arrov and I come to attention.

"My two favorite rebels." He sits at the edge of it, looking relaxed. "One failed mission. One failed warning about a night raid from our favorite overseer. Am I missing anything else?"

Xor stares at us with all three of his eyes. I look away first.

A distant muffled explosion sounds, and the ground shakes under our feet. A thin layer of dirt falls from the low ceiling and saturates the humid air with the smells of soil. Is Xor expanding the underground camp?

A makeshift door of syn-plastic bursts open and bangs into the dirt wall. Belthair marches through, followed by Jorha. Great—I was so hoping for an audience. *Not.*

"We found even more cave drawings in the tunnels," Jorha says. "You were right. The tunnels were there but blocked off."

Cave drawings? I exchange a confused look with Arrov.

Xor nods. "Good."

Jorha turns her attention to us, studying us with an unreadable expression on her cooled-lava-toned face. Embarrassment burns my cheeks. She encouraged me to take a bigger role, and I failed her too.

Belthair says, "Tell me one good reason why I shouldn't kick both of your useless hides out of the rebellion."

"It was my fault, sir," says Arrov.

"It was my fault," I say in unison. "Sir."

Belthair sneers. "Didn't I predict she'd fail, Jorha?"

Jorha rolls her eyes. "You did, Major."

"That's what I thought. This botched-up attempt stinks of your spoiled, highborn self."

Don't let him rile you up. "We got into an asteroid field that destroyed our ship. If the Teryns hadn't rescued us, we'd be dead."

"It would have been better," Belthair mutters.

Xor pushes away from the metal table. "Did you say 'Teryns'?'"

I nod. "Technically, it was the Teryns' fault that we got into the accident that destroyed our ship. Their fleet is so enormous, it pushed an asteroid field ahead of them, causing us to run into it." I won't confess in front of Belthair that it was my panic attack that made us miss the code exchange *before* the asteroids arrived.

"I don't know why they're here, but it seems my fa—uh, the ma'ha—had invited them. And that's not the worst of it."

Jorha gestures with her hand. "Go on."

I hesitate. It's not that I don't believe in the rebellion's cause—to free the refugees from the camps. But it is one thing to go against Father, and another to betray state secrets. I have not crossed that line yet. Once I tell them what I know, that would mean betrayal to the monarchy. Treason. Punishable by death.

Isn't that the same fate that awaits the refugees? Thousands will be sent to certain death in the crystal mines. All because Father's profit line had a severe cut, and he desperately needs miners. To him, the refugees are nothing but numbers to shuffle around.

That's why Xor leads the rebellion. A rebellion that evolved from small skirmishes with the camp guards to missions that force Father to notice them. But they are losing.

"The ma'ha will limit the population of the camps to twenty thousand. The rest he is sending to the crystal mines."

"How sure are you?" Xor asks, running his hand over his bald head. Jorha leans to Xor, brushing her arm against his before she steps back.

"He signed the order this morning."

Belthair whistles without mirth. "I should be surprised, but I am not. Ever since Pigballs arrived to 'oversee' the camp, things are getting worse. I bet this was his idea, wasn't it?"

Pigballs? Overseer Irvine from the House of Swinestones. Fitting. "Yes, it was."

"I want you to find out why the Teryns are here and report back to me," Xor says.

"Yes, um, sir!"

Jorha watches Xor leave, her expression revealing. "Good news, you two can stay. Bad news, this room needs to be cleaned in an hour," she says and pulls from her pocket two small brushes with missing wires. She hands one brush to Arrov and the other to me. "Even worse news, you can only use that."

It would take forever to clean the room that way!

When Arrov and I don't move, she claps her hands. "Rebels, what are you waiting for?"

I drop to my knees, holding the fragile little brush like an idiot. Arrov drops down by me and mutters under his breath, "Kill me now."

CHAPTER 19

Arrov and I limp through the shadowy gateway and gingerly step onto the white carpet in my living quarters.

"That was the most brutal punishment I've ever had in my life," Arrov says with a groan. Cleaning the rebel meeting room was more than brutal. It was impossible.

"Gods, I just want to fall into bed and sleep through the night."

I glance at the sky with pink and reddish undertones visible through the balcony doors. "You mean day."

Arrov laughs. "I guess sleep has to wait." His expression sobers. "Listen, it's probably not my place, but—"

"But what?"

"You're making a mistake," he says in a rush.

"A mistake?" What is he talking about?

"Yes. It's a bad idea to become Xor's new puppet."

Oh, he's joking. "I'm no one's puppet," I say and laugh.

"This is no laughing matter, Lilla. He is risking your life for the rebellion. I'm worried about you."

I point at my chest. "About me? Why?" I can't decide if I should be happy about that or not.

"I'm worried that your guilt of being a royal will drive you too far."

"You are royal too, Arrov. You take part in the rebellion, doing everything I do." I wave his concern away. "Besides, I know what I'm doing. Or are you doubting me?"

Arrov drags a hand through his short dark blue hair. "I don't doubt you. But—"

"What? Just say it."

"Xor treats you differently," he says, his dark blue eyes imploring.

"You must be more exhausted than you look," I say, frowning. "Because you're making no sense to me."

"I'm not exhausted," Arrov snaps, then grimaces. "It's as if he is angry at your family for personal reasons."

"That's absurd. I never met him before that day in the camp six months ago." I doubt that Father ever met him.

He puts his hands on my shoulders. "Listen: just be more cautious."

I can do that. "Sure."

Arrov opens a gateway and walks through it with one last backward glance.

Yawning, I undress and limp to my bed. I fall down onto it, face-first, drifting off.

Someone knocks.

Maybe if I don't respond, whoever it is will go away.

The knocks turn into flat-out bangs.

Buckets and buckets of fishguts!

"Fine!" I shout and get up. Getting into clean clothes hurts a lot, and by the time I make it to the door I am in a terrible mood.

"This better be important," I say as I tear it open.

Glenna, her face pale, grabs my hand. "You have to come right away."

CHAPTER 20

Our footsteps crunch as we make our way down the rocky shore. Above us, the Crystal Palace looms, barely visible through the rolling curtain of marine layer. Dark silhouettes of a group are ahead. Captain Murtagh and five more guards gather around something I can't quite see.

When he hears our approach, the captain glances at us with a solemn expression and steps to the side.

I stumble on a rock when I see the prone bodies on the ground with General Callum squatting by them.

I run to the familiar body. "No, no, no!" My hands shake above the long gray hair that flows free without the chef's hat to cover it.

"Glenna, why aren't you doing something?" But my best friend shakes her head.

Captain Murtagh places a hand on my shoulder. "There is nothing anyone can do for her. I'm sorry."

No! Realization hits. Deidre will never smile at me first thing in the morning when I drop by the kitchen for a freshly baked boomberry tart. She will never give me one of her comforting warm hugs when I'm upset. She will never say how proud she is of me.

I reach out to her, but the general pulls me away. "You don't want to see her like that."

"I have to see her!" I shout and hit his chest with both hands in fists. "Please, let me see her!" I hit him once, twice, until I can't move. Until tears overflow, running down my face. Until my head falls forward on my fists, my body shaking in silent sobs.

General Callum puts his arms around my back, holding close. Giving me time to compose myself.

"What happened?" I ask in a hoarse voice after a while.

"I found her like this," the general says, "among the others."

Anger that clears my head burns the tears away. I push away from him. Someone went to great trouble to murder these servants. But why?

I wipe my face before I turn to Captain Murtagh. "What do you know so far?"

"Ma'hana, I'm not supposed to . . ." he falls silent when he sees my desperation. "They were murdered, but not here on the beach. There is no blood around the . . . around her, nor around the others."

"Did she suffer? Did any of them suffer?"

He looks away, and that's enough answer.

"Will you tell me, Captain, about everything you find out?"

He takes a deep breath. "I can't, Ma'hana."

"Do you mean you won't?"

Captain Murtagh shakes his head. "No, I mean I am *ordered* not to investigate this."

I recoil. "By whom?"

"By Overseer Irvine," he answers, confirming my suspicion. That ma'har was adamant about where servants stand on his priority list.

"Surely Father will tell you otherwise."

The captain shakes his head again. "The overseer was acting on orders from the ma'ha."

"I see." But I don't.

I don't understand how Father could let their killers get away with this.

As if the captain could read my thoughts, he pulls me to the side. "Ever since the, uh, visit of the general, they are the ma'ha's main concern. The murder of these servants doesn't have much priority right now—it's a domestic issue that can wait. But I am sure, once the negotiations are over, that that will change."

It's weak comfort, and both of us know it won't happen. Ever since that ma'har arrived at court, he brought nothing but suffering. I cannot fathom why Father allows the overseer so much power.

I look back at Deidre's prostrate body.

"If someone would look into these murders, where would they start?" I ask. "Hypothetically speaking."

He studies my expression. "They could start by figuring out where the murders took place."

I nod in thanks and turn away. Captain Murtagh stops me with a hand on my arm. "This could be dangerous, lass. Are you sure you want to do this?"

I look at Deidre again. "Yes, I am sure."

She deserves the truth. They all deserve the truth.

CHAPTER 21

"How on Uhna will you investigate Deidre's death on your own?" Glenna asks as she closes the door to her workroom.

"What would you do in my place?"

Glenna makes her way to the large tree trunk that serves as her desk. Its polished surface, with the rings of the tree's life visible, gleams in the light of Fla'mma-infused lanterns. "I don't know what I would have done if it was Great Healer Robley lying dead on that beach."

It was the great healer who adopted Glenna when she was only eight years old, bringing her to the palace with him. That's how I met her when I was six. She didn't like talking about her parents, and I could barely think past the pain of losing my mom.

As if sensing Glenna's distress, a large black mushroom comes to life at the other end of her desk. The creature mewls a high-pitched wail and crawls toward her on a multitude of thin roots. Its round cap slants to the right in an unnatural angle. Glenna's newest rescue.

Glenna lifts a brown jar off a shelf. Picking out a wiggling worm, she feeds it to the mushroom. It gobbles up the worm so fast, I can't even tell where its mouth is. I step back from it. Just in case.

Glenna rolls a large water-filled syn-ball out of the corner.

"Would you let some arrogant ma'har tell you that Robley doesn't matter because he was only a healer, a servant?"

I sit, ignoring the disgusting sloshing sound it makes, and wince when the sore muscles in my back light into me. Why Glenna can't use a regular chair is beyond me.

Glenna puts down the jar next to the mushroom. "I'm not sure I would have any other choice in the matter. I can't just go around breaking rules when I feel like it. You should be worried about the danger."

A root inches out from the mushroom, questing toward the still open jar. Glenna snatches up the jar right before the root can dip in and puts the jar back on the shelf.

"I'm not worried." Glenna scowls, and I lift a hand to stop her from lecturing. "How about this: I will be vigilant, and stop the second I encounter anything too dangerous?" I can't imagine there is much risk in searching poor Deidre's living quarters for clues.

"That would work," Glenna concedes. "Now let me look at you."

"Why?"

"I know you're in pain. I saw you limping."

She narrows her eyes as she examines me, coming to a diagnosis fast. With quick and efficient moves, she collects vials, jars, and pouches of dried herbs, putting them in a mortar and mixing them together.

"Do I have to?" I whine. I know all too well where this is heading.

"You know I can't use magic to heal you." Glenna is right. Every time she used her magic on me, we had less than ideal results. It was as if my body took her magic, twisted it, then spit it out in some terrible and unexpected way. The main reason I never really liked magic—too unreliable for my taste.

"That doesn't mean I can't complain about the bad taste." I take the glass of murky drink with chunks of herbs floating on top. I sniff it, and recoil from the pungent smell, which reminds me of, well, farts.

I try to hand it back to Glenna. "You drink it."

"We both know that you have sore muscles in both of your arms, legs, and abs, to mention a few. You can drink this and feel better within minutes. Or suffer for days. It's up to you."

"That's not a fair choice," I complain. Plugging my nose, I take a large gulp. A horrible bitterness hits my tongue, making me gag all the way until I finish it. Glenna hands me a cold glass of water and I chug it down to wash off the aftertaste.

"I'd rather vomit than drink your potions." I shudder. "No offense."

"You might—vomit, I mean—if the potion works as it should."

I stare at her in dismay.

"Just kidding." She waves a hand. "You won't throw up. Unless you're allergic to lemon root . . . but let's not worry about that now. Tell me, what did you do to get yourself in this state?"

"Uh . . . I just . . . you know . . ." I can't tell her that I had to clean the rebel meeting room with a brush as punishment for a failed mission.

"You were weeding the kitchen garden again?"

"Something like that." I wince inside. I hate keeping secrets from her.

She turns away from me, and I see transparent blue ribbons emerge from her, A'ris, heading toward the black mushroom creature.

"Why is your healing magic blue?"

Glenna finishes her check on the mushroom and turns to me. "You can see magic? With your bare eyes?"

How else? "Yes, with my own eyes. Can't you?"

"No," she says, shaking her head. "Nor can those charlatans, I mean mages."

Huh. "Do you think I can see it because I have magic too?"

"I thought only healers and mages have magic," Glenna says and leans a hip on her desk. "Maybe you're one of us, or one of *them*. Although I've never heard of a healer or a mage who couldn't receive magical healing. Maybe you're a fluke."

"Thanks Glenn. Do tell me how you really feel."

"Funny." She crosses her arms. "I can't believe I'm saying this, but you should ask that mage who officiated at your father's marriage. Maybe he'll know more."

"After I've searched Deidre's room, I'll go and talk to him." It's not a conversation I'm looking forward to.

"When are you coming with me to the refugee camp again? You haven't visited since—"

Since Eita and her family got beaten. "I'm not sure—"

Glenna wipes her hands. "I miss you coming with me."

"I miss it too." Maybe I should tell her everything. It would be such a relief not to have to lie anymore.

"You and your mom did so much for the refugees. The rebellion could learn a thing or two from you." Glenna's crimson eyes glint with anger. "Because of them, innocent people are suffering. Look at what happened to poor Eita. Look at what happened at the other camps. Where was the rebellion then?"

"But don't you think the rebellion is fighting for what's right? To help the refugees?"

"It doesn't matter if that's what they are fighting for," Glenna says. "Take the healers, for example. You don't see us going around poisoning people to get what we want. No. We adhere to our principles and act responsibly. Those are the right things to do."

I eye my best friend as if I've never seen her before. Now I know where she stands when it comes to the rebellion. Now I know I'll never be able to tell her the truth.

CHAPTER 22

I close the door to Deidre's room with a soft click. I take a deep breath to summon courage, inhaling sweet scents of vanilla and cinnamon that always seemed to cling to Deidre. I expect her to pop out and greet me any second, but the room remains dark and silent.

The pain of her loss hits, bringing tears and pressure to my forehead. Closing my eyes, I stuff down my grief. I have to focus. I have to find something, anything that can help me figure out who killed Deidre and the other servants.

I push away from the door. The Fla'mma-infused cones around the living area come to life at the motion.

Deidre's precious heirloom furniture that she treasured lays broken in pieces. The doors of her massive armoire are hanging off their hinges, its contents scattered on the floor. The carpet has small dark brown spots on it, enough to show signs of an attack.

Someone attacked Deidre here and took her to another place, where she got killed, then dumped her body on the beach with those of the other servants. They didn't even bother to hide the bodies, as if flaunting us by leaving the gruesome crime scene in plain view.

I check Deidre's bedroom, and then her kitchen, but it seems the worst of the attack happened in the living area. Who would do this? Deidre had no known enemies. It seemed that everyone loved her. She was strict but fair. Why would anyone want to kill her or the others? Are their murders connected, or was Deidre in the wrong place at the wrong time?

There are no answers here, only questions. I leave, knowing that once I close the door, I will never be back.

CHAPTER 23

Rubbing my arms for warmth, I stand in the center of the main level of the palace, with corridors leading in all directions. After leaving Deidre's quarters, I searched the other servants' rooms. All of them showed signs of struggle to various degrees, but none gave me any clues about how to proceed. Finished with my task, I ended up here.

Ma'hars and ma'haras flow by me, as if I am nothing but a large rock in their path. An obstacle not worthy of notice. I wonder if they know there are murdered servants and missing court members. Would they even care about it or worry about becoming the next to disappear? I study each non-chalant face, wondering if he or she is the murderer. But there are no hints there, just cool superiority.

A small commotion on my left has the ma'hars and ma'haras jumping out of the way to hug the wall, a rare sight—high society members are known to demand the right of way, not give it.

Black-clad Teryn warriors stride past, cutting through the crowd. General Callum glances in my direction, studying me without breaking his stride.

My mind seems to empty of all thoughts and gets stuck on the cruel fact of how powerful he looks. No one should look that good, with so much confidence.

Then I remember him crouching by Deidre's body. He was the one who found her and the others. I was too upset to talk to him then. But now I want to ask him questions. Before I can step in his direction, he is gone inside the royal negotiation hall. Colonel Teague winks, then follows after the general.

Nic bursts from the main hall with a slight limp, stuffing the last bite of a roll in his mouth. Now is my chance to find out what's going on. I step right into Nic's path, as if by accident.

"Sis! Watch where you're going," Nic says, then smiles, and all is right. He could never stay upset for long no matter what I did.

"Where are you going in such a hurry that you would barrel through your own sister to get there?"

"Just to be clear, it was you who 'barreled' into me." Nic nods toward the meeting chamber. "The negotiations with the Teryn Praelium start today."

"What kinds of negotiations?"

"I want to tell you, really, but I can't." Nic smiles in apology. "Father is already too stressed about this as it is."

That's a surprise. Father has the reputation of being a shrewd and calm diplomat in the Pax Septum Coalition. He worked hard to earn it.

"He seems worried," Nic continues. "It's as close as I have ever seen him of being overwhelmed."

"But why is he overwhelmed? Why are these negotiations different from any others?" Why are the Teryns here?

Nic shakes his head. "I wish I could tell you—"

"But it's not my place to interfere with politics." I roll my eyes. A proper ma'hana should know her place. Blah, blah, blah.

"Don't worry about it, sis. Father and I will handle the Teryns. Aren't you glad you don't have to be involved in this mess?" I already am, more than you know. I shrug my shoulders.

I watch the double doors close after Nic. I have to know what's going on in there, but I can't just barge in. Then my gaze lands on a much smaller door.

CHAPTER 24

Nobody notices when I slip into the servants' corridor. Breakfast has already been served, and there is no one here with me. I turn off the oil lanterns so I can find a crack large enough for spying.

My claustrophobia flares up in the dark, tunnel-like passage. My heart pounds and I break out in a cold sweat. The urge to flee clamors, but I cannot give in to panic. Who knows when I'll have another chance like this?

Leaning a hand on the stone wall, I take deep and deliberate breaths, inhaling the aroma of ancient bricks mingling with the aroma of baked pastries. Then I head off.

Fortune winks at the first turn of the winding corridor. A small shaft of light penetrates the darkness. I lean close to the narrow fissure, no wider than a finger, and peer through.

In the middle of the royal negotiation hall, two half-moon-shaped tables face each other. The first table's polished stone top shines in the two sunlight. Held up by thick legs carved in the likeness of river dolphins. Crystal trays piled high with mouth-watering pastries remain untouched in front of General Callum and Colonel Teague. Though the colonel eyes the finger foods in front of him, he doesn't reach for them.

Across from them, Father, Nic, and High Adviser Ellar, along with fourteen other advisers, pose at a similar table. This time supported by legs carved in the image of deepwater sharks. Terrible and enormous predators who snack on the river dolphins.

Silence rules the room, with a staring contest. The Teryns wear a bored expression, while the Uhnans sneer in condescension. But the worry lines on the foreheads of the advisers betray their unease.

"Why are you here?" Father asks.

General Callum leans back in his seat. "You know why we are here. You invited us."

"I invited you here because you were already on your way. Isn't that true?"

The general inclines his head.

"We know that you are on a 'warpath'—an action that your Wise Women sanctioned," High Adviser Ellar says, his distaste for the Teryns' quest clear. "What we don't understand is why."

"The Era War is upon us," Colonel Teague responds.

Disbelieving gasps and murmurs rise from the advisers.

"Why should we believe you?" asks Adviser Thom, whose prominent white beard reaches the table. "The last one was a millennium ago and the mages called it the "last" Era War. Yet here you are telling us otherwise."

The Uhnans laugh, mocking the warriors.

"How do we know," Adviser Goll adds, twirling the edge of his handlebar mustache between his thumb and forefinger, "that you are not using the Era War as an excuse to attack worlds without repercussions?"

All the advisers murmur in agreement, while Father, Nic, and the high adviser observe the Teryn delegation.

General Callum glances at a young warrior sitting on his far left. The warrior jumps up and leaves the room at a run.

The advisers exclaim in offense, but the warrior is already heading back, carrying a covered cage that's half his size, holding it as if it weighs nothing. The young man drops the rattling cage between the two tables and stands to the side.

"What is the meaning of this?" Adviser Vall, with one milky eye, snaps.

General Callum nods. The young warrior tears the cloth cover off the cage.

Vicious snarling rips through the air, and a hideous monster bucks against the thick metal bars.

With jaws dropped, the advisers stare at the nightmarish creature inside the cage.

Repulsion runs down my spine in waves at the sight of it. The thing inside the cage might have been a gray wolf once, but now it bears little semblance to the majestic animal found in most wintry worlds. Its twisted and grotesque body roils with corruption. Corruption that left behind bare and rotting skin, with raw sinew oozing black fluid. Black orb eyes full of rage bore into Father and Nic. Dark gray foam splatters from its huge fangs. Snarling, it claws the metal floor of the cage with long black talons, leaving behind thick gouges. Then the monster bangs its body against the metal bars, over and over, heedless of the damage to itself.

General Callum strides to the raging animal. He unsheathes a long-sword from over his right shoulder. With a quick motion, General Callum thrusts through the bars of the cage into the chest of the raging creature.

Everyone except the Teryn warriors jump to their feet, shouting in surprise.

The monster should be dead, but instead it is back on its feet, in the process of shaking off the stab wound. "*That's* how we know the Era War has started."

General Callum grabs his longsword in both of his hands and slams the blade through the creature's head. It doesn't get up again. The general wipes the sword with a rag and sheathes it. He nods to the young warrior, who covers the cage and carries it out of the hall.

General Callum faces Father and Nic. "That was a half-corrupted animal, a dark fiend—the first sign of the archgod growing an army. If this would have matured into a fully corrupted one, we couldn't kill it with mere weapons or mage magic. We found an inhabited moon full of these animals in Galaxy Four."

Nic pales. "You mean there are more of these corrupted creatures?"

"Most of them fully corrupted too," General Callum says. "Even though we blew up the moon to prevent the archgod from making more of them, we couldn't eliminate the already made ones. By now the archgod must have collected them and absorbed them into his army."

Father addresses the general. "You showed us that animal to prove that the Era War has started. I won't argue with you whether that claim is true or not. Not after what we've seen. I ask you again, what do you want from us?"

General Callum says, "I want you to decide whether you are with us or against us."

Nic slams his hand on the table. "How dare you threaten us!"

Colonel Teague says, "We are here to see how best the Pax Septum Coalition, with its nineteen worlds, can assist us in our efforts. The Teryn Praelium is committed to stopping the archgod from gaining more soldiers."

"By destroying worlds?" High Adviser Ellar says.

The colonel smiles at him, flashing even white teeth. "Only as a last resort."

The high adviser points at the general. "But it is you who decides what constitutes a last resort, isn't it?"

General Callum narrows his eyes. "When it's us on the front lines dealing with half-corrupted dark fiends and dark servants, then yes, we decide when to deploy drastic measures."

Nic glares at the general. "That's unacceptable!"

Colonel Teague waves another pastry in the air. "The Teryn Praelium is committed to do anything to prevent the Archgod of Chaos and Destruction from gaining power. Winning the Era War is in all our best interests, but it is by far not a guaranteed outcome. The Archgoddess of the Eternal Light and Order won the previous Era War at the last minute. It came at a terrible cost. Nearly sixty percent of the Seven Galaxies' worlds were destroyed."

"We all know those facts," High Adviser Ellar says. "Why should the Pax Septum Coalition get involved in any of this?"

A reddish-yellow light flashes in the general's gaze as he looks at the high adviser. "Just because you are hiding in the corner of Galaxy Five doesn't mean the Era War will spare you."

"That's absurd," Nic snaps. "Uhna is not hiding!"

"Whether we like it or not, we are all affected by this war," Colonel Teague says. "We learned much from the mistakes of previous era wars." He looks around the room, meeting every man's eyes before continuing, "First, banding together is the only way to stand against the growing number of half-corrupted dark fiends and dark servants. Second, stamping out the corruption before it matures into full level is paramount."

Father sits back. "What can the coalition do?"

General Callum smiles for the first time. "That is what we are here to find out."

I sigh. It seems Uhna is caught in the middle, between the Teryn Praelium and the archgods' war, and if we are not careful, we'll be ground up like dried shrimps crushed for feed.

Suddenly General Callum's head snaps up, and he stares at the spot where

I am hiding behind the wall, as if he heard me exhale. Could he really have heard that tiniest noise?

But then I don't have time to ponder it any longer. Colonel Teague heads toward the servants' entrance in a hurry, and I am sprinting out of the corridor before he can catch me spying.

CHAPTER 25

Closing the double doors to the royal library, I lean against the cold, hard surface.

After I ran out of the servants' corridor before Colonel Teague could catch me, I went into the kitchen out of habit. Seeing the empty spot where Deidre usually worked nearly undid me. Jossim, the head of servants, noticed me right away. The elderly man had known Deidre and the other murdered servants for many years. He conveyed his deepest sympathy and expressed his worry over the murders, and how much that fear affected the servants. I wanted to reassure him that it won't happen again, but that would have been a lie. Instead, I asked his assistance to gather any information from the servants that could provide clues to go on.

Using my crystal necklace, I send a message to Arrov, requesting a pickup so I can go to the camp. I have my first report for Xor ready. Well, sort of ready.

Arrov responds within seconds, and I exhale in relief when I read that he needs a few hours before he can fetch me. It will give me some time to organize my thoughts.

The royal library is a place I love. I inhale that wonderful aroma of ancient books and scrolls.

Ever since High Adviser Ellar gifted me my first tome—a story about a runaway princess who traveled the Seven Galaxies with her trusted sidekick, getting into all kinds of troubles—I never stopped reading.

The library stretches before me, two stories tall. Dark wood covers every surface—the panels on the walls; the curving arches on the ceiling; and the floor, which runs endlessly in this cavernous space. More arches highlight the jutting balconies on the left and right, perpendicular to the larger archways on the ceiling, with wide support columns connecting them, like waypoints. Beyond the balconies are dark bookcases, too many to count, bursting with tomes and ancient scrolls. A treasure trove of knowledge from all over the Seven Galaxies.

The heels of my boots click rhythmically on the shiny hardwood floor, echoing in the silence. But there is no one here to be bothered by it. No one in the court bothers to read these ancient tomes anymore.

I reach the end of the wide corridor, where it branches out. On my left it turns into a series of chambers used for art exhibition. Full-sized sculptures and marble busts surround priceless paintings displayed in the warrens of interconnecting rooms.

On my right an open atrium waits, with brown leather sofas scattered about. Long white marble columns support the frosted glass dome ceiling of this oversized sunroom. But the columns are for decoration only—the ceiling is built on a T'erra-infused iron cage, the very first application of magic-infused technology that the mages bestowed on us. I wonder if my father ever regretted this gift, one that set off a wave of technological advancements on Uhna and every other world in the coalition in turn. Which led to the Magic Cleansing War. Ending with the mages banned from the coalition worlds. Until now.

Until Father decided to use a mage to officiate at his wedding to Beathag. Since mages are the only ones who can infuse weapons with elemental magic, the timing is not so conspicuous as it seemed six months ago. Not since the arrival of the Teryns.

As I recline on the closest leather sofa, my gaze trails the dust particles swimming in the two sunlight, floating on an invisible breeze. The supple leather hugs my body like a warm embrace as I sink deep into the cushions. I gather my thoughts to work on a cohesive report, but my gaze lands on the magnificent and detailed murals under the glass dome, and I lose the strand of thought in an instant.

Maybe it's the threat of war that makes me compare our current situation with the past. On one hand, there is Xor and the rebellion against the monarchy. While on the other hand, there is the Teryn Praelium and the Era War. Both seem inevitable, albeit on a different scale. Yet Uhna is stuck in the middle, nonetheless.

I can't help but long for the simplicity of times shown in the murals. It is not that I don't understand the danger of fighting in the middle of a raging ocean against a squid monster with hundreds of tentacles, whose fangs are made even more threatening in the mural by flashing bolts of lightning that illuminate them. Neither do I misjudge the peculiar situation that the next mural depicts, a deceitfully sunny day with the water roiling around pirate ships from attacking hordes of spiked sea dragons with their turquoise mosaic scales that reflect the two suns' harsh light.

Still, I have no doubt that those long gone times were simpler. You knew exactly who the enemy was—a monster, or hordes of them. You fought for your life and then moved on. These battles had meaning, such as the last mural, which shows the famous battle where all the pirate houses, predecessors of our high society houses, fought each other for one to emerge as victorious and lead them all. Many found their graves in the Fyoon Ocean, while my great-great-many-great-grandfather consolidated his power and established the ruling House of Serrain.

In those times, you fought with honor. There was an unwritten code that they all lived by. There was none of this negotiation for alliance whalecrap the Teryn Empire hides behind, disguising their true intention, to conquer other worlds.

Why does the Era War have to happen now? What does it even mean for us?

I stifle a yawn. None of my family ever prayed to any of the gods, guardian or archgod. They trusted their own skills to get over whatever obstacles they had to contend with. Nor did I ever pray from true belief to the gods. Mom only taught me the basic prayer. I don't imagine the archgoddess would even notice if I asked for her help. Why should she? We mortals are specks of dirt under their immortal fingernails, too little to bother with, simple annoyances.

Another yawn pops up, and before I can reel in my thoughts, my eyelids slide shut and I plunge into a dream that has been haunting me for months.

CHAPTER 26

I stand on a grassy hill, facing a valley that's buried under thick and rolling fog. Beside me are a few hundred soldiers, but it's not my body that casts a long shadow on the ground, it's too tall and muscular. I survey the soldiers, who are all handpicked and battle-tried. Each and every man and woman loyal and capable. I fought beside them many times. *Dying by their side today will be an honor.* But it is not my own thought that pops in my head. It's too strange. Too confident.

"Where are the reinforcements?" a male voice asks from behind me. That voice belongs to my soulmate. The dream woman's soulmate.

The purest love flows through my heart. Love that makes life worth living, filling it with purpose and happiness.

Turning, I face the most impressive man I've ever seen. His face is the definition of handsome, with a straight nose and a square chin. Lush lips pull into a smile, begging to be kissed. His skin gold toned, glowing bright with power. His striking face framed by long blond hair that is so light, it looks as if sunlight is infused into every strand. His eyes, the color of molten gold, bore into mine with intensity.

"Triann, I . . ." His voice trails off, as if choked by suppressed emotions. He doesn't have to say it. I can see his never-ending love shining in the depths of his gaze.

"I know, Cadeon," I say in a raspy voice. "There will be no reinforcements. We wait no more. We'll make our stand here, on Stavhl."

I expect to wake now. The dream usually ends here. But instead, it continues.

Dread fills me as the thick fog lifts from the valley below.

Hundreds of thousands of monsters charge out of the fog. Rotting, terrible parodies of once-living animals. Deadly, filled with mindless rage and aggression that only killing could satisfy. The grotesque creatures shriek in a bone-chilling sound.

"We cannot let the Archgod of Chaos and Destruction gain another world for his growing army of dark fiends," I say to Cadeon. "The corruption must be stopped."

Readying for a charge signal, I raise my arm over my head, my skin glowing an eerie golden light. Then power stirs in me. Magic that I never knew I possessed flows through my veins. It is limitless, and intoxicatingly potent. It almost feels right to have it. I recognize each light element as they rise to my call: A'ris for air; T'erra for soil; A'qua for water; Fla'mma for fire; A'nima for all living things; and Lume for light. They coalesce into one wave, melding together, held in check by the dream body's practiced control.

Triann forces the raw wave of magic to obey her wish, and two blazing longswords form in our hands, swirling with currents of magical energy.

"In the name of The Lady," I shout, "charge!"

The valley, the monsters, and the soldiers fall away. I drop into blackness.

I try to wake, but I still can't.

"Lilla," a raspy female voice says, "don't be afraid."

I turn, even though I am bodiless in the darkness, facing a tall woman with bright golden hair and molten gold eyes and dressed in a flowing silver dress. I've never met her, but I have heard her voice multiple times in my dreams. Triann.

"What is this? How can you be here?" Why can't I wake from this dream?

"You are right that this is a dream. It's my only way to reach you. It is also my recollection—my last memory of the Battle of Stavhl, from the previous Era War, where Cadeon and I perished fighting the Dark Lord of Destruction, or DLD, as I like to call him. You know him as the Archgod of Chaos and Destruction."

It hurts to hear that they lost their lives in that battle a millennium ago. I always wondered what happened to the two of them, but I imagined it in a different way—getting married, having children, living a full and happy life, dying of natural causes. That's what I would want.

"I searched for Stavhl in all the known maps and history books, but I couldn't find it."

"There is no more Stavhl. Cadeon and I stopped the DLD's advancement, but it came at a price—we had to destroy the very planet with Lume to succeed."

"Why have I been dreaming your memory for all these months?"

"I have been sharing it with you on purpose."

"Why?"

Triann smiles, moving closer. "You are so much like your mother. Stubborn and relentless when you're focused on something."

"What did you say?" How could this woman who died a thousand years ago know my mother? Just how old was Mom? She didn't look a day over twenty-five in my holo-image!

"She was a fierce Lumenian. Just like you."

"Lumenian?" I've only seen that word in a few ancient scrolls, without much explanation and always in connection to the era wars.

Triann places her hands on my shoulders and studies me. I can feel the warmth and weight of her fingers, as if she is real. She picks up one of my dark violet strands. Repulsed, she drops it, and shakes her hand as if she got burned. "Eilish, what have you done?"

It takes all my effort not to snap at her. "Please answer me. What's a Lumenian?"

She snorts and steps back. "Not what, but who. There is so much Eilish hasn't told you, and I fear this will cost you."

Triann grimaces. "I don't have much time, so you must listen to everything I tell you. Your mother was from Lume, our home world. Lumenians are a legendary race, the children of The Lady. We were created to fight her enemies, the dark fiends and dark servants of DLD in the era wars. It is our sacred honor and duty. It is your duty, too."

"It is not *my* duty." Mom never told me anything about Lumenians or fighting in the Era War. Something doesn't add up. "If you are immortals, how come you can be killed?"

"It's true we can live a long life, thousands of years if needed, but we are not immortals. We can be killed if we are not careful. This is how balance is restored."

I have a hard time believing her. Especially since . . . "I don't look anything like you or Cadeon."

"Your mom ran away from Lume when The Lady prohibited us from leaving. The archgoddess thought that would stop DLD from hunting and killing us into extinction." Sorrow flashes in her eyes. "Eilish couldn't stand feeling imprisoned on Lume. Your mom ran away—"

"Mom ran away?" I am so much like Mom, more than I even thought. What I wouldn't give to have Mom alive!

"She did. Eilish believed in fighting. She thought hiding out on a planet was cowardly. Your mom must have found a way to disguise her true origins, and yours in turn. Not even The Lady could pinpoint her location. But I do wonder what price she must have paid for it. I detect something wrong in you. Something that shouldn't coexist with your Lumenian side. I—"

"There is nothing wrong with me!" I snap. How could Triann imply such a thing?

"No. Of course not." She shakes her head. "Anyway, no one would recognize you as a Lumenian now. It took me more than five hundred years to find Eilish's tracks. Once I learned of your existence, another nineteen to find a way to talk to you."

"But why did Mom want to hide from The Lady? Why didn't she wanted the archgoddess to find me?"

"We are out of time," Triann says. "There is so much to tell you, but I cannot. I have stayed too long as it is. The burden of finding the missing knowledge is on you." Her expression sobers as she adds, "I have to ask your forgiveness. I have broken my vow to Eilish to never look for her or any of her children. But I had no choice."

"Why?" Mom knew Triann would come looking for me?

Triann's eyes well up. "She has Cadeon."

"Who has Cadeon?"

"You must wake up before she arrives."

"Who are you talking about?"

Triann lunges at me, drawing her magical longsword. "Wake up!"

CHAPTER 27

I jolt awake on the leather sofa, in the royal library, and promptly roll off onto the floor. Triann's warning echoes in my mind, and adrenaline primes my body. I lay still, waiting for the mysterious "she" to jump from behind one of the marble columns and attack me.

My skin feels tight and burns with the hot-and-cold-and-hot-again of magic. For a long moment I stay frozen, straining my ears to listen for any telltale signs of movement. But all is quiet.

With a sigh, I sit up and lean back against the sofa. Of course nothing happened. It was just a dream!

No, it wasn't just a dream. It was too real, too specific for my mind to conjure something like that. But if indeed real, then all I've ever known just turned upside down.

How could Mom never tell me I'm a Lumenian? Why did she run away and hide? Did she really refuse her duty to fight against the Archgod of Chaos and Destruction? Or DLD or whatever his name is?

I close my eyes with an exasperated sigh. Who can help me find answers?

"What are you doing in my library?" a cool male voice asks above me.

I yelp and jump to my feet. When I see that my hands are still glowing with that eerie golden light like Triann, I hide them behind my back.

"*Your* library?"

The man's intelligent, storm-gray eyes observe me as if I am an annoying magical anomaly he has to deal with. High cheekbones, aquiline nose, and square chin make his face aristocratic. Wide shoulders stretch his black robe with multicolored emblems representing the six light elements. His black robe gapes open to reveal a dark gray suit underneath. He brushes his long, silver hair off his shoulder instead of answering me.

He might pretend not to recognize me, but I remember him. "You are the mage who married Father and Beathag."

He bows at the waist. "Royal Elementalist Mage Ragnald at your service, Ma'hana Lilla." Somehow I doubt that.

"Since when is this *your* library, Royal Mage?"

"Since the ma'ha appointed me to the new role of royal mage." He crosses his arms, making muscles bulge under the silky material. I haven't met a lot of mages—or any, to be precise—but from what I heard, most of them tend to be on the older and wrinkly side, with crooked backs. Maybe my informant, Glenna, was a bit biased.

"I waited months to receive an office. When I realized that wouldn't happen, I took the initiative and selected my own." He looks around approvingly, then his gaze lands on me, and his expression cools.

What is his problem?

Forcing patience, I ask, "Do you know anything about the Battle of Stavhl? I need help with some, uh, research I am doing on the Archgoddess of the Eternal Light and Order." After a thought I add, "I also need everything you can give me about the Archgod of Chaos and Destruction and the last Era War."

"Is that all?"

"If you could also provide me some information on the Lumenians, that would be great." If anyone, a mage should know something about the "legendary" race.

Royal Elementalist Mage Ragnald narrows his eyes. "Let me tell you what would be 'great,'" he says, heading toward me and pushing me to back away from him.

"In all my two hundred years I have never been so humiliated as I am now. I have no office, no apprentice, and my living quarters are on the servants' level. I am supposed to handle the diplomatic relations between the Academia of Mages and the Pax Septum Coalition. How do you rekindle political connections when doors get shut in your face before you can even open your mouth? I ask you, how?"

"I have no—"

"The Academia of Mages demands that all the destroyed temples are to be rebuilt, but the ma'ha allows half of what we had. Half! As if that's not enough, the ma'ha won't provide any workers, sending me to deal with your high society houses."

I snort. I can imagine how well that goes. The royal mage glares at me.

"Sorry," I say, but for what, I am not sure at this point.

"Those arrogant ma'hars wouldn't spare a single soul for my temples, and the ma'ha cannot force them. It's been months, and I have achieved nothing. Yet I am being commanded to infuse weapons—even though it's only supposed to happen after the temples were built. As the agreement between Uhna and the Academia of Mages dictates. This diplomatic task is impossible, doomed from the start. I have failed and there is nothing I can do. Because nobody cares. Not the ma'ha, nor the ma'hars, nor the citizens who were glad to see mages banished decades ago. No one!"

I can imagine how he feels. I've been dealing with Father and his court a lot longer than he has. "I care—"

"My title is meaningless. No one respects me. I am a social pariah at the court; everyone avoids me out of fear or distrust. I can't even take evening walks around the village on this island for fear of a mob showing up and chasing me away like I am some vermin. I've had enough. I feel so imprisoned in this palace!"

I know how that feels.

"I am ready to burst into flames!"

"Can you do that? Can you really burst into flames?"

"No," he says, and stops walking. "As a matter of fact, no one can."

"I'm sorry that you—"

The mage glares, as if to say he doesn't need anyone's pity. "All information on the Battle of Stavhl is classified. Accessible by special request, which the academia usually denies. Information on the archgods is classified—only ruling monarchs have the privilege to examine those records."

"But I need to know!"

"And I need to leave this horrible world, but I guess neither of us will get what we want," the mage says and resumes his trek through the library.

I jump out of the way before he runs me over. "If someone suspects they have magical powers, what should they do?" There. I asked, and it only hurt a little.

"If a person shows signs of magical powers, they must follow the clear magical hierarchy established in the Decree of Magic by the academia."

I have no idea what that decree is. The way he communicates, all mono-tonic and haughty, I'm not surprised no one wants to be his friend. "En-lighten me."

The mage sighs, as if everyone should know this. "If he shows aptitude toward the A'ris element, meaning toward the healing arts, then he should contact the Healer's College. Not that they would know much about mag-ic. Anyone can become a healer these days."

"Anyone? Really?" I remember Glenna struggling through her training years, and the relentless hard work she had to put in to graduate.

My sarcasm is lost on the mage. "On the other hand, if he has some-thing more useful, like the ability to set buildings on fire—"

"How is *that* useful?"

"Then I would recommend for him to immediately contact the Aca-demia of Mages, where skilled and knowledgeable elders will guide his future onto the most amazing path of becoming a mage."

Someone has a high opinion about the mages.

"What if that person's magic doesn't fit into either category?"

Royal Elementalist Mage Ragnald looks at me, his expression incredu-lous. "According to the academia, that would not be possible."

What is he not telling me? "Are you sure?"

"Of course I am sure."

I don't want to reveal to him that I have magic. Not until I know how he would react. So instead I ask, "What about a person who can manipulate another person's will?" That's what Beathag did. I think.

"That's not magic per se—it is only a slight affinity to the A'ris element. An offshoot of healing. We see this among the healers often, where care-less breeding dulls magical talent to the point where hybrids emerge. They have very limited magic and are insignificant in the eyes of the academia. In another generation or two, whatever trickle of magic they have would dry out altogether."

Then where do I fit in with my magic?

We reach the exit. The royal mage pushes one of the double doors open. "Now if you'll forgive me, I have work to do."

"But—"

With a loud click, he shuts the door in my face.

Oh, the arrogance! It takes all my effort to resist kicking the door. It's not the poor thing's fault that the mage behaved so condescendingly.

"There you are, Lilla," Arrov says, loping down the corridor. "Xor can't wait to see you."

CHAPTER 28

Arrov and I step through the gateway and into the underground rebel camp. I feel nervous and underprepared for this meeting.

We find Xor alone in the room, sitting on the wobbly metal table as usual. Arrov and I stop in front of him and stand at attention.

"What do you have for me?"

I open my mouth to speak. "I uh—"

Jorha pops her head in, asking, "Xor, do you have a minute?" He waves her in.

She hurries in, clearly upset, and hands Xor a transparent digi-scroll. "We've lost another few dozen rebels since yesterday. They failed to report this morning. But that's not the worst of it." She hands him another digi-scroll. "At dawn, as I was doing my rounds, I found twenty-five refugees and rebels. Murdered."

Murdered? Just like Deidre . . . all the servants from the beach.

She continues, "This must be Overseer Irvine's doing. But the guards went too far this time. They didn't even bother to hide this atrocity, leaving the dead behind, as if to taunt us. The overseer has to be stopped, or I will personally—"

Xor places a hand on Jorha's shoulder. "I will take care of it." She looks up at him, and something unspoken passes between them. Jorha nods, visibly calmer, then leaves the room as fast as she came in.

Xor then turns to me. "Continue."

"The Teryns are here to establish an alliance with the coalition, against the Archgod of Chaos and Destruction. They believe that the Era War has begun, and it's everyone's job to fight or to provide provisions for those who do. The coalition has been asked to choose a side. It was implied that if the coalition won't help willingly, then the Teryn Praelium is prepared to make the coalition 'help' by force."

Xor studies my expression. I feel as if he is judging me, only to find I've fallen short of his expectations. I recognize it, because I've seen such a disappointed look before. Father's.

"I see. What are your thoughts, Lilla?"

My eyes go wide. He's never asked for my opinion before. I can't decide whether to feel honored or put on the spot. Maybe a bit of both.

"I think that the Teryns are right about the Era War. They had proof—a half-corrupted dark fiend in a cage. They will do anything necessary to fight the Archgod of Chaos and Destruction. Even if it means going through Uhna and the coalition."

Lost in thought, Xor scratches his chin, the short bristles on his green face making a loud scraping noise as he stares past us. I wasn't expecting praise, but I would love to know what he thinks at this very moment.

"That's all, rebels," Xor says, heading out of the room.

That's it? "Wait!"

Xor stops with an eyebrow raised in question. "What is it, rebel?"

"Aren't you concerned about the Era War?"

Xor makes a noise that sounds like a snort of derision. "That's a funny question coming from you."

I don't see the humor. "I don't understand."

Something harsh shines in his dark green eyes. "I thought after your ancestor chased off the mages—not the first time something like that happened—from Uhna and from all the coalition worlds that any concerns about the gods went with them. After all, you did destroy all their temples, didn't you?"

I blink at him, speechless.

Xor shakes his head. "I will tell you this much. I have no care for the archgods' petty fight. My sole interests lie with the rebellion and with the refugees. And I will do anything to win. This new distraction is, in fact, to our benefit. While the monarchy deals with the Teryns, their attention is not focused on us. Couldn't have organized it better myself."

"But—"

"We are done here, rebel!" Xor strides out of the room, and I let out a frustrated exhalation.

"I don't understand. I thought he would be more worried about the Era War," I say to Arrov.

"Not here," Arrov says and raps on the worn leather cuff. As he hugs my shoulders, we step into the swirling shadows.

CHAPTER 29

The freezing cold hits the second I step through the gateway. A stark contrast from the hot air of the rebel camp.

My feet slide on snow-covered cobblestones, and my breath comes out in big puffs of clouds. "Where are we?"

I squint in the darkness. We seem to have arrived in a narrow alley, between two log houses, clearly not on Uhna.

"You'll see." Arrov takes me by my elbow and leads me out of the alley. "Now we can speak freely."

"I don't understand Xor," I say with teeth chattering and glance around.

Icicles hang from roofs covered in a thick blanket of pristine white snow. Their top layers are frozen and sparkle like crystals in the large moon's light. Quaint wooden houses line either side of the street, with Fla'mma-infused gaslights illuminating the way. Men, women, and children, dressed in attire more fitting for summer, spill from their homes, laughing as wolf dogs dart around their feet. They are heading away from us, with excited purpose. I know of only one world where this weather would be considered warm: A'ice.

A blast of wind cuts through my thin tunic dress and leggings, as if I wear nothing. It hurts to breathe the clean and frigid air that's scented with crisp snow and hickory wood smoke from chimneys. The tantalizing aroma of roasting boar mixes with the sweet fragrance of pastries filled with cinnamon and nutmeg. My belly grumbles.

"I told you not to trust Xor," Arrov says.

"This has nothing to do with trust. He should be more concerned about the Era War and its consequences for everyone in the Seven Galaxies."

"Why would he?" Arrov shakes his head. "He is far from the Era War."

"I just thought he'd be more worried about the Teryns. They were the ones who destroyed his home world, right?"

"I don't think so. From what I heard, Xor arrived on Uhna two decades ago, seeking asylum. He used to be an archaeologist, specializing in extinct cultures. That's why he had those umbrae travel gauntlets—used in deep excavations."

Oh. "I see." Is that why he has Jorha and the rebels excavating in the camp? For his hobby?

"You heard him. Xor will use the Teryns to his benefit. Even if it means allowing a couple of young royals in his midst, like you, the twins, or me."

"I understand that but shouldn't he—" A sneeze interrupts me.

Arrov walks backward. "Lilla, it doesn't matter what you think he should do. Xor will always do what *he* thinks best, so you might as well stop worrying about him. It's out of our control."

"That might be easy for you, but not for me." It irks me that Xor is making a mistake. I worry that the refugees will pay the price.

"Arrov, I shouldn't be here. I've been gone too long as it is. We should go back to Uhna."

Instead of answering, Arrov stops in front of a merchant's booth to buy some winter attire for me. Finished paying, he says, "This is a great idea, and I'll tell you why. It has to do with my personal philosophy."

"Really?" I accept the most exquisite, dark blue cape lined with faux black fur. With a big grin, Arrov helps me into the cape, and I pull its hood over my head. I button it up with numb fingers. It hugs my body like a streamlined dress, fitting perfectly, narrowing at the waist, and widening into a long skirt at my feet. The same faux fur lines the arms, the bottom of its opening reaching past my knees.

"You look great," Arrov says and clears his throat. He hands me a pair of dark blue leather gloves and gray boots.

I mumble thanks. "What's your philosophy?" I take my worn leather slippers off my frozen feet and get into the boots, hobbling in the process.

Arrov steadies me by the arm so I won't fall. "It's simple, really. I don't worry about things out of my control. I live only in the moment. Like this one. What could be better than being in the company of a beautiful girl at a festival celebrating the arrival of spring?" He gives me a dazzling smile as he takes off his white leather jacket. Hooking it on a finger, he drapes it over his shoulder.

Smiling, I shake my head. "I would love to stay, really, but I have to go back."

"Even if I wanted to, I can't take you anywhere. The gauntlets need to recharge for a couple of hours before they'll work again." Arrov takes my slippers out of my hand.

"What? We cannot stay here for two hours—"

"More like four hours," Arrov corrects me.

"That's too long!"

Arrov shrugs. "Nothing can be done about it. We'll just have to wait. Why not have some fun while we're here?"

Crossing my arms, I frown at him.

"Relax." With a careless motion, he throws my slippers into a metal can.

"No! Don't!" I lunge, nearly diving into the garbage can, but Arrov pulls me back. Just as flames burst from the can, incinerating its contents.

Tears well in my eyes as I whirl to him. "How could you do this?"

Arrov raises an eyebrow. "See? You are too stressed out worrying about every little thing. They're just slippers. I'll buy you ten pairs like them if that will make you happy."

"You don't understand." I stare into the flames. They weren't just any slippers. They were a gift from Deidre. She saved her credits for months to buy me those. They were the last things she gave me, and now I have nothing left of her.

I turn my back on Arrov.

He faces me, smiling. But I look away. I won't let him charm me out of my anger.

"Come on, Lilla. Don't be like this."

I glance away.

"I'm sorry I destroyed your shoes—"

"And made me stranded for hours."

"And made you stranded for hours. All I wanted was to spend some time with you. Can you forgive me? I cannot stand to see you sad. I would give anything to see you smile again."

He bends down until our noses almost touch. "Please?" He makes the most pathetic pleading face.

I smile. I can't help it.

"That's better!" Arrov grabs my hand. "Now let's go have some fun!"

CHAPTER 30

Arrov takes off in a jog, pulling me after him.

I try to keep up with his long strides. "Where are we going?"

"They are about to start the snow sculpting contest," Arrov says over his shoulder. "You'll love it."

We arrive just in time to join a long line of contestants, filling up the top of a hill, when a shout signals the start of the contest.

Wide-eyed, I stare at Arrov. "What am I supposed to do?"

He picks up a handful of snow, forming it into a ball. "Anything you want."

Around me, people young and old dive into the deep snow, shaping it with expressions of joy and concentration.

"I can't remember the last time I played in the snow."

Arrov, busy forming a brick out of snow, beams at me. "I've never stopped. This is the best part of spring!"

We spend the next hour side by side, our shoulders touching occasionally as we work. I try my best to sculpt a snow fish, but the head won't stick to the body. I look around for a stick, but there is none.

Unexpectedly, Arrov's snow fortress implodes, a huge chunk of its side falling off like a miniature avalanche. He looks so crestfallen, so unlike his cheerful self, that I giggle.

"You think this is funny?" he asks and forms a ball out of the snow. He throws it at me with a quick aim.

It lands on the side of my neck. I gasp from the cold as the snow splatter hits me. "So this is how it is?" I grab the stubborn fish head. "Then you better watch out. My revenge is coming!" I jump to my feet and hurl the large snow chunk at Arrov.

He scrambles to get out of the way, but he slips and falls on his bottom just as the snow fish head hits him in the chest. Slapping my knees, I laugh at his upset expression.

"If I were you, I'd start running now. You're talking to the best snowball champion of all of A'ice!" With eyes full of happiness, he picks up a large handful of snow and tries to shove it down the neck of my cape. We wrestle until we lose our balance and slip, rolling down the side of the hill.

I land on my back with an "oof," with a grinning Arrov on top of me, his hands braced by my shoulders. He studies my face, his smile disappearing. His gaze traveling from my eyes to my lips and back.

Leaning close, Arrov brushes his lips against mine. It is the lightest of touches, tender and soft. Then he kisses me.

My eyes close on their own. His kiss is full of desire, passion, yet it is lighthearted and playful at the same time. It's as if he is transferring all that he is, all that joyful abandonment, to me. To show how amazing life can be. To show that nothing matters at this moment except us.

A group of drunk people stumble down a hill not far from us.

Arrov and I pull apart. He jumps to his feet, helping me up as he assesses the situation.

I squint when I see General Callum's tall form among the group of men.

"Lilla? What's wrong?"

But it's just a tall stranger who resembles the general. Even so, the illusion of this evening is broken beyond repair. Shattered by reality.

CHAPTER 31

Loch Ramor

"There is really no need for the blindfold anymore." Loch blinks against the bright light of the white room.

This kidnapping routine is getting tiresome. Loch had worked too hard to get where he is only to be plucked from his own bed without notice. He'd killed people for less offense. Too bad he can't kill the archgod.

He did as he swore and sent suitable bodies to the archgod—twenty-one from the palace, and twenty-five from the closest refugee camp. It wasn't his fault that the archgod was picky about choosing a body. It is fortunate that Loch is excellent at disposing bodies while driving home the point. He made sure to block the investigation of the dead servants. As for the refugee camp, a healthy dose of fear would keep them in check. This way, Loch could kill two fish with one stone—putting added pressure on the slippery rebel leader while making sure everyone in the palace knew that a new age is upon the palace.

Loch glances around, taking in the white room, which hasn't changed since his last visit. He slants a look at the Archgod of Chaos and Destruction, who finishes the last brushstrokes on another beautiful landscape, this time a blooming meadow with yellow flowers in the middle of a forest.

The archgod seems shorter and different.

Loch nods in understanding. "I see the last young lord I sent you was satisfactory."

Loch had handpicked this minor ma'har, whom no one would miss, for this reason. The poor thing had no family left to look for him. He wasn't a rich lord, and he was always too quiet in the court, making few personal connections.

The body in question is five feet, ten inches, early twenties. A perfect mix of average characteristics. The height is not too tall, nor too short. The weight isn't too fat, nor it is overly thin or muscular, but average. It has hair that isn't brown or blond, but a modest dishwater color that won't stand out.

A blandly unassuming face matches the body with its unmemorable features. If the archgod decided to walk around the palace in this body, no one would blink an eye or would be able to recall how he looked. Only the eyes show the banked inhuman power of the archgod in their hazel depths.

The Archgod of Chaos and Destruction turns, and Loch lowers his eyes, catching the smile on the archgod's face. "Young and virile, just the way I like them. I took this body for a stroll a dozen times and no one bothered me. It was quite refreshing to walk around among the unsuspecting and ignorant. That reminds me, you have more bodies to take out."

Loch bows. "As you say, master." He ignores the bitter taste in his mouth. He thought he'd never have to utter *that* word ever again.

Memories of being a ten-year-old bubble to the surface of Loch's mind. Memories that are too horrible and too revolting to keep, yet Loch uses them to push himself toward his goal. To remind himself how close he got to ending up with nothing. Nearly dead. Like his mother.

He doesn't want to blame it all on her, but he cannot help it. It was because of her weakness that they ended up living in servitude in the home of a high society ma'har. An old and lonely man who took in the poor single mother with her young son. Nothing out of the ordinary on the surface.

But under the surface, the old lord was different. When Loch tried to refuse him, the ma'har threatened to kick his mother back to the street where they'd come from. Loch couldn't let that happen. She was already in a fragile state of mind, barely scraping by from day to day. Her artist soul suffering and dying in servitude. Loch did what he had to, in exchange for his mother's safety.

But it wasn't enough for the ma'har. He wanted Loch's mother, too. No matter how much Loch begged the ma'har to leave his mother out of this, it didn't achieve anything. The ma'har went after her.

She fought him off, refused his offer, but not before she learned the ugly truth that Loch had already been harmed by the ma'har. And she hadn't noticed it happening.

That stormy night, Loch found her lifeless body. He couldn't save her.

Rage, like nothing he ever felt, overtook him. He went into the sleeping ma'har's room, clutching the only memento his father left behind, a jeweled dagger with a spiral blade. Loch hated that dagger. It was a reminder of how his father didn't want Loch. Bribing his mother with it. But she refused, took the weapon, and ran away.

Loch dipped into that hate, drew strength from it as he gripped the dagger with both hands. Its point poised over the sleeping ma'har's chest.

Loch will never forget that night. It was the night he lost his mother. It was the night he first killed, and created a new identity for himself. It was the last night he ever allowed someone to use him and dominate him. Until the Archgod of Chaos and Destruction, that is.

"I had a humble start too," the archgod says. "I came first, as an entity at the beginning of time, created by the Omnipower. I ruled all twelve elements: A'qua and Murky A'qua; T'erra and Barren T'erra; Fla'mma and Black Fla'mma; A'ris and Dusky A'ris; A'nima and Diseased A'nima; Acerbus and Lume. I was darkness and light. I was neither male nor female. Just power. A dark energy. It took millions of years of worship to give me form, gender, and names that bring fear and awe to any who hear them."

"They called me 'the Slayer of Souls' and 'the Destroyer,' or my personal favorite, 'the Dark Lord of Destruction.' I ruled for many millennia, and as my true nature took over, chaos and corruption reigned free. That's when She was created. For balance."

A twist of the archgod's lips turns his expression bitter. "Suddenly I had no right to all the twelve elements. I had to share them with the Archgoddess of the Eternal Light and Order. She got all the light elements: A'ris, A'qua, Fla'mma, T'erra, A'nima, and Lume. While I got all the dark elements: Murky A'qua, Barren T'erra, Black Fla'mma, Dusky A'ris, Diseased A'nima, and Acerbus. It was as if someone tore away half my soul. She did nothing to deserve them."

The archgod shakes his head in frustration. "Where The Lady is light, I am dark. I could never win, while she could do nothing wrong in the eye of the Omnipower. I fought Her for control. In the first Era War."

Loch raises an eyebrow. So this is how the era wars started.

The archgod sighs. "But I lost. After a millennium of planning, I tried again. I nearly won that time. That is when the Omnipower allowed The Lady to create soldiers to fight me and to cruelly hunt all my children."

The archgod laughs mirthlessly. "She took Her five elements and formed them together into a being, Her first attempt at creating the Lumenians. But something was missing, and it wouldn't hold its form. Unlike my dark servants, whom I create by corrupting existing people, She created from scratch. Those first beings of Hers had nothing to hold them together. That's when The Lady broke the rules. She breathed Her sixth element, Lume, which was forbidden, into Her creations. Thus She made the all-too-perfect Lumenians, the very antitheses of me and mine. I expected the Omnipower to interfere, as the balance was tipping to Her side. But nothing happened. She came second, after me, yet She was the favored one."

"I didn't give up. I kept fighting in the next few era wars, learning all I could, and experimenting on my own to perfect my children."

An unusual and honest smile spreads on the archgod's face. "During the previous Era War, a rare child of mine was born. One who was a perfect balance of all the dark elements and Acerbus. The most powerful Ankhar of all, my right hand and general. Once again I had hope that we could win. Together."

"But She got jealous. The Lady couldn't share the Seven Galaxies with my son and Her perfect Lumenians. She hunted him and ambushed him. She killed my son, and then She won the Era War."

"From then on, all I felt was rage. And thirst for vengeance. I methodically hunted Her Lumenians, killing them one after the other. It took me six era wars to find the strategy that will make me, once again, the only archgod of the Seven Galaxies, as my right. This time I have a brilliant plan."

"May I inquire as to what that plan is?" Loch knows how it feels to long for more.

The archgod's young face takes on a maniac expression. "It is simple. My struggle with The Lady is a constant push and pull. A divine check and balance, if you will. As long as I push, She will always equally pull, undoing everything I achieved. This is meant to bring peace to the Seven Galaxies, but it only brings suffering. My children will never know peace as long as Her Lumenians are hunting them and killing them where they stand. The Omnipower is blind where The Lady is concerned. He doesn't see Her as I do. I know what She really wants. She is hoarding power, bending rules, cheating to become the only ruling archgod of the Seven Galaxies, even if it means killing me, while I have to obey the rules!"

The archgod slams his fist through the white marble right by Loch's head without any warning. White powder rains on Loch's shoulder as he stares at the raging archgod.

The archgod pulls back his unmarred fist, and the marble wall is as good as new. "I cannot keep playing Her game. It's time for drastic changes. As long as I attack Her on multiple fronts, She will only scramble to react. She will fall more behind each time, and inadvertently allow the balance to shift to my side. This is my chance to break this never-ending cycle through unstoppable momentum that will propel me to win this Era War. Finally I can avenge the death of my son and become the ruling archgod of the Seven Galaxies. Then it will be my children who are legendary, and not Hers!"

Power explodes out of the archgod. The far right wall shudders. A crack spreads through its middle, widening to six feet at the top. A huge chunk of white marble crashes to the ground with a loud bang. Fine dust scents the air with an unpleasant powdery smell.

"But now I am the one who's ahead. She has no idea where I am, and with this mortal body, She won't find me easily. I have the upper hand."

When Loch blinks, the wall is whole again. His face beads with sweat from the vortex of power. He craves it. If Loch could harness one hundredth of the power swimming in the room, he would be unstoppable.

"What would you like me to do, master?"

"The first part of my plan is almost complete. I have killed almost all of her children. Except for one I couldn't seem to find. This Lumenian is the only thing that can prevent my plan from coming to fruition. I followed the Lume magic trail to this very island. I know he is here, somewhere in this palace. I want you to find Her creation. I want you to find the last Lumenian."

CHAPTER 32

I knock on Glenna's workroom door at the Healing Center. The two sunslight has barely broken the thick gray clouds, ushering in the morning. But after the nightmare I had, I needed to talk to her.

In the dream, I was in the refugee camp. Xor and the rebels mocked me, telling me I'd never succeed as a rebel, that all I am is a spoiled ma'hana with nothing better to do. When I started to cry in shame, they all burst into laughter. Then the dream scenery changed, and I was with Arrov, at the Spring Festival, lost in a passionate kiss. But when the kiss ended, it was Cadeon, the Lumenian from my old dreams, who looked back at me with sorrow. He told me I'd never have love or happiness as long as I am bound in a marriage contract. Then, out of nowhere, thick cold chains wrapped around me, so tightly that my claustrophobia reared its head. I woke, shouting.

"Come in."

Scents of herbs and dried flowers make my nose twitch when I enter. I sneeze.

Glenna fills numerous vials with a dark potion from a pitcher with her back turned toward me. "Whatever you do, don't turn around."

"Okay," I say and turn.

Above the door perches the largest ungula spider I've ever seen. It is bigger than a dog, at least three feet wide and four feet high, with long, thin legs. Short hairs cover its yellow body. Mirrorlike eyes focus on me, and its forearm-size fangs gnash, as if in anticipation. Its two front legs end in sharp claws, hence its name, claw spider.

"Uh-oh." I stand paralyzed in the spot, even though all my instincts scream at me to run.

Glenna sighs. "You turned around, didn't you?"

"Maybe." I feel the paralysis set in deeper with each heartbeat.

"Tell me that you're not looking straight into its eyes."

"Mhmh mhmh!" I cannot properly form words anymore. My lips are too numb.

The pitcher clicks on the top of her tree-trunk desk. Glenna claps her hands. "Gwendoline, I told you to leave my patients alone, didn't I?"

The spider lets out high-pitched chitters. It moves higher up on the wall, breaking with my gaze and releasing me from the paralysis.

"Another pet of yours?"

"No," she says. "Winter came too fast this year, and she brought her off-spring to me for help, knowing they would all perish in the cold. I healed Gwendoline when she was little and broke one of her legs. Now she is back, every year, for one thing or another. I don't mind as long as she doesn't paralyze my patients." Glenna wags a finger at the spider.

"You look upset," she says, and puts corks into the vials.

"It's not every day a giant ungula spider paralyzes me with a death stare."

Glenna snorts. "It wasn't a death stare—not for another few seconds at least. Out with it."

I tell her all about my impromptu date with Arrov and the unsettling dream while we pack away the corked vials onto a shelf. "I know the marriage contract bothers me more than it should, but I—"

"What marriage contract?"

I duck my head. "The one I forgot to tell you about?"

"Just what else did you forget to tell me about?"

Too much—like the part where I am in a rebellion that she thinks is pointless. "Nothing." The lie burns in my mouth. It is safer for her this way. "Now it's only a matter of time before someone accepts the contract."

"It's not like you to give up so easily."

I blink at Glenna.

"I bet it didn't even occur to you to fight for yourself." She laughs when I nod. "You would fight the tiniest injustice any servant suffers, but you won't stand up for yourself?"

"It won't matter anyway."

"One way to find out. Maybe you could enlist Nic."

"Nic is too much of a peacemaker between Father and me. No. I'd need someone else, such as High Adviser Ellar. He might be able to help." I don't want to get my hopes up.

"That's a—" Glenna's crystal necklace beeps. She picks it up and reads the message with deepening worry lines.

I head toward the door. Maybe she is right. I gave in too easily.

"Where are you going?"

"To talk to the high adviser."

"You'll want to come with me, then," Glenna says. "I know where he is."

CHAPTER 33

It takes all my courage to keep walking down the rocky beach with Glenna. My mind knows it's not Deidre who lies on the ground, among many bodies, but I keep seeing her.

Gray storm clouds roll in and chilly winds whip the ocean. Our footsteps crunch on flat red rocks as we head down the beach on the western side of Fye Island.

I shiver in the cold, staring at the group of bodies as we stop by a somber Captain Murtagh. A dozen of his guards mill around, some talking to High Adviser Ellar, while others mark the area around the bodies. General Callum squats by them with an unreadable expression. Colonel Teague guards his back.

When I glance at the captain, he says in a low voice, "It was the Teryn general who found them. Again."

That's strange.

"Why is he here?!" a shout rings out. Overseer Irvine barrels past Glenna and me, heading straight for the general.

General Callum puts something in his pocket, then straightens to his full height, confidence pouring off of him, as if daring the overseer to take him on.

High Adviser Ellar intercepts the ma'har before the fuming lord can get an arm's length from the Teryn warrior. "It is all under control, Overseer Irvine," High Adviser Ellar says in an urgent voice. "There is nothing more to be done here."

The high adviser inclines his head toward Glenna, who is finally allowed to approach the bodies.

"He shouldn't be here!" the overseer shouts, sidestepping the high adviser. "It's not enough that he is here under false pretense, now he is sneaking around Uhna like he owns it. While working hand in hand with that rebel leader and killing our servants and high society members as well? You think you're so clever? That no one would figure out that you committed these murders? Especially since *you* found the corpses. One may wonder what reason you have to work with the local rebels. A lot! I know you're doing this to sow discord on Uhna! Shining focus on the murders and not on you while encouraging the rebels to undermine the monarchy until we're too weak to stand up against you. But you went too far this time, General Callum, and I will personally stop—"

General Callum crosses his arms. "You're insane. I had nothing to do with this or with any rebellion."

"How dare you call me insane? I know your kind! All brawn and no—"

"Overseer Irvine," High Adviser Ellar snaps, "you should head back to the palace now. Leave the work to Captain Murtagh."

The overseer sneers at General Callum. "It is not an accusation, just an observation. You may think you're unnoticeable, but it won't give you protection for long. I know that the rebellion is behind this somehow, conspiring together with this barbar—"

General Callum's face goes blank, and he heads toward the overseer. Colonel Teague jumps in front of the him, blocking him as if preventing the general from following through with whatever he planned.

With wide eyes, Glenna watches the Teryns. "Do you think General Callum is really connected to that rebellion?"

"I doubt it," I whisper back. "After all, the Teryns put more people into the rebel camps than anyone else. They wouldn't suddenly make friends with, uh, the rebellion."

"That is enough, Overseer," High Adviser Ellar says. "Captain Murtagh needs room to clean up the beach. You should leave now."

With a huff, the overseer storms away.

I eye the general. Now that the overseer blamed the general, it's as if he put the seed of suspicion in my mind.

General Callum meets my regard without any hint of guilt. He opens his mouth to say something when High Adviser Ellar steps in front of me, cutting the general from my view.

"A ma'hana shouldn't be around such tragedy," High Adviser Ellar says, offering me his arm. When I accept it, he escorts me from the beach.

I look back over my shoulder. General Callum stares after me, while Colonel Teague says something to him with a hand on his shoulder, as if preventing him from following us.

"What will happen now?" I ask as we climb the narrow dirt path that winds up the steep hill toward the Crystal Palace.

The high adviser pets my hand on the crook of his elbow. "Ma'hana Lilla, please don't worry about it. Captain Murtagh will take care of it all."

By not doing anything. Father won't lift a finger to find out who murders his own people, just like he didn't care about sending the refugees to die in his crystal mines.

Speaking of Father . . . "I need to ask your advice."

CHAPTER 34

"Now remember, let me do the talking, Ma'hana Lilla," says High Adviser Ellar and knocks on the door leading to the ma'ha's antechamber. "I'll do everything in my power to help you. It hurts me to see you in distress."

I give him a warm smile.

We enter. My stomach knots tighter with each step I take in the luxurious gold room, toward Father, who sits behind his enormous golden desk.

Nic paces in front of the desk, wearing a path in the gold-colored carpet. "I don't understand why you're letting the Teryn delegation set the parameters of this 'alliance.' And by 'alliance' I mean dictatorship. If you give in any more, they'll be our monarch, and not you!"

I glance at the high adviser as we stop at a respectful distance. "I don't think this is the right time—"

He puts a hand on my arm. "We don't know how long you have with marriage contract. It's better to ask now than wait until it's too late."

I grimace. "I guess so." I despise how little I feel in this room, the site of much humiliation. Like the time when I was eight and broke my arm in a riding accident with Fearghas, my battle horse. Father didn't seem to be upset that I was injured. No, he despised the fact that Captain Murtagh dared to gift a horse to me without his permission. Only the high adviser's tactful advice managed to cool Father's temper enough to allow me to keep Fearghas.

"Don't be overly dramatic, son. This negotiation will fail if we make a misstep. I don't have enough magic-infused weapons to arm the whole coalition armada." *Yet.* "Until then, we are not on equal terms with the Teryns and you best remember it."

Nic leans on Father's desk with both hands. "But we do have the coalition armada with ten million soldiers! I might not be a pilot anymore, but I could still lead a fleet—"

Father gets to his feet, forcing Nic to straighten as he does. "You won't lead any fleet, not with your injury. The Teryn warships outnumber our armada ten to one. They would obliterate us and subjugate whoever is left. Like they did with hundreds of worlds before us. They have been expending their empire rapidly while the coalition stayed the same. But I am about to change that."

"Why do you think I invited them to the negotiating table? I had to do everything to protect Uhna from such a fate and prevent an outright war." Father taps the glass with a finger, as if in emphasis. "Because we cannot win against them. Our most prudent choice is to go along willingly and get the most out of this 'alliance' while we can. At least that way, we will be partners rather than conquered subjects with no rights of our own."

"You're aware this is not a beneficial alliance we're getting."

"Of course I know, son. But we are the first to get them to negotiate as opposed to just absorbing us into their empire. It's a new and fragile position we are in. But as long as we are talking, there is hope that there will still be a monarchy on Uhna for you to inherit and rule."

"You know I never cared for ruling," Nic says and drops down on a sofa.

"You will once you're old enough," Father says and gestures to us to come closer. It's rare to see Father and Nic fight. And it's even rarer to see Nic lose.

The high adviser and I bow in front of Father before we take our seats across from Nic. I place my hands in my lap, trying my best to calm my racing heart. As long as I am nice, Father might listen.

High Adviser Ellar says," Your Highness—"

"Father, I don't want the marriage contract. Cancel it now because I won't go through with it."

Forget nice. He needs to know how I truly feel.

"You sent out a marriage contract for Lilla?" Nic looks at Father, astonished. "Why not for me? I'm your firstborn after all."

Father shakes his head. "I won't have a marriage contract for you. You're too young and too important to be sent away." Nic is six years older than I am! And I'm not important?

"But she is too young," Nic says, crossing his arms.

"She is nineteen years old and should have been married for three years by now. But I was too lenient with her." Father clasps his hands on the desk. "This will do her good. I'm sure of it."

"What a bunch of whalecrap—" I earn a sharp glance from Father. Right. A ma'hana doesn't swear.

"Your Highness, if I may—"

"I am not surprised, my daughter, about your stubbornness. You're trying to avoid your royal duty as always."

"That is not true! I do what is expected of me." Eventually.

"That's the problem, my daughter. You do just enough to get by. You think I don't know that you sneak out of the palace? I know everything that happens in my palace."

Not with that again! "We should go," I say to the high adviser. "This was a mistake. He will not hear reason."

"Ma'hana Lilla, if I may—"

"Do not talk in my presence as if I am not here, my daughter. I am still your father and your ma'ha."

"You mean you're my ma'ha first, then my father."

"What's that supposed to mean?"

"If you would be my father first, you would hear me out. You would let me out of this marriage contract simply because you know I don't want it. But I have no doubt it is part of some diplomatic bargain you've already made, and you won't be able to back out now."

I wait for Father to deny it, but he stays silent.

So this is how he plans to grow the coalition—through me. "You never cared about me. Not since Mom"—I choke up but push the words out—"ever since she's been gone, you don't know what to do with me. I remind you of her too much."

Father closes his eyes for a second, as if to prove that I am right.

"This is good, very good indeed," High Adviser Ellar says with an encouraging smile. "Talking about the past is the way to healing."

Nic scoffs. "I disagree. Talking about the past is what led to this festering situation. Father and sis need to put the past behind them. They need to start over if they are to have any 'healing.'"

I cross my arms. "How would you propose we start over?" Is it even worth a try after so many years of anger?

"You have to stop blaming Dad."

What? "I don't blame him."

"You always blamed me for everything, my daughter. You blamed me for that guard I 'shackled' you to. You blamed me for the way the court treats you. You even blamed me for your mother's . . ." He looks away.

"That's not true!" I don't remember the moment Father told me Mom died. All I remember is how the color seeped out of my life in those years. How nothing mattered.

"When I didn't hold you responsible for Nic's accident *your* carelessness caused."

"Who's blaming whom now, Father?"

Nic's face pales. "Dad, please don't—"

"Remember, my daughter? The accident that ruined Nic's military career?"

I swallow, staring at my clasped hands. The accident that left Nic with a permanent limp and severe vertigo. A constant reminder that he is lucky to have survived at all.

"You have nothing to say, my daughter? Aren't you going to tell me you were too young, only ten, and it's not your fault? That it was your claustrophobia that made you panic, causing your brother to crash his spacecraft?"

I clench my hands tighter until my nails cut into my skin.

"Dad, it wasn't her fault. I should have known better than to surprise her like that. I mean, I blindfolded her, for godsake! I thought . . . I could help her get over her claustrophobia."

"A weakness she has refused to deal with," Father snaps. "A convenient excuse to hide behind, if you ask me."

"But nobody asked you," I mutter.

High Adviser Ellar raises a hand. "Your Highness, please. Claustrophobia and the panic attack it triggers is a serious condition. It is known to have debilitating effects on the sufferer. One does not merely overcome it but also must learn to manage it."

Nic looks at the high adviser with surprise. "I have to say, I agree with Ma'har Ellar. I was pushing Lilla too far. It was a small ship, with the new type of harness. I didn't realize she wouldn't be comfortable. When she lost control, there was no room, and I should have paid attention to that mountain. It all happened too fast. I forgave her, Dad. Why can't you forgive her, too?"

Father eyes Nic for a long moment, then looks away.

"And Dad, you have to forgive her for what happened at your wedding. She didn't really mean to be so disrespectful. Can you really fault her after what happened between the two of them?"

Father and I take each other's measure coolly, then we say in accord, "I don't know what you're talking about." It seems neither of us is ready to discuss *that* crab's nest.

Nic throws his hands up. "You're both too much alike. Too stubborn to see reason!"

Father exhales. "When I was your age, my daughter, I was already married, and had my firstborn child. I never fought my duty, my responsibility as a ma'ha. Those ten marriage contracts are the reasons our coalition is as big as it is today. They brought peace and prosperity between the T'Hu Marauders and the Pax Septum Coalition that wasn't possible for hundreds of years."

Ten marriage contracts? I only knew of one, from which Nic was born.

Nic's gaze is sharp on Father. "What did you say, Dad? Are you telling us that Lilla and I have brothers or sisters we never knew about?"

"Sisters," Father corrects him.

"How many?" I ask.

"Nine," Father says.

"Your Highnesses," High Adviser Ellar says, "as per the contracts, no one was allowed to disclose any details. It was forbidden to have any connection between the royal siblings. No one wanted any diplomatic complications. The inheritance lines must stay clear, especially since the other children are females. This was all carefully negotiated."

Nic shakes his head. "None of this makes any sense. How could you keep this from us? We had a right to know! I had a right to know! Since when do you lie to me?" Nic storms out of the room with a limp.

"Son, wait—" Father cringes when the door slams with a loud bang. "This is all your fault, my daughter! When will you grow up and start acting like an adult? I hope you are happy with what you've done."

CHAPTER 35

"Ma'hana Lilla, wait!" High Adviser Ellar says as he hurries after me.

I stop in the middle of the corridor, fighting the urge to keep running, away from Father's antechamber. Away from his accusing words.

"Ma'hana Lilla, you sure are fast. I thought I'd never catch you."

I grimace in response, struggling to keep the tears from overflowing. I should have known better than to get my hopes up. By the gods I won't cry over it.

"Your Father loves you, Ma'hana. He tries his best to—"

"I'm sure he does." All I can think about is the nine sisters I have, somewhere out there, whom I never met and probably never will. And Father wants the same fate for me—to get married to a stranger, living far away from my family, and never to see my children.

A tear escapes, and I swipe at it. "What am I going to do?"

High Adviser Ellar tries to smile, but his sad eyes betray him. "This may seem like the end of the world, but it is not. I wish I could have done more for you, but no good will come out of wallowing in the 'what ifs.'"

With a respectful nod I leave him.

I don't have a lot of time to waste on Father and his senseless marriage contract. I will do anything I can, in what little time I have left, for the refugees. Knowing that this will hurt Father in the process is an added benefit.

Feeling a bit better, I increase my speed and hurry down the corridor. When I take the next turn, I run into a brick wall where there shouldn't be one.

CHAPTER 36

Hands grab me before I could fall onto my bottom. Brushing a long dark-violet strand out of my face, I look up. Into the smiling face of General Callum.

He is out of his usual black military uniform. Instead, he wears a white sleeveless shirt tucked into white loose pants. His toned muscles seem to be carved onto his arms and chest, powerful without being fake. He is in top physical form and not for sport, like some of the court lords with their inflated bodies, but for survival. And he has the scars to prove it.

"It seems I don't have to go looking for you anymore," he says.

"Get out of my way." I try to step back, but he tightens his fingers on my arms. He sure likes to use me as a crutch.

"Or what?"

Behind the general, a crunching sound attracts my attention.

Colonel Teague munches on a large, blue fruit, chewing it with gusto. He looks up and he winks. Then takes another big bite, then with the back of his hand wipes the clear juice running from his chin. *How can he eat all the time?*

General Callum clears his throat. "You were saying?"

"Get out of my way or, um, I'll call for the guards."

The three of us look around. There isn't a single guard, or ma'har or ma'hara, or even a servant in sight.

"Will they come if you whistle? If you can't whistle loud enough, Teague here would be happy to help you out." He thrusts a thumb over his shoulder. Colonel Teague grins, and I get a view of the half-chewed bite still clinging to his teeth.

With a quick move that Captain Murtagh taught me, I jerk my arms down and outward, disentangling myself from the general's grip.

Ignoring the general's impressed expression, I point at his chest. "Aren't you supposed to be somewhere else? I thought you had an important negotiation with the coalition. So why don't you go away and negotiate, *Your Generalness?*"

Colonel Teague snorts, earning a glare from the general, he shrugs it off while taking another substantial bite of his fruit.

"I can't go away," General Callum says with a growl.

"Does your warship not work properly? We have the best engineers on Uhna to help you. If you ask nicely."

Colonel Teague laughs, but covers it up with a cough.

"I meant there is no negotiation today."

I clap my hands. "You mean you're finished? That's wonderful! Then you should really be on your way back home." I wave bye-bye to get him to move.

Colonel Teague doesn't even bother to hide his amusement as his gaze travels between the two of us.

A muscle jumps on General Callum's jaw. "Today is *your* repose day, or have you forgotten?"

"It cannot be." Could it be the tenth day, a day reserved for rest, signaling the end of the week? How didn't I notice?

Colonel Teague nods. "But it is."

I bow my head in mock respect and step to the side. "Then I leave you to enjoy your free time."

General Callum grabs my forearm again, stopping me.

I glance at his tanned fingers on my arm. "You forget yourself, General."

He releases my arm and says, "It's you who forgot. You owe—"

"I know, I know. Three favors. How could I forget when you remind me every time you see me?" It's best to get it over with. "What do you want?"

General Callum smiles, baring perfect white teeth. "You."

He wants what?

I sputter. "That's not going to happen!" I don't care who he thinks he is, or how many favors I owe him, he won't get my body in exchange for his silence! Yet the image of us, tangled, pops in my head.

Colonel Teague hands me the chewed-up core of his fruit. "The general meant he wants you to teach him. About your culture. As you can see, he is in desperate need for help."

General Callum crosses his arms, making his biceps bulge. "I am not desperate."

Colonel Teague nods. "And he's in denial about it."

"Oh . . ." And here I thought that he wants to . . . that he wants to . . . Don't go there!

Colonel Teague chuckles as if he read my thoughts. "Will you help him?"

Instead of answering, I take the core of his fruit with two fingers. I bump my elbow into a marble tile on the wall that has a small leaf etched on it, to open a hidden trash compartment. As long as I appear busy, I won't have to look at the general. Lest he figures out the cause of my embarrassment.

I scrutinize the dark inside of the compartment, as if all the answers are written there. My first thought is to refuse his request, out of principle. But what if I can use this?

If all he wants is to know my culture, I don't see how that could be disadvantageous to Uhna. Not to mention, it wouldn't be a difficult favor to deliver. Plus I could benefit greatly from keeping him close, a chance to pry information out of him for the rebellion. Xor did task me to spy on the Teryns. This is an opportunity I should not pass up.

With a satisfied smile, I drop the fruit into the trash and turn to the general. "I guess I can do that." I wipe my hands on my leggings to get rid of the sticky fruit juice. "We can start to—"

General Callum smiles wide, and I have a feeling I walked into his trap. "We start now."

CHAPTER 37

"I'll leave you two at it," says Colonel Teague as the frosted glass doors slide open to reveal the palace training room. He steps to the side to let the general and me walk in.

"Wait—" I say, but the doors slide closed behind me.

"Are you afraid to be alone with me?"

"Of course not." Liar. I face him. "Don't be ridiculous." Fla'mma-infused lights in iron sconces make the rough gray stone walls shine in the room that's a cave really.

"That's the first time anyone has ever called me ridiculous." The general strides to the closest weapons rack and picks up a pirate sword. Shark-teeth serrations cover the short sword's lower side, with an elongated pistol attached at its top. He runs a thumb over one of the teeth, cutting a thin line of blood into the meat of his finger.

I stop by him and do my best to ignore his presence, which seems to fluster me from so close. "And lived to tell the tale?"

General Callum extends another short sword toward me. "What do you think?"

I shake my head to the sword. "I think that's a bit cliché." Instead, I choose a long staff. "Are you sure you want to train and talk at the same time?"

The general lifts an eyebrow. "Are the two incongruent?"

"That's a big word." I untie my indigo tunic and toss it aside, revealing a matching tank top underneath. I roll my head, then my shoulders to warm up, and catch the general staring.

I look down at my top, searching for a telltale spot of jam. I tend to drip it down my neckline every time I eat boomberry tarts.

General Callum clears his throat. "Now who is being cliché?"

I pretend to turn and attack him with an upward swing of the staff in answer.

He deflects it.

119

Smiling, I launch into fast combinations with the staff, meant to keep him off balance. I wonder if he'll underestimate me, like so many do.

He counters each move with ease. "You should have picked the sword. It's more effective."

He comes at me faster than I expected, his sword slashing close to my skin. He's not treating me like a fragile crystal.

It takes all my energy to redirect his attacks. "It might be effective for you, but I am not a murderer."

General Callum raises an eyebrow. "And I am?"

"If the sword fits . . ."

"A murderer is someone who kills without conscience," he says and lunges at me with a stab of his sword, then angles the blade up in a follow-up move. "In war, there are no murderers. It only means that you are the one left standing."

He lets my staff bounce off his shoulder, then taps my arm with the flat of his blade to signal a hit. "Tell me about Uhna."

Where to start? "The Crystal Palace was carved into the Piercing Mountain hundreds of years ago. The palace got its name from the diamond dust that's embedded in the bricks, making it sparkle in the sunlight. We usually export seafood, pearls, and—"

The general fakes an attack, then quickly follows it with a downward slash I can barely parry. "I've noticed there aren't any women in the negotiation or among the ma'ha's advisers."

He noticed that, didn't he?

I jab him with the top of the staff, expecting him to sidestep it, and when he does, I tap the butt of the staff behind his knee. "Women don't participate in politics. It's the job of the ma'ha, his high adviser, the fourteen assistant advisers, and a few trusted high society ma'hars to 'carry the burden.'" Even though many famous historical leaders were, in fact, women. Even if they were pirates.

"Is that a direct quote?" General Callum bows out with the sword by his side.

I return his bow. "From Father himself." We walk to the rack to return the weapons. I must admit it, I had fun.

"And you agree with it?"

I shrug my shoulder. "It doesn't matter whether I do or don't."

"If you aren't allowed to be involved with politics, then what *do* you do?"

That's a sore topic. "It's none of your business."

He takes a step closer, forcing me to back away from him. "Oh, but it is." A rare hint of playfulness glints in his eyes.

"Really? Since when?" I back up, playing along.

"Since you—"

"I know! Since I still owe you two favors." My back hits the wall.

He leans his hands on the wall by my head, caging me in. "Exactly," he says in a deeper voice, desire replacing mirth in his eyes.

Something awakens in response, and my face feels hot.

"Now what are you going to do?" He lowers his head until our breaths mingle. He may think he caught me. But it's not over.

I push away from the wall, forcing him to step back. Taking control from him.

Curiosity sparks in his eyes as I circle around him. He has no choice but to turn with me.

Without looking away, I back him against the wall, as if he is my prey. I know I should stop, but I need to know how far he'll let me go. I need to know how far I'll go.

My heart races, sharpening my vision. Reaching out, I place my hands on his chest, my fingers tracing the shape of his muscles.

Callum inhales sharply. "Lilla—"

I shake my head to silence him. If he says another word, I'll lose all my courage.

I slide my palms to his shoulders, marveling how strong he is. How much he is affecting me. Affecting my body. Craving his touch.

He exhales with force, his hands grasping my waist. He pulls me close into the heat of his body. His scents of sun and desert send tingles through my skin.

My gaze lands on his lips. *How would it feel to kiss him? Just once.* Anticipation and excitement grip me like never before.

I look back into his blue eyes. His gaze, focused on mine, burns with the same expectation and need I feel.

I rise on my tiptoes, but I don't have to go far. Callum meets me half-way. He wraps his hand in my hair, his fingers tightening. His lips press on mine, insistent and hungry. He kisses me like it's his last kiss—full of passion and out of control. He kisses me, claiming my lips, declaring them his. Encouraging yet taking everything.

My body comes alive, full of sensation, full of fire. Burning. His kiss is everything I imagined it to be. Addictive. Passionate. I can't get enough of him. I return his kiss with the same passion. Same need. Demanding more.

He growls into our kiss, breathless. His arms brace my back in answer, embracing me, his hands caressing.

My head spins and I don't want him to stop. Ever. I want more. I want . . .

He pulls back, gasping for breath.

Reality hits, clearing my head.

What have I done? I lost control like never before.

"I shouldn't have done that," I say and step back. I was supposed to spy on him, not fall for him, for godssake!

Callum reaches for me, his expression confused. "Lilla, wait."

"I can't." I turn away. I kissed him like I've never kissed anyone. I kissed him like I couldn't get enough. Like Triann kissed Cadeon.

Buckets of fishguts! I run for the exit. But I still see him in my mind's eye. His tanned face heated, his lips red from my kiss.

"Are you scared of me?!" he shouts.

But I don't stop. I can't tell him the truth of how scared I am. Scared of falling for him.

CHAPTER 38

My boots are eating up the white marble tiles as I rush recklessly through the corridors, away from the training room. Away from Callum.

It was a mistake letting my emotions take over. Now I'll never forget what it feels like when he kisses me. When he holds me in his arms.

I can only blame myself. I'll just have to avoid Callum from now on, damn the "favors" I owe him. I don't trust myself in his company. Xor'll just have to do without that information because there is no way I go back to spy on Callum. And risk losing control again? No, thank you!

Out of nowhere, hands grab my arms and pull me into one of the hidden alcoves the palace is peppered with.

My scream is cut off with a hand—a third one? over my mouth. The only person I know with more than two hands is . . . "Belthair!" My voice is muffled.

"Don't make a fuss."

When he removes his hands, I face him. "Why are you here?"

"I, uh, I have orders from Xor."

I cross my arms over my chest. "What orders?"

Belthair just stares at me unblinking, as if he'd never seen me before.

He's acting very strange. He hasn't shouted at me yet. Not once. "Are you okay?"

A deep blush colors his light-gray-toned face. His gaze keeps dipping lower until his eyes are glued to my chest.

I look down, too. With my arms crossed, my tank top does a poor job covering, leaving little to the imagination. Ugh! In my haste to run away from Callum I forgot to pick up my tunic.

I snap my fingers in his face. "Eyes up, rebel. What are the orders?"

Belthair tears his gaze away from my chest. "What orders?"

I exhale in exasperation. How on Uhna have I ever found this bumbling boy charming? I was a fool at seventeen.

Belthair clears his throat. "Xor wants to know what the Teryns intend to do on Uhna, especially regarding the refugee camps. He wants you to get close to him, by any means necessary, and find out everything you can." He aims his last words at my cleavage and steps closer to me. "Shouldn't be difficult for you. You always had a way with men. He won't be able to resist you. I know I couldn't."

I push him with one hand. "I didn't have *men* in my life. I only had you. And you're acting like an idiot."

"But at least I am good at it."

"Stop this," I say. "This is not you."

Belthair smirks. "You have no idea who I am anymore. Because of you, my life got turned upside down and I almost died. Had it not been for my friends on duty that night, I wouldn't have been able to escape." He leans closer. "I might forgive you for betraying me if you kiss me. See where that might lead us. At least we won't have to hurry, like that night. I'll never forget that night."

How could he have brought up that night, the *only* night we spent together? When we were desperate, fumbling, and trying our hands at passion. The night that convinced me that Belthair and I were in "love."

"You can consider this your practice. Kiss me like you kissed the Teryn."

"You're joking, right?"

Instead of answering, he buries his face in the crook of my neck, kissing it as he used to when we were together.

Buckets of fishguts! He is serious! He thinks he deserves this. That I owe him. But I am done feeling responsible for that night. I am done walking around him with regret. Done apologizing. Done respecting his hurt feelings as if I hadn't grieved over him for two years.

Plastering a smile on my lips, I ask, "You want me to kiss you?" I grasp his shoulders with both hands.

He swallows and nods.

"Are you sure you're up for practicing?"

He nods again, inhaling sharply.

Holding onto his shoulders, I drive my knee up between his legs. Once. Twice. Three times.

He muffles a cry and doubles over.

"Never threaten me again," I say and jab my elbow down on his back, ironically a move he taught me. "I owe you nothing!"

He crumbles to the ground.

Before I leave, I say, "If you ever try anything like that again, I will stomp on your balls until there is nothing left. Do you understand?"

Belthair gasps in pain and glares up at me, all six of his hands cradling his groin.

"I don't hear you. Do. You. Understand?"

He nods with eyes flashing in fury. "You're cold and heartless! You'll betray him too. It's in your nature."

CHAPTER 39

I shouldn't let Belthair irk me, but what if he is right? What if it's in my nature to fall for the wrong guys? What if . . .

From one step to the next, the white marble floor of the corridor disappears, turning into soft, green grass.

I stumble to a halt. What on Uhna is going on?

A gentle breeze tugs my hair. Long, yellow flowers sway, rustling. All around me a beautiful meadow stretches under a bright blue sky.

Dazed, I squat and run my fingers over the long stalks of grass, sure that this is some sort of illusion or hallucination. But each bright, linear leaf bends under my touch. As real as I am. The petals of the yellow flowers are silkier than the most expensive Evander spider silk. Their dark veins visible, like intricate webbing. Perfection marks every inch of the field, so well composed, as if drawn by a masterful hand.

"They are wonderful, aren't they?" asks a musical female voice.

I turn to face the speaker.

Two women in silver wrap-style dresses stand not three steps away from me. They project calm and peace with their hands clasped in front of them.

The taller woman, with shoulder-length blond hair, smiles. Cheerfulness that borders on outright elation spreads through my body.

Who are these women? I feel as if I've met them before, but I would remember them, wouldn't I? Another thought pops in my mind, but before I can grasp it, it drifts away, as if nothing matters but this perfect day, right here in this stunning meadow, with these stunning beings.

A silly smile appears on my lips, beyond my control, as I gawk at them, speechless. I must be dreaming.

The shorter woman, with long, blond hair that reaches her ankles, steps forward. "Lilla, this is not a dream. You are in the presence of the merciful, loving, and benevolent Archgoddess of the Eternal Light and Order. You may refer to her as The Lady. I am her acolyte, and you may call me Aisla. We are—"

A warning bubbles up from somewhere in the recesses of my mind. Triann's warning. About a mysterious "she."

I point at the tall archgoddess. "It is you." The joyful feeling retreats. Adrenaline pumps in my veins and fear floods my body. "Have you come to kill me?"

She laughs, and her laughter is the most beautiful sound I've ever heard.

"Killing you, my child, is the farthest from my thoughts. I am here because of you."

I point at my chest. The idea of the archgoddess stopping by to visit me, of all people in the Seven Galaxies, is beyond hilarious. I laugh until tears run down my face.

"I am a nobody." I snort after a particularly long laugh, the sound harsh in the peaceful meadow. "You have wasted . . . your time . . . over nothing!" I burst into a guffaw, doubling over and slapping my knees. What is wrong with me?

Aisla's amber eyes glint with anger. "Has your mother not taught you to respect your archgoddess?"

"She is *not* my archgoddess, and respect is earned."

The petite acolyte's palms start burning with bright light.

"There is no need for that," the archgoddess says. "Lilla, my child, you are right. I forgot you weren't raised traditionally, like my other Lumenian children. You don't even look like us."

She smiles again, and it's as if someone turned on happiness in my mind. I am full of joy again, choking on it. "When your mother left—"

"Stop it! I know it is you who are making me feel so . . . strange."

The artificial "happy fog" lifts from my mind. I exhale with relief.

The archgoddess continues, "When your mother left Lume—"

"You mean when she ran away." I remember when Triann explained to me that The Lady prohibited the Lumenians from leaving Lume, their home world, for a while.

"Either way, you weren't raised as a Lumenian and simply don't know better."

She dodged my question. "Everyone keeps telling me that I am a Lumenian, as if that should mean something."

The Lady glances at her acolyte. Aisla explains, "The Lady is the mother of all Lumenians. She created her children to fight against the forces of the Archgod of Chaos and Destruction—the only protection against his spreading corruption. As a legendary Lumenian, it is your honorable duty to fight in the era wars, on Her side—"

It's well-practiced propaganda, the exact version I heard Triann recite. "Now if we're done, I'd like to get back to the palace."

I turn to leave the meadow, not that I would know how or where to go.

The Lady asks, "Why are you turning your back on your heritage and your duty? What more could you want from life than an honorable and true purpose?"

How about love? Happiness? Family? "I have better things to do than fight in the archgods' war. *Your* war."

"That little rebellion of yours, my child, is of no consequence in the grand scheme of the Seven Galaxies. The Era War, on the other hand—"

"That 'little rebellion' matters to me."

"That's a weak excuse that doesn't eradicate your duty, my child. Nothing else matters when the fate of the Seven Galaxies is in question. Besides, you of all people have a personal stake in this."

I turn back to look at the archgoddess. "Continue."

"It was the archgod who chased your mother all the way to Uhna, where she met her tragic end. So far away from my protection."

"Are you implying that the Archgod of Chaos and Destruction killed my mom?"

The Lady touches my shoulder. Love, like the softest and warmest of blankets, envelops me. "I care for all of my children, just as I cared for Eilish, your mother. Her death remains unavenged, and it pains me."

Love intensifies to an overwhelming degree now, suffocating me, shutting all thoughts out. "Stop it!"

The Lady removes her hand. All that love dissipates with it. For a second I feel a physical longing at the lack of it, but I shrug it off. "What do you want from me?"

"I want you to embrace your Lumenian heritage and your duty. I want you to fight by my side. As my right hand. My sybil in this Era War—"

"I already told you that I want nothing to do with the Era War. Find someone else."

"You don't understand, my child. This is our *only* chance. The archgod is missing, hiding from me, probably in a mortal form while hunting my children, no doubt. He might even be here, on Uhna, looking for you as we speak. Do you want Him to find you first?"

"No, but—"

"Then it is settled," The Lady says.

"Nothing is settled. Why don't *you* do something about him? Why don't *you* stop the Era War?"

"I cannot participate directly in the Era War, just as He can't. We can only act through our children or avatars. That is why I need you, my child. I need you to find Him and—"

"What? Kill Him?"

"The archgod broke the rules and is in mortal form. Do you want decades of war to wage? Millions of lives lost? You could change all of that."

"I cannot even squash a spider, and you want me to kill a god? An archgod at that?" It's surreal how casually we're discussing a cold-blooded murder.

"Before He finds you and kills you, my child."

"No."

"Why, my child?"

Because this is insanity. Because I have the rebellion to fight in. Because of the promise I made to Mom. "You have my answer. Now let me go."

CHAPTER 40

From one blink to the next, I am back to the palace. I head straight to Glenna. She won't believe the news I have!

Nic leans in Glenna's doorway, talking to her. Charm pours off him as he drinks in her words, beaming at her with an animated expression. He says something low to her and Glenna giggles, flustered. She glances in my direction and jumps. With a hand at the base of her throat, she hisses at Nic. He raises his head and mutters under his breath. His eyes glint hard, and the message *Go away!* is clear.

I need her more. I don't move, just stare back. In a game of willpower, Nic has no chance against me.

With a curse, he pushes away from the door frame. Touching Glenna's cheek, he leans down and kisses her. "I'll come back later."

As he passes me, I stop him with a hand on his arm. "She is not one of your dumb, shallow flings. She deserves someone who will—"

"I know she is a once-in-a-lifetime girl," he says. "I intend to give her everything she wants."

"You *are* serious about this. But what will Father say?"

"I'll deal with Dad if it comes to that." Nic rubs the top of my head, which he knows I dislike, and leaves.

Glenna studies the ceiling with forced fascination. "It's not what you think—"

I pretend to be stern about it. "Are you telling me you didn't kiss my brother?"

Wide-eyed, she looks at me. "I did, but I swear I haven't encouraged him!"

"Why not?" I crack a smile.

"Lowly servant. Heir to the monarchy. It could never last. I keep saying no to Nic, but he doesn't seem to care."

"You should try to say yes and see what happens."

"I thought . . . I mean I shouldn't . . . Are you not mad?"

"No, I am not mad! You deserve to be happy." I hug her thin shoulders.

We make our way into her living quarters. An enthusiastic cacophony of barks, meows, chirps, and all kinds of screeches greets us.

I bend down to pet a three-legged A'ice wolf, Anton, who tries to lick my face. Then Buck the old hunting dog presses forward. Two fat gray cats with long fur wind themselves around my legs. Cataracts make their eyes shine milky, but they still have that look of feline pride. Glenna calls them Isa and Bella, her princesses, to the chagrin of our friends the twins, who also happen to have those names. The black mushroom pushes its way through the cats and tilts its cap toward me. Taking a hint, I pet it. It doesn't bite me. But I don't have time to marvel at it before Angie, a waist-tall and thin-legged redbird, rubs its unnaturally bent beak on my arm. I run my fingers over the soft feathers above its eyes. Then Bobby, a small white bear who isn't a cub but who will never grow taller than knee-high due to some genetic disease, vies for my attention. I take a big chunk of honeycomb from a bowl on a shelf and hand it to him. The bear scurries away, dropping on its bottom in a corner and chewing on his treat with gusto. Three butterflies the size of small children—Itty, Bitty, and Missy—with transparent wings in pastel hues and small breaks in their membranes hover awkwardly in a shy greeting. They flutter away into Glenna's bedroom.

A prickling feeling at the back of my neck makes me glance around. A vine-covered wall divides her kitchen from the living area. Birds of all shapes and sizes flutter under the huge, green leaves. A yellow spider moves from under the largest leaf.

"Oh, it's Gwendoline. I see you moved her in with you." Two long and thin legs extend in my direction, either as a warning or as a greeting. I hope it's the latter.

"I had to. She kept scaring the patients. But she seems happier here, with the other animals."

Glenna and I sit on a long sofa, next to a curled-up purple island snake, Betty. She is too old to do much besides sleep, which is a good thing. Island snakes are the most aggressive of all snakes, and the most venomous too.

Three chubby puppies dash into the room, appearing guilty and happy at the same time. "Oh, you rascals!" Glenna lifts them up, one after the other, onto the sofa. "You escaped your crates again, didn't you?"

A pure white puppy scrambles up into my lap, dropping down with a little puppy sigh. I rub its soft fur. "They're new."

Glenna raises a brown and white puppy to her face, letting it lick her cheek. "Someone abandoned them in Deidre's herb garden. You know how she is . . . how she was about her herbs." Deidre could spend hours in there, weeding it, and talking to her plants.

"How is your, uh, investigation going?" Glenna asks to break the silence.

"There isn't much for me to go on." When Jossim sent me his findings, following up on the other servants, he ended up with nothing. No one saw anything. No one heard anything. No one knew anything. "More than fifty people murdered, and Father just ignores it. I don't understand why."

I thought I could find out the truth, but I ended up with nothing. I am no better than he is.

Glenna reaches over and squeezes my hand. "Don't give up, Lilla."

I give her a halfhearted smile. "I won't." But with each passing day, there is less and less chance of ever finding the murderer or murderers. "But it's not why I came to see you. I've just met the Archgoddess of the Eternal Light and Order."

"You're joking." Glenna laughs. But when she sees my expression she says, "Tell me."

I recount my strange meeting with the archgoddess and her acolyte. I sit back, waiting for Glenna to say something, but she is in deep thought.

Something heavy, and quite large, crawls across the back of my neck on multiple legs, then curls around it, settling in. Keeping my eyes forward and my mouth shut so I won't scream, I poke Glenna.

"What?" Glenna asks, looking up.

I gesture toward my neck with silent urgency. The urge to scream is getting overwhelming, but I've learned the hard way her pets don't react well to that. Not at all.

"Oh!" Glenna reaches over. With a grunt she lifts something off of me, pulling it close to her. It's a black millipede, the length of her forearm and at least eight inches thick. "Bobo, I told you to stop crawling over people," she coos, and kisses the millipede's shiny black head before placing it on the ground.

The millipede crawls in circles, confused for a few seconds, then beelines to a high-backed chair. It scrambles up fast and slips between the blue cushions. I make a mental note *never* to sit on any of her chairs before checking for Bobo.

"I'm surprised you said no to the, uh, The Lady. I saw how you were at the refugee camp. How you embraced helping them and worked hard. You were a natural at it. It sounds to me that being a sybil is helping others, only on a larger scale."

"Glenna, being a sybil is more than that. I'd have to be a general. In the Era War. It's a ridiculous notion."

She makes a "pfft" sound. "Anyone can learn to be a general." I wonder what Callum would think about that. Then I remember our kiss. *For two godsdamn seconds stop thinking about him!*

"I meant you are kind, honest, and genuinely interested in the welfare of others." I have to look away to hide my guilt. Glenna has no idea how honest I am. "You could have been a wonderful healer."

"Healers generally don't go around murdering gods."

Glenna's expression sobers as she pets her sleeping puppies. "Speaking of healers, what I am about to tell you is something we kept secret for a long time. This is the most shameful and proudest part in our history. In the first Era War, all the healers fought, and yes, we killed, using our magic. We fought side by side with the battle mages. Our healer's magic, A'ris, was the perfect complement to the mages' Fla'mma and T'erra magic. Together we did a lot of good. But we also killed half-corrupted people, preventing them from becoming fully corrupted dark servants. Technically, the healer's oath only covers beings who are *not* corrupted by the Archgod of Chaos and Destruction. Half-corrupted fell outside that protection. Some healers took issue with that distinction and refused to participate in killing them. Suffice it to say, it is a sensitive topic even up to this date."

"I had no idea."

"Don't judge healers or sybils until you know more about them. Not everything is as straightforward as they seem on the surface."

CHAPTER 41

"You're kidding, right?" I ask Arrov, staring at the small device in his palm. Thin green wires wrap around a two-inch black square. Arrov's job is to place it on the engine above our heads.

"I wish," he says in a frustrated voice. "My hand is too big for this and we are running out of time." Then he looks at me and wiggles his eyebrows. "Of course, it is just right for everything else."

A blush creeps up my cheeks, and I'm grateful he can't see it. The early afternoon's light doesn't reach under the float. It might as well be night, it's so dark here.

"Just let me do it," I say with impatience and take the small gadget from him.

Arrov bumps his head when he straightens up, cursing in a whisper. "Fine, but keep your voice down."

He shouldn't worry so much. The float stretches thirty feet long and twenty feet wide, hovering five feet off the ground. The luxurious and overly decorated float dominates most of the wide main street, leaving only a narrow path between it and the cloudscrapers on either side. Civilians crowd all around the nineteen floats. The clamor of loud conversation mixes with raucous music from each float, stifling any noises we could make.

"Look for a small place between the metal pipes and blue wires." Arrov holds up his necklace to shine a dimmed light on the T'erra-infused float engine. Without the magical infusion, the small engine would be ineffectual to operate the multiton monstrosity. "Ship! We're out of time."

"See the royal sentinels out there? Father hasn't boarded the float yet." The procession won't start without him no matter how late the ma'ha is.

I squint at the engine. There! I lift up the device but hesitate. "What if this is a—"

"It's not a bomb," Arrov says. "It's too small to be effective."

"Have you seen many bombs?" I joke and slide the device between the pipes and wires.

"Enough to know the difference," he says. A click sounds as the device's magnetic hold engages onto the metal pipes. "But I'd like to know what this one does, though."

"Why?"

"I'm worried about you." He drags a hand through his hair. "You are on the float, and I have no idea what Xor's plan is. Maybe you should skip the parade."

"Don't be ridiculous. You know I can't do that." I wave his concern away. "Besides, I can take care of myself." Xor wouldn't hurt me, would he?

"Let's hope you won't have to. Time for us to go."

Hunched, we head toward the light. Arrov checks if the coast is clear, then reaches down to pull me out after him. I straighten, wiping my hands.

A throat clears near me. I jump and turn to see General Callum and Colonel Teague.

Fishguts! "What, uh, what are you doing here?"

Arrov crosses his arms. "Don't you have anything better to do than sneaking up on us? Or are you here to invade our parade too?"

Callum narrows his eyes. "The real question is, what were you two doing under the float?"

Buckets of fishguts! He did see us. "I, um, was looking for . . . um . . . you know—"

Teague snorts. "No, we don't know."

Arrov snaps his fingers. "She, um, just dropped—"

"My earring!" I rub my earlobe.

"Her handkerchief," Arrov says at the same time, and pulls a white, embroidered silk square out of his pocket, handing it to me. "Here, I found it."

Teague barks a laugh and pops a tiny purple boomberry into his mouth as his gaze travels among Callum, Arrov, and me.

Callum wipes something off my ear. Engine grease.

Buckets and buckets of fishguts! "I uh . . . I mean it's—"

"We don't have time for your stupid questions." Arrov grabs my hand. "Let's go, Lilla."

A reddish-yellow light flashes across Callum's blue irises.

I disengage from Arrov as if I got burned.

"Is that so?" Callum says. "She will come with me." He extends his arm.

When I put my hand on Callum's, he places it at the crook of his elbow, holding onto it.

Callum must have picked up the gesture from High Adviser Ellar. Except there is nothing formal about the way he is holding my hand. It's more personal, like a proud proclamation that we're together.

I tug to free my hand, but he won't let go. Why do I even bother?

Callum heads toward the float's stairs, with me in tow.

"Hey!" Arrov says. "You can't just drag her around like a piece of luggage."

Teague blocks Arrov's way, bodychecking him every time he tries to step around the colonel.

"You ran away before I had a chance to talk to you," Callum says.

"There is nothing to talk about." Not a thing. Definitely not about the kiss. Nope.

We climb up the stairs, all the way to the end of the float, stopping by the ten-foot-tall aquarium, which houses a baby deepwater shark. One day it will grow up to be a two- or three- hundred-foot-long predator, reigning the ocean—*if* it's ever allowed to be free.

In front of us stretches the float. The theme this year is "white," and not a single inch of the float is left uncovered. White palm fronds wave in the cold winter breeze, crystal diamond dust sparkling on the leaves in the two sunlight.

Callum turns to me, releasing my hand. "There is plenty to talk about, starting with what you and that boy were doing under the float."

"Shh! Not so loud." I look around to see if anyone is close enough to overhear. But Teague and the rest of the Teryn warriors manage to keep the growing crowd of courtiers from reaching the back of the float with their sheer presence. "As I said—"

"You dropped your earring-handkerchief." Callum rolls his eyes. "I want to talk about our kiss."

For a second I lock eyes with the baby shark. The large, black orbs in the round and flattened head reflect no emotion or thought. It is too young to comprehend its prison. Its wide mouth gapes open. Row upon row of sharp fangs glisten, while dozens of tentacles float around its head. The tentacles catch any prey that swim too close, then pull it into the shark's waiting mouth. Like they do now, with a big fat fish in their grasp.

"I told you already." I turn away, unable to watch the fish's struggle. "It was a mistake. It won't happen again. Now, as your cultural guide, I should tell you—"

"Go ahead," Callum says with a glint in his blue eyes, knowing full well that he interrupted me in doing so.

"As I was saying, this is the hundredth annual celebration of the Pax Septum Coalition's existence. It started out simple, with each of its members presenting a decorated float to showcase their planet's culture. But with every new world that joined, the parade bloated into a longer and slower procession, each world trying to outdo the other. As the capital of the coalition, Uhna has been hosting the past thirty celebrations." An honor that hasn't been sitting well with the other coalition worlds.

"What's with the half-dressed lady at the front?"

The lady in question is the twenty-five-foot-tall sculpture of a voluptuous piratess captain. Lifelike and awe-inspiring. Although I doubt the real captain dressed anything like the sculpture. The sheer toga-dress seems to run out of material and only covers one of her breasts. A'ris magic is infused into the heavy alabaster marble to lighten its weight for the float. Fla'mma-infused floodlights shine on it, igniting thousands of embedded crystal diamonds into tiny fires. Those crystal diamonds could support a small planet. For years.

"That's Captain D'anna, Patron of Fortunes and Riches." I point at the figure. "See how she's holding a bag in her outstretched hand? It's full of coins for riches. In her other hand, which curves over her head, is a rare seven-petal starflower to symbolize fortune."

"Very subtle."

He has no idea. "Technically, by the Academia of Mages's spiritual regulations, no world should have patrons. Every year, Father selects a famous pirate and makes him or her our patron. Since the Magical Cleansing War, more worlds follow Father's example."

"It's Magical *Cleanse* War, not Cleansing War," Royal Elementalist Mage Ragnald says as he climbs up and over the side of the float, using the maintenance rope ladder. "I wish people would stop confusing the Magical Cleanse

War with detox, as if it were self-induced diarrhea and not a bloody battle. It is really *not* the same."

The mage studies the float with a sour expression and purses his lips when his gaze lands on the half-naked piratess. After a deep exhale, he heads up to the second level, where the royal family will gather.

"Who was that?"

"The only mage allowed on Uhna and on most of the coalition worlds." Probably the most despised, too, from what he told me. "Royal Elementalist Mage Ragnald."

"He seems like a cheerful fellow."

I laugh. "About as cheerful as that diarrhea he just referenced."

Callum crosses his arms and leans onto the glass aquarium. "Maybe the mage is just concerned about the lack of respect Uhnans have for their guardian god."

I do a double take to see if he is joking, but he wears a serious expression.

"We have an important connection to our Guardian Goddess Laoise. Without Her we wouldn't exist."

"Exist? That's a bit much, no?" All life originates from the Omnipower, with the two archgods governing over them. Everyone knows that.

"I guess it's hard for me to imagine life without the protection of my goddess."

"I respect how you feel, but not all goddesses are the same."

"You speak as if you've met one," Callum says with laser focus.

"That would be crazy." I step around Callum. "If you'll excuse me—"

He reaches for me. "Are you running away from me again?"

"The parade is starting. My place is by the ma'ha."

"You didn't answer my question."

I turn away from him and resume walking. "For your information, I'm not *running* away from you. I'm *walking* away from you. Big difference."

CHAPTER 42

"Someone is smitten with that Teryn general," Beathag says. She waves to the crowd, smiling.

I turn my head to the right, smiling and waving too. "Someone needs glasses. Only the blind would confuse mere tolerance with attraction." I'd rather die than admit that she is right.

The float jolts into motion, rising nine feet above the ground, then moving forward at a slow pace, leading the procession down the wide main street. Around us, the cloudscrapers reflect the floats like grotesque mirrors, all that luxurious decoration out of place amid the sober steel and glass.

Beathag slants a look at me as cheers go up from the spectators below. "You keep falling for the wrong males. All it takes is for them to pay attention to you. So desperate. Not that I care, of course."

I roll my eyes skyward. "For someone who doesn't care, you sure are obsessing," I mutter while keeping the smile in place. Only three more hours to go.

"I can't imagine how hard it must be for you. To not have any say in your own life. I know I wouldn't let *that* happen to me."

"Your lack of imagination isn't my problem." Why won't she shut up?

"Tell me, how does that feel? Do you feel sorry for yourself? Or are you secretly planning to run away? Again?"

She dared to go there! "As if I would tell you."

If I have to keep smiling like this, my face will be frozen in a painful grimace for the rest of my life.

"It is so easy to get a rise out of you." Beathag grins widely. "Did I tell you it was I who convinced your father to send out those marriage contracts?"

It was? "I am not surprised."

"Then it won't surprise you to know it didn't take much convincing. I was expecting more resistance from my beloved, but he was ready to be rid of you. He cannot even bear to look at you."

Don't let her rile you up!

"You never fit in the court," Beathag continues. "Didn't even try. Always acted as if no one could understand how hard it was for you. But you have no idea what hardship is. You're spoiled, and don't appreciate what you have. I can't wait for you to be sent off to a world where you'll be all alone. Then you'll truly know what it means to be an outsider."

"You vicious—" I raise my hand, but Nic steps between Beathag and me. "I have no idea what she said to you, but you cannot act like this in clear view of the public. Why don't you get some air, sis?"

"We *are* outside," I say. The wind whips a long white palm leaf in my face, and I push the leaf away.

"You know what I mean," Nic says and leads me to the steps of the second-level platform.

"Fine. But that doesn't mean she won."

"Of course not."

I march down the steps to the main level of the float. Could Beathag be right? Does Father hate me so much that he would send me away? Since Mom died, we hadn't gotten along, but has it come to this?

As I reach the main floor, Callum strides toward me with purpose.

Fishguts! I take a step back, but Nic blocks the top of the stairs. I have no choice but to head to the back, around the second-level platform.

A loud boom sounds, like a rifle shot.

Screams and shouts echo from the high society members. Everyone drops down, expecting the worst. I stand rooted to the spot, trying to figure out what or who caused it.

Callum tackles me to the ground. "Whoa!" I say and try to get up, but he drapes himself over me.

"Don't move, Lilla," he says by my ear, his body tense above mine. He scans the crowd for threats. "Why hasn't the float stopped?"

"They would never do that." I push against his shoulder. "Get off me, will you?"

Callum looks at me. "When I judge the situation safe."

"Do you have to lean on me so heavily, then?" I say, pretending that his closeness has no effect on me. None whatsoever! "I can't breathe."

"Am I taking your breath away?"

Yes! No! I inhale his scent of sun and desert, and it transports me back to the training room. I remember the feel of his kiss on my lips. Anticipation builds, as if my body craves it.

Something shifts in Callum's expression, and he lowers his head. "If you keep—"

"I apologize for the confusion!" Royal Elementalist Ragnald shouts. "There is no threat. Please do get up."

That was close! I exhale and look away. I almost kissed him. *Again!*

Callum curses and flows to his feet, then helps me up. All around us, the muttering high society members get back to their feet, looking perplexed.

"What is the meaning of this?" Father asks the mage from the raised platform.

The royal mage bows from the waist, then gestures toward the marble sculpture of Captain D'anna. "Manipulating such a heavy mass sometimes can cause a magical backfire, if you will. But all is well now." He flicks his wrist, and the massive sculpture comes alive, sashaying in place.

The high society guests watch Father. For an intense second, Father stares down at the mage. "Make sure this sort of thing doesn't happen in the future, Royal Elementalist Mage." Then Father claps in appreciation. All the high society members start clapping too.

"Yes, Your Highness." The mage's expression shows no regret. Red ribbons of Fla'mma magic shoot out from him toward the sculpture. The bag in Captain D'anna's right hand bursts open.

Crystal diamond specks shower down, to the excitement of the crowd. The ma'hars and ma'haras crawl on hands and knees or jump up trying to gather the tiny, expensive pieces, all composure forgotten.

A thin young waiter appears next to me. He stumbles, seemingly over his own feet. He shoves an empty serving tray into my hands as he tries to regain his balance.

I take it while he grasps my right shoulder, pulling me in front of him. "What—"

Cold steel touches my throat. "Don't move, Ma'hana."

CHAPTER 43

I raise my hands in placation. "I won't—" The waiter presses the blade more into my throat, making me rise on my toes to avoid getting cut.

Callum's expression turns threatening and walks toward the waiter with hands outstretched in clear view.

"Don't move or I'll kill her!"

"There is nowhere for you to go," Callum says. "Why don't you let the ma'hana go and we can forget about this?"

"I don't need the ma'hana. I only need the Lumenian. If you come with me—"

Callum moves fast before the man can finish his sentence. He twists the waiter's hand, snapping bones, taking the knife while he shoves me out of the way.

The attacker cries out in pain but doesn't give up. He lunges at Callum with a left hook.

Callum ducks, then counters with a terrible uppercut as he straightens. The force propels the waiter over the metal railing of the float.

Both Callum and I rush to the railing. The attacker's unmoving body sprawls on the walkway below. A small crowd gathers around it with shocked interest. More than one maintenance crew or waitstaff had fallen off the floats due to the poor protection offered by the railings. But these railings obstruct the view to the decorations the least.

I close my eyes against the horrible image, shivering. It happened so fast, fewer than ten seconds, yet the loss of that young man's life will last forever.

"Are you okay?" Callum asks. Teague and six warriors come running from the front of the float, but Callum shakes his head and they stand down.

I swallow bile. "I'm fine."

"Why would this man think I am a 'Lumenian'?" Callum asks.

"I have no idea." I look away. Another lie. The Archgoddess of the Eternal Light and Order was right. The hunt has begun. Sooner or later the Archgod of Chaos and Destruction will figure out that Callum isn't the Lumenian.

Another boom sounds, reverberating through the whole float, making everyone stumble.

All eyes turn toward Royal Elementalist Mage Ragnald. The mage raises both of his hands in the air. "It wasn't me."

With a loud screech, the float jars to a halt.

"Why did we stop?" Callum asks, his voice raised over the discord of the court.

The court fidgets, looking baffled as we hover in the middle of a long turn, with no one in front of the float or directly behind it.

I shrug as I glance over the railing. There isn't a single onlooker below. Strange.

"You don't look too surprised."

I duck my head. "It's probably an issue with the, um, engine or something."

"Or something," Callum says, not bothering to hide his disbelief.

"If I may have your attention," High Adviser Ellar says from the platform, "it seems we have some technical difficulties."

"See?" I say. Callum studies my innocent expression, unconvinced.

"We'll be on our way any minute," High Adviser Ellar says. "Nothing to—"

Fla'mma-magic-magnified laughter sounds, interrupting the high adviser. At the nearest cloudscraper, a tall window opens, ten stories above us. Xor and Jorha appear—Xor laughing, and Jorha with a serrated laser gun trained on us. They are disguised with hooded jackets and bandanas over their faces, but I recognize them anyway.

Four royal guards aim their weapons at the pair. All around us, more rebels appear at various windows, with laser guns focused on our stranded float.

Callum steps in front of me, with his own laser gun in one hand, while his warriors surround us in a protective circle.

"Don't listen to the monarchist scum," Jorha says. "He lies. You *should* be worried."

Gasps and shouts erupt from the court guests on the float.

In the chaos, High Adviser Ellar points at Royal Elementalist Mage Ragnald. "What are you waiting for? Protect your ma'ha!"

The mage crosses his arms. "The Academia of Mages cannot and will not get involved with national disputes."

"What is the meaning of this?" Father demands.

High Adviser Ellar leans to Father. "I have informed the city guards. They should be here any minute, Your Highness."

Father nods, staring at the rebellion leader. While Beathag looks around as if preparing to flee, Irvine takes cover behind his ma'ha, like the coward he is.

"Is it true that you're planning to send us to work in your crystal diamond mines?! I thought it's illegal to enslave your citizens!" Xor shouts.

The court quiets and turns to face Father, waiting for his answer.

"You are refugees, not citizens," Father corrects him. Then he asks the high adviser, "How does this rebel know about this? I just signed the order yesterday morning."

High Adviser Ellar looks lost. Irvine hisses, "There are less than a dozen who are aware of the signed the order, Your Highness. It shouldn't take long to find out who betrayed you. I will personally oversee the investigation."

Father inclines his head. "Harming us in any way is punishable by death!"

"Harming you? I wouldn't dare," Xor says and spreads his arms, just as the first city guards emerge running on the street, a hundred feet away. "I thought I would give you all a taste of how caring Uhna has been to us. I hope you enjoy it as much as we do."

More windows snap open, as if on cue. In them rebels appear, holding onto thick and wide tubes.

Before anyone can move, a torrent of rank mushroom-colored fluid bursts from the tubes, raining down on us.

CHAPTER 44

For the first time in history, the parade failed to complete its circuit. The cloudscrapers stand silent witnesses of the marooned floats.

The rebels made a well-executed exit before the city guards could catch them. The ma'hars and ma'haras screech and shout in panic, covered head to toe with the rancid "meal" Father supplies to the camps.

The floats lay scattered in the street. Abandoned. Their decorations hanging dishearteningly as if they too feel the dismay of this historic disaster.

I refuse to board the passenger craft back to the palace with Father and decide to stay behind. Father and Beathag seem all too happy to escape the chaos, and they take my refusal without comment. My gaze trails the small craft as it takes off, disappearing from view.

"Are you okay?" Callum asks.

No, I am not okay. But I can't tell him that. I didn't expect Xor to share the crystal mines issue so publicly. Now that Irvine will investigate the situation, it's only a matter of time before he discovers who betrayed Father. Traitors don't live long on Uhna to regret what they did.

"I am fine." Thanks to Callum, Teague, and the Teryn warriors, the foul-smelling spray only landed on me in a few spots, while they took the brunt of it.

"We should leave too," Callum says, extending a hand. He doesn't seem to be bothered by the slime on his uniform.

I reach to take the hand when the high adviser appears, giving me a disapproving look.

I yank my hand back. "High Adviser Ellar! I thought you left with Father."

The high adviser nods toward Callum. "General," then offers an elbow to me. "If I may ask for a minute of your time, Ma'hana Lilla."

"Um . . . sure." I take the high adviser's arm and we walk a short distance from the float. I turn to face him with a questioning look.

"I just wanted to make sure Your Highness is doing well. It is not every day we come under attack from the rebellion." His whole left side is covered with the stinking "meal."

"It wasn't an attack, but a harmless demonstration. They are rightfully upset, wouldn't you say? Father provoked them, and now *we* paid the price."

High Adviser Ellar grimaces. "I am afraid it is not so simple as the Ma'hana makes it sound. Your Father is trying to do what is best for the whole nation, not just what is good for a small group. Hard decisions are always made by those who have the burden to rule, while others have the easy job of criticizing it." He smiles as if to lessen the sharpness of his words. "That being said, I am still advising the ma'ha to divert from this course of action."

"Good." I cross my arms. "I don't condone what Father is doing."

"I would be surprised if Ma'hana would feel any other way. But these are challenging times. With the arrival of the Teryn delegates, the ma'ha is overcome. Which brings me to my next point."

The high adviser steeples his fingers and raises them to his chin as if to think how best to proceed. "I wasn't sure if I should interfere, but now I see that I must."

He sighs. "It seems that the Teryn general has been spending too much time in your company, to the chagrin of the court. I have dismissed these concerns before, but after today . . . even I have noticed how he acts casually around you, following you like a lost fish."

Complaints? "I can assure you—"

"Your Highness," the high adviser says and lifts a hand, "it is my duty as a high adviser to always look out for the royal family's best interests. I am fortunate to have been there during the early years of Ma'hana's life, and my duty comes as much from care as from obligation. I must warn you about the Teryns."

"Warn me? I am in no danger from them."

"I've always known that Ma'hana's kindness knows no limits, but the Teryn general clearly takes advantage of it. It is unfortunate that I need to remind Ma'hana of not one, but two incidents where General Callum interfered with Uhnan matters directly, making him seem suspicious."

"High Adviser Ellar, I appreciate your concern, but I don't think—"

"Your Highness, it is easy to forget common sense when one is young like yourself. But it would be best for all concerned to avoid the general's company."

My temper rises, bringing with it the all too familiar sensations of hot-and-cold-and-hot-again, burning deep under my skin. I rub my arms to ward it off. "I will take your advice into consideration."

"That's all I am asking." He bows and leaves to check on a group of courtiers.

A wave of dizziness washes over me, and I stumble into the closest alley.

CHAPTER 45

"Lilla!" Arrov shouts as he runs by the entrance of the alley. "Where are you?"

"Here," I say with effort. The hot-and-cold-and-hot-again feelings sap my energy and I lean on the dirty wall for support. Just until I get my body back under control.

"What are you doing here?" Arrov asks.

"I could ask the same."

"Xor has a mission for you. Tonight you will meet with a refugee—"

"Tonight?" Will this day never end?

Arrov makes a sympathetic face. "Yes, at this location." He sends the information to my necklace. "You will receive a necklace crystal."

"At least I have a couple of hours before the meeting," I say. Enough time to get rid of this magic "problem."

"I heard what happened with your float and Xor's announcement," Arrov says with disapproval.

"Xor showed Father that the rebellion is holding him accountable."

"Don't protect him," Arrov snaps.

Anger spikes at the reminder. New waves of hot-and-cold-and-hot-again wash over me. "I am not defending him. I'm sure he did it in the best interests of the refugees."

"You're crazy if you think he acted in anyone's best interests other than his own. There was nothing to gain by this little stunt. Except severe retaliation. But all is well—Xor had his fun by shaming the ma'ha! He might as well have pointed you out with that information. How long do you think it will take the overseer to figure out—"

"Probably not long," I joke, fighting the hot-and-cold-and-hot-again feelings, which refuse to let up.

"This is serious, Lilla!"

"Don't snap at me." I can't even muster the energy to feel offended.

"You misplaced your loyalty in Xor," Arrov insists. "He doesn't deserve it. If I were you, I would leave the rebellion."

I look him in the eyes. "You're not quitting. Why should I?"

"It is too dangerous for you," Arrov says and places his hands on my shoulders.

"You're risking your life, too."

"It's different. I can handle myself."

"And I can't?" I step back from him.

Arrov lets his hands fall. "All I am saying is that you're risking treason. The stakes are higher for you. Now is not the time to be a hero. Now is the time to think of yourself."

"You are wrong. This is the time to fight for what I believe in." I scratch my arms, leaving behind deep, red grooves. The hot-and-cold feelings intensify. It is as if the sensations turned into bugs marching under my skin.

Arrov pulls me into a quick hug. "I don't want to fight with you. I just want you to be safe." Someone calls for Arrov outside the alley, and he hesitates.

"Go ahead." I gesture with my hand, wincing at the effort it takes. "I'll be heading back on the next shuttle, too."

Arrov kisses my cheek, then lopes away.

I move to follow him, but sharp pain pierces my temples. Grasping my head in my hands, I collapse to my knees. My heart beats as if it is trying to free itself from my body. Away from my magic, which devours me alive, incinerating from the inside.

My skin, glowing now with bright golden-white light, seems to melt from my bones. Pressure builds to unbearable levels.

I throw my head back and scream.

CHAPTER 46

Strong hands pull me to my feet. I struggle to open my eyes against the overwhelming pain. Through the curtain of tears, I see two black and blurred shapes. I blink. The shapes turn into Callum and Teague.

My body shivers and panic wells. "You cannot . . . be here! Too . . . dangerous." I sway on my feet. It won't be much longer.

Callum scoops me up in his arms. He shouts something to Teague in their own language.

The alley whirls around us and the cloudscrapers disappear in a green blur, held in a protective bubble.

"What—" I double over my stomach.

"Let it go!" Callum shouts.

"Lilla, it's okay! Teague says, straining as if he is holding us in this strange place by his sheer will. "Just let it go."

Then there is no more time to think. My back arches in Callum's arms.

Vivid golden-white torrents of magic burst out of me, cascading from every pore. Unchained, uncontrollable, unstoppable. Wild. I try to scream, but I cannot even take a breath.

Then, after what feels like forever, but only a few seconds, it stops. I collapse against Callum's chest, panting, my whole body raw and glowing with that eerie golden-white light.

He holds me close. "You're fine. I've got you."

I lift my head and look into his eyes, which hold relief. "You could have died." I brush a few strands of black hair from his eyes. "I could have killed you—" My voice hitches, and I look away.

"I'm immune to most magic," he says.

"*Most* magic? Are you telling me that you didn't know whether *my* magic is a danger to you before you decided to shut yourself in with me?"

"It didn't matter," Callum says, smiling. "I wouldn't have left you alone."

The fact that he didn't care for his own safety because he didn't want to abandon me stuns me. I slap his shoulder and return his smile. "You are too stubborn."

He grins wider. "Don't forget handsome, too." His gaze studies my face, lingering on my lips. When he looks back into my eyes, the blue of his irises seems to darken.

My fingers slip into his hair as he moves to close the short distance between us. Ready for—

Teague clears his throat.

With a sharp exhalation, Callum lifts his head, glaring at the colonel. A reddish-yellow light flashes across Callum's eyes.

The hazy bubble around us disappears. We find ourselves on Fye Island. On a snow-covered plain, with quaint, colorful houses nestled into the hillside, not far from us.

"I hate to interrupt this tender moment," Teague says, but he doesn't sound the least bit sorry. His tanned skin looks too pale, stretching too tight on his cheekbones. "But can we take this somewhere else? Preferably some place where there is food?"

"The village up ahead has an inn with a diner. It's closer than the palace."

"That sounds good enough for me."

I disengage from Callum, and he puts me down. I say to Teague, "Thank you."

He winks. "You are most welcome."

"What is it that you did? Exactly?" I shiver as the cold island wind tears into my thin and ruined dress. Callum, seeing my discomfort, takes off his jacket, shakes the dried "food" off of it, and drapes it over my shoulders. I burrow into its warmth.

"I am not sure I can translate it into your language. I have some ability in teleportation, and I can also manipulate time-space to a small degree. When I combine the two," Teague says and claps his hands, forming a ball with his curled fingers, "I can form it into a time-space-displacement pocket, if you will."

"You have magic, too?"

Teague shakes his head, then he pales even more, as if that much movement fatigued him. "It is not magic like yours—I don't use elements. It is an ability I was born with."

"Oh." It would have been nice to find someone who also possesses magic that doesn't fit into the known hierarchy.

Teague puts a hand on my shoulder. "I may not be a magic user, but even I can recognize signs of repressed magic. When I don't use my ability for a while, I have a harder time controlling it." He squeezes my shoulder. "Something to think about?"

I nod.

Teague heads off in the direction of the village, with a predatory glint in his eyes. I pity the innkeeper who'll come across him. The colonel looks downright ready to kill for food.

Pulling the jacket tighter, I move toward the dirt path leading back to the palace. "I should go, too." I have only a few hours before tonight's mission.

"He is right, you know," Callum says as he follows after me. "It's not a good idea to let your magic take control over you."

That's easy for him to say. "It's not like I wanted to lose control. It just happened. The stupid thing snuck up on me, and by the time I realized it, it was too late to stop it." Why anyone would want to have magic is beyond me—it's too unreliable.

"That's just it. You are not familiar with your own magic. What kind of mage magic is it, by the way? I've never seen anything like it."

I can't tell him that I have "Lumenian" magic, not when I don't even know what that entails. "I am not a mage. What I am is tired and would like to go back to the palace now."

Callum stops me with a hand on my arm. "I don't understand why you won't talk about it with me."

"Because it is embarrassing. Because I am ashamed that I lost control and nearly destroyed the whole city with my godsdamned magic. Is that a good enough answer for you?" I turn away from him and resume heading up the path.

"Lilla, I meant—" Callum tilts his head, listening.

"What is it?" I look around, then I hear it too. A faint beep sounds from somewhere nearby. Then another. And another.

I turn in a circle, searching for the sound, when Callum pulls me to him by the lapels of the jacket. He reaches into one of the pockets and takes out a small gray device, no bigger than a three-inch square—the source of the beepings.

Shiny black coils cover most of the gray device's surface. He rubs a thumb over the coils, and they retract. A message in an unfamiliar language appears on its small screen, running past fast. Then the whole device turns dark again, and the coils move back into place. Without any change in his expression, he puts the device back into his jacket.

Whatever message he received, I know it would be smart to get it. But I can't just take the device in plain sight.

Callum faces me. "Lilla, if I was out of line—"

I loathe what I am about to do. Manipulating him in such intimate way is the only way I can think of to distract him. "No, you weren't." I place a hand on his chest. "I overreacted. Forgive me?" I bite my lips, the way I've seen my twin friend Bella do it a hundred times to get what she wants.

He lowers his head. "Nothing to forgive."

Rising on my tiptoes, I kiss him. The kiss is meant to be chaste, just long enough for me to snatch the device from the jacket's pocket. But then his arms brace my back, and he returns my kiss with such passion and need that I forget all about the damned device, almost dropping it.

I fumble to keep hold of the device and pull free from Callum, feeling guilty. Wishing the kiss would have never had to end. Wishing that it would have been for a better reason.

"Lilla—"

I don't give him a chance to finish what he wants to say for fear that I won't be able to resist him. "I have to go." Without looking at him, I take his jacket off, making sure the device in my left hand stays out of sight, and give the jacket back to him.

"Keep it."

I want to but . . . "I can't. The court—"

Callum's expression turns blank as he takes it from me. I regret giving it up.

But I've taken enough from him already.

CHAPTER 47

"I'm sorry, boy," I say, patting Fearghas, my battle horse, "but you can't come with me."

Exhaustion weighs heavily on my body after my magical fiasco, and I rest my forehead on his warm neck. I barely had time to change out of my stained dress and get ready for my meeting with the refugee.

Fearghas neighs and stomps in place. Patience isn't his greatest virtue. His whole body tenses, not used to being left behind. Not since Captain Murtagh rescued him as a foal, nearly starved to death, badly beaten. The captain paired us—two injured souls to heal each other. It took time, and a few broken bones, to earn his trust, but it was worth it.

I scratch his neck under the coarse black mane. "I know you didn't mean to attack that stable boy earlier, but I cannot risk this mission, buddy. You'll just have to wait for me." That poor boy got lucky that most of Fearghas's bite encompassed his uniform and only a bit of skin. Others hadn't been so fortunate.

Fearghas bobs his head up and down, as if disagreeing, but stays put. His is a huge black shape—eighteen hands, or six feet, at the withers—blending into the night, and practically vibrating with aggression. It's not his fault that he was bred for war, with sharp fangs meant to tear the throat out of any enemy who gets too close. His clawed feet, instead of hooves, can rend like sharp daggers, and have webs between the claws for swimming. His thick hide, which even laser shots cannot penetrate easily, covers robust muscles. Making him better than any other horse. Capable of running longer than any other animal in the coalition. Fearghas's mean temperament earned him the nickname of "Nasty Beast," and I swear he knows it. He proudly owns it.

Cold wind sweeps snow off the edge of the cliff. Ahead of me is a slush-covered path leading up to the infamous Curved Moon Bay, known as Reckless Bay for all the tragic deaths that have taken place there. A strange meeting place Xor picked.

I pull up the inner snow-protection cover of my cloak from under its hood, leaving only my eyes visible. The cloak itself is plain dark gray, almost black, and reaches the tip of my black boots. Everyone on Uhna has one like it.

As I climb the steep path, loose soil scatters with each step. Either side of the curved cliff ends in a sheer drop, with jagged cliffs below. I keep to the middle of the pathway, to the illusion of safety. When I reach the small rocky top covered in snow, I find it already crowded by two men.

In front of the rickety fence stands a short young man with a small beak for his mouth, his feather-covered face visible under his ragged gray cloak—the refugee I am supposed to meet.

The other is a tall man, with long silver hair, who seems to burp and snigger at the same time. A feat I didn't realize was possible until now. Royal Elementalist Mage Ragnald hugs the refugee's shoulders, forcing the young man to support the mage with both of his hands.

This complicates matters a bit.

I move closer to the two men and quickly rattle off the identification number that should prompt the exchange.

The short man grimaces, and his knees buckle when the mage swats and tries to look into his face with a finger raised, as if wanting to touch his beak. Rude!

"Top pocket," the refugee says.

I step next to the young man, looking for his pocket, but they keep moving around. It's as if all three of us are locked in a strange dance where none of us knows the steps.

"I can't get to it," I say.

The mage falls toward me, and I push against him with one hand. He nearly scratches me when he tries to peel the winter protection cover off my face, murmuring nonsensical words to himself as he does it.

"Stop it!" I snap at him.

I reach for the refugee's pocket again when the mage decides to burst into a loud ballad, singing "Life can be dreary, and life can be cheerful. But life ain't worth living if you are alooone! Or tearful? I can't remember the words," he mumbles. The mage looks at me with bloodshot eyes, hiccup-burps twice, and adds, "Something is very wrong with me." He staggers to the right, forcing the young man and me to stumble with him while he keeps singing.

"You are drunk, that's what's wrong with you," I say.

"Be quiet," the refugee begs him.

"I can't stop," the mage slurs, and tries to move his long, silver hair out of his face, but his hand misses the strands by a mile. "I don't remember getting drunk."

"That what all drunks say." If only he would stop moving around in circles! I'm getting dizzy.

"No, no, no, NO," the royal mage insists. "You don't understand—"

"I understand just fine," I say. "You are a closet drinker who can't hold his alcohol."

Strange and loud clicks reverberate behind us. We all turn to look.

"Don't move! You are all under arrest!" a stern male voice barks.

CHAPTER 48

We stare at four men clad in white and cobalt cloaks. Their weapons trained on us don't waver in the guards' hands. None of us, even the intoxicated mage, dares to move.

How did they find us?

Fla'mma-infused flashlights blind me. "Let me through," a self-important male voice commands. The four men part to let Overseer Irvine through.

The ma'har examines the group with a satisfied expression. "I knew that injecting trackers into the refugees would come in handy." He gestures toward the young man. "He led us straight here."

Royal Elementalist Mage totters on his feet, almost tripping the young man. "I am not with these two"—he swallows, then continues—"I have no idea what is going on . . ." His voice trails off, and he hiccup-burps again, looking green in the face.

"You're lucky to be under diplomatic protection, Royal Mage. Although being drunk is not something the ma'ha will appreciate. I'll deal with you later," Irvine says with disgust, then turns toward us. "These two are not so fortunate. You are under arrest. Give up your leader, and I may grant you a quick death."

With mind racing, I take a step back, only to have part of the ground give under my foot. Rocks fall into the gaping abyss.

The young rebel, cursing, shoves Ragnald forward, right into the overseer, then turns and jumps over the rickety fence.

The ground shakes and Fearghas barrels through the guards.

Irvine jumps out of my horse's way, pushing the mage into the hands of one of the guards, and slips on the muddy ground, falling on his face.

I climb onto Fearghas's back, holding him by his reins as he stomps around, agitated with nowhere to go.

The guard grasping the inebriated mage stumbles behind Fearghas, who kicks out with his clawed feet, propelling both the guard and the mage into the rickety fence.

For a moment it seems as if the fence will hold their combined weight, but with a loud cracking sound, it gives way.

The guard and the mage plummet off the cliff.

"No!" I stare after them as Fearghas dances under me. No one pays us any attention, but I cannot make myself escape.

Buckets of fishguts! I turn Fearghas toward the broken fence and urge him to move.

Fearghas leaps off the cliff.

CHAPTER 49

The wind whistles by my ears as we plunge into the Fyoon Ocean, just past the jagged outcropping of rocks.

The cold, hard ocean hits like an unforgiving stone wall. All air gets pushed out of my lungs, and a long stream of air bubbles surges as we sink.

The salty black water laps over us, freezing me to my bones. Pain screams through every inch of my body from the shock of it. Liquid blackness blinds me, and the need to take a breath becomes unbearable.

Fearghas kicks his legs, slowly at first, then faster and faster.

We break through the rolling surface of the water.

I wheeze in a shuddering breath just as lightning illuminates the darkness. On my right, two dead bodies, one of the refugee and the other of the guard, bob facedown, out of my reach.

I could make Fearghas swim over and try to search the refugee's body for the necklace crystal, thus completing my mission. Then the death of the young man wouldn't be in vain, and Xor would be happy.

But I would never be able to live with myself knowing I chose a piece of crystal over saving a person.

I turn away from the dead. I don't see the mage anywhere. Where could he be?

A huge wave crashes over us, nearly shoving me off Fearghas. Only the reins, wrapped around my hand, prevent me from being dragged away.

Coughing, I urge Fearghas to swim forward, like we used to do in calmer summer days. Keeping his head above the water, Fearghas obeys. He fights against the onslaught of waves, heading out into open water.

Two back-to-back waves sweep over us. They shove us to the side like flotsam, tearing my hood off my head. I drag my wet hair out of my frozen face and rise in the saddle, searching for Ragnald.

Another bolt of lightning illuminates the dark sky, shedding a white-blue-and-purple electric glow. I see something up ahead.

Thunder booms, then blackness returns. Near-gale force winds cut through us, and salty foam whips into our faces. Snow falls sideways around us. Then the next moment freezing rain pelts us, as if the weather itself went insane tonight. Unable to make up its mind.

More waves crash over us, Fyoon Ocean bucking wild, trying to drag us away from the mage. "Come on!" I scream in frustration as my strength wanes. With quivering muscles I urge Fearghas to keep swimming, but he slows, tired now. "Come on, boy. Just a little bit longer." My words sound incoherent, and my eyelids close.

My head jerks painfully, and I wake up. I have no idea how long I was out. Fearghas, exhausted, barely moves. We are going to die here.

No! I slap my face against the exhaustion. I won't give in so easily!

My eyes close again. This time something that looks like a bright light calls to me. My magic. With desperate mental hands, I grab at it. I am clumsy, clueless, and unskilled. It slips away at first. But I try again.

The hot-and-cold-and-hot-again feelings signal my success. My magic bursts through me, driving away the ocean's chill in an instant. Strength floods my muscles and my skin glows with golden-white light. My mind clears of the hypothermia-induced fog. All the fears and doubts fall away, leaving behind a centered calm.

I open my eyes, and with crystal sharpness I see Ragnald just to my right. I turn Fearghas toward the mage's direction. His body floats, as if his magic were keeping him buoyant. I grab his ankle and pull him closer. I drag his unconscious body over my lap with muscles saturated with magical strength.

A weak nicker sounds from Fearghas. The added weight is too much, sapping my horse from what little of his thew is left. As if driven by instinct, I plant my hands on Fearghas's neck, channeling my magic into his tired muscles.

Fearghas shakes his head from side to side, almost giddy with his new-found energy, soaking it all up.

Then Fearghas moves.

He swims with newfound strength, as if he is galloping in a spring meadow and not wrestling with a raging ocean. We head straight toward a narrow ledge, not exactly a beach, but it's the closest land to us. It is so long and narrow that I can't see its other end, obscured by a thick white fog that cuts off visibility beyond a few feet.

Fearghas's clawed feet find solid ground, and soon we are climbing out of the water and up the tapered slope.

Relief spreads through me, and my magic retreats, slipping out of my mental hands. All strength and warmth leave my body, letting in the frigid cold.

Fearghas drops to his knees, and both the mage and I slide off the saddle, onto the cold ground.

Exhaustion closes my eyes. If I could just sleep a little . . .

† ‡ ∞

Something wet and cold pokes my face.

I swipe at it, but it returns, more insistent.

"Lemme be just a little longer." I don't want to wake up.

A complaining neigh sounds right by my ear. My eyes pop open. I see Fearghas's nose inches away.

For a second I have no idea where I am or what I'm doing here. Then I remember.

We are still in Curved Moon Bay, with Fearghas and Ragnald. In the middle of the night. After a failed mission, and a stormy ocean rescue that almost killed us.

I rub my face with numb hands and sit up to look around. I have no idea how long I had dozed off, but all my muscles and joints ache. My teeth chatter as I suck in the cold air. We cannot stay here any longer.

Groaning, I get to my knees and crawl to Ragnald, who still seems to be sleeping. With shaking fingers, I check his pulse as Glenna taught me, but I can't feel any.

Maybe my hand is too cold. I should probably slap him, just to be sure. As gently as I can, I tap his face.

Nothing.

I slap him again, harder.

Still nothing.

In my mind, I hear Glenna shouting at me to stop wasting time and do mouth-to-mouth resuscitation. I scoot closer to the mage and take a deep inhale. I clamp his nose between two of my fingers.

Ragnald's eyes snap open just as I am about to swoop down on his mouth. I can see the red veins in the white of his eyeballs. His gaze focuses on me, and he shoves me away. "Ah! What are you doing? Are you trying to kill me?"

I land on my bottom next to him. *Kill him?* Has all that drinking turned his brain into mush? "You're alive."

"No thanks to you," Ragnald complains as he struggles to sit up.

"You do realize Fearghas and I spent godsknow how long in the stormy ocean, trying to fish you out?!" Crossing my trembling arms, I add under my breath, "If I'd known you'd be so ungrateful, I would have left you there."

It seems I didn't say it as quietly as I thought, because Ragnald glares at me.

But before he can say anything, a serrated pirate sword appears out of the thick fog, only to land on the throat of the mage.

CHAPTER 50

The pirate sword is followed by an arm, attached to the body of a burly thug who holds it.

Ten more men dressed in dark brown wool cloaks follow after the first thug, each burlier than the last. They surround us within seconds, glaring in threat as if to dare us to move.

Fog lights on a boat turn on, making the mist morph into a yellow, smokelike curtain. A small boat's silhouette becomes visible, bouncing on the water right by our rocky ledge.

A wave cutter! The fastest ship on Uhna, favored by smugglers, and the bane of the port authorities.

With a grunt, the closest smuggler, the size of a small house and with a red beard on his rugged face, drags Ragnald to his feet, shaking the mage.

"We can pay you—" I say in a placating tone as my mind races for a solution.

But the thug with a blue captain's hat interrupts, "We no' need no money. We al'dy been paid f'r the Teryn general here."

They think Ragnald is Callum? This is the second time in one day someone attempted to kidnap Callum!

"How do you know he is the Teryn general?" I ask as much from procrastination as curiosity.

The eleven thugs stare at me. A tall man with legs like tree trunks scratches his long brown hair. "We 'ere following 'im from the palace just as we 'ere told."

"Tall man, wearing black," another smuggler adds, showing missing teeth. "Clearly, we found 'im."

Clearly. "Why don't you take me instead?" I bluff.

"We c'nna take you," a bald smuggler retorts. "Yo' not the Luman-uh Lumin-uh—"

"Lumenian," I say, just as three other smugglers correct him, too. They scowl at me, frowning in suspicion.

"Maybe best if yo's n't alive to tattletale," says Captain Thug.

"Yea'," the others respond.

I raise my hands. "I won't tell any tale."

The smugglers advance on me, set on their plan. Fearghas neighs, stomping his front legs. He rears and bares his fangs at the approaching men, blocking the thugs from getting to me.

Ragnald collapses into a lunge, as if his knees gave out. He slams his hands onto the ground, fingers sinking in deeply. The mage's eyes burn with cerise light, and his long silver hair floats around his face as magic saturates the air around him. He makes a guttural sound, an incomprehensible command that makes the hair on my arms stand up.

The ground shakes and bucks under our feet, like a wild and living thing. A wide crack opens, spreading fast. It circles the thugs but never reaches Fearghas and me.

The smugglers scatter from the gaping rift that chases them, but they are not fast enough. One after the other, they all fall into the deep chasm.

Then, in the blink of an eye, the ground is flat again. There isn't a single sign left of the smugglers.

Drained, Ragnald sits back.

Fearghas shakes his long mane, as if he is impressed, then bumps his nose into my arm. I scratch his neck. "Thank you for saving us."

"Don't thank me. I didn't do it for you."

That's good to know. "Why are you so rude to me?"

He rises to his feet, his expression full of anger. "Because this is all your fault!"

I reel back, unsure if I heard him correctly. "My fault?"

"Had you not come to my library—"

"*Your* library?"

"I never would have attracted the attention of your healer friend. She was the one who harmed me."

"Glenna would never hurt anyone," I say, seething. What is wrong with this mage to blame others for his own mistakes? "She didn't get you drunk. You did this to yourself!"

"Why do I even bother?" Ragnald throws his hands up and turns to leave.

I grab his arm. "Take it back." I cannot let him smear Glenna's reputation with lies.

Ragnald yanks his arm away from me. "Why would I? It's the truth. Everybody knows that healers hate mages. This was no mere drunk 'escapade'—I was poisoned. Correct me if I am wrong, but isn't your friend exceptionally famous for her knowledge with herbs? Herbs that can be easily used in the right dosage for poison, especially when mixed into wine?"

Poison? "I don't believe you!"

"I am so tired of hate and fear wherever I go. You should have let me die. I would have been happier dead."

I curl my fingers inward before I give in to the urge to slap some reason into him. "Is this why I risked my life? To save a crazy and selfish man?"

"Think what you want. You don't know what it's like for me here." Reaching inside his black robe, he takes something out, then throws it toward me. It bounces off my soaked cloak and falls to the ground. "Just take that thing and leave me be."

"Wait! Will you tell anyone what happened tonight?"

Ragnald regards me with a cold expression. "I've told your father before that the Academia of Mages does not involve itself with state issues. You can rest assured." He plods into the fog, leaving me staring after him in disbelief.

Bending down, I pick up the small item Ragnald threw my way. It's palm-size and covered in sand. I wipe off the sand until it shines in the moonlight.

It's a necklace crystal! The one I was supposed to get from the refugee but thought lost.

The mission was a success after all. But at what price?

CHAPTER 51

I rub my eyes to get the last remnants of sleep out of them as I shuffle toward the main hall early the next morning. Every inch of my body aches from last night's incident.

I enter the cavernous hall through one of the open double doors. The main hall, where the royal family and a few esteemed high society members dine, is one of the oldest rooms in the Crystal Palace. Stone floor, stone walls, and stone columns support the wood beam ceiling soaring high above. Glass tables line the floor, arranged in a U shape with elegant silk chairs around them. Most of them empty except for a few ma'hars and ma'haras lingering over their breakfast in the back.

Ancient woven tapestries, depicting battles of our pirate ancestors, flap in the ever-present breeze between tall windows on my left. On my right, private dining nooks with open glass doors invite anyone to sit in quiet comfort. These nooks were added later to bring a modern flare to the hall.

Scents of freshly baked pastries make my stomach grumble, and I don't pay attention to the two men facing each other in the middle of the room until I am almost next to them.

I stumble to a halt.

Belthair, wearing a plain dark-gray winter cloak similar to one I had on yesterday, glares down at Irvine. Only the top two of his six arms are visible, as if in precaution. There weren't that many six-armed guards in the palace. While he has changed much over the two years since he worked as my guard, he probably wouldn't want to risk anyone realizing that he isn't dead after all.

"For the last time, I demand that you show your necklace and identify yourself right now," Irvine says, reaching toward Belthair's neck, as if to take matters into his own hands. "You might have thought you got away last night, but I recognize you. You were there, at Curved Moon Bay, weren't you? Admit it!"

Belthair slaps Irvine's hand away and laughs into the ma'har's face, which is turning purple now. "You have no right to demand anything from me."

Irvine pulls himself up straight, as if trying to look taller, and puffs out his narrow chest. "I am the Overseer of Refugee Affairs. No one is exempt from scrutiny. I have every right to demand your identification, by the order of the ma'ha. Or are you hiding something?"

Belthair opens his mouth when two nearly identical young women glide up to him and drape themselves over his sides, like living curtains.

Bella, the younger twin by two minutes, shakes her black hair styled in a short bob and coos, "You left without waking us." She rises on her tiptoes and gives Belthair a steamy kiss that he seems all too happy to return.

Isa, looking impatient but otherwise a mirror image of her sister, puts a hand on Belthair's cheek and forces him to disengage from Bella to turn toward her. She also kisses him. "We were looking for you everywhere."

Irvine gapes at the twins and stutters for a second, then bows at the waist. "Princess Isa and Princess Bella! I greet you respectfully. I had no idea he was with Your Highnesses. Uh . . . how was your trip from Barabal?"

Belthair puts his arms around the two petite women's waist, smirking at the confused ma'har.

Isa and Bella glance at Irvine. "Uneventful." Then they turn away from the ma'har, dismissing him.

Isa grasps Belthair's chin and pulls him close to her to engage in kissing again. Noisily.

Irvine, still purple-faced, bows again from the waist, even though neither of the twins pays any attention to him. The ma'har hesitates. Uncertain what to do, he finally decides to leave, muttering under his breath. He notices me, and embarrassment mixed with frustration flicker across his expression, as if he is ashamed that I witnessed his pitiful treatment. He bows his head, just barely, and tramps toward the exit.

I step next to the threesome. "You can stop now." But Isa and Belthair remain locked at the lips.

I look back to see if Irvine is gone, but I catch the ma'har lingering in the hall, scrutinizing the four of us with suspicion. When he realizes I see him leering, he hurries away.

Bella giggles. Isa and Belthair pull at each other's clothes, as if they are alone. The few ma'hars and ma'haras take notice, and grumble in upset. Great, we needed more attention.

"I repeat, 'You can stop now.'"

Still no reaction. With a low curse, I clap my hands. The loveygulls jump apart.

Belthair wipes at his mouth as he straightens, glaring at me. "Jealous?"

I huff, and head toward the closest eating nook. "You forget that I've been there and didn't go back for seconds."

Tittering, Isa and Bella follow after me. "Ouch."

I shrug. They don't know much of my history with Belthair beyond a fallen-out friendship, and I don't plan to enlighten them.

The small nook, encased in transparent glass with stone floors, has a round wooden table sitting in the middle with six chairs around it. On the tabletop, a crystal bowl bursts full of fresh fruit next to a crystal pitcher of boomberry punch with six wooden mugs.

I close the doors and engage the nook's privacy setting, frosting all the glass surfaces. I turn to find Belthair, still fuming, looming over me.

"Are you insane?" I ask him. "What are you doing here?"

"I had no choice but to come." He leans down so only I hear his words. "Because every time we send someone else to meet you, they end up dead."

My stomach drops at the reminder of the disastrous events of last night. I wish I could go back and prevent the young refugee from jumping. But wishing changes nothing.

"Irvine knew the young refugee would be there," I say, "because he injected a tracker into the refugees. Did Xor or you know about this and failed to warn me?"

"Xor and I suspected Irvine would try something like that, but now we know thanks to you."

I take a step toward Belthair, not sure what I'm intending to do. He covers his crotch with his hands in reflex.

I smile sweetly. "Oh, by the way, how are your balls, Major?" Belthair narrows his brown eyes in response. "I hope there isn't any *lasting* damage. Brain damage, that is."

Isa clears her throat, and Belthair and I separate from our huddle. "What are you two whispering about?"

Both Belthair and I say, "Nothing." We sit down at the table next to the twins, as far away from each other as we can.

I turn to Isa. "You two are back early from Barabal."

Their home world, Barabal, was the last planet to join the Pax Septum Coalition. They have visited the Crystal Palace many times, but when Glenna was away at the Healer's College our acquaintances morphed into a friendship. When they caught me in a lie and learned I'd joined the rebellion, they joined too. They claimed they had nothing better to do anyway. They've been away on a mission to get more financial support for Xor.

"We had to leave in a hurry," Isa says.

Bella adds, "It might have been because a few million credits disappeared mysteriously from the royal treasury."

"Some of it even made it to the rebellion," Isa says, and elbows Belthair. "You're welcome, Major."

Bella spreads her hands when I frown. "Technically, it's part of our inheritance. We just accessed it early."

"Decades early," Isa adds.

"What will happen when the Barabal authorities figure out that it was you two who liberated those credits?" I ask, worried. The last thing we need is the Barabal authorities to descend on Uhna, demanding the release of the twins along with those credits.

Isa waves away my concern. "That won't happen."

"No one will ever find out we did it," Bella insists. "That 'little surprise' we left in the planet's central network will take care of it."

I lean back in my chair. They might be impulsive, but there is no doubt the twins are the best hackers in the whole coalition. Which reminds me . . .

I put the communication device on the table.

Isa and Bella both "ooh" seeing it. "Where did you get this?"

"I—uh—borrowed it from Callum."

The twins look at me, puzzled. "Who?"

"She means *that* general, from the Teryn Praelium. Remember? I briefed you two at the camp. And by borrowed," Belthair says, sneering, "she means *stolen*."

"I fully plan to return it to him." If I return it, it won't be stealing anymore, right?

Belthair snorts. "I never thought I'd live to see the day when I find the goody-goody ma'hana steal."

"Oh, please!" Bella says, mocking. "I'm sure you've done worse, Major. You forget you have a certain reputation among the wealthy coalition ladies. An *impressive* reputation." The twins snicker.

I had no idea about Belthair's, um, tactics. But now that explains a lot.

"Can you figure this out?" I ask Isa to change the topic.

She picks up the small gray device with the black coils on its top. When she rubs a finger over the coils, the device vibrates. She yanks her hand back, as if it had zapped her.

"This is a live one," she says with wonder. "Literally. Technology combined with a living creature." She points at the coils. "It's some kind of electric worm. If I have to guess, it acts as a security measure. Probably reading the oil levels on the skin. It zapped me, only lightly, when I touched it. I am sure next time the zap would be worse, until it might even kill the unauthorized user."

That thing is a bug? And it was my pocket the whole time? "Can you, um, bypass it without hurting it?" I might not like bugs, but that doesn't mean I want it to suffer.

She sucks air through her teeth. "I'll need to bring out 'the hammer.'" She reaches into one of her hidden pockets and takes out an unassuming box, much smaller than the gray device on the table.

I point at it. "That thing is 'the hammer'?"

Bella leans back from the table. "That *thing* is Isa's invention. *Nothing* can withstand it."

Isa glances at me when she picks up the communicator. "Sweetie, I am afraid there won't be much left of it for you to return once I am done with it."

I grimace. I had a feeling.

Isa pops open the middle of the box and places the gray communicator on top of it. The box shakes and stretches to swallow up the whole device, as if it is made of a flexible fabric. She puts a pair of glasses on her pert nose, then presses the side of the box.

Flashes of color run over the box's matte top, which Isa reads out loud. "It's a message to the general. Something about a blood analysis done on— that's not right, is it?—dead bodies?"

"What else?" I prompt Isa, and she glances up at me over the edge of her glasses, noting my anxious tone before she turns back to reading. "The result is"—she falls silent and adjusts something on her glasses—"it's inconclusive. Then the message ends with, 'need more.' Of what, I am not sure."

I pinch the bridge of my nose. The dead bodies must refer to those poor souls Callum found. I had no idea he took blood from them. But why? What was he looking for? And he needs more of what?

With its task done, the hammer peels back from the communicator, leaving behind a melted and smoking gray chunk. Isa drops the chunk into a wooden mug. "That's all I could get out of it."

Belthair pushes his chair on its back legs. "This was a waste of my time."

Fed up with his complaining, I remove the necklace crystal from my pocket and throw it at him. "Why don't you take this thing, and leave us then?"

Belthair, nearly toppling backward, fumbles to catch the crystal before it falls to the stone floor and shatters.

With furious brown eyes, he glowers at me as he slams his fist on the table. "Are you insane, throwing that thing around? It's more valuable than you can imagine." He slides the crystal back to me. "Besides, you'll need this to complete your mission."

"I thought the mission was over!"

"No, it's not. You'll have to—"

The glass doors rattle.

CHAPTER 52

With quick reflexes Belthair taps the leather gauntlet on his left arm and leaps into a freshly formed shadow. But instead of disappearing, the shadow stays in the corner just as the doors burst open.

"There you are, Lilla," Glenna says. "I've been looking for you everywhere." She rushes into the nook, then halts when she sees the twins. "Oh. You two are back. I thought I smelled something cloying."

Bella—ignoring Glenna's verbal jab—jumps to her feet and hugs the stiffened healer, which she knows how much Glenna despises. "We've missed you!" She moves to kiss Glenna on each cheek, in greeting.

But Glenna pushes Bella away, which she always does, tilting her head out of reach. "Like I've missed you two. *Not.*"

Snickering, Bella drops back onto her chair, pulling her legs up, clearly not offended by Glenna's grumbling, as usual.

The healer eyes the twins. "Staying long? I hope not," she says. Then her gaze snags on the winter cloak draped over the empty chair next to Bella. "Is someone else here too?"

All three of us say "NO!" with such vehemence that Glenna takes a step back. When she sees the necklace crystal on the table, I casually put the crystal away, as if it's nothing important. "So," I say, "what brings you here?"

Glenna hesitates, wringing her hands.

Isa and Bella exchange meaningful looks. "Yes, Glennie, do tell us."

"Stop calling me that! You know I dislike it."

The twins grin. "We know."

"What are you two doing here anyway?" Glenna asks. "Did you steal something? You both have that shifty look about you I know so well. One that doesn't bode well."

Isa and Bella burst into laughter. Isa says, "Of course we did! Do you want to know more?"

Glenna raises both of her hands. "The less I know, the better off I am. Of the four of us, I have to work." She looks at me apologetically. "No offense meant."

I shrug. "None taken."

Isa glides over to Glenna and hugs her shoulders. "Glennie, I've told you many times, Bella and I are not criminals."

Bella nods. "We only take advantage of rising opportunities, if you will. And who could fault us when we're having so much fun?"

Behind Glenna, Belthair starts re-forming from his shadow disguise.

"You two will give me a heart attack one day from worry. If you weren't such a bad influence on Lilla," Glenna says and hugs Isa back, "I would even go so far as to say I like—"

Without thinking, I pick up an apple from the fruit bowl and lob it in the direction of Belthair. The fruit flies by Glenna's cheek, missing her by a hair, and hits Belthair in the chest. He grabs the apple, mouthing a curse at me, then disappears back into the shadow.

Relieved, I lean back in my chair.

Glenna points at me. "See? That's exactly what I mean! Bad influence."

Isa shrugs. "You have to admit, it was a great throw."

Bella adds, "Unless Lilla was aiming it at your head. In that case . . ."

Isa continues, ". . . she missed badly."

Glenna throws her hands up and stares at the ceiling. "*No one* should put up with this much whalecrap."

"Listen, how about I catch you at the Healing Center later?" I suggest. "Then we can talk. All right?"

Glenna sighs. "I guess it can wait a bit longer." I lead her to the exit, then close the glass doors behind her. Locking them this time.

Next to me, Belthair materializes again, picks up his cloak, and rubs his chest. "You didn't have to throw so hard, you know."

Yes, I did. "Just tell me what the rest of the mission is."

"Tonight, at the delegation ball your father is holding for the Teryns, you'll meet with a secret supporter—"

Secret supporter? Is he joking? "How will I know this 'secret supporter'?" I ask in a mocking tone.

But it goes over Belthair's head. "You won't. They will find you. You'll give them the necklace crystal and you'll receive a bag in exchange."

"*A* bag? That's it?" Could this mission be any vaguer?

"As far as you're concerned," Belthair says and opens a gateway from the leather gauntlet. Heading toward it, he adds, "Try not to get anyone killed this time."

The arrogance! I throw another apple from the bowl, but he disappears before it could hit him.

I face the twins. "He is unbelievable," I mutter, but Isa and Bella shake their heads in disapproval at me.

"What did *I* do now?"

"You should have told Glennie already," Isa says. "About the rebellion."

"Don't you think I tried?" I say. "Many times! But you know how she is. Besides, I would only put her in unnecessary danger."

"Sweetie," Bella says and puts a hand on my shoulder, "you have to try harder, or you'll lose her."

CHAPTER 53

I enter Glenna's small office in the Healing Center. I find her by the tree-trunk desk, grinding away dried herbs in a stone mortar, with fingers grasping the stone pestle in a white-knuckled hold.

"If you keep up like that, there won't be anything left of those herbs."

Glenna glances up, then back down into the mortar, as if seeing it for the first time. "Oh, you're right." She wipes her hands on her healer's cloak.

The twins' warning echoes in my mind. Maybe they are right. Maybe I shouldn't keep Glenna in the dark about me being a rebel. I'll just have to phrase it very carefully.

"Glenna, I have something to tell you—" I say, just as she blurts out, "I'm ruined!"

Ruined? "Are you expecting Nic's baby?"

"No! Why would you think that?"

"Uh . . . then what is it?"

She closes her eyes for a moment, clearly struggling. Then, to my surprise, she rolls up the wide sleeve of her cloak. Underneath, she wears her usual long-sleeved dark blue shirt. For a second she hesitates, then pulls up the shirtsleeve too.

Pale red, angry-looking welts, two fingers thick, crisscross Glenna's alabaster skin all the way to her elbow, disappearing under her shirt.

"Oh, Glenna!" I reach out, but dare not touch her arm.

"It's okay. They don't hurt anymore."

"How did you get those scars?" She had never shown them to me before. I always assumed that was how she dressed, like me with my leggings and tunics.

She rolls her sleeve back down. "I got them on the day my whole family died in a Fla'mma fire."

"What happened?" I know Glenna was adopted by Great Healer Robley, but I didn't know she had lost her family in such a tragic way.

"My parents were healers. We lived with my two older sisters in a small cottage in Evander Forest. We had no weapons. Nothing. They came in the middle of the day."

"Who came?"

She looks up, but her eyes don't see me, as if they are looking into the past. "Elementalist mages. They found us because I used my magic to heal one of the orphan pets. It was suffering. I couldn't help it . . . I had to . . ."

"Oh, Glen! I'm so sorry!"

She clears her throat. "I didn't know they were pursuing us. I wish I—"

"But why were the mages after your family?"

"They weren't after my family. Not exactly. The mages always thought that our healing magic, A'ris, is the weakest element, and prone to cause healers to turn. But that's not true. It's easy to underestimate how much we channel into our patients, trying to save their lives."

I had seen Glenna working hard at the refugee camps, doing her best to heal everyone, sometimes to the point of exhaustion.

"Turning is a complex regression affecting both healers and mages," Glenna continues. "When one overdoes magic, he risks becoming addicted to it. From that point, he will crave it. Abuse it. Allow it to corrupt his soul. Once corruption sets in, it will eat the magic user's soul from the inside out, leaving behind a shell. A monster bent on killing."

"These turned are under the rule of the Archgod of Chaos and Corruption, right?"

She nods. "One turned could destroy many cities with its magic and be nearly unstoppable. The mages call them 'Hounds of the Dark Lord of Destruction,' because to them, these lost souls are nothing more than mindless animals that need to be put down."

"Were your parents turned?"

Glenna laughs without mirth. "No, they were not."

"Why would the mages kill your family? And how can they do that when they were banned from the coalition worlds?"

"They were banned with the only exception to hunt turned—as long as they are on their holy mission they can come and go as they please." She takes a deep breath. "The mages hunt the turned, but when there isn't one, they focus their attention on where a turning *might* happen. They don't care how low the possibility is—if there was someone in your family who turned, no matter how many generations back, they will methodically go after all of your relatives to eradicate the risk. Like they did to my family."

"That's horrible!"

Glenna turns away from me and picks up a handful of herbs from the stone mortar. "I thought I was over it. That I didn't harbor any prejudice against them. But when I saw that royal mage at your father's wedding"— she clenches the herbs in her fist as she looks at me—"it all came back. I thought I could resist. . . . I thought . . ."

I place a hand on her trembling shoulder. "What did you think?"

"I thought that I could find peace if I . . . I don't know . . . if I just taught one of them a lesson."

"But instead you almost poisoned the royal elementalist mage. Was he the one who killed your parents?"

"Yes. I mean no. At least I don't think so—I didn't get a good look. Oh, gods! I almost poisoned the royal mage!" she wails and buries her face in her hands.

"Oh, Glenna." I hug her to me. Her whole body shakes from the force of her sobs.

Minutes pass before she finally calms. "I don't know why I did it. I never thought I was capable of such an act . . . to almost break my healer's oath . . ." She trails off and looks at me with a deep frown. "How did you know that I poisoned the mage?"

"I, uh, I had to rescue him, last night, from drowning."

"Drowning?"

"Yes. By Curved Moon Bay."

Glenna steps back. "What were you doing at Curved Moon Bay last night?"

This is it. This is my chance to tell her everything.

I open my mouth. But I don't know what to say. What if she can't accept it? What if she'll never trust me again?

"Is that why you were with the twins, in a secret meeting?"

"I—uh . . . it's not that—"

Glenna raises a hand to stop me. "Don't think I haven't noticed that you're up to something. You've been acting different, avoiding me ever since that incident with that poor refugee girl from the kitchen."

"Eita. Her name is Eita."

"You would tell the twins but not me."

"Glenna, I—"

She laughs bitterly. "It's all clear to me what's going on."

"It is?"

"Yes. I am not good enough for you and your royal friends."

"That's not true! How could you think so little of me? Would you just listen for a second? I can explain—"

"Don't bother." She walks behind her desk. "It doesn't matter anymore."

"Glenna, please! I've never meant to hurt you." I am losing her, and I don't know how to stop it from happening!

"There is nothing to understand, Your Highness." Glenna points to the door. "I'm afraid the Healing Center is closed for the day."

CHAPTER 54

"Walk with me," Jorha says. "I have to examine the newly excavated tunnels."

Arrov dropped me off at the refugee camp so I could deliver some food from the kitchen. Since I have a few hours to wait for him until he finishes his inspection of the rebellion's "new" spacecraft, I follow after Jorha.

We enter a narrow dirt tunnel supported by slim wooden beams that seem too weak to do the job. Torches light the way, making the air smell of smoke, which is an improvement over the putrid smell that seems to hang in the hot air of the underground rebel camp.

The ground shakes, and a thin layer of dirt showers on top of my head. Here's hoping that the tunnel won't collapse while we're still in it.

"I thought Xor would be done with the excavation by now." I swipe the dirt from my hair.

"This is the last tunnel. We're done once we're finished digging."

I glance at her. "I'm surprised Xor can afford to send rebels to work here."

Jorha shines her Fla'mma-infused torchlight on a crack at the top of the tunnel. "It's been hard to find volunteers, I'll give you that. After our 'appearance' at the coalition parade, the whole of Camp One has been sent into one of the crystal mines." She mutters a few choice words.

I stumble. "What do you mean, the whole camp?"

"Adults, elderly, and children. No exceptions," she grinds out the words.

That can't be! All those poor people sentenced to hard labor and a slow death. That explains the eerie atmosphere in Camp Seven today. The usual hustle and bustle were missing. Everyone walked around with their heads ducked, as if trying to be invisible.

"I had friends in that camp!" I had assisted Glenna in issuing immunization potions more than once to the children there. We spent time with the elderly refugees to make sure their everyday needs were met.

Jorha's expression tightens. "So did I. Most of the refugees are scared to help us now, even with minor tasks. And the rest of us are dwindling in numbers. Every day we are losing many who abandon their posts. If this keeps up . . ." her voice trails off.

I had no idea things were so bad in the rebellion.

Jorha flashes her light on a set of petroglyphs. Three groups of stick figures are shown in scenes portraying their daily life. In the first one, women and children are gathering fruits from trees. The second one depicts figures fishing with stones and rudimentary fishing rods. In the third one, a large group is sitting around a fire, as if telling stories to each other.

These must be the cave drawings Xor wanted to find. "I wonder how long ago they were made. How did Xor even know they were here?"

Jorha shrugs. "My guess is as good as yours."

I squint at the last petroglyph. Is that a third eye? I lean closer. Nah. Just a smudge.

"I wish they could be made public, so they can take their rightful place in Uhna's history," I say. These could be the first cave drawings of life before the time of the pirates.

"That would be a trick, since we can't exactly betray their location without betraying the rebellion." Jorha resumes her trek.

She is right. "What was Xor's response to Camp One?"

"Nothing," Jorha says. "I wanted to retaliate, but Xor decided not to."

That's a surprise. "Will he start evacuating the refugee camps soon?"

Jorha scoffs. "And how would he do that? We barely managed to replace the spacecraft that you and Arrov destroyed, making our 'fleet' grow to all of five craft. The second we start moving people, the overseer would be on to us. Same with the umbrae travel gauntlets. We have no more than half a dozen of those, with a maximum capacity of three people. They won't be of much help. Do you want the rest of the refugees punished or immediately sent to the mines, too?"

"No, of course not!"

"Xor does his best with what little is available. Our job is to deliver on our missions to make sure he has all the support he needs." She shines her torchlight into my face. "Successfully. Especially the mission you have tonight."

CHAPTER 55

I pull at the tight collar of my sleeveless evening gown as I stroll toward the royal ballroom. The dress is suffocating, too close-fitting for my taste, spiking claustrophobia and irritation. My feet already ache from the high-heeled shoes. I wish I could turn back and skip this event. After the spat with Glenna, I just want to hide in my room. But I can't. I assured Jorha I'd do my best, and by the gods I will.

I pat the hidden pocket that contains the necklace crystal on the wide belt around my waist. The one I need to complete the exchange.

A muffled curse stops me in my tracks.

"Every godsdamn time," I hear Nic's voice, but I don't see him.

Following his curses, I find him behind the door of the royal ballroom, leaning his forehead on the wall.

"Nic? What are you doing?"

He whirls to face me, covering his mouth with a hand. "It's embarrassing."

"Do you have a cold sore? Or bad breath?"

"Ha-ha." He lowers his hand. "*This* is embarrassing."

He sports a fake mustache. On the left side of his mouth, it is narrow and curving at the edge, and I recognize the artistic style of Isa. On the right side, it is thick and bushy, drawn with coarse lines that show the impatience Bella is known for.

"At least the twins didn't draw a beard like last year." I examine his "mustache." I thought they used black ink, but it is actually navy blue, and seems to reflect the light when Nic moves his head. "Or muttonchops, like the year before that. Or the three-day stubble a year before that." You would think Nic would be prepared for this by now.

"I know, I know! No need to remind me. I was there."

"Have you tried to wash it off?" I clear my throat from the laughter that wants to escape.

"Of course I tried! I scrubbed it for ages but nothing helps. See?"

I look where he points, and the skin does look red and irritated around the drawing. "You really should start locking your door when the twins are visiting."

Nic groans. "I did! I even had guards assigned to my living quarters. And if I find those two—"

"Were they male guards?"

"Yes, as a matter of fact. Why?"

I laugh at his crestfallen expression. "That explains a lot. You forget, the twins are experts in all males." And sometimes females too.

"What should I do? I can't go in looking like this!"

I push him out of his hiding place. "Go find Glenna." Thinking about her makes all my mirth dry up.

"Good idea," he says, heading to the Healing Center.

At least one of us is happy. With a sigh, I enter the royal ballroom.

Elegant, airy, and just the right amount of melancholy music drifts above the cloud of buzzing conversation interspersed with trilling laughter.

All the monarchs and their entourages from the parade, visiting from the eighteen other coalition worlds, mingle with Uhna's high society members in the hexagonal room. Tall mirrors on the wall make the room seem bigger than it is. White silk curtains, with colorful bouquets of flowers tied on them, frame the floor-to-ceiling windows that reveal the darkness of the early evening. A beige marble floor with gold veins bumps against the same tiles on the walls. Oil paintings depicting the happy moments of past pirate life hang around the room, trying to bring it cheer. But the free-flowing and synthetic boomberry wine takes care of all that.

When a purple-uniformed servant offers me a flute of the red bubbling drink, I gladly take it from the crystal tray. Not that I like it. Too acidic for my taste. But holding onto it gives me something to do with my hands.

Up ahead, the crowd seems to swell like the ocean tide, making my stomach clamp into knots with a rising panic. I have no choice but to wade in, be visible so the mysterious supporter can find me.

Ma'hars and ma'haras bump into me from every side, and I splash my drink on my dress while pushing forward.

My claustrophobia rears its selfish head. There isn't enough air in the overcrowded room. The urge to flee has me spin on my heels toward the exit.

"Are you quitting already?" Belthair asks before I can take a few steps.

Forcing calm, I turn to face him.

Wearing a dark gray suit that emphasizes his athletic form, Belthair eyes me with a mocking smirk. His black hair is slicked back, and only two of his six hands are visible.

"Are you here to supervise my mission?"

"Yes," he says. "This is too important for you to ruin it."

"Thanks for the trust."

"Just because Xor doesn't hold you responsible for the death of that courier doesn't mean I give you the benefit of the doubt."

"There is nothing you can say that will make me feel any worse than I already do." I shove my drink at him so I won't smack him.

Blindly, I plunge into the crowd, and run into someone.

"*Excuse* me," I say with impatience, only to realize it's Arrov.

"There you are," Arrov says, oblivious to my rudeness, looking impressive in a white suit with silver motifs of snowflakes embroidered on it. "Isn't this ball great?"

Right now, nothing feels great. "If you've seen one, you've seen them all." I thread my arm into his. "Come with me." Having him by my side helps me deal with the crowd. A crowd that gives way to Arrov much more easily than it did to me.

"Belthair got to you, I see."

I fill him in on last night's fiasco. "He thinks it's my fault, and I agree. I should have been more careful. I—"

"There is nothing you could have done differently." He drags a hand through his midnight blue hair. "Xor shouldn't have sent you. I should have been the one who—"

"What's done is done," I say. There nothing I can do to change the past. "Let's just get through this night."

"How about I grab us some drinks?"

"That would be great." I envy Arrov as he weaves through the ballroom with ease and his usual cheerfulness. What I wouldn't give to be just a little like him.

"How is it that I always find that boy around you?" Callum asks as he takes the spot Arrov vacated.

I jump in surprise. "You scared me!"

"Guilty conscience?" Callum asks with a half smile. "What are you up to this time?"

"I am *up to* nothing." Why does he always have to rile me up?

"Then why are you with him?"

"Are you jealous?"

He gives me a look full of confidence. "That would mean I consider him a threat. Which I don't."

"Good to know." I glance around. I can't be seen with Callum. What if the supporter decides to abort the mission because of him? "I have to go. I'm busy."

Callum's expression turns to suspicious. "Doing what?"

Fishguts! "Um, dancing?"

"Are you asking me?"

What? "No!"

Callum takes my hand, and as if on cue, the music switches to a romantic song. He strides to the middle of the floor, towing me after him. He pulls me into him with a flourish, and I land in his arms, with my hands on his shoulders. Holding me by my waist, he leads us into a swaying dance with surprising skill.

An amused smile appears on Callum's face. "You didn't think I could dance."

Caught! "It's not that—"

"Just admit it. Disbelief is written all over your face."

"Fine! I assumed you can't. Are you happy now?"

His gaze locks on my mouth before slowly looking back into my eyes. "Very."

The dance floor fills with couples. They are nothing but a haze in my vision. I inhale Callum's scents of sun and desert. They are intoxicating.

"If you keep looking at me like that, I won't be responsible for my actions," Callum says with a growl. His hands tighten on my waist, and he slows us to a near stop.

184

"I thought you had more self-control," I whisper. With his face so close, I can practically *feel* his kiss.

"I am about to reevaluate that fact." Heat radiates from his body, engulfing me. I really shouldn't encourage him. I shouldn't . . .

Before I can stop myself, I rise on my toes, everything forgotten.

A throat clears at our right.

I falter.

"I am cutting in!" Arrov declares, glaring with hostility at Callum.

"No, you're not." Callum leads me away by my hand.

Arrov grabs Callum's shoulder, shoving him backward. "I said, 'I am cutting in!'"

Callum shakes off Arrov's hand. "*Make* me."

Arrov gets into Callum's face. "Gladly."

"Stop this!" I hiss. "You're both acting like children!" Already half the dance floor stares at us with unveiled curiosity.

But the men don't listen. They're locked in their staring contest, tension thick and charged between them.

I contemplate stomping my feet when a gentle touch on my arm interrupts. "What is it?"

A tall woman with light blue skin, long dark blue hair in a braid, and dressed in a light silver pantsuit, smiles at me. Her posture regal and commanding.

My eyes widen as I recognize her as the ruler of A'ice. I bow in respect. "Queen Amra, forgive me. I didn't know it was you."

She waves a hand. "Don't worry about it, my dear." She gestures toward the men. "Let us leave the boys to their games."

Games? "I am not sure that's such a good idea."

She extends her arm. "Believe me when I say, and I did raise seven sons, including my baby, Arrov, it's best to let them get this off their chests."

"But—" I take her arm out of politeness.

"Before we know it, they will be best of friends." She leads me away.

I glance back over my shoulder. Callum and Arrov face each other, their bodies rigid, a hairbreadth from violence. "I doubt that would ever be the case."

"Trust me. Besides, they are providing a nice little distraction for us. Exactly what we need."

I increase my steps to keep up with her. "I'm not sure I understand."

Queen Amra pats my hand on her arm. "I believe you and I have some business to take care of."

CHAPTER 56

My jaw drops. The queen of A'ice, who is Arrov's mother, is the secret rebellion supporter?

Queen Amra is the only female monarch in the nineteen-planet coalition. A formidable queen who had wrested power from the previous ruler, a tyrant, via a bloody coup 120 years ago. She ended hundreds of years of reign. A ruling house that was plagued by madness from inbreeding. They were destroying A'ice as a nation while terrorizing the populace. A queen who has kept her power ever since, despite being common-born, against violent opposition, and who led A'ice into its current prosperity that many call its golden age.

Queen Amra smiles wider seeing my expression, making the crow's-feet around her dark blue eyes deepen. "My dear, do close your mouth. We don't want anyone to wonder why you look so shocked."

"I would never . . . I mean—"

"That's why this is perfect. No one would guess looking at the two of us, now would they?"

Queen Amra turns her head as she greets a coalition monarch, the thick braid of her dark blue hair falling forward onto her wide shoulder. Here and there silver strands glint, betraying her age, but the pale blue skin of her face still looks decades younger than her 150 years.

We reach a glass door leading to a small, private balcony. I step outside with the queen. Cold air hits me like a slap. The crescent-shaped balcony is barely wide enough for the two of us, but it will do for this meeting.

"How is this . . . and wouldn't Arrov . . . *why?*" My teeth chatter and I step in place to ward off the cold.

Queen Amra leans her elbows on the banister and gazes out, unfazed by the cold. "Arrov has no idea about my involvement, and I would like to keep it that way. He also doesn't know I am aware of *all* of his adventures."

When I grow up, I want to be just like her—so confident, and so in control.

"As to the why," she continues, "it is complicated, to say the least. Your father has been altering the balance in the coalition, bribing his way, and forcing his will on the rest of us as our leader. He does the same to his subjects here on Uhna, whether they live in cities or in camps."

She extends a hand, palm up, partially hidden under her other arm. With a quick motion, I retrieve the necklace crystal from the hidden pocket of my dress and drop it into her hand, trying to be as surreptitious as she is, and probably failing.

She pockets it. "Let's just say that sometimes it takes a lot of wrong to make things right again." She pulls out a silver pouch that looks like an evening purse, matching the exact fabric of my dress.

Shocked, I stare at the bag. How did she manage to match the color when I had no idea what I'd wear until the last minute? I couldn't be more in awe of her even if I tried.

Queen Amra loops the leather handle over my wrist. "This has all things a ma'hana might need during her night at a ball, and a bit more." She turns and leans against the banister, crossing her legs at the ankle, like I've seen Arrov do many times.

"You and Arrov would make beautiful babies."

Babies?! I choke as I inhale and burst into a coughing fit.

She pats my back helpfully. "There, there. It's the truth."

Feeling heat bloom on my cheeks, I tighten my fingers around the pouch. "Thanks, uh, I guess. But . . . um, I am not free to choose. There is a marriage contract out with my name on it."

She makes a clucking sound. "How silly that your father still engages in such an outdated tradition. These contracts are notorious for prompting young princesses and princes to run away."

Surprised, I look at her. "Run away?"

The queen smiles. "Have I ever told you what an amazing pilot my youngest son is?"

I stutter. "I—uh—know . . . I mean he is."

"He is too much of a free spirit to settle on A'ice right now. That's why he joined the rebellion. The cause is worthy, don't misunderstand me, but it is the call of adventure that sings to him, like it did to our fabled A'ice heroes of ancient times. You could tame him. Make him put down roots."

Roots with Arrov? "Um . . ."

"I've always believed a young woman should have options." Queen Amra straightens. "Speaking of options, I believe there is a six-armed man, your ex, anxiously awaiting your company. Best to wrap this up before he decides to take matters into his own hands. No pun intended."

Is there anything she *doesn't* know?

I nod, and with haste I head back inside.

"Don't rush, my dear. It is not fitting for a ma'hana, and only makes you look guilty."

CHAPTER 57

When I reenter the royal ballroom, welcoming warmth envelops me, spreading through my cold skin. My fingers tighten on the small silver pouch. Now all that is left to complete this mission is to find Belthair and give it to him. I search for him in the overcrowded ballroom.

I spot his slicked-back hair. He is looking around for me, too. We lock eyes and I wave, letting the pouch dangle around my wrist. He nods in understanding and makes his way toward me, cutting through the crowd. But after a few steps he frowns and changes direction, hurrying toward the exit.

No! Where is he going?!

Belthair leaves the ballroom, turns right, and disappears from my view.

Fishguts! I search for the cause of his sudden escape. My gaze lands on Irvine on my right, who pushes past ma'hars in rude haste.

Buckets of fishguts! Why can't this mission end easily? Why?

Fortune listens to my complaint, and a white-haired ma'har steps into Irvine's way, engaging him in conversation. It gives me just enough time to get a head start, and I rush toward the exit without looking like I am in a hurry. Irvine tries to untangle himself from the elderly ma'har, but the older man is oblivious, and clamps a hand on the overseer's shoulder.

Resisting the urge to keep looking back to check on Irvine, I wade through the ballroom. But the now inebriated ma'hars and ma'haras keep wandering into my path, blocking me like mindless fish. One drunk man slows me down to a standstill. He steps in the same direction as I do. Three times. Frustrated, I shove him out of my way.

Glancing over my shoulder, I push past another intoxicated ma'har, who seems to be all hands. The overseer leaves the elderly ma'har and now hurries with purpose, not far behind.

I pick up my pace, fighting my way through the crowd. When I reach the open double doors, I follow after Belthair, turning right, too.

Kicking my shoes off and wrapping my skirt over my hand, I sprint down the corridor after Belthair, hoping to catch up to him before the overseer catches up with *us*.

My bare feet slap on the cold marble tiles as I dash past a few milling court members. Pointed and sharp comments follow after me, insinuating that I must be blitzed to act like this. I hiccup loudly and giggle, as if they are right in their assumption.

Just as I take the first bend in the corridor, I catch sight of Irvine exiting the ballroom. The overseer shouts for his guards but turns left, as my luck would have it.

Up ahead, Belthair makes a second turn.

Damn him and his long legs! I'll never catch up.

"Wait!" I shout, thankful that there is no one at this part of the corridor.

He glances over his shoulder.

"Haven't you forgotten about something?" I shake the pouch.

He jogs back to me. "Pigballs wouldn't stop following me."

"And you were going to abandon me before we could finish the mission? Now who's the quitter?"

"Why do you always have to be such a—"

I raise my hand to silence him. Shouts and running footsteps echo behind us. "We don't have time for petty fights." I shove the bag into Belthair's hands. "Now go! Get out of here!"

He hesitates. "What about you?"

"Half the court already thinks I'm drunk, so I'll just pretend I've passed out."

"You won't have to pretend if it's real."

"Wha—" Belthair's hand flashes toward me. Sharp pain bursts near the base of my neck.

My knees give out.

The last thing I see is the ground rushing toward me.

CHAPTER 58

I am hovering in the middle of Fyoon Ocean, seven feet above its raging waters. A terrible dark storm whips the waves into a boiling tempest. Buckling and wild. Restless. Out of balance.

I know I am dreaming, but I can't break its hold on me.

Unnatural lightning strikes, thick and straight as a rod. It lights up the sky for a second before spreading horizontally on the surface of the water, making a splashing sound. A handful of dead fish float to the surface, electrocuted. Horizontal rain tears ruthlessly at my thin nightgown, plastering it to my body.

"This is His doing," the Archgoddess of the Eternal Light and Order says, appearing by me.

"Whose doing?"

The Lady stares straight ahead with her golden eyes, her white-blond hair floating around her exquisite face, unaffected by the out-of-control storm. She is Light itself. Her white flowing dress illuminates the darkness, only adding to the archgoddess's ethereal beauty.

"The longer the Archgod of Chaos and Destruction infects your world, the more He disturbs its natural balance. Your world is dying because of Him."

Gale-force winds blow my hair into my face, as if to prove her words. The air is charged with tension, smelling sulfuric and briny.

"Then make him leave Uhna."

"I've told you, my child, I cannot interfere. The fate of your world is in your hands now."

"And I've told you, this is not my fight."

"It became your fight the moment you were born, my child. You cannot run from your destiny. You cannot hide from your responsibility. It is time to face your Lumenian heritage and act."

"Why can't you leave me alone?!" I shout, but the visage of The Lady is gone, replaced by the deadly image of a tremendous deepwater shark jump-

192

ing out of the ocean, right under me. Its terrible open mouth full of rows and rows of sharp fangs, ready to swallow me whole.

I scream, staring into the face of certain death.

Then the shark freezes in midair and knocks. *Bang, bang, bang!*

I jar awake, into a sitting position, with a muffled scream. My arms flail, as if to fight the shark. It was just a dream!

Before I can lay back down, the door to my living quarters bursts open, slamming into the wall. Hurried footsteps ring out, heading toward my bedroom.

Grabbing a pillow, I raise it in my defense. I strain my eyes to see in the darkness. When someone enters, I throw it, with a shout meant to be threatening.

The intruder steps to the side, easily avoiding my pillow, and claps to turn on the Fla'mma cones in the room. "Were you planning to kill me with that?" Beathag asks. "How pathetic. How *you.*"

"Why are you barging into my room in the middle of the night?"

Dressed in a body-hugging red dress that's more like a sleeve really, Beathag looks fresh and rested, with her hair in an immaculate knot. How can she not be tired? After last night's ball and my "fainting episode," it took forever to convince Irvine, and then Father, who showed up with Beathag, to let me go back to my living quarters. Father was so concerned that he wanted me to go to the Healing Center right away. I'm sure it was more for appearances. I refused. Knowing Glenna and her grudges, I wasn't sure if she would cover for me.

"It *is* dawn," Beathag says, smirking.

Oh, goodie—I got a whole two hours of sleep. No wonder I felt kicked in the head.

"I have good news."

"Father is divorcing you?"

Beathag tears the bedsheet out of my fingers. "Why don't I show you this good news? You'll appreciate it much more in person. Guards!"

"Wait a minute!" Six burly guards rush in. They look more like thugs with scars on their bald heads.

I scoot back on my bed. "You can't make me go."

"Oh, yes I can!" Beathag says and claps her hands.

CHAPTER 59

"You can let go of me now." I tear my arm out of the red-faced guard's hold when we enter the green parlor. With all the varying hues of green furnishing, the room looks as if a meadow had thrown up all over it.

A feeling of being watched prickles my back. I turn.

On the spring-green sofa sits a man. He gets to his feet.

He is taller than me by a head, with a compact build that shows through his black suit. He wears a brown cape embroidered with gold motifs, draped over one shoulder. Short dark-brown hair frames an angular face, with just enough wrinkles to put him in his midforties. Dark brown eyes full of calm intellect observe me. The slightly tanned skin looks unnatural, almost grayish, as if he is suffering from a chronic lack of sunlight and has to use other means to compensate.

"What's going on?" I demand.

Beathag spreads her arms. "This is my surprise. Your marriage contract, after a long wait, has been accepted. I think—"

"Ma'hara Beathag," the man says, interrupting her, "I would like a few minutes in private with Ma'hana Lilla."

Beathag's expression turns calculating as her gaze goes between the man and me. "I don't think it is wise for me to leave the ma'hana alone. Fortunately, I, as a representative of the royal family, would be happy to stay and facilitate the first meeting."

The man bows his head to her. "I appreciate your offer, Ma'hara, but there is no need for you to inconvenience yourself. This won't take long."

Beathag irks at the title Ma'hara, as if the man just diminished her self-appointed importance.

He clucks his tongue. Two men, dressed in brown capes similar to his, appear from outside, ready to escort Beathag out. She frowns at them. "This is highly irregular, Your Highness." She pronounces the man's honorary title as if the words are sour-tasting. "I firmly believe I should stay here and—"

194

The man bows again. "Ma'hara Beathag, I assure you, this is all customary on *my* world. As I understand, Uhna values tradition. This is no exception."

"Uhna custom dictates that an unmarried man and woman cannot spend more than five minutes unsupervised," Beathag says. It's a lie, but I don't correct her. I don't want to stay here a second longer than I must. "I hope that is enough time for Your Highness."

"More than enough, Ma'hara."

With a last searing look, Beathag leaves with the foreign guards. I face the man, with my heart beating in my throat.

"I am Crown Prince Anthelm the Third, son of High Ruler Anthelm of Aak. Please call me Anthelm." He makes a complicated series of gestures with his hands that must be his cultural greeting.

"I don't want this marriage contract," I blurt out in response. Best to get it out of the way.

"I understand your reluctance."

Does he now? "If you understand it, then break off the contract."

"I can't, I'm afraid. It's not that easy."

It should be that easy! "Why not?"

"Commonly, we don't accept marriage contracts from outside worlds, but yours had pleased my Guardian God Amth'Aak."

Again, with the gods! "How do you know it 'pleases' your guardian god?" I say with forced patience. Shouting at this stranger won't help my case. Not at all.

Anthelm looks at me with surprise. "Do the people of Uhna not have any spiritual connection with their guardian god?"

"We never did." Asking for assistance with the fickle ocean currents was one thing, but my pirate ancestors *never* allowed the guardian god to interfere with their day-to-day business. I see the wisdom in that more every day.

Anthem's expression turns uncomprehending. "I know my Guardian God Amth'Aak approves of this marriage contract, because he told the Saage women, our wise women."

I blink at him in disbelief. "That's it? You won't fight this contract because your guardian god told you to accept it? Does your guardian god think for you as well?"

Anthelm clears his throat, ignoring my jab. "I don't have much time to tell you what you need to know—"

If he won't hear my rejection, then . . . "I don't want to know anything."

Anthelm sighs, the first sign of his irritation showing. "Ma'hana Lilla, you are not making this easy for either of us."

You think? "No, I won't make this easy for you."

"You don't understand, Ma'hana. There is so much you need to know before—"

"No, you don't understand me, Anthelm. Let me explain it better for you: I. Don't. Want. The. Marriage. Contract!"

For a second, humor glints in his eyes, as if in any other circumstance he'd find this exchange humorous. "Ma'hana, if only you'd stop acting like—"

The door of the parlor bursts open and Beathag sashays in. "Time's up."

CHAPTER 60

Beathag keeps the door open until Crown Prince Anthelm leaves. But before she can close it, Father enters. Dark circles stand out under his eyes, his expression blank. For a second, he looks lost.

"Father? What are you doing here?" I doubt that he is here to tell me he changed his mind.

"I'm—uh . . . I'm not sure—" Beathag interrupts Father's stuttering. "My beloved husband is here to officially initiate the marriage contract."

Father rubs his forehead. "Yes, that's exactly why I'm here. Consider it initiated." He waves his hand weakly.

"Father, please—" I take a step toward him.

Some of the fog lifts from his eyes, as if my words slapped him. "Do not beg, my daughter. We, from the ruling house of Serrain, never beg." He heads to the door, dismissing me.

Five women file in. They line up in the middle of the room, with their green eyes locked on me. They must be the Saage women. The wise women of Aak.

Their bright yellow outfits are an unlikely cross between a shapeless sack and a tight bodysuit. The smooth fabric is loose around their body, held close at the waist with a wide yellow belt. Around their legs and arms the fabric is tight, with ribbons wrapped around them, forming gloves and knee-high boots. They wear strange trapezoid-shaped headdresses, four yellow and one red, left open at the top of their heads with stiff material draping down all the way to their shoulders. Thick scarfs, part of the headdress, cover the lower part of their faces, leaving only their eyes visible.

They stand in front of me, in order of height: from shortest to tallest—with the red headdress, then back to the shortest. Their eyes convey no feeling or emotion as they face me.

Beathag shuts the door with a loud bang. She drapes herself on the sofa, anticipation pouring off her.

The tallest woman squints at her. "You no stay. Out!" she snaps in broken Uhnan.

Beathag frowns at the Saage woman. "You must not know who I am. I—"

"Is matters not. Out!" From a pocket on her leg, she pulls out a long gray stick. Without any warning, she whips it at Beathag's arm.

"Ow!" With furious eyes, Beathag stares at the tall woman and rubs her forearm. "You cannot treat me like this! I arranged this marriage contract, and I can have it nullified too, like that." She snaps her fingers.

"Gods, please do," I mutter.

The stick flashes; it bites into my left forearm with a sharp sting.

I glare at the tall Saage woman but say nothing else. Wrinkles appear at the corners of her eyes, as if she is smiling under her headdress. Then they disappear when she looks at Beathag.

"Aak marriage contract only ends by death. If you 'null' it, Aak will come and make war. Is war you want?" the Saage woman asks. Judging from the way she takes charge she must be the leader of the group.

One of the shorter Saage women leads Beathag to the door. "I will inform the ma'ha, my *husband*, about this, have no doubt." She leaves before the stick heads in her direction.

The tall Saage woman laughs. "Doubt it not. The purification process begins. Shall we?"

What on Uhna is that? "Purification process?"

The leader sighs. "You talk with Crown Prince Anthelm, no?"

I nod, then shake my head.

The Saage women exchange looks of significance. The shortest one says, "She too willful. Like prophecy say."

"Prophecy? What prophecy?" I ask, but I might as well ask the wall for all they reveal with their blank eyes.

The gray stick flies. It stings my right forearm this time.

This is getting tiresome. *Fast.*

Another Saage woman, with a small potbelly, adds, "No outside-Aak is blessed for hundred years, by Amth'Aak the ever-knowing. Now we see wisdom where there was none." The other Saage women mutter their agreement.

"Is matters not. We are like stick." The leader bends the stick in both of her hands. "We bow to our guardian god's wish, but we don't break."

All the Saage women nod and repeat the last sentence, as if it's their mantra.

The leader turns to me. "You must understand Aak to understand purification process. Our world is not 'nice' to live above. Too cold and die fast. Nothing live above surface. Aak live under surface, in caves. Is better, but no easy. All must have discipline to survive. We Saage women create purification process. It help live in caves. All must do purification process if to live on Aak. Is no exception." She makes a quick swipe with her stick in the air for emphasis. "Purification process prepare body. Prepare soul for royal marriage and life in caves. It purify and cleanse. It lock all magic in."

"But why lock magic in?" I ask, surprised.

The tall Saage woman nods. "Is good question. Magic in caves is danger. It destroy Aak. No good. But now we protect Aak from magic."

"How is locking magic even possible?"

"Saage women know how. With three purification process: we find, we collect, and we lock."

The idea of "locking magic" bothers me more than I would have thought possible. On one hand, not having magic could be a relief. I wouldn't have to worry about losing control, like at the Coalition Parade. On the other hand, there is something utterly wrong about having someone "lock" my magic in, only because of a marriage contract I want nothing to do with.

Suddenly I feel suspicious about this lock. "Once you 'lock' my magic in, is the process reversible?"

They all look at me as if that's answer enough. Just as I thought. Irreversible. Final. No more. "I cannot explain this to you," I say. I doubt I can explain it to myself. "But I cannot let you do this to me."

The Saage women exchange another look. One of them mutters, "Another sign! 'With heart full of qualm,' like prophecy say."

"What prophecy?" The Saage women ignore my question again. Instead the tall one asks, "Why not?"

"I am a Lumenian." The Saage women gasp, clearly familiar with the term. "The Archgoddess of the Eternal Light and Order tasked me with, uh, higher purpose than a marriage contract. She asked me to be her sybil in this Era War." They don't have to know that I declined the offer.

The Saage women huddle, discussing something in their own language, before their leader turns back to me. "You spoke to Lady in person, yes?"

I nod.

"And Lady want you Her sybil?"

I nod again.

"Then you have proof."

"Uh . . . proof?"

The Saage women untie their headdresses in response. Each has a starlike scar on her left cheek, with long points that seem to curve back to its body.

Once they are satisfied that I see what they mean, they all retie their headdresses. "We pledge love, servitude to Guardian God Amth'Aak only. We get His blessing. And life lasting long as our faith. Now show us proof."

"I, uh, I have not received any, um, 'blessing.' Yet."

"Until you have proof . . ." the leader says and gestures to the shortest Saage woman with a flick of her wrist.

The shortest woman undresses me, ignoring my protests. She helps me into an outfit similar to theirs, except in white, with a back that opens from the neck down to the waist. Two Saage women restrain me by my arms, presenting my bare back to the leader.

Something sharp touches my skin. Something that is heavy, pointy, and feels like many insect legs, probably belonging to a huge bug. With my luck it's a spider.

Then sharp fangs pierce at the base of my neck, pumping cold liquid under my skin.

". . . we continue purification process."

CHAPTER 61

A short Saage woman pushes me out the doorway. On legs that feel like boomberry jelly, I stumble outside.

"We done. You go now." She shuts the door in my face.

My back, now covered by a see-through lacelike material, feels cold and itchy one second, burning and tight the next from whatever "poison" their insect injected into my skin.

Passing courtiers stare at me with open curiosity. Shame makes my cheeks ignite hot, all the way down my neck. I need Glenna, but she is still upset with me. I wish I could seek comfort in the kitchen. But Deidre is gone.

Fishguts!

"Lilla, are you okay?" Callum asks, appearing at my left.

"Go away." I turn my back on him, but that only makes me face the door to the green parlor. A dead end.

Callum mutters something under his breath that's a mix of a curse and awe. "What happened to your back?"

He just can't let me wallow in self-pity, can he now? "Will you leave me alone?"

"Not until you tell me why you're so upset."

"Don't you have anything better to do?" It is not fair to have him receive the brunt of my anger. I know that. But *he* is here.

"Lilla, what's going on?"

"Fine, but not here."

CHAPTER 62

When the coast is clear, I open a section of the wall by the royal library. It leads to a small, windowless area. Yet there is plenty of light from an opening in the white-paneled ceiling where a spiral metal stairway leads upward. Its railing is black metal, with starflower patterns. The red hardwood stairs and red back paneling make the stairway look like a ribbon curling down to the floor.

"Where are we?" Callum asks.

"You'll see." We climb the steps all the way to the top and enter a round glass room.

"Welcome to the royal observatory." I head to a curling wooden bench with colorful pillows on top of it that runs along the edge of the floor-to-ceiling glass. I drop down and pull a round pillow into my lap. Not many know of this place, which is why Mom and I would come here to disappear from the eyes of the court.

I point out the window. "On a clear day you can see all the way to the Olde Capital City." Today is not one of those days. Dark gray clouds hide the two suns, and a rising fog swallows up most of the view.

Callum sits next to me. He doesn't say anything, just waits for me to speak when I am ready.

"I cannot even see more than a few days ahead in my life," I say, despising the self-pity I feel for myself.

"Why is that?"

"Because soon I am to marry a crown prince from Aak." Meeting with the crown prince and going through the first stage of the purification process really drove that point home. "My father already signed the marriage contract."

"Do you love this crown prince?"

I snort. "No! I only met him once, today."

"Then why are you marrying him?"

"Because of the marriage contract. Aren't you paying attention?"

"It's not my fault your beauty makes it difficult for me to focus."

I stutter, not expecting that response.

Callum laughs out loud. "Don't look so shocked. I can be nice too."

If this is what he calls nice . . . "Anyway, there is no way out of this contract. Not unless we go to war with the Aak. I'll be shipped off once I complete this purification process. Ready for life underground, and without an ounce of magic left. The process will 'lock' it in forever and irrevocably."

"Is that what happened to your back?"

I nod.

"May I see?"

I turn. With the gentlest touch, he pulls down the lacy material to reveal what that bug did to my back.

Callum stays silent for a long time.

"Is it that bad?" I ask, imagining awful scar tissue that will never heal.

"It's not that," he says in a strange voice.

"Then what?" I face him, really worried now. "Worse than bad?"

Callum takes out two small triangularly shaped mirrors from the pocket of his jacket. He hands me one while keeping the other. "See for yourself."

I angle my mirror until it lines up with his. I gasp when I see my back.

It's horrible!

It's terrible!

It is the most exquisite thing I've ever seen.

Silver markings sparkle in the light, starting from the base of my neck all the way to the middle of my back. Intricate lines of branches, complete with leaves, vines, and flowers make the beginning of a vast treetop appear almost three-dimensional.

"Doesn't look like it'll wash off anytime soon," I joke. If only the beauty of the markings could take away the shock of intrusion the purification process left behind.

I hand the mirror back to Callum. He takes it, his fingers brushing against mine. "On my world, there are no marriage contracts," he says. "It is the woman who claims her mate. We call it the bride's choice."

Bride's choice? "Tell me more."

Callum smiles. "It's a very old tradition, created by necessity. There were always more men than women on my world. Which caused vicious fights to break out, as men tried to win their women's heart. But our first empress stopped that by giving the power of choice to women. Men had to give up fighting and learn . . ." he trails off, searching for the right word.

"Dating? Courting? Wooing?"

He snorts. "All of the above, to ensure that they'd win the women's favor in the end. Once a bride's choice is announced, it's final. No other man may compete for her."

"That's great . . . I mean that must be . . ." I clear my throat to hide my amazement. I can't even imagine what that would be like. "Is there someone—um, back on your home world—you were trying to, um, woo?" I stare at the pillow, as if his answer is not important.

Callum lifts my chin with a finger. "No one."

I let out a breath I didn't even realize I held. "I see." Not that it matters one way or another. Really. *It doesn't!*

"You look relieved."

"No. I mean, why would I—"

"It's as if you cared."

"Don't be ridiculous!" I throw the pillow at his head, but he bats the pillow away.

"Now who's being ridiculous? I know you care about me. Admit it." Callum leans only a couple of inches away from me.

"Yes. I mean only as, um . . ." I forget what I meant to say. I can't think past how he's affecting me. How tempting he is.

Grabbing me by my waist, he pulls me all the way into his lap, until I straddle his legs. Our lips lock, as if this is our last kiss. Our last chance. As if—

A throat clears behind me.

CHAPTER 63

I squeal and scramble off of Callum's lap. Teague leans at the rail, grinning.

"How did you find us? I mean, why did you find us?" I'm nineteen years old, for godssake! I shouldn't feel *this* guilty!

"Am I interrupting something important?" Teague asks and winks. "Like the start of an intergalactic conflict between Uhna and Teryn?"

Callum glares at Teague. "Don't you have somewhere else to be?"

"No." Teague bites into an apple he had in his pocket. "Just think of me as your conscience," he says with his mouth full.

"I don't need another conscience," Callum says. "Mine works just fine."

"You forget their culture is not so open about 'dating' as ours. Especially when you two spend such a long time together. Unsupervised. Without weapons to keep you preoccupied. It would be easy for anyone to misconstrue this, and use it as an excuse to cause trouble. Just proceed as if I am not here."

"But you *are* here." A reddish-yellow light flashes across Callum's irises. "Leave!"

"Try again," Teague says, all joviality gone from his expression.

I get to my feet. "I'll leave." Before they break into a fight.

Callum puts a hand on my arm. "Stay. It's he who should leave."

My necklace chimes. I read the message and curse under my breath. "I have to go." I push past Teague to the staircase, taking the steps two at a time.

"Lilla, wait!"

But I can't. The rebellion needs me.

CHAPTER 64

Arrov and I step out of the gateway into a grimy alley between two cloudscrapers in the Olde Capital City.

"Why are we meeting with Xor in an alley?" I pull my gray winter cloak closer to me to ward off the chilly wind. Too bad the cloak can't defend against the smell of rotting garbage.

Arrov opens a rusty metal door. "He is in here."

As I walk through the doorway, I notice an unlit sign proclaiming the establishment as the Greasy Worm Canteen. "Charming," I mutter.

We weave among wobbly metal tables and mismatched syn-plastic chairs with stuffing hanging from their red seat cushions. Tiles that used to be white but now black stick to the foot of my Saage outfit. I wish I could have taken it off before coming here, but there wasn't time. Now I wonder what the hurry was.

"It's Xor's favorite place," Arrov says over his shoulder, heading to the only occupied table in the corner. It's good to know that the rebellion leader can leave camp long enough to develop a "favorite" place while the rest of the refugees are imprisoned. Although how anyone can favor this place is beyond me.

Something sizzles in the kitchen behind a pair of swinging metal doors splattered with unidentifiable stains. I try my best not to gag on the fumes of repulsive smells pumping out.

"I'm sure it must be the cuisine," I say.

Xor wipes his fingers on a paper napkin and looks up at Arrov. "You're late."

Arrov grinds his teeth but says nothing.

Across from Xor, Jorha nods in welcome and plucks a fried insect with multiple long legs from a steaming bowl. She bites off half of the insect, crunching on it. "Want some? They're still hot."

My stomach turns, and I shake my head. Fried insects are an acquired taste. One I've never managed to acquire.

"More for me." She pops the other half into her mouth.

Xor pushes his empty plate away, dropping his wadded napkin in the middle of it. "What do you have for me?"

"Um, nothing new." I've just carried out the last mission yesterday. What does he think I have to report? "I trust you've received the silver bag from Belthair?"

I slant a look at Arrov. There is a dark yellow and purple bruise visible on the left side of his jaw, which Arrov insists didn't come from Callum when they faced off against each other. Though I don't recall seeing any bruises on Callum's face.

"According to Belthair, you've been spending every minute of your time with the Teryn general, yet you have nothing to say. I find that fascinating."

"Are you accusing me of neglecting my duty to the rebellion?" I glance at Jorha. She leans back from her plate, her expression blank. Right. No help from her. "You must be joking."

Xor raises an eyebrow. "Is this rebellion a joke to you?"

I recoil. "No. Of course not!"

"Good. Then it won't be a problem to acquire the codes."

"Codes? What codes?"

Xor gives me a flat look. "What do you think?"

For the palace's defense armament. I am not stupid. He needs the codes to attack the palace. My home. "I thought—"

Xor sighs with impatience. "You thought *what*?"

I look him square in the eyes. "That the contents of the bag would be spent on ships to evacuate the refugees before any more are sent to the mines."

Xor jumps to his feet, slamming his hand on top of the table, making the plates clatter. "Are you questioning my orders?!" he shouts.

Jorha gets to her feet as well, her hand on her sidearm, as she looks between Xor and me.

"It seems to me that rescuing the refugees should be a priority," I say, not letting him intimidate me. There was a time when I worried about upsetting him. But not anymore.

"I should have known better than to allow you to play rebel. I knew you weren't cut out for this."

Allow me? "I have followed every inane and menial order you gave me. I lied and I stole. I risked my life. But it was never enough for you, was it? I never could do anything to make you forget who I am or where I came from. But I put up with it because I believed your cause: helping the refugees. Now I know that was a lie. You don't care about them—"

Xor looms over me. "Be careful, Ma'hana."

"You only care for you!" I shout. "I quit!"

"You can't just quit. I forbid you!"

"You don't get to order me around anymore." I move away from him. How could I have not seen this selfish side of him before?

Xor lunges and grabs my shoulder. "Don't you dare walk—"

A loud bang rings out, and the window on my left shatters.

CHAPTER 65

Shots explode around us.

Jorha falls backward, like a broken doll, her arms floating around her as laser shots tear through her body. Xor jumps to catch her, his body shuddering from the laser bullets, green blood blooming on his shirt.

Shots whistle by me, one grazing my shoulder. Arrov tackles me to the ground, using his body as a shield. Plaster and chunks of wood rain on top of us, leaving behind a cloud of smoke and dust.

Then there is silence.

Arrov rolls to the side, scanning for threats. I raise my head, and my gaze lands on Jorha's unseeing eyes. Xor, unconscious, lies next to her, embracing her.

"This is the Overseer of Refugee Affairs," Irvine says into an A'ris-infused loudspeaker from outside. "You are surrounded! I know you harbor the rebellion leader. Escort him out and give yourselves up. This is your first warning!"

There is no way we're walking out of this canteen alive.

Arrov crawls toward Jorha. I follow after him. When he hesitates, I search for Jorha's pulse, but there is nothing. With gentle fingers I close her eyes.

He curses when he sees Jorha's umbrae travel gauntlet. Bright sparkles pop from it, crackling. "It's broken."

"Can you repair it?"

"I repeat, you are surrounded!" Irvine's voice booms. "Escort out the rebel leader and give yourselves up. This is your last warning!"

Arrov shakes his head. "I cannot take more than three people. We take Xor back, then I'll come back for Jorha."

"No! We cannot leave Jorha here! Her father will lose everything if she's branded as a rebel. I'll stay."

"Lilla, you can't stay! That's insane!"

It sure is, but there is no other choice. "I'll come up with an excuse. Don't worry about me."

Arrov hesitates. "There has to be another option. I can stay and—"

"No, you can't. I don't know how to use the umbrae gauntlet and we don't have time for me to learn it," I say, and push Arrov's shoulder to get him to move. "Go! Leave now!"

Cursing under his breath, Arrov opens a gateway. "I'll come back for you. You hear me? I'll . . ." He hauls both Xor and Jorha through it. Then the gateway closes.

I drop my head on my arm. There is no one to call for help. There is nothing to say that would explain what I am doing here.

This. Is. It.

Something crunches on my right.

CHAPTER 66

I lift my head in time to see a black shadow move. I inhale deeply to scream, but a warm hand covers my mouth. I inhale scents of sun and desert.

"Are you so anxious to meet with the overseer?" Callum's voice says by my ear.

I push his hand off. "Callum? What are you doing in here?"

Instead of answering, he picks me up. He barks a command to Teague in his language.

From one blink to the next, the remnants of the assaulted canteen disappear. Everything speeds into a green blur as Teague takes us into a pocket of time and space. Within seconds we arrive at the lowest part of Fye Island, on a rocky beach.

"Put me down."

Callum complies, then lifts my injured arm. "You're bleeding."

I glance at the shallow wound. "I'll live." Unlike poor Jorha. I close my eyes for a moment against tears that threaten to burst. If I hadn't quarreled with Xor, she'd still be alive.

I yank my arm out of Callum's hand. "I have to go." I head for the flight of stairs carved into the sheer cliff, leading to the palace.

Callum turns me back to him before I can get far. "Is this how you thank me?"

"Thank you? How do I know it wasn't you who betrayed us?" I ask. "After all, you came to my rescue at the perfect time. Just a coincidence? I think not!" I say the exact words he threw at my head during our first meeting on his spacecraft.

Teague clears his throat. "Oh, look—nice, big shells. I'm just going to go over there and . . ." He strides away from us to a short distance.

"From kissing to betraying on the same day—I sure am indecisive," Callum says and crosses his arms, his expression dark. "Why would I do such a thing?!"

I wave my arms in agitation. "You came to my home world with threats. You blackmail me with the favors I owe you. You keep popping up wherever

I go. You find dead bodies and take blood from them. What *should* I think?"

"Guys?"

"Not now, Teague!" Callum snaps, and a reddish-yellow light flashes across his blue irises. "What are you implying here, Lilla? Just say it!"

Fed up, I say, "I am not implying anything but the facts! If you have nothing to hide, then tell me what were you doing snooping around on the beach!"

"Guys? Listen—" I raise my hand in Teague's general direction without looking. "Not now, Teague!"

"I don't snoop! Besides, there is no crime in finding dead bodies."

"No crime? How do I know it wasn't you who . . . that it wasn't you . . ." I can't make myself say it.

Callum leans close until our noses almost touch. "Go ahead. Finish your sentence."

"Guys!" Teague barks.

"What?" Both Callum and I snap.

"That!" Teague points over his shoulder as he calmly heads back.

CHAPTER 67

"Oh." I take in the not-so-empty beach.

Hundreds of creatures that were once human but now senseless rotting beings flood the beach, surrounding us. Their ragged and tattered clothes hang on their emaciated bodies. Bodies that are pale gray, with large open wounds, oozing black liquid. Showing sinew underneath. The creatures growl in menace and advance on our small group, malice and hatred emanating from the creatures in waves.

Callum pulls his longsword from his back. "Why didn't you say it sooner?"

Teague pulls out his longsword, too. "I tried. It's not my fault you two were busy flirting." Both men position themselves in front of me as we back away from the perilous crowd.

There are so many of them! I recognize most of the missing servants, and many minor ma'hars and ma'haras from the palace who disappeared. Dozens of missing rebels march among them, wearing the tattered brown maintenance uniform of the rebellion. The smell of rot hits like a physical slap, and I gag, covering my nose with a hand.

I guess they are not missing anymore.

We reach the cliff wall, with nowhere to go. We're trapped.

Callum twirls his longsword with a smooth flick of his wrist. The creatures follow his every move, their eyes glued to him as if getting to him is their main goal.

Callum and Teague charge into the crowd. They turn into a whirlwind of blades, cutting and slicing, clearing a wide circle around them. The creatures fall down in pieces, their black blood drenching the white sand.

A twitch of movement attracts my attention. A fallen body lurches and the dark fluid flows back, along with parts of its body, rejoining and remaking it whole.

CHAPTER 68

Teague curses. "They are regenerating."

Callum says with a snarl, "I've noticed."

Teague curses some more. "These are fully corrupted dark servants."

"I've noticed that too." Callum steps back from the fighting. "Cover me." Teague takes Callum's spot.

Callum jabs his sword into the sand. Placing his hands on my shoulder, he says, "I wish I could have prepared you for this."

"Prepared me?" I ask.

"Callum, don't do it," Teague says. "That's a *last* resort."

"Last resort?" I ask. I'm starting to worry.

"I don't have much choice," Callum says without taking his eyes off me.

"Callum?" Really worry.

"I could try to take us out of here," Teague argues, still fighting the creatures.

Callum shakes his head. "You can't do back-to-back transport in such a short time. It would kill you."

"What's going on!" His blue eyes hold such a jumble of emotions that I can't even guess what bothers him.

"Just remember, it's still me," Callum says and steps back.

He raises his arms outward, palms up. Standing with eyes blazing in that reddish-orange glow, he is the very image of a warrior god. Light spills from his eyes like a torrent, encompassing his whole body. Heat radiates from his strange light-cocoon, making the air shimmer around him as if he is on fire.

From one blink to the next, the cocoon implodes, sucking all of that reddish-orange light back in.

With jaw dropped, I stare at Callum, who isn't Callum anymore.

His new body stands more than seven feet, with corded muscles and short black fur. His fingers end in long black claws. His uniform, stretched into a thin black layer of material, covers him like a protective bodysuit to accommodate his new shape.

His face, sheeted in the same black fur, is a perfect blend of some ancient feline predator and human male. Steel-colored stripes run down his high cheekbones, stripes that remind me of the white tigers of the Caoimhe jungles. Yet he is more than those tigers.

The thick, shiny black mane cascading from his head is like a magnificent shroud. Framing his elongated face, it reminds me of the black lyons of the Amnag Desert. Yet he is more than those lyons.

The wolfish muzzle with sharp, white fangs reminds me of the white wolves from the A'ice tundra. Yet he is more than those wolves.

He is a manifestation of the deadliest and the most ultimate predator. Something primal—that's beyond thinking and logic—shifts in the deep recesses of my mind. Adrenaline pumps in my body, as if preparing for the lethal threat he now represents. I take a step back.

He studies me with intent blue eyes, tinged with reddish-orange. It's as if another entity is looking at me, one that is merciless and ruthless.

"Scared?" Callum asks in a deep, grumbling voice.

His joking tone breaks through the fog of primal fear. It takes only a split second to know the answer to his question. To see behind the threatening surface and to find the man I know. Stepping close to Callum, I reach up with a hand.

He lowers his head. I trail my fingertips over soft fur. He clasps my hand in his, holding my hand to his face for a moment.

He tries to hide it, but I detect vulnerability in his expression. "No, I am not scared."

Callum exhales as if in relief.

Striding to his longsword, he picks it up and slams the heel of his palm into the hilt. The blade opens. Four more blades that are twice as long emerge out of it and snap in place. They form a sharp cage around the original, with red Fla'mma fire dancing on their edge.

Callum leaps into the crowd of dark servants, giving Teague a much-needed break. He whirls and slashes faster than I can follow with my eyes. A fiery blur. Body parts rain and black blood oozes over the beach.

Within minutes, Callum decimates the throng of dark servants. He stands over the fallen creatures, the once white sand black around him. He strides back to Teague and me. Before he can reach us, the broken and cut-up bodies re-form, advancing on us yet again.

Teague snarls. "Now what?"

Callum cracks his neck. "I'm out of ideas."

How can they not be dead? I refuse to let them win!

Something in me snaps. The hot-and-cold-and-hot-again feelings rush through my veins, and I welcome them. The pulsing sphere of my magic waits, ready. I gather it until pressure builds under my skin.

With glowing arms I shout "Begone!" and throw all my magic into the horde.

The brilliant golden-white light turns blinding. My magic blasts at the dark servants. They lurch to stop, cowering as it rushes toward them.

The magical explosion engulfs them, incinerating each of their dark molecules. The Lume magic blazes through them until they disintegrate into dark gray smoke.

Once the glaring flare of magic clears, the beach stretches in front of us, empty. Not a drop of the black blood mars the white sand.

Teague whistles. "What do you know."

I stagger, and Callum catches me before I fall. He smiles with awe shining on his new face. "So *that's* what it takes to kill a fully corrupted dark servant."

I sigh in relief, but it's short-lived. My magic soars too close to the surface, the pressure surging. I press down on it. *Willing* it to go back.

Callum frowns. "Lilla, you're still glowing."

"I know!" I battle for control.

Pain intensifies. My magic swells.

"Remember what happened after the parade?"

Understanding shines in Callum's eyes. "Lilla, you can fight it!"

Teague curses. "Not again."

"Lilla, you can't!" Callum says. "We're too close to the palace!"

"I can't!" My head snaps back as the magical torrent bursts out of me, shaking the ground.

CHAPTER 69

The torrential magic streams, reaching the edge of the dark clouds until there is nothing left in me.

Cracks open by our feet, widening into a canyon. The sheer cliff wall on my right melts from the blast, sliding down like an avalanche of mud, heading straight for us.

Then everything freezes.

The wide explosion of magic shrinks, as if collapsing on itself.

Royal Elementalist Mage Ragnald, with his long silver hair flying around him, appears out of the brightness. With his hands extended, he strides toward us, reeling in the blast until the magical shock wave vanishes.

Ragnald turns where the cliff used to be. He makes a fist with his right hand. With T'erra magic, he forces the mudslide to move in reverse until the steep cliff wall re-forms to its original state. Complete with stairs carved into it. Then he kneels down by the gaping canyon. Using T'erra magic, he moves his hands close, as if he is about to clap. The canyon's two edges shift toward each other until the ground is smooth again.

"What are you doing here?" I ask. I'm grateful for his help, but I still remember his harsh words from last time.

Callum, now back to his usual self, narrows his eyes on the mage.

"I was on my usual walk," the royal mage says, "when I felt wild magic building up. I came running, and it was a good thing I did."

"Thank you for the magical intervention," I say.

"It's the least I could do," Ragnald says, "considering what you've done for me."

"What have you done for him *exactly*?" Callum asks.

"Yes, Lilla. Do tell us." Teague digs into his pocket and pulls out a stick of dried meat. He bites into it as his gaze travels over the three of us.

"She saved my life."

"Really?" Callum says and crosses his arms. "How did she save your life?"

"It's not important," I say, shaking my head, hoping the mage doesn't go into details.

"After I was poisoned," Ragnald says, oblivious, "and I fell into the Fyoon Ocean, she rescued me. I blamed her, unfairly, for the circumstances. It didn't help that those goons showed up, confusing me for you, General."

I cover my eyes with a hand. He just had to share all that, didn't he?

"Poisoned?" Teague asks around a large bite.

"Goons?" Callum asks with a raised eyebrow.

Ragnald flicks his hand. "The poisoning was a minor misunderstanding between me and Healer Glenna. I realize now that Ma'hana Lilla had nothing to do with it."

"Do these 'misunderstandings' happen to you a lot, Mage?" Teague asks.

Ragnald grimaces. "More than you can imagine."

"What do you mean those 'goons' were looking for me?"

"They thought I was you, General," Ragnald explains. "Not sure why they would confuse us. Clearly, we don't look alike."

"I agree," Teague says, still chewing. "Callum doesn't have such pretty silver hair."

"As opposed to having pretty streaks like you?" Ragnald retorts.

Teague laughs and offers a stick of dried meat to Ragnald.

"This is the second time someone was 'looking' for me," Callum says.

"Third," I correct him. "The dark servants were trying to get to you." I explain to the mage what happened to us on the beach.

Ragnald pales. "Dark servants? Here?"

"They were fully corrupted," Callum says.

Ragnald's head snaps up. "That's impossible! That would mean the Era War is advanced farther than the Academia of Mages declared." Muttering, he starts pacing up and down the beach.

I turn to Callum. "I haven't had a chance to thank you for getting me out of the city . . ."

He cups my cheek with a hand. "There is no need for that." His blue eyes are warm as his gaze traces my face. "I'm glad that you are not . . . I thought that you—"

"Lost for words?" I tease. "Were you *that* worried about me?" I rise on my toes to brush a quick kiss on his lips.

When I pull away, he grasps the back of my neck and lowers his head for a much more thorough kiss, taking my breath away. Literally.

"Aw," Teague says. "All that's missing is a bride's choice."

"This is not . . . I mean we're not . . . uh . . ." I stammer.

Callum grins. "Now who's lost for words?"

I hit him on the shoulder.

"You didn't look surprised," Callum says.

I frown at the quick change of topic. "Surprised about what? That the mage showed up?"

"About the dark servants' attack, directed at me," Callum says.

Nothing gets by him, doesn't it? "Maybe because you are the biggest threat out of the three of us?"

"Hey!" Teague says with mock indignation.

"You know why someone is looking for me," Callum states.

I guess it's time to come clean. "Yes. The Archgod of Chaos and Destruction."

Teague whistles.

Callum rubs his chin in thought. "That makes sense."

"It does?"

"It's only the archgod who can fully corrupt people to create dark servants."

"I wish we could have saved them." They were once living, breathing people before corruption took them. "They never had a chance, did they?"

Ragnald, done with his pacing, joins us. "Once a soul is corrupted by the Archgod of Chaos and Destruction, there is no saving them."

"The Archgod of Chaos and Destruction must be stopped before he can make any more of those dark servants," I say. There was nothing human left in them. Just pure, mindless hatred. "No one deserves to end up like that."

"That's why we killed them," Teague says and pats my shoulder. "So they don't have to suffer any longer."

"More like *her* magic killed them," Callum says.

Ragnald studies me with interest. "There is only one type of magic capable of disintegrating dark servants. Lumenian magic."

Does everyone know about this Lumenian thing but me? "Yes."

Ragnald's frown deepens. "You don't look like a Lumenian. They are . . . I mean—"

They are the most beautiful, amazing, and fierce people I've ever met, and I've only "met" two of them: Triann and Cadeon. "I know."

"You can't even control your magic," Ragnald says.

"I know!" Does he have to rub it in?

Ragnald closes his eyes. "We're doomed."

CHAPTER 70

Teague slaps the mage's shoulder. "Friend, tell us something we don't already know."

I wish I could deny it, but they're all correct. If it depends on me, then we are indeed doomed.

"I have to do some research," Ragnald says and hurries up the stairs toward the palace. At least *he* knows what to do.

"I should go too." Exhaustion catches up with me, and I yawn. "It's late."

Fla'mma-infused small lights illuminate the curving and steep stairs. The idea of climbing them is enough to make me curse. Which I do. Under my breath.

"I'll scout ahead," Teague says, and sprints up the stairs, taking two at a time. I envy his energy. All I want to do is curl up on the beach and go to sleep. I yawn again.

I catch a whiff of my dirty Saage outfit that's now covered in dried blood, dirt, sand, and a few spots of black stains from the dark servants that somehow survived my magic. Maybe shower first, then sleep.

I glance at Callum. "I owe you an apology."

"What for?"

"For assuming that you had something to do with the dead bodies. Once I learned that you were taking blood samples . . . I guess I jumped to conclusions." Funny how anger can create logic where there isn't any.

"So that's where my communicator vanished."

"You knew it all along!"

"You're not exactly a stealthy thief," Callum says, laughing, "and I got a kiss out of it."

"Is that all you can think about?" I probably shouldn't confess that's what I'm thinking about. I clear my throat.

Callum grins. "I'm not sure how to answer that politely."

I stumble. I'm not going to go there!

"Why didn't you say something?" My cheeks sting from shame. Lying, stealing—I sure showed him my best side!

221

"I wanted to see where all this was going," Callum says. There isn't any judgment or condemnation in his voice.

"You don't have to worry about me stealing from you again." I mean it. I am done with that. "I only did it for the rebellion, but I'm not a rebel anymore."

"You sound disappointed."

"It's complicated," I say, avoiding the answer.

"Try me."

"I quit. I was a fool to think Xor wanted me in the rebellion for my help. I should have known it was all about getting access to the defense codes of the palace."

"Is that why you quit?"

"I thought I was protecting the refugees, but in the end, I've failed them." I failed my promise to Mom—to protect those who cannot protect themselves.

"It's only a failure if you stop trying altogether," Callum says and stops me with a hand on my arm. "There are other ways to help them."

"I guess." I resume the climb. "So why did you take those blood samples?"

"I was checking for signs of corruption. Wherever the Archgod of Chaos and Destruction spreads his corruption, it always starts like this: large numbers of people disappear; then dead bodies with low-level corruption appear—those whom the archgod failed to corrupt; then half-formed dark servants appear—some of the missing who started their transformation: and once they show up, it's only a matter of time before they transition into fully corrupted dark servants. Once that happens, that world is lost."

Poor Deidre! She got caught in the archgod's net.

"Lost?" I ask. No hope? No help?

"Yes. Since we don't have access to Lumenian magic, the only thing left to do is to obliterate the planet. Even that only slows the archgod and prevents him from corrupting more of the planet's inhabitants. He can still collect the already corrupted ones."

"I had no idea," I mutter, shocked. "The Lady was right."

"You've met the Archgoddess of the Eternal Light and Order?" Callum asks in disbelief. "Although I shouldn't be surprised. You are a Lumenian after all."

I didn't realize I said my thought aloud. "Yes. She asked me to be her sybil."

"That's the highest rank and greatest honor to have in the Era War."

Just not for me. "I said no."

Callum's expression turns incredulous. "Why would you do such a thing?"

"I have my reasons, okay?" I say. "There must be other, better Lumenians she can choose for that 'honor.'"

Callum shakes his head. "You don't think you can do it."

"That's not it." At least not completely it.

"Then why?"

I send a sharp look at him. "Maybe it's easy for you, but I am not a warrior."

"Did you know that in the era wars, all nations, all races, mages, healers, everyone fought to stop the Archgod of Chaos and Destruction?"

I'm not sure where he is going. "Yes. Uhna sent soldiers, too, in the last one."

"Teryns never fought in any of the era wars."

Surprised, I look at him. "Why?"

"We only came to existence after the last Era War ended. We dedicated all of our resources and efforts to prepare to fight in the next one."

"It's that important to your praelium?" We reach the top of the cliff. The Crystal Palace is only a short distance from here, standing proudly and sparkling in the moonlight.

"More than anything. We took it upon ourselves to fight the spreading corruption of the Dark Lord, whether there is an Era War or not."

"And DLD was busy giving your praelium plenty of work." When Callum frowns, I explain that DLD stands for the Dark Lord of Destruction. "I'm sure you're eager to jump into fighting."

Callum turns me to face him. "DLD always preys first on those who are the most vulnerable. You want to protect the refugees? This is your chance. Become the sybil."

I open my mouth to protest, but then I hear my name.

"Lilla!" Arrov shouts as he runs toward us. "You have to come quickly!"

CHAPTER 71

The three of us run into the palace, right into a large crowd in the main hall.

"It's my fault," Arrov says as we elbow through the throng of loud courtiers.

I go around a group of snickering ma'haras. "What happened?" The court does seem more malicious than usual.

"I shouldn't have just quit on the spot," Arrov says. "I should have waited for Glenna first, but I didn't think. After you left, I didn't want to keep, um, 'going.' But I didn't expect to get kicked out of the, um, you know, the 'place' right away."

"You *not* thinking is a problem, all right," Callum says.

"What are you talking about, Arrov?" I have difficulty following his story. Especially as more excited ma'hars and ma'haras rush past us. What's going on?

"You know, the 'place,' where we were, um, 'working' together?" Arrov says.

Oh! He means the rebellion!

"What was Glenna doing in the, um, 'place'?" I ask, ignoring Callum's eyeroll. Clearly, he caught up sooner than I did.

"Our *friend* needed immediate medical attention," Arrov says, "and I thought Glenna is the best there is and . . ."

I tried to keep her from the rebellion, but she still ended up mixed with them.

"There you go *thinking* again," Callum says with a growl.

Arrov glares at Callum. "In the heat of the moment, I simply forgot about her."

Poor Glenna!

We reach the edge of the perfume-saturated crowd and I see my worst fear come true. Glenna, white-faced, stares up at the overseer, who has her arm in his grasp.

Irvine looks around as if to make sure he has everyone's attention. "You think you can keep hiding behind the ma'hana's goodwill and protection? You're mistaken! I've caught you. You are a collaborator with the rebels; just admit it!" He points into Glenna's pale face as he adds, "You shouldn't have gone into the camp, healer. Not when I know the rebellion leader was gravely injured in a raid mere hours ago."

Glenna, unfazed, glares at the ma'har. "I did nothing wrong. I lost track of time dispensing immunization potions to those poor refugee children. Potions that you have delayed for months with your new regulations. It is your fault that I had twice as many patients than before."

Irvine shakes Glenna by her arm. "You lie! You have blood on your healer's robe." He points to various blood spots. "Since when do immunization potions cause bleeding?" He looks victorious.

Oh, no! I move toward Glenna, but Callum stops me. "If you go to her now," he says, "you'll implicate yourself."

"But I have to—"

"I know you do," Callum says with a serious expression. "Wait for the right time."

Glenna attempts to free her arm but without success. "Since I am the only healer volunteering to help the sick, I also have to deal with broken bones, severe injuries from beatings your guards mete out, and other ailments." She points to a greenish smear on the sleeve he holds. "That's puss I had to drain from an infected wound. Will you hold that against me, too?"

The overseer cocks his right arm and slaps Glenna across her face.

One of his many rings draws a thin line of blood on Glenna's already reddening cheek. He holds her arm at an unnatural angle. "I am your better, an esteemed member of high society. You do not take that tone with me, sh'all."

Glenna holds her cheek, while she stares up at the ma'har. "You are no one's better, especially not mine," she says.

Irvine raises his right arm again, his expression a mix of fury and a strange pleasure. My vision turns red. I lunge at the ma'har, intercepting his arm with mine.

Irvine reacts without looking—bringing his left arm up in a sloppy punch. Something rushes by me, fast.

Callum, holding Irvine by his throat, slams the ma'har into the closest wall, dangling the overseer three feet off the ground. "Don't you raise your hand to Ma'hana Lilla," he says with a snarl into the ma'har's ashen face. "She is *your* better, is she not?"

The court falls silent, staring at us. Behind the overseer, his guards snap to attention, aiming their serrated pirate rifle-swords at Callum. Teague and six warriors with laser guns surround Callum, ready to defend their general.

Tension and violence hang thickly in the air.

"Stand down!" I say with a raised hand. "Do not escalate!"

It is not until High Adviser Ellar, who appears and repeats the same command, that the guards stand down. Teague and the Teryns reholster their guns.

While the high adviser is busy dismissing the crowd, I touch Callum's extended arm. His corded muscles don't shake from the effort of holding up the other man.

"Callum, please. Let the ma'har go. He is not worth it."

Callum looks at me for a moment, his blue eyes flashing reddish-yellow in his fury.

"This is not the right time," I say.

"You're right." He drops the purple-faced ma'har to the ground.

Irvine crumples to the white marble tiles, rubbing his bruised neck and gasping for air. "How dare you touch me, you filthy—" he says, but when Callum stares down at him, the ma'har shuts up.

Ignoring a pointed glare from the high adviser, I go to Glenna and put an arm around her shoulder. "Let's get out of here."

CHAPTER 72

"This is all my fault," Arrov says as Callum, Glenna, and I file into my living quarters.

"You're damn right it is," Callum says and drops down on one of my sofas.

"If it is anyone's fault, it's mine," I say. Arrov settles down across from Callum.

"It doesn't matter who's to blame," Glenna says. With a sigh of exhaustion, she takes the only chair in the room. "It won't change what happened."

I lean on a bookcase, facing the room.

Glenna frowns. "Aren't you going to sit down?"

Arrov pets the sofa next to him. "There is plenty of room right here."

Callum raises an eyebrow. "Or she can sit next to me."

I clear my throat. "I, uh, I'm good here."

Two quick knocks sound and the twins burst into the room.

"We heard what happened," Isa and Bella say, "and we came as fast as we could."

Isa sits next to Arrov, and Bella next to Callum. They gaze at the men in fake adoration. They love getting a rise out of all males—and females too.

"I'm fine. Don't concern yourselves." She turns to me, and all the mirth disappears from her expression. "How long?"

Isa and Bella say, "Six months, give or take a few days."

Glenna's dark crimson gaze flashes toward the twins. "They know?"

"Of course we know," Isa says, and flicks a thin hand. "We've been rebels alongside Lilla."

Glenna raises an eyebrow and looks at Arrov and Callum. "And them?"

I hang my head in admission.

"Why wouldn't you tell me, Lilla?" The hurt in her voice nearly undoes me.

"Because I wanted to protect you." The words pour out, getting jumbled together. "Because I didn't want you to lose your dream. Because I love you too much to let you risk your life and turn you into a traitor. I would have done much worse if it meant keeping you safe," I say.

Isa crosses her legs. "But it doesn't matter anymore."

Bella says, "Lilla quit the rebellion," then adds, "We quit, too."

I can imagine that made Xor very happy, losing his best pilot in Arrov and losing his best hackers in the twins in quick succession. If he hadn't hated me before, I'm sure he does now.

"Glenna, I know I made a mess of this. Can you forgive me?"

The anger drains from her expression until only compassion is left. "There is nothing to forgive."

She gets up from her chair. I meet her halfway, and we hug. "I've missed you."

She hugs me tighter. "I've missed you, too." She wipes the corner of her eye as she sits back down. "Now someone please tell me what's going on."

We take turns recapping.

Glenna rubs her cheek, wincing. "What's our plan?"

Callum leans forward, placing his elbows on his knees. "We have an advantage, for now. It seems DLD thinks I am the Lumenian, and not Lilla. But we don't know how long that will last or when his next attack will be. So far we've been lucky."

"Even though it was my magic that got rid of those dark servants," I say, "it's no good for us as long as I have no control over it."

"Then it seems to me that figuring out your magic is our top priority," Arrov says.

I nod. "I'll talk to Ragnald about it. I'm sure he can help."

"It boggles my mind that, uh, DLD is here on Uhna. Hiding in a mortal form, no less," says Glenna.

"At least we won't have to go too far to find him," I say. "This is our only chance to save Uhna and prevent the Era War from advancing to the rest of the Seven Galaxies."

"What about the marriage contract?" Glenna asks. "Won't your magic be locked soon by the purification process?"

"You're right. I can't let that happen." But to stop the Saage women, they need proof. I guess I can't avoid The Lady any longer.

CHAPTER 73

I close my door after everyone leaves and stand there in a daze. I know that this must be done, but I really, really wish I wouldn't have to.

If I proceed, not only do I admit that I was wrong all along, but also there will be no going back. Ever. My path will be set.

There is no point prolonging this. "Archgoddess of the Eternal Light and Order," I say, then hesitate. How does one summon an archgoddess? "Um, reveal yourself?"

From one moment to the next, I am hovering in space, somewhere in the Seven Galaxies. I wait for the choking and the freezing to start, but nothing happens.

"What is it, my child?" asks The Lady.

With awe and a surge of humility, I gape at the cold and merciless beauty of the Seven Galaxies. Its vastness full of planets, life, and mystery nearly inconceivable to me. This is what the archgods must see every day of their never-ending lives. No wonder they see us as insignificant and unimportant.

"I accept."

She smiles, her eyes glinting with a harsh light. "Accept what, my child?"

"Don't make me regret this."

"You have no idea what regret is, my child. Say it."

"I accept the role. I will be your sybil." Now there is truly no going back.

The Lady bares her teeth in a smile. A burst of love cascades over me, like the unforgiving waves on a beach, dragging sand away until nothing is left. "Stop it!"

She turns down her broadcast of love and extends her hand. What comes next is very much in the hands of The Lady. Literally.

After hesitating for a second, I take it.

The planets and stars flick by us. Moving fast until they are nothing but a dizzying haze. Then they all come to a sudden stop.

A huge globe looms in front of me, easily a hundred times bigger than my home world. One half of it is covered with lush greenery and small lakes. The other half is desolate and blackened.

"I don't understand . . ." The black half grows in size, from one breath to another, like claws extending. "What's happening?"

The Lady, instead of answering, waves her hand over the planet.

We are hovering near the ground. Around us there is no life. Just black smoke, like an oppressing fog. Curling and drenching the whole area with the smell of rotting, charred meat.

Horrific beings materialize from the smoke. Dark sinews ooze black fluids from open wounds that cover their bulky bodies. They resemble a grotesque fusion of humanoid and predatory animal. Bone spikes grow out of their bodies. Blood drips from their black fangs, protruding from their long, repulsive faces. Their eyes glare, full of menace and hatred, leaving no doubt that they will show no mercy to their victims. They are malevolence embodied.

My mind struggles to take them in. How do you fight these monsters when you're so terrified you can barely even breathe?

More of the creatures ramble out of the thick fog of smoke. Dozens turn into hundreds. Hundreds into thousands. Until all I can see is a never-ending army of beasts.

"Those are dark fiends, the foot soldiers of the Archgod of Chaos and Destruction. His first creations before the more advanced dark servants."

The Lady grabs my hand and takes me to another planet. And another. And another. Small. Big. One with forests. Another with volcanoes. Each more different than the previous. Except for the corruption that blackens every one of them to varying degrees. The grotesque dark fiends keep spawning, while life disappears in their wake.

I turn to look away, but The Lady grabs my chin and forces me to watch. "This is what you should regret. Witness what happens when you don't act. Every second of your hesitation costs hundreds of thousands of lives. The least you owe them is to behold their destruction."

The enormity of the situation sinks in. Innocent souls who had no chance against DLD die suffering or end up corrupted into dark fiends. And all because of my indecision.

"Enough, please!" I cannot bear to see another planet falling under the corrupt power of the archgod. Those planets will haunt me for the rest of my life.

"Now you understand, my child. Now you know what you have to do."

The Lady lifts her arm with her hand closed in a fist. She opens her long fingers to reveal a golden jewel. It's small, the size of my forefinger, and oval-shaped. Under a transparent cover, gold filaments are interwoven into an intricate pattern. At the top it has two tiny gold claws curling inward, while at its bottom are two longer claws pinching.

I study the jewelry. "It's beautiful."

"This is the blessing of the sybil I will bestow upon you. You'll wear it from now on."

There is no necklace attached to it. "Wear it how?"

The Lady motions for me to turn around. When I do, something cold pierces the back of my neck in two places.

I cry out in pain. Thin tendrils burrow under my skin. I try to move, but my body doesn't obey.

"This will be over soon, my child."

The thin tendrils wrap around my spine. Around my brain. They light up all my nerves in blinding pressure-pain for a moment. Then all discomforts evaporate, as if nothing had happened.

"How dare you!" I say and face The Lady. "I didn't give you permission to do this!"

"Now you wear my blessing to signal your position as sybil." She smiles, an image of benevolence. "A talisman, if you will."

"Is that all it is?" My skin crawls. It takes all my effort not to reach back and rip it out. "A talisman?"

"It does a few more things, but you'll figure it out as you go."

"But—" The Lady leans over and kisses my forehead, cutting off any more protests.

Overwhelming feelings of love burn in ever-intensifying waves. Worse than I've felt from her before. Until my body shakes under the torrents of joy and bliss.

I conjure anger, fighting the artificial happy feelings. But the suffocating clouds of oppressive happiness spread nonetheless.

It must be the talisman's effect! Then all thoughts fade, drenched by the bursts of love. Until I want to beg for more. Like a pathetic devotee.

"I'm glad you see my way, child. Now take care of the Archgod of Chaos and Destruction."

CHAPTER 74

I stifle a yawn as I enter the royal library early the next morning. I head to the atrium to meet with Ragnald. I had no sleep last night. I tossed and turned, my mind occupied with my new role and the unforeseen consequences.

I reach back to touch the talisman. It sends a sharp jolt of zap down my spine. As it did dozens of times, and I dared to touch it.

Ragnald, unseeing, peers up from a scroll in his hands.

"I'm here for the magic lesson," I remind him. "You asked me to come 'right away' in your message."

"Yes! Yes, I did." Ragnald lets the scroll roll back on itself. He picks up a dozen more from a table by him. As he takes two steps, half of the scrolls drop.

As he bends to pick them up, I squat to help. "Nervous?"

Ragnald laughs. "Is it that easy to tell?"

I smile. I know *I* am. Two uncontrolled magical explosions aren't exactly what I'd consider promising or successful.

He straightens up, holding the scrolls to his chest. "No one has ever had the fortune to test a Lumenian's magic before. Today will go down in mage history as the most important magical discovery."

"I'd wait till the end of the lesson to judge that if I were you."

"It's been rumored that a Lumenian has command of all the light elements. Many elders speculate that it's because of how the Lumenians came to existence. *From* the elements. But we've never had a chance to prove or disprove this theory. Until now."

Great. Now I am a magic-test vermin. "Can't mages, um, command all the elements?"

Ragnald stumbles on his own foot. "Of course not! A mage may command two elements, while healers only one: A'ris. I can command three—a first in centuries," he says, distracted. "I just need to figure out where to start."

Ragnald shuffles through the scrolls, discarding one after another. "Somehow I have to condense two hundred years of magical knowledge into a few lessons for you."

Sounds complicated. "You're not very good at pep talks, are you?"

"I have no doubt you'll catch up fast. After all, you are a—"

"Please don't say it—"

"—a legendary Lumenian."

I cover my face. I have no idea how I'll live up to that high a level of expectation.

Ragnald smiles. "Now let's get started!"

CHAPTER 75

Rubbing his hands together as if to clean them of any residual magic, the mage moves to the center of the atrium. His eyes glow with a cerise light, lit from inside. His long, unbound hair floats around him as his power steeps the air, which suddenly smells like ozone.

"Wait," I say. "Will the magical markings I've received in the purification process interfere?"

He lowers his hands, and an invisible wind dies down. "What stage of the process are you in?"

"First."

He shakes his head. "Then it shouldn't be a problem. In fact, it'll help your magic to amass. It's only the third stage that locks it in. I would recommend you get to the next stage's markings—it will boost your abilities significantly."

Great. More bug tattoos. "I'll keep that in mind."

He raises his arms, his hair once again floating around him as his magic intensifies.

"Wait!"

Ragnald sighs, lowering his arms, his magic deflating. "Yes?"

"Will the talisman I received from The Lady affect our lesson?" I rub the back of my neck in reflex and get zapped with a sharp current.

Ragnald's expression turns to shock. "You have the sybil talisman?"

I grimace in affirmation.

"That's amazing! You are truly a lege—"

"Stop calling me that!"

"It's what you are," Ragnald insists. "No, the talisman shouldn't cause any issue. At least I think." He rubs his forehead and mutters under his breath, "Gods, I hope so."

He starts raising his hands but stops and asks, "Any more questions?"

I shake my head.

"Then to begin, I will set the elemental circles." Ragnald holds out his right hand. A small, azure blue ring appears, hovering over his palm. He flicks his hand as if to throw it, and the ring lands by my feet, growing into a two-foot-wide circle. Suspended an inch above the white marble tiles, it glows pale blue. Misting tiny magical particles vanish once they land on the ground.

"A'qua, representing the water element," he says in a ceremonial tone.

He holds out his left hand. A garnet red ring, similarly transparent and misting, appears above his palm. He flicks his hand and it lands outside the first circle, encompassing the smaller one inside its four-foot-wide space.

"Fla'mma, representing the fire element."

He repeats the motions, adding ever-widening circles, and calling each out:

"T'erra, representing the soil element." A dark brown circle joins the others.

"A'ris, representing the air element." A sky blue circle.

"A'nima, representing the animal element." A straw yellow circle.

"Lume, representing the light and energy element." A golden white circle joins finally.

Ragnald wipes the sweat off his face and shakes his arms out. He takes out a pair of eyeglasses. Their frames are a thin metal with no bottom edge, the lenses green. He puts them on, then examines the circles with a content expression.

"These are the light elements. They are the domain of the Archgoddess of the Eternal Light and Order, and the guardian gods. The dark elements, such as Murky A'qua, Barren T'erra, Black Fla'mma, and Dusky A'ris along with Acerbus are the domain of the Archgod of Chaos and Destruction and the turned ones. We won't invoke them here, for they are antitheses of the light elements."

"The light and dark elements are in a constant push and pull. Just like the archgoddess and the archgod are against each other. Thus creating the balance that governs our Seven Galaxies. Neither element dominating the other. Neither archgod dominating the other."

"Could it be that DLD amassed too much power?" I ask, remembering all those planets covered in black. "Is that why this Era War is happening? A power struggle between the archgods?"

"We, mere mortals, are not informed why an Era War starts," Ragnald says. "Our duty is to partake on the side of The Lady."

A troubling thought occurs to me. "How do we know that we are not fighting on the side of the archgod who has too much power?"

Ragnald looks taken aback. "If the Seven Galaxies ever become a place where the Arch- goddess of the Eternal Light and Order should lose, then I don't want to live here. Not that there would be much life left to live anyway. You've seen the dark servants."

I did. "But what if this is what DLD wanted? What if he tricked The Lady somehow?"

"Lilla, you're giving too much credit to DLD. Do you honestly think he is capable of any superior tactical planning? He did lose six Era Wars after all."

I open my mouth to tell the mage that he underestimates the other arch-god, but his expression invites no argument. "I guess you're right."

"We have a chance to restore balance before the Era War can devastate the Seven Galaxies. What if *this* is the plan of the Omnipower? Who are we to question it and as such blunder it?"

Ragnald is right. I don't want to be responsible for ruining the plan of the Omnipower. Which means back to my magic.

I gesture to the circles. "How does this work?"

Ragnald steps in the middle of the smallest one, which represents A'qua. "If you can light up the circle with your magic, like so"—he demonstrates it, and the azure blue circle sparkles brighter than before—"then you have control over that element."

Two more circles light up: the ruby red one and the dark brown one. "As you can see, I have command over A'qua, Fla'mma, and T'erra." The three circles lose their brightness, going back to their original state once Ragnald pulls his magic back.

He steps out. "Now it's your turn." With a resigned sigh, I take his place.

"Close your eyes and feel each circle in your mind's eye."

I do as the mage instructs. For a moment nothing happens, and all I can see is the neon-bright afterimages of the circles in the back of my eyelids. Then a sparkle grows, until it expands into the six elemental circles, each bright in its own colors. "I see them."

Ragnald stammers. "You can see magic?"

I nod.

"How marvelous! It must be a le—uh, Lumenian characteristic. Without the help of my amplifier glasses I wouldn't be able to see them at all."

"Now that you feel—I mean see—the circles, it is time to find out how many elements you can control. Dip into your magic. See if you can find each element. Then, by using the tiniest amount of that element's magic, channel it into the appropriate circle."

Forcing calm over my body, I wipe my sweaty palms on my leggings. The hot-and-cold-and-hot-again feelings rise under my skin, making it glow with a golden white light.

I find the pulsing bright white sphere, which seems to be alive. My magic. For the first time, I feel each light element inside the sphere resonate, as if answering the call of the magic circles. As I get closer to the sphere, I realize that the bright white is actually composed of millions of tiny threads. Threads of elemental magic that sparkle in the hue of their elemental colors, like light does inside a crystal.

With an imaginary finger, I poke a strand with an azure blue hue. It separates from the others, lifting up just enough for me to grab hold of it. I unravel it and imagine threading the smallest amount into the first circle at my feet. In my mind's eye the circle lights up brightly.

"That's it! Keep going!"

I continue, handling each elemental thread with the utmost care. Channeling them into the appropriate circles until I am done. "Can I open my eyes now?"

"Yes," Ragnald whispers in a strange voice.

Worried, I ask, "Why are you whispering?" and open my eyes.

CHAPTER 76

All the circles turned into individual domes. The smallest is as tall as I am. Each of the following domes are ever taller and wider than the previous one. Until the last one, the Lume dome, arches beyond the ceiling, as if it cannot be contained by the mere roof of the library.

I ruined the test! "I must have misunderstood—"

"No, no!" Ragnald says, shaken out of his reverie. "You did great!"

He walks around the dome circles, staring in awe. "Never in my whole life have I seen anything like this."

"This is progressing much more quickly than I thought. Clearly you have no trouble using all the light elements. Now we have to find out how much control you have over them." Ragnald lifts his hand with finger extended and adds, "For without control, a mage is as good as turned."

"I think we both know the answer to that. Or do I have to remind you of what happened on the beach?"

"That was only a minor loss of control." Ragnald waves away my concern. "Didn't even last longer than a few seconds. You clearly overused your magic that time. It's perfectly understandable. You were fighting for your life. It can happen to any mage—instincts take over, and we draw too much magic."

Maybe this time will be different. And maybe crabs will fly.

"As to the 'control' part: there isn't a mage who has equal control over their dual, or in the rare case triple, elements. Usually one is their major element, while the other is their minor element. For me, Fla'mma and T'erra are my major elements, while A'qua is my minor. I always do better with the first two in power, control, and effectiveness than in the third."

"Let us start with Fla'mma," Ragnald suggests. "There is something delightful about lobbing fireballs back and forth."

I think that his definition of delightful is different from mine.

I grasp a thick thread of Fla'mma from the bright white sphere of my magic. With growing sureness, I pull more of the Fla'mma thread, forming it into a makeshift ball in my mind. Then, without any finesse, I let it loose.

"That's too much! Reel it back!"

The Fla'mma ball keeps growing in size, as if feeding on the thread I failed to sever from the magical sphere. I reach for the thread to tie it off, but it bucks out of my grasp.

"I can't control it!"

"You must!" Ragnald urges.

The pressure keeps increasing, crushing me from the inside. I change tactic. Instead of severing the Fla'mma thread, I shove at it, trying to press it back into the bright magical sphere. Both the thread and the sphere rear out of my control, resisting all my attempts.

Pressure pain builds, stretching my skin too tightly. Hot-and-cold-and-hot-again feelings beat inside my arteries, in rhythm with my frantically beating heart.

Suddenly images of blood surface in my mind. Echoes of screams reverberate in my ears as the blood spreads on the white tile.

"I can't hold it anymore!" I scream.

CHAPTER 77

The pressure bursts, taking the pain with it. All the elemental magic erupts from me, gushing hotter than the combined cores of the two suns together.

A terrible explosion rocks the library.

Blinding light, hued with colors of azure blue, ruby red, sky blue, dark brown, straw yellow, and bright white saturates the atrium.

A'ris whirls like a raging storm, fanning the flames to a frenzy. Tossing the debris around. Tearing at my clothes and hair with vengeful fingers as shards of broken glass shower from the ceiling.

Fla'mma burns white hot. Devouring every surface. Filling the library with smoke as burning pages of books and pieces of curtain flutter in the air.

A'qua crushes waves of foaming water at the walls. Dragging my feet to the side.

T'erra shakes and cracks the floor under my feet. Opening wide. Shaking all the white marble columns until they come crashing down around us.

A'nima breathes life into the inanimate objects. Furniture rushes at us in a wild attack.

Lume explodes upward in a thick column of golden white light, tearing off the ruins of the glass roof. Shattering all the windows outward in a deafening boom.

Then the chaos freezes. The explosion suspended in midair. Hovering unnaturally.

Ragnald strolls through the destruction, moving his hands in circles over each other.

The explosion jars in place, then slowly crawls backward, as if sucked by a magic vacuum.

The glass shards flow back into their place. Re-forming into windowpanes, as they were before my magical eruption.

The ground stops shaking and melts into a seamless close, with the tiles re-forming on top of it.

The ceiling reverses in millions of pieces, until it is whole again.

The wild and attacking furniture revert to their inanimate state, the pieces sliding to their proper spots.

The floodwater evaporates, leaving not a single drop behind.

The fire extinguishes. The curtains and books re-form, unburned, and the books are back on undamaged bookshelves.

Even the art and sculptures are restored as if nothing had happened.

Ragnald, finished, bends over double, gasping.

My knees give out. I land on the floor. Sitting and utterly exhausted. "After this debacle, I have no doubt that the DLD knows where the real Lumenian is," I say, not bothering to hide the bitter undertone in my voice. "You better run, before it's too late."

"My magical words held, just as I knew they would," the mage says. "In my experience, when a mage struggles so much, it's because they have an emotional block interfering with their control. Do you know what that might be for you?"

"I'm not sure . . ."

"Until you dissolve your block, I cannot teach you anything." Ragnald folds his arms over his chest. "I can't believe I am saying this, but you need to see a healer."

CHAPTER 78

A knock sounds on the door of my living quarters.

I put down the holo-picture of my mom. I've been staring at it for hours, trying to figure out what trauma blocked my magic. I've gotten nowhere. I have no choice but to see Glenna and ask her help. Apologize first, then ask.

Another knock sounds, more persistent.

"I'm coming, I'm coming. Hold your ships." I open it to find Arrov standing there. He beams. "May I come in?"

I let him enter. He leans down to kiss me, but I step back to avoid it.

"Something changed," Arrov says. "I can feel it."

I close the door and look up at him in despair.

I still like him. I still care for him. He is the most handsome man I've ever met. But when I close my eyes, I don't see his face in my mind. When I wake up, he is not my first thought.

"It's him, isn't it? That Teryn general. You've been spending a lot of time with him. You've fallen in love with him. Don't deny it. It's plain to see."

"I'm not in love with Callum." I would know if I was, wouldn't I?

Arrov puts his hands on my shoulders. "Then why are you so distant with me?"

"I've come to rely on you as a friend, Arrov, and I'd hate to lose you. But I also cannot lead you on." Pathetic. It's not you, it's me. "I cannot commit to you more than as a friend."

Arrov looks away and stays silent for a long moment.

"I am sorry that I hurt your feelings," I say, tearing up. "That was never my intent. Please say something."

"I know, Lilla." He wipes an errant tear off my cheek. "I can't lie and say it doesn't hurt. But I also can't say I didn't see it coming."

"Please don't hate me," I say.

"Hate you?" He smiles, shaking off his melancholy. "I could never hate you. Truth is, I really am not ready to commit. Just give me some time to get used to being friends only."

He leans on my fireplace and crosses his feet at his ankles. "Speaking of commitment, there is chatter that Xor plans to attack the palace by the end of the week."

"That's three days away!" I haven't had a chance to search for the archgod. Nor have I learned to control my magic. "It's too soon!"

"Ever since Jorha died, he is obsessed with the attack."

Buckets of fishguts! "I never told Captain Murtagh about his daughter's death."

"Lilla, don't worry. I'll handle it."

"Please tell the captain about the rebellion's attack. He would know what to do. We can trust him." Arrov nods and leaves my living quarters.

I have three days to somehow find the archgod, figure out my past trauma, and control my magic. Easy. Not.

The most important thing is to get rid of that magical block. Glenna should know how. With newfound purpose, I head to the door and swing it open.

Only to find Beathag blocking my way. With her usual thug guards.

Well, Ragnald did recommend getting the second stage of the purification process.

I head toward the stairs. I glance back when I hear no footsteps following after me.

Beathag stands entrenched, gawking at me.

"Aren't you coming?" I say, smirking. "The Saage women don't like to wait."

CHAPTER 79

When we reach the green parlor, Beathag waves her guards away. She stops me in the doorway with a hand on my forearm. She searches my expression, but I give her no clue.

"Why are you in such a hurry?" she asks.

"It should be obvious." I remove her hand from my arm. "The sooner I am here, the sooner it will be done." And the sooner I'll get that magical boost.

Beathag frowns, but lets me enter the parlor ahead of her.

The five Saage women wait patiently inside. They stand out like sour lemons among all the green.

The two shortest women step forward. They face the furniture, lifting their right knees and rising on their toes. Extending their arms and stepping out in an angle toward the furniture, they open their arms in a shoving motion.

Two emerald sofas, the two sea green chairs, and the khaki coffee table slide smoothly all the way to the wall.

"I thought you're not supposed to use magic," I say.

"No magic," says the leader. "Harness energy of room. Use energy move large things. Now we do lesson. You will—"

I raise my hand. "You asked for proof that I'm the sybil."

"Have you proof then?"

I turn, lifting my hair from my neck to show her The Lady's talisman.

The Saage women gasp. When I face them, they are on their knees, with their heads bent in prostration.

I lean down with a hand extended. "Please, don't." It's strange to see their open devotion to The Lady, and by extension, toward me.

The leader accepts my hand, and I help her to her feet. The others straighten, too.

"You the sybil," she says in awe.

"Now can you help me dissolve the marriage contract to your crown prince?"

"No can do such a thing," the leader says. "No contract brings war." She shrugs her shoulders. "Eh. How you say? 'It is what it is'?"

She would know that saying, wouldn't she?

"But much time pass before war, no? Men talk long. Argue much. War may not happen, no?"

"I guess so."

The leader pats my shoulder, then points at her chest. "I am Saage Antha."

As I saw them honor their crown prince, I bow over my two fists that are angled in a "V" shape, extend my elbows twice, and clap without sound.

Saage Antha returns my greeting. Then she does something unexpected. She grabs my hand and bows over it until her forehead touches the back of my hand briefly. With her eyes closed, she first turns her right cheek, then her left cheek, above my hand. As she straightens, she murmurs, "I see you Sybil a'k Order."

Chills run down my spine as I hear the ceremonial title. The first time anyone has acknowledged my new role and with such reverence.

The other four Saage women introduce themselves and repeat the traditional greeting, complete with the ritual at the end. Their blessings humble me.

I turn to Saage Antha. "I need a favor."

"How help Saage women the sybil?"

"I would like you to keep this new development between us."

The Saage woman nods. "Of course."

"I would also like you to complete the second phase of the purification process." After a short thought, I add, "And could you teach me how to manipulate energy?"

All the Saage women bow and say in unison, "Anything for sybil."

CHAPTER 80

I head to the exit once the Saage women leave, pulling at the tight neck of the ceremonial outfit. This time it's blue. We all agreed that I should keep up the pretense and wear their traditional attire, as if everything is progressing as it should.

The new magical markings, from my shoulder blades to my waist, itch like crazy. Getting them via the Aak spider bug was just as horrible as the first time. But knowing that these markings will amplify my magic makes the discomfort worth it.

Before I can leave the room, Beathag storms in, shutting the door behind her. "I've come to talk to you."

"It will have to wait." I don't have time for her bickering. I have to go see Glenna.

Beathag steps in front of me. "It's important."

I sigh with unveiled impatience. "I don't know what games you're playing, but I am busy. Now get out of my way, or I'll move you." And I won't even have to touch her, thanks to the energy manipulation trick the Saage women taught me.

"I was concerned for your well-being—"

"Please! The only person you care about is yourself."

The haughty expression disappears from her face, and she pats the pocket of her wide skirt. "There was a time when you thought the best of me."

"Those times are gone." I shoulder past her. "I really don't have time for this."

She stops me again, with an outstretched hand. "All I ever wanted is the best for you."

With those words I am transported back to two years ago.

When Father decided to fetter me with guards, he had assigned Belthair. It didn't take long for me to develop a crush on the handsome guard, who made me laugh when I felt miserable. His dark gray eyes watched me with compassion and understanding that my life lacked. He made my heart flutter every time he was around. Those accidental brushes against his hands—and he had six of them!—soon became secret touches, stolen at every chance we had.

I thought I had fallen head over heels in love.

We planned to run away together that night. With Glenna off at the Healer's College, I shared my news with only one person: Beathag, who was a good friend at the time. Or so I thought.

"We had plans to live away from Uhna," I say. "Away from Father. I was bursting with happiness when I told you that I was supposed to meet him by the stables. I trusted you."

"I didn't want you to ruin your life," Beathag says with uncharacteristic vulnerability as she heads deeper into the green parlor. "I was worried about you."

Following, I turn her to face me, my fingers gripping her arm tightly. "It was my life! It was my choice to make, not yours. You betrayed me. What else is there to talk about?"

I'll never forget that night. How Belthair stood by the stables, under the moon's light. Ready to start a new life with me. Only to have guards fall on him. Beating him, while Father looked on. Ignoring my desperate screams as I begged him to stop.

Beathag reaches into the pocket of her skirt, hesitates for a moment, then pulls something out. "I can't change the past . . . but I can make amends." She shoves an object at me.

Frowning, I accept the grimy thing. Ready to throw it out, when I recognize it. It's Mom's journal.

"How is this possible?" When I confronted her about her betrayal, later in my living quarters, she grabbed it off my desk. "I saw you throw it into the fireplace. I thought it was destroyed." I turn it around with shaking hands. Its dark purple cover still feels plush in places, while in others it is charred but otherwise intact.

"After our fight, I went back and dug it out of the ashes."

And she hadn't given it back for years.

I look up at Beathag. "Why now?"

"We are both at crossroads in our lives. If this is not the time to start fresh, then when?"

"Whalecrap." She wants absolution.

"I don't want us to part as enemies," she tries again.

Too late. "I should have known this is all about *you* and what you want."

"That's not true—"

"Do you think I can forgive you for all of this? Your betrayal, your marriage to Father, and now my marriage contract to the Aak crown prince you've arranged? You think, because you decided we should be friends, it will be so?"

"No, I mean—"

"You haven't changed."

Beathag's expression darkens. "You don't know me. You have no idea what I had to go through to get here. We could have been allies. You're making a mistake by refusing me."

I step around her. Letting her into my life again would be a mistake.

"You'll regret this!" Beathag shouts.

I look over my shoulder. "I already regret the day I met you."

CHAPTER 81

After leaving the green parlor, I go straight to Glenna's quarters and knock on her door, hoping she is still up so late into the night.

Glenna opens it a crack, wearing a thin, yellow silk robe that reaches above her knees.

"What is it?" Her eyes widen. "Oh, it's you, Lilla!" She pulls the front of her robe closed with one hand while holding the door with the other in a white-knuckled grip.

"Were you sleeping?"

"Uh, no. Not exactly."

"Good." I walk past her into her living area, wading through her numerous animals, birds, bugs, and plants. "I need your help."

"My help?" She slants a nervous look toward her bathroom, where the shower is running.

"Ragnald thinks you can help me deal with a past trauma that's blocking my magic." I point toward her bathroom. "Aren't you going to shut it off?"

"In a minute." She leads me to the exit. "Why don't I meet you at the Healing Center later?"

"You're acting strange. Are you okay? You do look a bit flushed."

"I'm perfectly fine," Glenna says. "Now if you'd only—"

The bathroom door bangs open, letting out a thick cloud of humidity. A naked man strides out, his face buried in a small pink towel.

"Glenna," he says, "who was it?"

I know that voice! "Eek!" I put a hand out to block the view of naked Nic. Glenna ducks her head.

"Sis!" Nic yelps and drops his towel. "This is not what it looks like." He bends to pick it up, keeping the pink fabric in front of his hips when he straightens.

I wiggle my eyebrows. "I'm pretty sure it's beyond just *looking.*"

"Lilla!" Glenna slaps my shoulder, blushing.

"Joke all you want," Nic says, grinning, "but nothing can diminish the fact that it was the best night of my entire life."

Glenna groans in shame.

I cover my ears. "La-la-la! I don't need to know details!"

Muttering and red-faced, Glenna hurries to pick up clothes strewn all over the ground, then propels Nic into the bathroom. "Excuse us for a second." The door shuts.

It was about time they got together. They were circling each other like deepwater sharks in mating season.

"Ow!" Nic says. "Are you going to kiss where you pinched? Ouch! Stop hitting me, Glen! I'm hurrying!"

The bathroom door opens, and they return fully dressed. Leaning down, Nic kisses Glenna. "I'll see you later," he says, and caresses Glenna's face.

Nic rubs my hair as he goes past me, leaving.

Glenna stares at the ceiling as if it's the most interesting thing. "So . . . this happened."

"I've noticed."

"For the first time in my life, I'm bursting at the seams."

I laugh. "It was high time. Speaking of time—"

"Right! Your magical block. Let's head to the Healing Center."

CHAPTER 82

"I don't like this," Glenna says in the Healing Center.

"You've said that already." She did. At least half a dozen times.

"It's too dangerous!"

"You've said that, too."

Glenna paces in front of me. "For memory retrieval I usually have to use my magic. Except you don't respond to it, so that's out of the question."

"I know."

"Which means I must use alternate ways to bring you under, so we can access your repressed memories."

"I know." I am all too familiar with her alternate ways.

"There are so many things that can go wrong," Glenna says, glaring at me as if it's my fault. "You could even die."

I didn't know about that, but I say, "I know."

"Would you stop saying that?" Glenna snaps. "This is serious!"

"I kn . . . I mean of course it is. But what choice do I have?"

With a crestfallen expression Glenna says, "Fine," then leads me to a hovering patient bed. "Just don't come crying to me when you die."

"That would be a great feat." Even for a *legendary* Lumenian.

Cheerful bamboo and vines cover the walls, with carpet that looks like white sand—all very reassuring. I wish I could relax, but all my instincts tell me to stop prying at my past.

Glenna tucks a thin blanket around me. "At the first sign of danger, I will pull you out. Got it?"

"Yes, *Mom*."

She pulls the hovering metal tray closer to her. Vials and potions in all colors are lined up neatly, along with a large mixing pot and a stone pestle.

"To replace the magic catalyst, I have to create a good enough potion to do the trick," Glenna says.

"A pinch of sleeping fungus mixed with the calming lily petals and the bark of the dreaming ash tree," she says and measures out small pinches of dried mushroom, flower petals, and a white-gray bark into the clay pot, "that will get you to a long sleep—step one."

"The difficult part is creating a potion that will keep you in a meditative state but not put you into deep sleep." She lifts one of the vials and uncorks it with her teeth, spitting the cork into her palm. Tilting the vial, she counts out seven drops into the disgusting-looking mixture. "That's step two."

"Punch-out tonic mixed with sour oil should do the trick, but they are not stable enough on their own without some help." She picks up a green bottle and adds an oily-looking yellowish liquid. After a thought, she pours in the rest of the bottle's contents.

"What kind of help?" I ask, trying my best not to gag.

Glenna bends down and lifts a pink bottle. "This." She pours out three fingers' worth of the sparkling purple liquid.

"Sparkling boomberry wine? Are you kidding me?"

"I'm dead serious about my potions." She brings the bottle to her lips and takes a few big gulps before placing it back under the hover bed.

She picks up the clay pot, and using a stone pestle, she grinds the ingredients together. Finished, she studies the swirling and hazy-looking concoction. "I did my best, but I cannot overmix it, or it will lose its potency. I'm afraid it will be chunky."

I plaster a smile on my face. "Who doesn't like a good chunky potion from time to time?" Said no one ever.

Glenna puts a glass straw into the mixing pot and hands it to me. "I am fresh out of lemon slices and tiny umbrellas."

I take the rancorous-looking drink. "Very funny." The pungent odor is even worse up close.

As I lift the mixture, Glenna puts a hand on my arm. "It's still not too late to stop this."

Instead of answering her, I close my eyes, hold my nose with two fingers, and take the first gulp.

The liquid is so chunky-bitter-sour-oily-grimy that I almost spit it out. I force myself to swallow. Then to take another gulp. And another. And another. Until tears run down my face and my stomach churns. Finished, I lock my teeth together to prevent the potion from coming back up, holding the nausea at bay by sheer force of will.

Something cold and soft touches my face. Glenna wipes my cheeks with a cold, moist towel. "The worst part is over." She takes the clay pot from me.

I lie back. "Now what?" I don't feel anything. "When will it—"

The room spirals, and darkness swallows me up.

CHAPTER 83

I am bodiless. I am everywhere and nowhere. I am in the darkness of my mind. But the darkness isn't absolute. It's more like a swirling dark gray storm, with ripples of memories flashing brightly, like lightning.

My childhood plays out for a few moments, on the dark winds of my thoughts.

Here I am, smiling on my fourth birthday, looking up in adoration at Mom.

There I am, riding Fearghas into the ocean, when I am twelve.

Here is Father, kneeling by me when I am three, holding my hand with a nasty cut, and talking to me as he cleans the wound.

Here is Nic chasing me with two wiggling frogs in his hands when I am seven, his laughter ringing out loud.

There is Glenna in the woods, instructing me at age nine to pick the correct herbs and mushrooms.

Here are the sixteen-year-old twins Isa and Bella giggling as they draw on Nic's face with squid ink. Only to run away when he wakes, leaving me behind, laughing.

One memory after another appears, randomly chosen across my life.

Nothing hurts here. There is no hurry, no pain, no exhaustion. No rules. No roles to play. No responsibilities. Or perils to fear.

Glenna's voice drifts down through the eddying storm in my mind. "Focus, Lilla, on my voice. Find your deepest, most hidden memory. Find the memory that causes you the most pain."

The images speed up, whirling past me faster and faster. *There isn't a secret memory!* I want to shout, but I have no voice here.

Then the images dissipate altogether, except for one.

No, no, no! I don't want that memory! There is nothing bright about this one, with blood rising at its edges.

I fight back, trying to flee from it. With every fiber of my being, I know I don't want to go there. But the pull is relentless. Dragging me into its gaping blackness.

CHAPTER 84

In the memory, I am five years old, skipping down an empty corridor. My bright yellow dress floats around me, and it's fascinating to me.

Then I burst into a run, ahead of a tall woman with dark violet hair and dark violet eyes.

Mom's laughter rings out. "You're such a silly little girl," she says. "So much energy! Maybe all you need is some tickling to get it out of you." She pretends to chase me.

I squeal in laughter and speed up, while a small Fla'mma ball forms in my palm.

Without warning I turn around and throw the Fla'mma fireball at Mom.

She catches it, juggling it before she closes her fingers over it. When she opens up her hand, the fireball is gone. Vanished.

I stop to stare in wonder. How did she do it?

Mom bends down, placing her hands on her knees to face me. "Do you remember what we discussed?"

I nod with such vehemence that my long strands of hair bob around my face. "No magic in public."

Mom tucks a loose strand behind my ear, smiling with love. "I knew you'd remember." She straightens.

Her gaze lands on something behind me, and her expression hardens.

Six men block the other end of the corridor. Their purple servants' uniforms are ill-fitting. They are unkempt, not like the usual palace servants. The men scowl at my mom, and the hair on the back of my neck rises.

Mom bares her teeth at them in a vicious snarl in response. She pulls out a long dagger, the length of her forearm, from the sheath attached to her belt, as if she is ready to fight the men right on the spot.

My heart races. Each beat flickers the memory, blurring the edges.

"Lilla," Glenna's voice floats down. "You have to stay calm! Your body is already in too much distress."

My heartbeat slows and the memory sharpens, coming into focus again.

The six men advance on us, picking up speed with each step.

Changing her mind, Mom grabs my hand and turns around. We race away from them, taking the stairs down. My feet keep sliding off the round edges, but Mom's firm hold keeps me upright. I whimper but dare not cry.

"It's going to be all right," she says, but the running footsteps that are getting closer defy her calm words.

As we turn right, taking a narrow corridor, we run into a dead end.

Mom drops to her knees, putting down her dagger. She slams her hands on the wall. "Where is it?"

"Mommy?" I ask.

"In a minute, baby." She keeps hitting the wall. "There has to be one!"

Her right palm sinks in. A brick shifts out of its place, and a small section of the lower wall creaks open. Revealing a cubbyhole barely big enough for one person curled up.

The running footsteps are getting closer.

She looks into my eyes. "Lilla baby, you have to hide in there and stay quiet. No matter what. You understand?"

I nod, but I don't want to leave her.

Mom kisses my cheek and hugs me for a moment, her wonderful flowery scent enveloping me. "Everything will be fine."

I crawl inside the hiding hole. Mom shuts the section of the wall, and darkness descends. My breath rattles as I breathe in the hot and stinking air. My body burns, and the urge to pee has me squirming. I hit my head, and something sharp cuts into my skin, drawing blood.

I shiver and gasp for air. Blood rushes in my ears, blocking all other sounds.

Blindly, I claw at the wall, breaking nails off. My arms and legs flail. Then the wall moves, and I stumble forward.

Bright light blinds me as I lay on my belly, panting.

Holding a bloody dagger, Mom looks down on me, with two prone bodies at her feet. "No, Lilla! Get behind me!"

But I can't move. My muscles are locked.

One of the attackers lunges at me and wrenches me to my feet, holding me in front of him with a bleeding arm across my throat.

"Move and I break her neck," he says in a pain-filled voice.

I sob, staring up at Mom.

Mom freezes. "What do you want?"

"First, drop your weapon," the man says with a sneer.

She hesitates, gripping her dagger tighter, but when her gaze lands on me, she lets it drop to the floor.

"Our master warned you. Told you not to meddle. Told you to leave the ma'ha alone. If you come with us, we'll let your daughter live."

Mom's gaze shows recognition, as if she knows who their master is. "If I come with you, you'll kill my daughter and then kill me."

"I assure you—"

A spear of Lume magic bursts from her right hand, flying into the throat of the man holding me. He falls down, dragging me with him, and landing half over me.

She squats to pick up her dagger. A tall man rushes her. Rolling to the side, she slashes across his hamstrings. The man cries out, tumbling to the ground.

A third man, with black hair, swings at her. Stepping to the left, she lands a vicious kick into his knee. With a loud crunching sound, his kneecap shatters. Screaming, he curls up on the floor, holding his leg.

The fourth man, with a balding head, charges, raising his short sword to strike. Mom ducks under the strike. Swirling away, she cuts the man across his throat.

She scans the corridor. No one left standing to fight her.

"Mommy?" I cry from under the heavy weight. The man smells bad, crushing my lungs, and I cannot move.

Breathing hard, Mom hurries to me. She pushes the dead man off. Kneeling, she asks, "Lilla, baby, are you okay?"

"I'm so sorry, Mommy, I—"

"It's okay, baby." She brushes my hair off my forehead. "You're safe now."

A loud bang resonates, ear-shattering.

Mom looks down at her chest in surprise. Dark red blooms in the middle of her white tunic, spreading fast.

Behind her, a man sits with his back to the wall, his trousers soaked in blood. Smoke swirls from the barrel of his serrated pirate pistol.

Collapsing, Mom angles her body and hurls a Lume spear at the sitting man.

It slams in the man's heart. His dead body thuds on the tile floor, his pirate pistol dropping from his hand.

Mom gasps in pain, struggling to breathe.

"Mommy, I'm sorry!" I hug her, crying. "Please get up!"

"It's not your fault, baby. Just remember, don't use your magic . . ."

I shake Mom's shoulder, but she doesn't move. She lays there. As the light fades from her warm eyes. As the pool of blood around her body becomes wider. Amid my screams.

CHAPTER 85

"No!" I shout as I come to, in the Healing Center. My chest heaves from stifled sobs as the memory releases its hold.

The scent of bamboo blends with the coppery sweet smell of blood from the vivid memory. For a long second, past and present intersperse, and I see Mom's unmoving body, right on the sand-like carpet, lying in the pool of her own blood. Then the vision dissolves.

She sits on the edge of the hovering patient bed. "What happened?"

I wipe my face with both of my hands. "My mom and I got attacked by six men. They came out of nowhere." I look down at the thin blanket, my mind replaying the chain of events. "She told me to hide in a small cubbyhole . . ."

Glenna nods, squeezing my hand in silent reassurance.

"She was so capable and fearless with her dagger. She moved with it like a fighter, cutting her enemies down. But I couldn't stay hidden any longer . . . I panicked for the first time." An errant tear escapes. I wipe it, frustrated. I don't deserve to feel self-pity.

"Lilla, I'm so sorry!"

"Don't be. Now we know." Now we know that I killed my mother. Me and my claustrophobia.

CHAPTER 86

"This is a good start to understand the five light elements in their basic formation," Ragnald says, gesturing toward the colorful illustrations he set up on easels in the atrium of the royal library. The early morning sunlight shines through the glass dome ceiling, illuminating the five digi-posters stretched tightly on the easels.

I yawn as I study the illustrations. I didn't get much sleep after I left Glenna.

The first one shows a flying fireball with Fla'mma written on it. The second one has a whirling dark gray tornado and the word "Ari's." The third one displays a crack opening wide in a small patch of ground for T'erra. The fourth one presents a cascading ocean wave for A'qua. The last one has a gaping wolf maw, full of fangs, dripping blood and saliva and the word "Anima" on it.

"Fireball," Ragnald says and points at the first digi-poster, then at the rest, calling each one out by their name: "tornado, quake, wave, fangs."

"Sounds simple enough."

"They are. But they are potent in their own right."

He strides to four large urns, lined up next to each other on wooden crates with small wheels. Hints of azure rust peek through their navy blue color, hinting at their age.

Ragnald grabs the first one and wheels it to the center of the room.

"What are those?"

He straightens. "Precaution." Then heads toward the second one.

On an impulse, I focus on the second urn. As the Saage women taught me, I lift my right knee high and spread my arms wide. I step out and close my arms in a pulling motion toward my chest.

The heavy urn glides past Ragnald, past the first urn, seemingly on its own.

"I see someone has learned the famous Saage women's energy manipulation," Ragnald says and adjusts the second urn, aligning it precisely with the first one.

"It does come in handy, doesn't it?" I say, grinning. "Where do you want that one?" Ragnald indicates a spot on the floor.

While he rolls the third urn, I repeat the motion. Redirecting the fourth one's energy, I move it where the others are. Focusing to be more precise. This time it stops where I want it.

"How do they work?"

"They absorb any unwanted surplus magic. They are a new invention with a double infusion of A'qua and T'erra, a first of their kind, directly from the academia. I agreed to test them and report back. I haven't had a chance to fully recharge my wards, so it's a good thing they arrived this morning." Seeing my fallen expression, he adds, "Not that we'll need them, of course."

I am not sure I like the fact that the urns are untested. "Shouldn't we postpone the lesson? It might be safer, all things considered, to wait for your wards to recharge."

"It would take weeks. We simply don't have that much time." Ragnald pats my shoulder. "Besides, you've seen the healer, so there shouldn't be any issue now."

He raps the urns, and a loud click reverberates in the atrium. A shimmering, transparent wall of magic spreads up and out from the urns in the shape of a cube twelve feet wide.

Out of nowhere, I see my mom staring up at me as she lies bloody on the white tiles, asking me not to use my magic. Then I blink, and the fragment of the memory is gone.

It's only my grief acting up. I don't have the luxury of not using my magic. Without it, the Archgod of Chaos and Destruction wins.

Ragnald puts on red glasses and then rubs his hands together. "Now the fun begins!"

CHAPTER 87

Ragnald gestures for me to enter the space between the protective urns. I do so, resisting the urge to roll my eyes. The combination of magic and fun is an oxymoron for me.

"Now that you see the base forms of each element, it is time to get creative, if you will," Ragnald says as he studies the digi-posters. I really hope he won't choose Fla'mma, given the debacle last time. "Let's start with A'ris to create a basic tornado."

A'ris should be fine.

He moves his hands in a horizontal circle, overlapping them faster and faster until a miniature tornado appears in front of him, barely reaching his knees. "Now you try."

With a deep centering sigh, I concentrate. Hot-and-cold-and-hot-again feelings alight, making my skin glow. I find my bright sphere of magic much faster than the previous time. I separate an A'ris thread with my imaginary hand and form it into the shape of a miniature tornado.

It appears in front of me, an exact duplicate of Ragnald's. I tie the thread to the ground and look up at him.

"Well done!"

So far the lesson is going as it should. Using my magic felt easier too. I didn't even have to close my eyes to find my magic sphere.

"Most mages stick to the basic forms because it is easy to remember them, but I was always a bit of a rebel. I liked lightning as a child. There is something divine about the way a lightning bolt lights up the sky, branching into all directions." He steeples his hands together, the fingertips barely touching. Making his fingers close and open in quick succession, as if generating power, he then shoves his hands toward his minitornado.

The tornado changes, now whirling with lightning bolts.

"That's amazing," I say, studying the new tornado.

"I'd like to think so. It's one of my specialties." Ragnald smiles with a humble and proud expression. "Now you try."

"Okay." I can do this.

Separating another A'ris thread from my magical sphere, I imagine it stretching into the shapes of lightning bolts. Then I add the new thread, weaving it in carefully with the existing one.

My minitornado changes! Whirling full of lightning bolts.

"First try! You make it look easy. It only took me years to learn it."

I crack my knuckles and shake my hands out. "Watch this." I focus on the minitornado as I select an A'qua thread, shaping it into finger-size ice shards and adding it to the mix.

The tornado now swirls around, full of lightning bolts and hail.

"How remarkable!" Ragnald says. "I never thought to combine more than one type of element together without a technology to anchor it. They tend to be too unstable on their own, but that's clearly not the case with yours. Now why don't we move on to—"

"In a moment." I narrow my eyes on the minitornado. There is only one true test here—one element that caused me the most trouble.

I don't even have to look; the Fla'mma thread appears right in my imaginary hand, ready to be used. I shape the thread into small fireballs, no bigger than crystal marbles, and feed them into the whirling mix.

The miniature tornado spins with lightning bolts, ice shards, and fireballs in it.

"That is . . . I've never . . . I mean this is . . . " Ragnald says. "Keep going, Lilla! Don't stop now—you are breaking magical grounds that no mage ever achieved before."

Who knew? Me, the magical groundbreaker.

I glance at the digi-posters for inspiration. A'qua, Fla'mma, T'erra, and Anima threads float up to me, following my thoughts as if I commanded them. I shape each element into a separate miniature tornado.

Twisters of burning fire, sloshing water, whirling rocks, and twirling vines appear next to my first combination tornado.

"That's . . . uh . . . that's uh . . . five elemental tornadoes?" Ragnald's knees give out, and he lands sitting on the ground. "I think you should slow down—"

"I don't have time for slow progress." I have to push my boundaries.

I untie all the threads of the minitornadoes. I separate each one into their very essences, driven by an instinctual understanding.

The five miniature tornadoes disappear, replaced by shimmering and sparkling spheres of the elements. No bigger than melons.

"Lilla, maybe we should analyze this before—"

"I don't think so." I gather all the sparkling transparent spheres until they interpose each other. Then I shape all five elements into one twister, ten times the size of the mini ones.

A beautiful tornado swirls in front of me with all the elements harmonious inside it. Shining with all the elemental hues, like a swiveling rainbow.

Ragnald gets to his feet and strides around the urn-protected space. "I have no words to describe how astonishingly well you are doing. I think we should stop now, while we are still—"

I shake my head. "That's only five."

"Beg your pardon?"

"It's missing the sixth light element. Lume."

CHAPTER 88

Ragnald raises a hand. "I'm not sure it's a good idea to—"

"There is one way to find out." I reach for the Lume thread and weave it inside the new tornado. Shining brighter now than before, it swirls at my feet, like the most perfect creation of magic.

"It works," I say. "They all blend together as I thought." Surging blood fills my vision, replacing the image of the tornado.

Pressure builds from the magical sphere, pouring a torrent of my magic into the combined elemental tornado, fueled by the magical markings on my back.

I wrestle for control. "Not again!"

"Lilla? What's wrong?"

"What *isn't* wrong?" The pressure cracks. Wetness drips from my nose. I touch it, and my trembling fingers come away red.

No! This cannot be happening! I'm in control! I'm in—

Another wave of pressure builds. My skin glows golden white. Scorching hot and too tight.

The tornado builds, bulging. Expanding into a shapeless blob.

My control shatters.

CHAPTER 89

The magical shock wave swells, reaching the shimmering barrier from the urns. It freezes, suspended inside the protected space.

Ragnald jumps to his feet. "Lilla, get out of there!"

I leap out. The detonation stays behind.

The urns light up, emitting a sharp, piercing noise. They suck the explosion into themselves, like a giant magical void.

"Will this work?" I ask. They progress slowly, as if reeling back my magical expulsion is a lot of work.

Ragnald wrings his hands. "There is nothing to worry about."

"That's not what I asked."

A small pop sounds, and a thin crack develops on the first urn.

"Uh-oh."

When a mage says "uh-oh," is it as bad as when a healer says "oops"?

"Can you do something?" I ask. "Anything?"

He shakes his head. "Once they are activated, no one can interfere." Another small pop sounds. Another crack forms.

More popping rings out. A crack appears on the second urn. And on the third. And on the fourth.

"What happens if the urns, um, overload?"

The explosion is halfway inside the urns when the fissure on the first one widens.

Ragnald turns to me, his face pale. "It would be best if we don't find out."

We both look back at the explosion. More popping noises reverberate, and more cracks emerge on the urns while the magical blast crawls toward them ever so slowly.

Come on, please don't break on me!

Finally, the last bit of the explosion disappears.

Both Ragnald and I exhale in relief.

The first urn wobbles, vibrating faster and faster, while emanating a shrill hum. Then it disintegrates into dust at Ragnald's feet.

Then the second, third, and fourth commence to wobble, vibrate, and crumble to dust.

"I have no idea how I'll explain this to the academia."

I cringe. "Sorry I broke your, uh, protection urns."

"Don't worry about that," Ragnald says. "We have a bigger problem to deal with."

My control.

"Lilla, you are brilliant and skilled with the light elements. Not even the academia elders can do what you just showed me during this lesson. But you have less control than a first-day novice."

He is right. I can just see it—my magic exploding in my face at the worst possible time, while DLD laughs himself to death. One can only hope.

"I hate to say it, but it must be obvious even to you—I don't think you fully eliminated your magical block."

I cross my arms. "I did exactly what you told me to do."

Ragnald looks at me with a solemn expression. "I wish I knew why it's still there. But whatever you decide to do, you better do it fast. Or you won't have a chance to defeat the Arch- god of Chaos and Destruction."

CHAPTER 90

I stumble out of the library, right into a black brick wall. Ready to punch or kick something.

"Whoa there!" Callum says, catching me. "What happened, Lilla? Are you okay?"

No, I'm not okay. Instead of answering, I grab his hand and pull him after me. I don't trust myself to say anything nice right now.

Dodging the milling court members, I hurry down the corridor. As if each step could burn away my irritation with magic. Every time I make progress, it betrays me in the end. As if my magic is untamable.

When no one is looking, I duck into a private circular niche. A curving stone bench hugs the wall under a narrow window. No one can see us in this alcove unless they stop right at the entrance, but I don't expect that to happen.

"Now will you tell me what's going on?" Callum asks as we sit, frowning.

"I've failed with my magic," I say with hands in fists. "Again!"

"The palace is still standing. You sure it was a failure?"

"Not funny!" I explain to him how the second magic lesson turned to be a bigger disaster. Even after reliving that tragic day. "All this trouble for my cursed magic that's still unreliable and useless."

Callum nods, listening with full attention. As if there is no one else in the whole Seven Galaxies he'd rather be with. "Would a kiss help you feel better?" he asks, humor glinting in his blue eyes.

I pretend to think about it. "I won't know until we try."

With both hands, he clasps my neck and kisses me. Gentle but insistent. As if conveying how much he missed me. How much he needs me.

Now I know what women mean when they say a man took their breath away. "You're right. It did help."

"I feel so used now."

I pull back and slap his arm. "Because you got nothing out of it."

Callum shakes his head with mock sadness. "Not a single thing."

269

But all this joking still can't diminish the enormity of the failure I had with my magic. I don't know what to do with it anymore.

Sighing, I put my head on his shoulder. He hugs me close, stroking my back.

"Lilla, I don't think you fully dealt with your pain."

"But Glenna and I recovered the memory," I say, lifting my head to look him in the eyes.

"That's the first step."

"First? As in there are more?" I snap, losing patience. "Are you kidding me?!"

"What you experienced is still raw and new for you," he says, as if searching for the right words. "You haven't processed it yet. You seem . . . vexed. I recognize the signs of guilt."

"Is that what you think?" I ask, crossing my arms. "That I am angry?"

"You know that's not what I meant." He shoves a hand through his hair. "I won't lie to you just to spare your feelings. If that's—"

"No!" I say and reach for his hand. "I don't want you to lie to me. Ever."

"Good. No lies." Callum looks at our hands. "Which is why I wish I had better news."

"What news?" I ask.

"The rebellion will attack at the first light of dawn tomorrow."

"But that's two days earlier than what Arrov said!" The blood drains from my face. "That doesn't give me much time to find the archgod or to learn to control my magic!"

"That's not the worst of it. After the attack on the beach, I'd written a full account on the dark servants." At my alarmed expression he adds, "But I haven't sent it, because I knew it would condemn Uhna. I knew that the Teryn praelor would send his armada to clean Uhna from the corruption at all costs."

That would have been a terrible catastrophe. "Well, it's a good thing you haven't sent the report then."

"*I* didn't. Someone else did, without my authorization," Callum says with withheld anger. "And when I find out who—"

I interrupt him, "Are you telling me an even bigger Teryn armada is heading to Uhna?"

"Yes."

To devastate my home world. I have lost before my fight has even begun.

I glance away from him. A few ma'hars and ma'haras saunter past the alcove. I envy them for a second. They have no idea what's coming. Their ignorance is their shield.

But I have no such luxury. I have run out of time.

A couple of servants hurry past, unnoticed as they dash among the ma'hars and ma'haras. The court may look down on them, but without servants, the palace wouldn't be able to function.

My eyes widen.

"What is it?" Callum asks.

"We have to go." I jump to my feet. "Now."

Callum flows to his feet. "You have a plan."

"More like an idea." But it will have to do.

CHAPTER 91

"I called you here for a reason," I say and survey the large gathering in my living quarters, holding my mom's journal to my chest.

Callum leans on the wall with his arms crossed on my right, alongside his six warriors. The hilts of their swords poke above their shoulders. Their expressions emit menace, as if they're wound too tightly to wait a second longer before the action begins. Teague winks at me, ruining the tough-guy image.

Next to the Teryn warriors looms a somber Captain Murtagh with his two dozen most loyal guards. They are out of their uniforms for the first time I can remember.

Around them fidget fifty servants from all over the palace, never meeting anyone's eye longer than a second.

On my left, Arrov holds his hefty A'ice crossbow. The heavy weapon holds three layers, as if someone glued three increasingly large crossbows on top of each other to form a giant one. Dressed in white leather pants and jacket, he looks more striking than usual. He busies himself with the crossbow's aiming mechanism. A short sword by his side, and seven throwing knives, strapped to his arm, complete his arsenal.

Next to Arrov, Ragnald buries his head in a yellowed scroll, his long, silver hair falling over his shoulder. With his black mage robe that has dark brown leather straps crossing over, like a vest, he looks more like a warrior than a mage.

Glenna stands by the royal elementalist mage; she seems to have put aside her dislike of mages for today. She is dressed in black; I almost don't recognize her. She has a thin leather strip in her right hand to throw rocks with the help of her A'ris magic. Every pocket of her clothing is bulging with rocks, her ammunition. Bound by her healer's oath, she is not allowed to kill, but she is allowed to defend herself. Those rocks whirled at high speed with her magic can do some serious damage.

The twins, on the other hand, are not bound by any such oath. Dressed in identical brown leather pants and sleeveless leather vests over black shirts, they give "armed to the teeth" a whole new meaning. There are small laser pistols tucked into their boots; bigger ones strapped to the outside of their thighs; two large laser guns clipped on each side of their narrow hips; and ammo belts crisscross their chest. Each twin holds a pirate shotgun—a serrated short sword with a laser shotgun attached to its top—in their black leather gloves. Secured over their shoulders are tall rifles on leather bands. On their necks they wear black leather chokers full of finger-long shotgun shells. They grin at me, their expressions full of excitement.

Silence blankets the room, with all eyes fixed on me.

I hesitate. Do I have the right to ask them this favor? Who am I to gamble with their lives? What if this is the last time I'll ever lay eyes on them?

Suddenly there isn't enough air to breathe.

A hand comes to rest on my shoulder. Callum's.

"Somewhere inside the Crystal Palace hides the Archgod of Chaos and Destruction. He is infesting Uhna, like an island kraat. He is spreading his corruption. Killing innocent people. Our friends and family. I must stop him. But to do that, I have to find him first. I can't do this alone. I need your help."

I take a deep breath and scan the room once more. "I cannot ask you to risk your lives. You have to decide for yourselves. If you want to leave, I won't hold it against you." I pause to let the words sink in.

Nobody moves.

"What do you need us to do?" Arrov asks.

I open my mom's journal to two maps. She discovered many hidden passages in the palace and recorded them here. When I first found them, they made no sense to me. Until I overlaid the maps on top of each other.

I show the maps to the group. "With the help of these maps, we can use the hidden passages to find him."

Ragnald rubs his chin. "Even for all of us, combing the hundreds of tunnels and smuggler holes would take forever."

The mage pulls out a blank scroll and tears off a small piece. Without any warning, a thin black strand of magic rises from his palm. A keen awareness spikes my vision. Something resonates in me before repulsion takes over. He must have invoked the chaos element. Acerbus.

I grab his arm. "Ragnald, are you insane?"

He grits his teeth but keeps his eyes focused on the scroll piece. "Trust me, Lilla; I know what I'm doing." After a long moment, Ragnald disengages the Acerbus element and wipes the sweat from his forehead. He shows me the scroll. "A magical compass that will sense the presence of Acerbus—"

"Leading us to DLD faster," I finish Ragnald's sentence. "Brilliant!"

"Well, yes, I mean it would seem so," Ragnald says. When he sees Glenna's impressed nod, he practically preens. "Just happy to help."

"Break into groups of two and take to the tunnels," Teague says to the servants. "See if you can detect any signs of movement. Don't engage the dark servants. Don't take any unnecessary risks."

Jossim steps forward. "We can do that."

Callum points to a few spots on the map. "I'll have my men wait at these places for you to report. They'll follow up any leads you provide."

Jossim nods. Using his necklace, the elderly man takes a copy of the map. He organizes the servants into pairs while waiting for Ragnald to duplicate the magical compass. They leave with the six warriors.

Captain Murtagh approaches me. "May I see the map?"

I show it to him. "My guards and I will investigate all the smuggler holes." He too takes a copy of the map with his necklace.

While he is waiting for the mage to give him the magical compass, I pull the captain to the side. "Were you able to warn my, um, the ma'ha of the impending attack?"

Captain Murtagh sighs. He seemed to age a decade overnight. Arrov must have delivered the tragic news of Jorha. "I'm afraid not. Overseer Irvine wouldn't let me speak to the ma'ha or High Adviser Ellar. I couldn't even request a meeting with any of the other advisers. I had no choice but to deliver my warning to the overseer instead. But it didn't go well."

I am not surprised. "Let me guess: he didn't believe you."

Captain Murtagh shakes his head. "No, he didn't. When I refused to tell him who would provide me with such information, he relieved me of my duties 'until you can remember.'"

Now I know why his guards are all out of their uniforms. "I'm sorry. Is there no hope he'll at least prepare for an attack?"

The captain shakes his head again.

It's as if the overseer *wants* the rebels to attack the palace. To what purpose? To come out as a hero in the end somehow? Or to prove his point about the refugees and use this attack as an excuse to finally rid Uhna of them? Could *he* be the archgod disguised as a mortal?

Ragnald hands the scroll compasses to the captain, who bows his head before leaving with his guards.

Callum says, "The warning didn't work."

"No, it didn't," I say.

"The negotiation is over," Callum says, "but I am afraid the alliance between Uhna and Teryn won't happen now. Not with the report about the dark servants. But I could still try to warn the overseer—"

"What makes you think Irvine would listen to you?" I interrupt Callum. "What proof do you have? With the Teryn armada on their way, it's in our best interests to purge Uhna of DLD's corruption so the alliance can go through. We can't save the palace from the attack, but we have a chance to save Uhna from all-out destruction." And stop DLD from advancing the Era War.

"What about us?" Isa and Bella ask. "What should we do?"

Callum points at the map. "You could take the dungeons with Glenna and Ragnald, while the rest of us—"

A loud bang sounds, as if someone's trying to break down my door.

Ragnald looks up from his scroll. "Are we expecting anyone else?"

The door flies off its hinges. Irvine marches in, followed by a long line of his men.

The overseer surveys the room, smirking. When his gaze lands on me, he rubs his hands together. "Ma'hana Lilla, you are under arrest."

CHAPTER 92

Within moments, two dozen guards file into my living quarters, gripping strike-stopping rifles with long nozzles that split into two at the end. The top nozzle throws nets and paralyzing gas, while the bottom sprays concentrated A'ris-infused gel to knock everyone off their feet.

Callum pushes me behind Teague while they draw their longswords. Glenna cocks her leather strap, filled with rocks. Arrov aims his crossbow, while the twins level two pairs of laser guns at the men. Ragnald, with his eyes burning in a cerise light, balances a Fla'mma ball in each hand.

I step around Callum, refusing to hide. "What is the charge?"

Irvine's smile grows wider. "I have proof you are a known collaborator and rebel. That it was you who betrayed the classified information about the crystal mines to the rebellion leader. Ma'hana Lilla, you are a traitor."

It took him long enough to figure it out. Couldn't he have waited just a few more hours to arrest me?

I put a hand on Callum's arm, forcing him to lower his longsword. "There is no point fighting them. You have to carry on, even if it means without me."

"Lilla, you can't—"

"Stand down," I say and turn away from him with raised hands. "I surrender."

Sneering, Irvine waves to his men to step back. "Keep an eye on the others." He pulls out a pair of rusted, ugly cuffs that are five inches wide and connected by a ribbon of straw-yellow magic.

A'nima-infused cuffs? But why?

"I'd like to say I'm sorry for doing this, but I cannot stand a traitor. I never thought you, the ma'hana, would go so far as to betray your ma'ha so blatantly. You must have thought yourself above the law. But societal order must be restored, even if it means the ma'hana gets punished. If you think your father will interfere, think again. It was he who signed your sentence to the crystal mines. At least you'll get to work side by side with your precious refugees."

A reddish-yellow light flashes in Callum's eyes. I stop him with a glance before he could decide to attack. They cannot win against the superior strike-stopping weapons.

The overseer raises the cuffs. "These were invented to drown their victims in their own fear. It's the infusion of the A'nima that makes the victim's worst fear turn into pure terror. Amplifying it until their mind breaks. Rendering the wearer into a docile, drooling *thing*. Too insane to consider escape. Effective, wouldn't you say?"

"For decades, the guards were forbidden to use these cuffs, but I authorized them again. They had been banned because people died if they wore the cuffs too long. Of course, no one really knows what 'too long' means. Everyone has their own capacity for unfiltered terror. I wonder how long you'll last."

I yawn into Irvine's face. The twins snicker in appreciation.

Irvine, with face turning purple, slams the cuffs on my wrists, locking them with a loud click.

I feel nothing. I smirk at the lord. "Is that the best you've got?"

The overseer raises an eyebrow in superiority just as thin, transparent yellow ribbons of A'nima rise from the cuffs. The tendrils quest in the air before smashing into my skin.

Fear, all-encompassing and bone-chilling, washes over me. The room turns hazy in my vision. My mind screams with thoughts: *This is the end! You failed! There is no way out!*

I fall to my knees, clasping my head as if I could silence the torrents of terror.

The twins cry out. Arrov catches Glenna when she leaps toward me. Teague gets in the face of the overseer, shouting and causing a commotion.

Callum drops down by me. "Lilla, talk to me." His voice sounds distorted in my ears, deafened by the sound of my heart's beating. I try to talk, but only a whimper escapes.

Ragnald says, "It is the oldest and the worst of our magic infusion. It's nearly perfect, and there is nothing I can do with my magic to disable them. Help her before they take full hold of her mind and she goes insane, or worse."

Callum clenches his hands. "Help her how?"

Another wave of fear cascades over me. Thoughts induced by the cuffs reverberate in my mind: *You are pathetic and useless. You failed the refugees and you failed your world! You are worthless!* I tear at my hair to silence the blame.

"Make her focus on you instead of the cuffs," Ragnald urges. "Hurry!"

"Lilla, listen to my voice," Callum implores. "Fight! I know you can do it!"

Ragnald covers his face with a hand, muttering, "Pathetic."

I curl my fingers into fists until my nails draw blood. The momentary pain is enough to cut through the fog of terror. "I can't!" I already sound crazed.

The cuffs jab more ribbons of A'nima into my wrists in response. *You are PITIFUL! Weak and useless! You can't even control your magic! Why don't you just give up?*

It's not working," Ragnald snaps. "Try harder!"

"What is going on there?" The overseer peeks around Teague, but the colonel bodychecks him. The twins with Arrov join Teague, causing a louder ruckus, yelling, "We demand to see the ma'ha!" while Glenna blocks the overseer's view by casually taking a step toward me and standing in the eyeline of the overseer.

Callum's face, wearing a determined look, comes into my view again. He grabs my shoulders. "Lilla, I need you to fight this for me. You hear me? Fight the cuffs for me!"

You can't help Uhna! Everyone will die! Because of you! I rock back and forth. "No! No, no, no, no, no!"

Callum holds my face in his warm hands. He kisses me, hard, as if he could pour all his feelings, all his strength into that one kiss. "I never thought I would feel this way. I never thought that I would find you on this strange planet. I never thought that I would fall in love. You hear me? I love you, Lilla! Fight the cuffs for me!"

For a blessed moment, my mind is clear. "Callum . . ." I whisper and reach for him. "Callum, I—"

Then the cuffs flare up with thick ribbons of A'nima, sending a torrent of dread. *You killed your mother! You'll kill him too! That's what you do! You're a killer! Die! Die! DIE!*

Something snaps in my mind. Wetness gushes from my nose, and my eyes roll back in my head.

CHAPTER 93

You hear me? I love you, Lilla! Fight the cuffs for me! Callum's words echo in that sleepless and unconscious place that's neither dreaming nor awake.

The power of those words shines like a beacon. Cutting through the fog of fear I am drowning in, they shine brighter and brighter. Leaving no room for anything but that love. Until I am no longer terrified. Until the cuffs have no more power over me.

The weight of the cuffs falls off my mind. Receding. Leaving behind a colossal headache. Tingling heat emanates from the sybil talisman on the back of my neck. It trickles into my spine, into my veins, healing whatever damage the cuffs had done.

"*Now* you're helping me?" I mutter and rub my neck, earning a painful zap from the jewel.

I open my eyes to see filthy gray stone tiles. Island kraats scattering on eight legs in front of me.

Oh, fishguts! I'm in the dungeon!

I sit up. My grimy cell is barely big enough for me to stretch out my legs.

"Took you long enough to wake up," Beathag says from the other side of the metal door.

Instinctively, I reach for my magic, but I can't find the bright sphere. The cuffs must be blocking it.

I get to my feet. Through a tiny window in the cell, I see that darkness has fallen. I must have been passed out for hours.

Oh, buckets of fishguts! There has to be a way out of here! Dawn is only hours away, when the rebellion will attack. Any second now, the Teryn armada will arrive to take care of Uhna's corruption problem. I cannot waste any more time!

Beathag smirks. "There is no escape from here."

I face her. "You have to let me out!"

To my surprise the metal door opens, its hinges creaking loudly. Beathag steps into view with two beefy prison guards at her back. "You're right. I won't keep you here." She gestures to the guards.

The two men drag me out of the cell. I struggle against their hold. "Let me go!"

"He wants me to take you to him," Beathag says. "But I have something much better in mind. Something that will make you suffer more. You won't get off that easily."

He who? "Let me go and fight me!"

"I won't fight you," Beathag says, "not like that. You think you're better than I am? That you get to judge me?"

"You are a sea vip—"

She slaps me across my face. "You're no different than I am! I tried to make up for the past, but you couldn't forgive me. Who's the cruel one now?"

My cheek burns where she hit it. "You had no right to interfere in my life!"

"Oh, I had every right." Beathag's expression turns cruel. "I am your sister, after all."

CHAPTER 94

"What did you say?" I recoil from Beathag, but the two prison guards restrain me, their meaty fingers digging into my skin.

"Well, *half* sister," she corrects.

"You lie," I stammer. "You cannot be my sister!"

"Let me tell you a story—it's a bit cliché, but true. There was a young, gullible maid working in the palace twenty-three years ago. She admired the ma'ha. Naturally, her admiration grew into adoration. When he chose her from among the many, she was so happy. But that happiness only lasted until the ma'ha learned that she was pregnant. He had her thrown out of the palace by one of his advisers because he was too cowardly to take care of it on his own."

"I don't believe you!"

"I fought, clawed, and crawled my way here. I had a plan to avenge my mother. Then I met you, my half sister, who clearly needed my guidance."

"Enough with rehashing the past!"

Beathag grabs my chin, her nails digging in painfully, and forces me to look at her. "You will hear me out! At first I didn't want to be your friend. Friends only cause complications. But you were pathetic—falling in love with the first boy who was nice to you. Planning to run away with him. You had everything, and you didn't even know it. Despite what my instincts told me, I acted on your behalf. I should have known you wouldn't appreciate it! You derailed my plans for years when our father sent me away to spare your feelings. But I found my way back in the end, didn't I? Who knew he'd be so happy to see me that he'd marry me right away? Well, I did."

Realization sinks in. "If what you're telling is true, then you married your own father. *Our* father!"

Suddenly bile rises in my throat, and I throw up.

Beathag jumps out of the way before it can land on her feet. "I see *now* you believe me," she says, then gestures to the guards. "Bring her."

"Where are you taking me?"

281

Beathag leads us out of the dungeon, heading down a dim path toward one of the smuggler tunnels. "It seems once you sign a marriage contract with the Aak, they take it very seriously. The crown prince's father doesn't care how you get to their world, willing or not. And once you're there, you'll wish you were dead."

"You can't do this to me!"

Beathag turns to me. "Oh, yes I can! It's a pity you won't be here, though, to see my revenge."

"What are you going to do?"

She grins. "I am finally close to completing my goal I started all those years ago. I will be queen of Uhna, hailed for thousands of years as the monarch who brought prosperity—"

"You can't be queen. Uhna already has a ma'ha. You'll have to go through Father first."

"What makes you think I haven't already done that? Poor, *poor* Father. He hasn't been feeling all that well lately. Not even Great Healer Robley can figure out the mysterious illness that has him wasting away."

"You are poisoning him!" I lunge at her, but a sweaty arm slams across my throat, nearly choking me.

Pink, transparent ribbons rise from her. "It's not 'poison' per se. It's not my fault his brain can't handle my constant persuasion. And there is nothing you can do about it."

Something whistles by my ear. The guard behind me groans in pain, his arm loosening on my throat.

Then an explosion resonates through the tunnel.

CHAPTER 95

I push away from the slackened hold of the guard. The beefy man collapses to the ground, his eyes unseeing.

"You!" Beathag, pale-faced, stares into the darkness. "I thought you died!"

Taking advantage of the distraction, I swipe at her with both of my hands still confined in the cuffs.

The second guard grabs my arm, preventing me from reaching her.

Beathag runs past me, escaping down the tunnel.

"Let me go!" I kick and hit the guard with everything I have.

Another loud bang sounds.

The stocky guard's eyes roll back into his head. He drops to the ground.

I poke him with my foot. He stays unmoving.

Running footsteps ring out.

I lift my cuffed hands in front of me in preparation for a fight. "Who's there?"

Belthair appears, holding a still-smoking pirate rifle. "Who do you think?"

"What are you doing here?" A terrible thought pops into my mind. "Has Xor sent you to do away with me?"

Instead of answering, Belthair pulls a small dagger from the sleeve of his leather jacket. Its blade shimmers with A'nima.

I shy away from him.

"No one sent me 'to do away' with you." He grabs my shoulder. "Now will you stop fidgeting, for godsake?"

Oh. "Fine." I lift my hands. He cuts between the cuffs.

The cuffs fizz with electric yellow light, then crack open. They fall off, clattering to the ground. I kick the vile things away. I pull a thin thread of Lume, now accessible, from my magical sphere. I wrap the thread around my hand for comfort. I never thought I'd be so happy to have it.

Belthair puts his dagger away. "Nice glow you're sporting."

"Why are you here?" I ask, lowering my hand.

"Is that the thanks I get for saving you?" He shoulders the leather strap of his pirate rifle.

I'm not going to admit to him that I needed help. "I was doing just fine without you."

Belthair snorts. "As if."

I turn my back to him and head toward the dungeon. At least I *think* I am going in the right direction. "If all you want is to gloat, you can do that alone. I have things to take care of."

"Don't act so snooty, Lilla," Belthair says and joins me. "I came to apologize."

I stumble. "Could you repeat that? Something must be wrong with my ears."

"I deserved that. I know I haven't been treating you nicely—"

"Try 'nasty.'"

"But when I heard from Arrov what happened the night Xor got injured, I've been doing some thinking. You were right. Xor has only one goal in mind: to attack the palace. He completely ignores the needs of the refugees. Jorha's death only made him obsessed with his plan. Like it's his revenge or something. This is not what I signed up for. He's abandoned all that we fought for. So I quit, too."

"Are you going to blame me for your quitting, too?"

"I deserve that." Belthair drags his top right hand through his hair while crossing his lower four arms. "I know I've hurt you. I was still angry at you. I believed that you changed your mind. Then I remembered how shocked you looked, as if you didn't know that the guards and your father would be there."

"I didn't. I swear."

He gives a half smile. "I realize that now. It was easier to stay angry at you than letting go of my grudge."

"Does that mean you forgive me?"

He nods. "I should have done it sooner. I came to talk to you, but before I could leave the gateway, I saw you getting arrested. I figured I'd stick around to see where all this goes."

"I'm glad you did." I mean it. It's a nice change not to fight with him for once. "Thank you."

Belthair shrugs. "Don't mention it. It seems I am fresh out of causes to fight for."

I resume my hike. "How about fighting the Archgod of Chaos and Destruction?"

He turns me ninety degrees around, correcting my path. "I thought you'd never ask."

CHAPTER 96

"Where is she?!" Callum bellows.

Something hits the dungeon wall with a metallic bang, near the hidden passage where Belthair and I are. It sounds as if Callum has torn the door off of my cell and then thrown the door in his tantrum.

"There is no need to dismantle the dungeon," Teague says in a calm voice. Yep. I was right. "I'm sure Lilla is not far away."

He has no idea. Now I just have to figure out how to open this wall. I push at the bricks until something clicks.

A small segment creaks open. Belthair and I step through. Blinded for a moment by the bright light of the dungeon's Fla'mma torches, I halt.

"See?" Teague says as if he conjured us personally. "There she is!"

From one blink to the next, I am lifted by my waist. Callum hugs me so tightly that a few vertebrae pop in my back. He buries his face in the crook of my neck. "I've found you."

I hug him around his neck. "It seems that you did." I move to kiss his cheek, but he turns his head until our lips meet.

"Get a room, you two," Arrov says with a growl. "We don't have time for this."

Callum pulls away. "Jealousy ruins your cool image." He lowers me to my feet. "Are you okay, Lilla?"

"I'm fine."

"What is *he* doing here?" Arrov asks.

Callum glares at Belthair. "That's a good question."

"If it weren't for Belthair, I would be on my way to Aak by now." I fill in the others of Beathag's visit and her plans. When I get to the part that she is my half sister, everyone looks stunned and a little green around the edges.

"That's horrifying," Isa and Bella say together, and dry heave.

"I'm so sorry," Glenna says, shaking her head.

The Teryn men and Arrov curse, each in his own language, while Belthair spits to the side in disgust.

"I knew I shouldn't have married those two," Ragnald mutters.

Hurried footsteps sound, and everyone tenses.

Jossim bows his head when he reaches us. "We found it, Ma'hana. We found the tunnel leading to the Archgod of Chaos and Destruction."

CHAPTER 97

"You don't understand, uh, Colonel, uh, sir," insists Jossim. "You can't get to the secret tunnel's entrance that easily."

Teague raises an eyebrow. "Why is that?"

The older man wrings his wrinkled hands. "Because it is hidden in the main support column, in the middle of the main hall, sir. At this time of night, the hall is full of ma'hars and ma'haras. There is no way to sneak your group in without being seen. You'll just have to wait a few hours."

Callum shakes his head. "We cannot wait that long. There has to be another way." He gestures to Ragnald. "Show me the map." The mage unfolds the scroll, holding it in front of him.

Callum asks Jossim, "Where is the entrance to the secret passage?"

With a trembling hand, the older man points at the scroll. "Right here, General."

He traces the passage while Teague glances over Callum's shoulder. The two men exchange a look, then crane their heads to stare at the ceiling.

Ragnald frowns at the scroll, then he too looks upward. "Huh."

"What?" Arrov asks, taking the scroll out of the mage's hand. Belthair steps next to him so he can see it too. After a moment they both say, "No way."

I look up but see nothing special. "What is it?"

"Could it be that easy?" Arrov asks.

Callum nods. "It's right there."

"What's there?" I ask.

Belthair frowns. "But how are we supposed to—"

Teague pulls his longsword from its sheath. "Easy."

"Will someone please explain what's going on?" Glenna demands.

Teague slams his palm on the hilt of his sword, making it open into a weapon that looks like multiple longswords fused together. In the middle of it is a bright green laser core. Standing in a wide stance, Teague blasts the ceiling with multiple green shots. Chunks of stone rain at our feet.

The twins giggle and jump out of the way while Glenna asks, "Are you out of your mind?"

Teague puts away his now back-to-normal sword. "We don't need an entrance when we can make our own."

Ragnald nods. "Brilliant."

I point at the gaping hole twenty feet above us. "How are we going to get up there?"

Teague winks at me, then jumps. It's as if he has springs for legs—he makes the distance with ease and catches the jagged edge of the hole with his right arm. Dangling for a moment, he pulls himself up, then squats by the opening. "Next."

"What does he mean, 'next'?" I ask, but Callum grabs me by the waist and without any preamble propels me up with one big throw.

For a second I fly, as if I've grown wings. Then Teague grabs my hands and pulls me up.

"A little warning next time," I say, breathless.

Teague laughs. "Don't tell me you didn't like it."

I did. "That's beside the point."

The twins squeal in delight below us. Isa says, "My turn!" and steps up to Callum with her arms raised.

Glenna rolls her eyes. "Brat."

Callum repeats the process with her, then with Bella, and lastly with Glenna. Teague pulls each woman up with ease.

Jossim smiles at Callum, embarrassed. "I wish you all good luck, but—"

Callum interrupts him by putting a hand on the older man's thin shoulder. "We couldn't have done it without your help."

Jossim bows and then leaves the dungeon.

Callum turns to Ragnald, but the mage waves him off. "I'll have none of that." Using his T'erra magic, Ragnald builds stairs out of the rubble. With his hands crossed behind his back, he strolls up and through the hole. The steps turn to dust behind him.

"Show-off," I say to Ragnald, who shrugs with mock humbleness while checking to see what Glenna thinks.

Arrov smirks at Callum. "As if I need your help." Lifting his A'ice crossbow, he taps on its side to reconfigure it. Then he shoots a small dart with a thin wire attached at its end into the ceiling. With the crossbow's retracting mechanism, Arrov has it pull him up until he is close enough to climb into the hole.

Belthair appears next to us, stepping out of a gateway, just as Callum jumps up, clearing the distance in a single leap.

We all look into the swirling gloom of the tunnel that leads to the Archgod of Chaos and Destruction.

There is nothing left but to follow it.

CHAPTER 98

"How much farther do we have to go?" Isa asks. Her voice is loud enough to carry in the near-pitch darkness of the narrow and twisting tunnel.

"For the hundredth time," Glenna snaps, casting a weak light with her necklace, "we'll get there when we'll get there. Now be quiet!"

The tunnel opens up a bit. We all straighten from our hands and knees. My foot slides on a slippery patch of stone, and I bump my head on the low protrusion of the ceiling. "Ouch." I rub the spot. Me, strong warrior. DLD should quake in his boots.

Callum steadies me by my waist. "I'd kiss it better, but it really isn't the time."

I lean back into him. "Since when did that ever stop you?" He chuckles.

Isa cries out at the front, "Eek! Cobwebs! I'm not touching them."

"That's what she said," Bella says.

The twins and the men snicker.

"My gods, you two are idiots," Glenna says. "Would you just grow up and shut up already? Your voices are sharp, like dying island kraats. I bet the dark servants know we're coming by now because of you!"

"If they knew we were coming," Ragnald says from the back, "they would have already ambushed us at the last turn. Picking us off one by one."

A thud sounds. Ragnald says, "What was that for?!"

"Stop scaring the women!" Arrov says with a hiss.

"Everyone shut up!" Belthair snaps. "This is not a stroll down the beach. It's a deadly mission."

Isa and Bella snort. "Someone still thinks *he* is in charge," they say in singsong voices.

Teague snaps his fingers at the front of our line. "Children, stop bickering. Or this is the last time I'll ever take you into battle."

That shuts everyone up as reality sinks in. We are heading into battle. To defeat the Archgod of Chaos and Destruction. While he is still in his mortal form and vulnerable. Should be easy.

"Ugh! What's that smell?" Isa asks, making retching sounds. "Glenna, was that you?"

"I'm behind you, you imbecile!" Glenna gags, too. "That's horrible! You should own it, instead of blaming it on others. Also, a change in your diet might be in order."

"What are you talking about?" I sniff. The smell hits me like a punch in my nose. It is rotting and putrid. It churns my stomach. I know this stink: dark servants.

"We're getting closer," Ragnald says, his voice muffled as if he covered his mouth with a hand.

The tunnel ends, widening into a small area that branches into four tunnels. I look at the map my mom made, but this area is not on it. "I have no idea which direction to go."

We all come to a stop and study the four gaping openings and the darkness beyond.

Isa and Bella ask, "Now what?"

Belthair crosses all his arms. "We could split up and—"

"Out of the question," Callum interrupts him. "We are not separating."

Teague raises a hand. "Someone's coming."

Glenna frowns. "How do you know that? I don't hear anything."

Then we hear it.

Footsteps. Multiple footsteps, heading toward us.

CHAPTER 99

Callum, Teague, and Belthair unsheathe their swords, while Arrov aims his crossbow, all taking up defensive positions at the tunnel entrances. Ragnald readies his magic, holding a huge Fla'mma ball in each of his hands, his eyes blazing cerise. Isa and Bella drop to one knee, each clutching a pair of laser guns. Glenna, using her A'ris magic, has rocks hovering in front of her while she cocks her loaded leather string at shoulder level. I tense, readying for a fight.

We stare at the four openings.

Out of the first tunnel steps an average-looking man, same height as I am and not much older. He wears a long white coat over a white shirt and pants. He studies our group with an unfazed expression. Dozens of rotting dark servants surround him, like loyal dogs.

This must be the Archgod of Chaos and Destruction.

From the second tunnel, two dark servants drag an all-too-pale Father. His expression is confused, as if he is unable to process what's happening or still is under Beathag's persuasion. "Daughter, what are you doing here? What is going on?"

From the third tunnel, a dozen dark servants march High Adviser Ellar and Nic, with their arms raised in surrender. Nic tries to get to Father, but the dark servants restrain him. "Who are you and what do you want from us?"

High Adviser Ellar looks around with wide eyes. "You cannot do this to us!"

Through the fourth and last tunnel, Beathag glides out, holding Irvine's arm and looking satisfied and not a bit scared.

"You!" Nic points at her. "I should have known you were behind this!"

Beathag laughs. "I've chosen the winning side. I told you I'll be queen. All I had to do is prove my loyalty." She glances at the high adviser, then bows toward the archgod.

Irvine lifts Beathag's hand and kisses it. "Together we'll rule more than just Uhna as long as we serve the Archgod of Chaos and Destruction. Someone who'll appreciate our talents."

293

"Enough with chitchat," DLD says.

Fear washes over us, radiating from the archgod in thick pulses.

"Your camouflage is good, I must admit," the Archgod of Chaos and Destruction says to Callum. "I expected the last Lumenian to be more . . . special. Give up now. I have ruined your plans of alliance with these people. You won't get any help from them."

Last Lumenian?

"You're the Archgod of Chaos and Destruction," Callum says and laughs. "I thought you'd be smarter, but I'll have to live with that disappointment."

More ripples of shock and fear and terror inundate us.

The men clench their teeth. Their muscles strain as they fight the effects of the archgod. Ragnald shrugs his shoulders, as if getting rid of a muscle cramp. Glenna grimaces in pain, while Isa and Bella shake their heads, looking dazed. I chant under my breath "It's not real!" until the effects wear off.

"You wouldn't know a Lumenian if she stood right in front of you," I say.

"You? It can't be you!" The archgod's expression turns incredulous. "You are nothing like a Lumenian!"

If I had a credit every time someone pointed that out . . . I reach for a thread of Lume, wrapping it around my arm. "How is this for proof?" I raise my arm, which glows golden white and bright.

"Loch Ramor, I must wonder how you made such a mistake," the archgod says.

Loch Ramor? Who is *that*?

"I have hunted the Lumenians to near extinction," the archgod continues, "but it doesn't have to end here. Join my side, with your magic at my service, and I leave you alive and your planet untouched. Or suffer the consequences."

I behold my family.

Nic shakes his head. "Don't do it, sis! Don't—" A dark servant grabs his hair, jerking his head back and silencing him. Glenna cries out in anger.

Father returns my gaze, and for a second his eyes are clear. "Remember, you are more resilient than you know. Remember that you are from the proud ruling house of Serrain. We don't give in to threats. Ever."

High Adviser Ellar opens his mouth, but a dark servant shoves a blade at his throat, preventing him from speaking.

My gaze travels over my friends.

Callum and Teague, wearing expressions of outrage, glower at the arch-god, clearly itching to attack. Arrov moves his crossbow from side to side, as if unable to decide whom to shoot first. Ragnald narrows his eyes on the archgod, his magic flickering in his hands. Belthair snarls at the dark servants, brandishing short swords in his three right hands. Glenna and the twins are the only ones looking at me. Understanding, fear, and fury mix in their expressions.

"What's your answer?" DLD demands and waves a hand.

A dark servant presses its blade deeper into Father's throat, drawing a thin red line.

My heart beats so hard, it's as if it relocated into my throat. It doesn't matter how much Father and I fought, how much we disagreed, and how far we drifted from each other. He is still my family. I still love him. I can save him and Nic. I can save my friends, the refugees, and everyone on Uhna if only I join the side of the archgod.

Part of me aches to accept this deceptively simple offer. The part of me that's a young ma'hana at heart.

But I am not that person anymore. I've been a rebel. I accepted the role of sybil. I joined this fight to save billions of innocents in the Seven Galaxies.

"I won't accept your offer. You had my mother killed. You killed Deidre trying to corrupt her. You killed millions, corrupting life in your image. I will stop you."

DLD laughs. "You think I had your mother killed?"

"The Lady said—"

"She blamed me, didn't she?" The archgod smiles. "She lied."

"How do I know you're not lying to me now?"

"You don't." The archgod smiles wider. "I said there will be consequences, didn't I?" and snaps his fingers.

As if in slow motion, High Adviser Ellar lowers his hands. He pulls a curved dagger out of a hidden sheath under his jacket. Like a graceful dancer of death, he grabs Nic by his shoulder and slashes my brother's throat.

CHAPTER 100

"NO!" Glenna and I scream as red sprays in a torrent.

Ellar drives his dagger into Father's chest, stabbing him three times in quick succession.

"That's enough, Loch Ramor," the archgod says.

Swaying, Nic presses a hand against the wound. Glenna lunges toward him, but Teague restrains her.

"My master doesn't lie," Ellar, or rather *Loch Ramor*, says and lowers his dagger. "I was the one who had your mother killed."

"Why?" I ask. All I want to do is rush to my family and save them. But I can't.

"I had absolute power over the ma'ha until your mother came along. I warned her many times to stay away from him and not to interfere with Uhnan politics. But she was too stubborn. Like you. I had no choice but to kill her."

"How could you do this?!"

"It was quite easy," Loch says. "Everything that happened to you was by my design."

The realization of his treachery hits me as memories unfold.

After Mom died, he was always there to support me. Like a friend.

When I was fifteen, I received a few ancient tomes from Ellar. Stories of faraway adventures where the hero ran away from his oppressive family to become free. I remember how Ellar consoled me after I fought with Father, only to have "meaningful discussions" afterward about those stories, to further plant the seed.

When I was sixteen, Ellar was there in Father's antechamber, when Belthair was first assigned to guard me. It didn't take long for Belthair and me to plan our "grand escape."

When I was seventeen, Ellar encouraged me to leave the palace with Glenna. He told me it would do me some good, as if he knew Glenna and I would end up in the refugee camp.

A day before Father's marriage, Ellar sat down with me to help me face the difficult feelings of getting a new stepmom. He hinted how wrong it must feel that Father never married Mom. How Ellar wished he could voice this. And I did. I spoke up at the wedding, like a mindless puppet.

To escape my humiliation, I ran to the kitchen. Which Ellar probably knew would happen, since I often showed up for our discussions holding still-warm pastries. I confided to Eita who, was then caught by Irvine, which led me to the refugee camp trying to save her. But my claustrophobia made me bolt—straight to Xor, and to the rebellion. As if per design—a perfect chain of events architected by Ellar.

My hands curl into fists. "You!"

"Exactly," Ellar says.

"Why?" I say with a snarl. I never thought I could hate someone. Until now.

"I had to fix the problem your stubborn mother created. You were so much like her—stubborn and defiant. There was a small chance that you could ruin all my years of work. Especially once you figured out your magic. I had to make sure you were under control. My control."

All those years I trusted him and listened to his advice. All were lies. Manipulations.

"Now everything is progressing as I intended," Ellar continues. "The rebellion will attack at the same time as the Teryn armada will arrive. They can kill each other off, then my master will finish the rest. In all this chaos, no one will be surprised when the heir disappears and the ma'ha ends up gravely injured, creating an opening for a new regime. A queen with her faithful adviser."

"I won't let you!" I shout.

I take a step toward them, but the DLD and his entourage withdraw into the tunnels, hauling Father and Nic with them.

Glenna wails next to me, collapsing to the ground.

"There is no time for this," I say and pull her to her feet. "We're going after DLD."

We race through the closest tunnel, bursting into a large cavern. We stop at the edge of a deep chasm, a hundred feet across. Around the circumference of the cavern runs a narrow ledge, barely wide enough for two people.

It spirals down, disappearing from view. From the ledge, a multitude of tunnels twist off, like a hive. All empty of dark servants.

"Where are they?" I demand.

Teague points up. "There."

Twenty feet above us, a rock platform floats in midair. On that platform, the Archgod of Chaos and Destruction, Ellar, Beathag, and Irvine gather. At their feet lie Father and Nic, motionless.

Stone steps appear descending from the platform all the way to us.

Ragnald eyes our surroundings. "We need a plan."

"They're going to bleed to death!" Glenna cries. "I have to get to them!"

Arrov shakes his head. "We can't just run up there."

Teague kicks a stone step, but it stays in place. "If they had a sign with the word TRAP written on it, it couldn't be any more obvious. We should—"

Fog the plan! I sprint up, taking the steps two at a time.

"Lilla, no!" Callum shouts, following after me. When his feet land on the first few stones, they disintegrate, falling into the canyon. There is no sound when they reach the bottom.

Callum jumps back, and Teague pulls him to safety.

I reach the rock platform. "I'm here. Now let my family go."

Beathag laughs. "She still thinks she can make demands."

Ignoring her, I kneel by Father and Nic, pressing my hands to the worst of their injuries.

Beathag sniffs. "It's too late for them. Look at you, soaked in the blood of your family. Tell me, does it hurt knowing *you* killed them?"

I lunge at Beathag. Irvine intercepts me before I can reach her.

Callum and Teague land on the rock platform, crouching by my family. Callum catches my eye, his expression torn. "Lilla—"

Save them! I implore him with my eyes.

He picks up Father, while Teague scoops up Nic with the utmost care. Before any of the others can react, they leap off, clearing the canyon. They place the injured by Glenna. She drops to her knees, channeling her healing magic into them.

"Now you can't hurt my family anymore," I say. "What *can* you do?"

"I'll show you," Irvine says with a leer and grabs my arm. When I move to twist away, he slaps me across the face.

The Archgod of Chaos and Destruction stops Irvine with a raised hand. "That's enough for now."

Glaring down into the cavern, the archgod says, "Kill them, my children!"

CHAPTER 101

Dark servants fill the cavern, swarming around my friends on the thin ledge. They attack with claws, teeth, and blunt weapons.

Callum and Teague cut down many, while Arrov shoots crossbow darts into the eyes and throats of their attackers.

Belthair, Ragnald, and the twins guard Glenna and my family, blasting the mindless servants with laser shots and Fla'mma balls.

For every dark servant that falls, three new ones take its place, giving the fallen enough time to regenerate and attack again.

"No one will interfere anymore," the Archgod of Chaos and Destruction snaps. Dark smoke emerges from him, stabbing into the platform under my feet.

The platform shakes. Jagged rocks, conical in shape like stalagmites, burst out of the ground at the edges of the platform. They shoot up all around us, meeting at the top and then curving downward to form a lethal cage. More rocks, like terrible thorns, proliferate on every surface of the stalagmites, leaving no room to get through.

Irvine stumbles, releasing me. I step back from him. A sharp rock thorn pricks my back. I jump away. My claustrophobia screams, *Run! Flee!* but there is nowhere to escape to.

DLD lifts his hands palms up. The platform rises higher, until my friends seem like nothing but small figures. Dizziness from the height blurs my vision. Great. I needed another phobia.

Beathag smirks. "There is nowhere for you to go."

"Is pointing out the obvious your new role?" I ask her, pretending to be calm. But my claustrophobia clamors at me. Robbing me of air. I force myself to take even breaths. I can't panic now!

"You've always struggled with your claustrophobia," Loch says, as if commenting on the weather. "Such crippling weakness. So easy to take advantage of it."

"At least I am not a psychopath," I say, "hiding behind a web of lies!"

"The road to power is forged with lies and lives," Loch says. "I have no regrets. The truth is, you're too small-minded. Can't grasp the cleverness of my actions. I manipulated you for most of your life without you even realizing it. I know you better than you know yourself."

"Stop pretending that you're some kind of mastermind," I say. "All your false logic hides a coward. How is that for truth?"

His eyes glint with anger. The first real emotion. "I have no use for the truth. I buried it deeply a long time ago. Lies are natural to me. Something you and I have in common."

"We are nothing alike!" As a rebel I lied to protect my friends, but those days are over. "You are a cold and calculating killer!"

"I reinvented myself," Loch says, ignoring my jab, "to fit in among the overindulged and entitled highborns. I derived my new name from my initials 'L' and 'R' to be reminded that I can only count on myself. To keep myself focused on one goal: making Uhna great again, where merit speaks louder than credits. I am but a hairbreadth away from completing it."

"You never cared for Uhna!" I shout. "You'll sacrifice everyone until there's no one left to enjoy the 'greatness'!"

"Some casualties are unavoidable," Loch admits. "It's the only way to liberate Uhna. A chance to start over. On the side of the Archgod of Chaos and Destruction."

"Your father's tampering almost derailed my plans." Loch bares his teeth. "He invited those Teryn barbarians, allowing them to bully us into an alliance. One that would have made Uhna a vassal to them. Enslaving us. Everything was spiraling out of control. But I righted it just in time."

"You are insane!" I spit at Loch. My saliva hits his chin and slowly drips to the ground.

He raises his curved dagger to strike, but the Archgod of Chaos and Destruction intervenes. "Enough! Now that I have the correct Lumenian in my hands, I have to ask, Loch Ramor: Did you never wonder how I would take your manipulation of me?"

Loch pales. "Master, I can explain."

I take advantage of their lack of attention. Looking down at my arm, with the thread of Lume still on it, I gather more magic on top of it.

Beathag narrows her eyes. I school my expression into one of grieving until she glances away.

I shape the Lume into a spear and cock my arm, aiming at his chest.

Beathag shouts, "Watch out!"

Loch pushes the archgod out of the way.

The magical spear goes wide, grazing the god at the shoulder. Dark blood blooms on his shirt.

The archgod shrieks in pain, stumbling a few steps. His hand shakes as he touches his shoulder with an expression of utter shock.

Irvine grabs me by my shirt. "You stupid wench!"

Pinching the flesh between his thumb and forefinger, I twist his arm.

With a surprised shout, he releases his hold.

Purple-faced, he lunges for me again. "I'll teach you obedience!"

Before Irvine can reach me, I kick him in the middle of his chest. The force of the kick propels him backward, right onto a jagged, sharp stalagmite. It pierces through the overseer's chest with a terrible squelching sound.

Beathag screams, rushing to Irvine's side.

He flails on the stalagmite, blood pouring from his mouth. With a loud crunch, the rock breaks off. Irvine tumbles over the edge of the platform, into the gaping abyss.

"No!" Beathag shouts and attacks me with her hands raised like claws. "I'll kill you for this!"

As she rushes me, I jump up and kick out with my right leg. She flies back, straight through the hole in the stalagmite cage. Plunging off the rock platform.

"Enough of this!" the Archgod of Chaos and Destruction yells. The jagged stalagmite re-forms over the gap.

"Give me power, master!" Loch demands, grabbing the archgod's arm. "I will defend you!"

The archgod shakes off Loch's hand. "If you are waiting for The Lady to show up, don't bother. She is too spineless to be here. Instead, she'll let you die in Her name. Joining my side would hurt Her more than anything. You would be the most formidable Ankhar in the Seven Galaxies."

"Never!"

The archgod points at the cavern walls. "Let me remind you of the consequences of your refusal."

CHAPTER 102

Every surface of the expansive cavern flickers, and images appear. They reveal glimpses of terrible chaos the archgod wreaks all over my home world.

There is Xor, leading his rebellion forces with a determined expression to attack the Crystal Palace, only to run into a horde of dark servants and dark fiends.

The next image depicts hundreds of ships, the Teryn armada, all converging on Uhna, bombarding the ground with laser fire.

The next one displays the inside of the palace, where dark servants attack anyone who stumbles into their way. Servants, ma'hars, and ma'haras—the mindless creatures descend upon them without mercy. The Saage women, alongside their crown prince, fight against the tide of dark servants, a tiny group in the center of a raging storm.

I turn away from the carnage.

"You think this is terrible?" the Archgod of Chaos and Destruction says and squeezes his blood-smeared hand into a fist. "I haven't even started."

Suddenly the images show people all over Uhna falling to the ground, writhing in pain, as black tendrils of corruption infect them. The tendrils seep into their bodies, transforming them into dark servants or killing them outright.

Everyone, no matter their gender, age, or social status, shrieks in terror and pain, as corruption takes over. Black veins pulse on their tortured faces and graying bodies. Life and reason flee from their gaze. They fall down as humans, but they rise as dark servants.

"Stop!"

The archgod laughs and turns his attention inside the cavern. Onto the small group of my battered and exhausted friends.

"No! Don't!"

Black tendrils of his magic slam into each of them.

Arrov groans, doubles over, and drops his crossbow. His body twists and grows until he rises more than nine feet tall, as an ancient A'ice giant of old fables. His thick frame, covered in long light-blue hairs, bulges with tremendous muscles. Arrov roars, showing sharp white fangs the length of my hand.

Next, Glenna screams, throwing her head back in pain. Her hair turns fully white, her eyes gleaming mad, like a Turned. Then her hair turns back to crimson, her expression tortured, and her eyes full of fear. Still, she channels her healing magic, the blue ribbons of A'ris flowing into Father and Nic. Another wave of corruption hits her, turning her hair white again, making her chest bow. Ragnald grabs Glenna's shoulders, his eyes blazing with immense force, battling the spreading corruption.

Black threads of magic hit Callum and Teague. The men shrug as if they are in pain, and both transmogrify from one blink to the next. Callum stands tall, his face a perfect blend of ancient lyons, tigers, and wolves. Teague emerges too; his face is serpentine. His body is a mix of poisonous snakes from Evander, the terrible lyzards of Raghild, and dra'agons of old myths. He's covered with incandescent scales. A pair of wings that runs his full height open wide. A thick tail with thorns flicker behind him as he scans the ledge with slitted eyes.

When DLD focuses on Isa and Bella, I shout, "Just stop!"

CHAPTER 103

"Will you join me?" DLD asks.

I will never join his side willingly. I shake my head.

"Master, give me the power of an Ankhar!" Loch begs. "I will make her do whatever you need."

"No," DLD says. "If you won't join my side, Lumenian, then I have no choice but to take all your power by force. Just as I did with the other Lumenians. The essence of your magic will make me stronger than before."

I back away from him, but there is no escape from the stalagmite cage. Blindly, I reach for my magic, taking any threads of elements I can, blasting the archgod with them.

He bats away the elemental barrage with one hand. Thick tendrils of black Acerbus rise from the archgod, cutting through my magical torrent. Binding around my body like coils of a chain. The light elements retreat in reaction to the Acerbus's closeness. Gathering them is a struggle, as if I'm trying to pull molasses.

The rock platform and the stalagmite cage vibrate and shake as the pressure intensifies. With sheer force of will, I amass all the elemental magic in me. Building it up, until pain intensifies. Until my control is slipping. The explosion should destroy the platform. It's my only chance to take out DLD. None of us would survive the fall.

"I see what you're trying to do." From one blink to the next, the archgod is by me with a hand raised to strike. Sharp black talons burst from his fingertips. "But you are too late." He shoves his talons into my temple, sinking them deep. Into my soul.

CHAPTER 104

Agony, so much agony, threatens to shatter me as black strands of the archgod's magic burst forward, questing for my magical essence.

I push against the archgod, fighting him. Blood drips in rivulets from my eyes and ears. But the black strands of Acerbus speed through me.

"There it is," DLD says as the dark tendrils drill into the magical sphere.

My magical sphere rears against the intrusion but the Acerbus overpowers it.

The archgod begins to siphon my magic.

Unbearable pain, white hot and burning, cascades over me.

My knees give out.

Loch grabs me, holding me upright when my eyes roll back into my head.

CHAPTER 105

So this is it. This is how I'll die.

Failing to defeat the Archgod of Chaos and Destruction. Failing to protect my family. My friends. The refugees. My home world. Billions of innocents throughout the Seven Galaxies. All those deaths, all those sacrifices were for nothing. I'll never avenge my mom's murder now, or Deidre's.

I'll die as a failure.

My eyes are still closed, yet I see the satisfied face of the archgod in front of me as my magic seeps into the Archgod of Chaos and Destruction. Making him more powerful.

Trickles of warmth spread from my talisman on the back of my neck. Healing warmth spreads through my mind and body.

"It's not over," The Lady says, her voice drifting into my mind, "as long as you're fighting him."

But I can't. "Why did you lie to me about my mom's murderer?"

"We don't have much time to waste," the archgoddess says. "You cannot let him get your magic. You must defeat him. Use your power, my sybil. Use your Lumenian heritage. Stop him before it's too late."

Every time I use my magic, my control slips. I have nothing left to fight with.

"I can't. I am too weak."

The Lady's face appears in my mind, smiling with encouragement. "You are not weak, my child. You have your mother's persistent streak. She'd be proud of you."

"No. She wouldn't be. I killed her. With my claustrophobia. You should have picked someone else as your sybil." The joke is on me—there is no one else for The Lady to pick but me.

I should have listened to my mom. I never should have used my magic.

"Was your friend Glenna guilty for using her magic, which attracted the mages to her family?"

"No, she was only a child. Too young to understand what was happening," I say.

"Just as you were only a child." The Lady's hand touches my face, the gentlest and kindest warmth emanating from her palm. "My beloved child, this is your destiny. Accept your role and fight the Archgod of Chaos and Destruction."

She is right. I am the sybil. I am the last Lumenian.

"I need you to be true to yourself and fight for all you love."

Callum's face swims into my mind, and all doubt evaporates.

I strike the black tendrils of Acerbus away from my magic sphere. I gather as many elemental threads as I can. My magic obeys me, pliant, all the elements glowing like a beautiful rainbow as they rush to me, ready to burst out.

There is no more struggle. My control is absolute.

I open my eyes.

CHAPTER 106

The Archgod of Chaos and Destruction recoils with a cry of pain. He stumbles away from me, shaking his hands as if he just got stung.

My magic smolders under my skin like a torrent of the hottest lava. The silver markings on my back pulse to life, fueling my magic. Amplifying it.

"What's that on your neck?" DLD asks.

I form the mixed elemental magic into a deluge of vines. "It's time for you to meet the new sybil!"

"Give me the power of Ankhar, master!" Loch says. The archgod shoves his claws into Loch's chest.

Without hesitation, I let the magical flood loose.

Bright light in the hues of all of the five light elemental colors shine in a magnificent kaleidoscopic pattern, exploding over the archgod and Loch.

The magical blast takes all of the stalagmite cage out in a vast explosion, showering rubble everywhere.

I drop down, covering my head with my arms, protecting it.

When the dust clears, I straighten. This can't be!

CHAPTER 107

A terrible twelve-foot-tall nightmarish monster rises in place of Loch. Oily black smoke swirls around the monster, as if its power is still settling. Behind it sneers DLD, unaffected.

Dark gray muscles bulge on the Ankhar's colossal body, covered with patches of fur in some places. In others, raw muscle and sinew shine, oozing black slime. His head, larger than my torso, is fanned with black horns that curve inward, pointing down into its horrible face. A face that reminds me of A'ice bears and devastating ancient mythological dra'agons. Its elongated maw is filled with sharp fangs in multiple rows. Its massive body stands on four legs like thick tree trunks. A multipronged tail flicks behind it, covered with black bone-spikes running all the way to its back.

Involuntarily, I retreat a step, then another.

A rock thorn jabs into my back just as the stalagmite cage re-forms around us, accommodating the monster's new size.

The beast's eyes, like huge black orbs, track my movements.

Reaching into my magical sphere, I pull up elemental threads, shaping them into hundreds of daggers. Like a barrage, I lob them at the Ankhar.

The elemental magic shots hit the beast, slamming into it. Each one whipping its face from side to side, like physical punches. Forcing it back a few steps, but not enough for it to hit the stalagmite cage.

Breathing hard, I double over, panting from exertion.

The Ankhar growls, looking no worse than before. It swipes at me with a massive arm. I dodge to the left, nearly running into one of the rock spikes.

It swipes again.

I dodge to the right, but the monster anticipates my move. I run straight into its slashing paw.

Enormous claws rip into my side, leaving weeping gashes behind.

The sybil talisman struggles to heal the damage. Pain floods my body and I stumble.

Callum roars, an ear-shattering and outraged sound.

I reach into my magical sphere and grab multiple threads of A'qua. I shape them into jagged shards and throw them at the beast.

They bounce off of him without any effect. Why isn't my magic working?

The beast whips its spiked tail at my head.

I duck, but not low enough. Spikes tear strands of hair out of my scalp. Blood pours into my eyes, blinding me, and I cry out in pain.

A huge paw slams into me, piercing deep into my body, tearing a scream from me.

I wipe the blood out of my eyes as the beast lifts me up.

"Is this how a legendary Lumenian fights?" the Ankhar asks, the words perfect in its deformed maw. "Where is your legendary power? I should have killed you along with your mother. I won't make the same mistake again."

Agony shoots through my body as the monster tightens its grip, digging deeper. Crushing my bones.

I pull a thick thread of Lume from my magical sphere, shaping it into a spear.

"You want Lumenian power?" I release the Lume magic, aiming it into its open maw. "You shall have it!"

It tears through him, taking most of its throat and lower jaw off.

The Ankhar chokes. It drops me and claws at the gaping hole, gurgling.

I roll to my feet, ready to jump out of its way.

A piercing death shriek echoes through the cavern. The monster vibrates as if all of its atoms have been aggravated by Lume. Then it explodes into a thick, oily smoke, leaving behind the naked and bleeding corpse of Loch Ramor.

I look up, right into the Archgod of Chaos and Destruction's bewildered eyes, gathering more of my magic. "Here's a taste of consequence!"

CHAPTER 108

Thrusting all of my Lume power into a magical spear, I aim at the archgod. DLD's eyes widen, terror shining in their depths.

I let my Lume spear fly.

The archgod explodes into a column of smoke before my magical spear could hit him. The skin of his mortal body falls to the ground as he bursts through the ceiling of the cavern, shattering it.

"Godsdammit!" I scream.

Rock spikes of the stalagmite cage rain down, shaking the platform. I dive out of the way, landing on the ground.

Suddenly the platform tilts on its side. I claw the ground for hold, my nails breaking off. I slide over the edge of the shaking platform, catching the ledge with bleeding fingers at the last minute and dangling off it.

The cavern quakes as if it's imploding now that DLD's hold is gone.

With straining muscles, I pull myself up a few inches before falling back with a cry. All my wounds catch up, leaving me with no strength.

My fingertips slip. I close my eyes as I plummet into the gaping canyon.

Callum's agonized roar tears at my heart.

I'm sorry, Callum.

Before I lose consciousness, the prayer to The Lady drifts through my mind: *We are made of light, and we will return to Lume at the end of our time. We are made of light . . .*

CHAPTER 109

"Wake up," a distant yet familiar voice says, breaking into the darkness of this unconscious place.

I groan, trying to open my eyes, but to no avail. My body feels as if it's been through a grinder.

"Wake up," the voice repeats, with more urgency. I recognize that voice: Callum.

Waves of pain reverberate through every part of my body. I want to wake up, but it's so difficult. It's much easier to drift toward the light. Toward Lume.

I try to swallow so I can answer, but my throat clicks with a dry sound. Unconsciousness threatens to pull me under again. My body seems to float. *We are made of light, and we will return to Lume at the end of our time.*

"Come back to me, Lilla!" Callum says. Something sharp jabs into the base of my neck. Cold liquid is forced into a vein. Shattering the pull of the light. Tethering me to the here and now.

My heart drums in my chest. A rapid *Bam! Bam! Bam!* Frantically at first, then gradually slower.

My eyes flutter open to see an angular face framed by short black hair. The hair doesn't cover the long and jagged scar that runs from the edge of his left eyebrow all the way to his jaw. A lopsided smile stretches kissable lips, and intense blue eyes gaze lovingly at me.

"I thought I lost you there," Callum says, relief clear in his voice. He leans down and kisses me gently.

I return his kiss, hugging him close, inhaling his scents of sun and desert. We survived.

EPILOGUE

The next few days pass in a blur.

Father lived, but Nic didn't. We buried my brother next to Mom, as he would have liked.

I released all the refugees who ended up working in the crystal mines against their will. I visited every camp, opening their gates. Giving freedom to all. A choice to stay as Uhnan citizens or move on to another world as free travelers.

A heartbroken Glenna and the twins supported me and kept me company. Just as they are with me now, as we return to Fye Island. Back to the ruins of the Crystal Palace. I am meeting Callum, who's been dealing with the Teryn praelor, keeping the emperor from further destroying my home world.

The two suns set, painting the wide wooden entrance doors in a vermilion-yellow light. They are just about the only things left intact of the palace, surviving miraculously.

I enter after Glenna and the twins.

Callum stands with his back toward me, talking to Teague, who's eating an apple.

My pulse picks up and I break into a run.

The twins giggle, while Glenna shouts after me, "Don't run, Lilla! It's too soon for your injuries!" As if to prove her right, my side starts hurting, forcing me to slow after only a few steps.

Callum turns in time to catch me when I jump into his arms. He lifts me off my feet and embraces me in a tight hug. "I missed you."

"I've missed you too." I kiss him, holding his face in my hands.

A light blue mound moves on our right, and I pull away. It waves. "Don't mind me," Arrov, still in his A'ice giant form, grumbles.

"I doubt they do," Teague says around a large bite.

Ragnald hurries in. "Glenna, you are not supposed to be out unsupervised with, um, your condition." He stops next to an embarrassed Glenna. Holding on to her shoulder, he channels his magic into her.

She tucks the thick white strand of hair—the reminder of her run-in with DLD—behind her ear and bats his hand away. "I'm fine, I'm fine. Stop fussing."

But she isn't fine. Gone is the happy, confident healer. Glenna is constantly on edge, beyond what is normal for grief, fighting the seed of corruption that has taken root. Without Ragnald's relentless administrations, she could end up turned. I know how much she hates depending on a mage's help, but she has no other choice.

The double doors burst open. Xor treads through. "Where is your father? Where is the ma'ha hiding?"

Callum hugs my shoulders as we turn to face the ex-rebellion leader. "I see you're fine after all," I say. He was nowhere to be found after the battle, leaving the refugees to their own devices. "Come to repent?"

"I demand that the ma'ha hand Fye Island over to me!" Xor says, his face flushed a feverish dark green. "I am the rightful owner! My ancestors were here before yours; those space pirates kicked them off this island. There is proof in the tunnels, under Refugee Camp Seven. It's full of cave paintings. This island is mine and—"

So that's why he had those tunnels dug. "You can have it." I was right. That stick figure *did* have three eyes.

Xor stutters, "Don't you dare dismiss me!"

A gateway opens next to us, and Belthair steps through.

Unaware of the newcomer, Xor continues, "Don't try to trick me with dishonorable assurances. "I have rights and I want it in writing—"

Belthair grasps Xor's shoulder and punches him in the face with a vicious hook. "This is for abandoning the refugees," he says. Then he punches Xor again. "This is for Jorha." And again. "And this is for using Lilla."

Xor's eyes roll back. Belthair drops the unconscious ex-rebellion leader to the ground.

"I came as fast as I could when I heard," Belthair says, wiping all six of his hands, "that he was heading here."

"That's great—" I say, only to be interrupted by the double doors bursting open. Again.

This time a tall, muscular man, who looks like an older version of Callum, strides through, wearing the black uniform of a Teryn warrior. His expression is thunderous as he heads toward our small group.

Teague's eyes widen, and he drops his apple. "Oh, boy."

"Who is he?" I ask.

Callum curses under his breath. "The Teryn praelor."

Oh, no! "What is he going to do now?" I ask Callum, but he just stares with hands in fists at the older man. Who nearly destroyed Uhna. What more could the praelor want with us?

Teague turns to me with a mischievous light in his eyes. "If only there was someone here who could invoke an old tradition."

Could I do it? Should I do it?

"You don't have to do anything you're not sure of," Callum says. "I don't want you to feel pressured—"

"I remember what you said to me," I say and place my hand on his cheek, interrupting him. "Do you still remember?"

Callum clasps my hand. "I remember."

"Did you mean it?"

"Every word of it," Callum says and kisses my palm. "I love you, Lilla."

"Callum, I have you, uh—"

"No!" the Teryn praelor bellows. "Stop this insanity right now!"

Teague whispers helpfully, and I repeat it, "By the tradition of the bride's choice."

Callum leans down, his breath mingling with mine. "Are you claiming me?"

I rise on my toes and whisper against his lips, "I love you, too."

ACKNOWLEDGMENTS

When I started on the journey to write this story, I thought it would only take two years to finish. It's a good thing I didn't know it would take six years...

Here are all the fortunate ones (or unfortunate – it really is in the eye of the beholder) who encountered this story over those six looong years. I hope I remember all of you (I mean, I am not getting any younger here).

Thank you, my wonderful read and critique group: Tammy, Shannon, Rhianna, Dahlia, Carla, Terri, Neal, Steve, Arend, Dave and many others, for all the laughs and inspiring comments.

Thank you, Marni, for being so awesome and patient.

Thank you, La Jolla Writer's Conference, for the warm and encouraging workshops. You taught me that not every writer's conference has to be terrifying.

Thank you, John Truby, for revitalizing revisions and providing a trustworthy roadmap out of madness. After five rewrites, it was much appreciated.

Thank you, Matt, for the valiant effort to prevent the bad eating habits from taking effect. It was an uphill battle from the start.

Thank you, Leslie, for the first look at the content. Your encouragement and insight was much appreciated.

Thank you, Julie and William, for the amazing editing you both provided – more than once!

Thank you, Dan and Natasha, from NY Book Editors – your help of ensuring everything running smoothly was invaluable.

Thank you, Mario, the best project manager and mentor in the whole Galaxy One.

Thank you, Melissa, the best assistant and friend in the whole Galaxy Two.

Thank you, Clif, the best map designer in the whole Galaxy Three.

Thank you, Tim, the best cover artist extraordinaire in the whole Galaxy Four.

Thank you, Stephanie (karate sensei), Elizabeth (leader of tutors), Lydia (magnificent illustrator who read it in 5 hrs.), Marty (retired ranger), Ruth (Marty's wife), Patty and Peggy (twin scientists who reread it without forcing them at laser gun point), Japi (great brunch companion), Brian (young man in his 20s who likes reading Sci-Fi & Fantasy), Harry (Harley Davidson biker and Marty's neighbor). You are the best beta readers in the whole Galaxy Five.

Thank you, Ray and Abigail, the best web design wizards in the whole Galaxy Six.

Thank You, dear readers, for being the BEST READERS in the whole Seven Galaxies. It is not an easy job and definitely not for the fainthearted. Congrats to you all!

Last but not least, thank you God, for giving me the weirdest brain – it does have a use after all.

Family – see dedication page. (I love you but no need to be attention hogs.)

GLOSSARY

A

Aice – Rich world where winter rules nine months a year. It is part of the Pax Septum Coalition.

Amra, Queen – Queen of A'ice, mother of Arrov.

Arrov, Prince – Seventh son of Queen Amra, a great pilot. From A'ice. Very handsome.

B

Beathag, Ma'hara – Ex-best friend of Lilla.

Belthair, Captain – A six-armed rebel, ex-boyfriend of Lilla.

C

Callum A'ruun, Second War General in the Teryn army – An imposing Teryn warrior and general. Handsome, too.

Coalition, Pax Septum – A nineteen-planet-strong coalition with Uhna its capital.

Crystal or Crystalline – A transparent crystal that is used in the crystal necklace.

Crystal Diamonds – Most valuable export of Uhna.

Crystal Necklace – A necklace with a crystalline, or crystal for short. It is a personal computing and communication device. The shape of the crystal and the color of the chain signal status. Lilla's necklace is a hexagonal shaped crystal on platinum chain = ruling house; diamond-shaped crystal on a platinum chain = high society; a square-shaped crystal on gold chain = low society; a circlularly shaped crystal on a gold chain = all civilians; crescent-shaped crystal on a bronze chain = servants such as Glenna.

The back of the crystal is etched with blooming trees and star flowers that represent house families. This helps to identifying the heir of each house.

Crystal Palace – The palace where the ruling family lives. It has crystal diamonds embedded into its walls, hence the name.

D

Deidre – A mother figure for Lilla and head chef. She makes amazing boomberry tarts.

DLD – The Dark Lord of Destruction—the favored nickname of the Archgod of Chaos and Destruction.

E

Eilish – Lilla's mom. A Lumenian.

Ellar, Ma'har – high adviser to the king. Very smart.

Era War – A devastating and recurring galactic war between the two ruling archgods that happens when the imbalance of power between them becomes too great.

F

Fearghas, Battle Horse – He is Lilla's powerful horse. He can swim well.

Fye Island – The name of the island where the Crystal Palace is.

Fyoon Ocean – The name of the ocean on Uhna.

G

Gertrude – A huge spider that likes to visit Glenna ever since she saved it. Has a paralyzing gaze.

Glenna – Best friend of Lilla and a talented healer.

H

Houses – There are three types of houses on Uhna: ruling house, high society house and low society house. Each has a territory and jobs assigned to them.

I

Irvine, Ma'har – The overseer of refugee affairs. Not a nice person.

J

Jokes – You will find many in the story . . . some cheesier than the others.

Jorha – Lieutenant in the rebellion. Lilla knows her.

K

King Niall, Ma'ha – Lilla's father.

L

Loch, Ramor – Mysterious person. See story.

Lumenian – Legendary race that the Archgoddess of the Eternal Light and Order created. They don't like dark servants.

M

Ma'ha – Title: King

Ma'har – Title: Lord

Ma'hara – Title: Lady

Ma'hata – Title: Queen

Murtagh, Captain – Captain of the guard, father of Jorha. He is a nice person, too.

N

Nasty Beast – Fearghas's nickname he earned by biting others and being not so nice.

Nic – Lilla's half brother. He is great.

O

Omnipower – An unknown power that governs the Seven Galaxies.

Overseer of Refugee Affairs – That's Irvine as I said before. Pay attention.

P

Praelor – Title: Emperor

Q

Queen – Uhna has no queen.

R

Refugees, Camp Seven – A camp full of refugees from all over the Seven Galaxies. Also, the secret location for the rebellion.

S

Seven Galaxies – It is the name of the universe this story plays out in. There are seven galaxies in it: Galaxy One, Galaxy Two, etc. It's a pretty big place.

Sha'll – A derogatory term for servants. Lilla's great-grandfather forbade its use.

T

Teryn – It is the name of the world Callum is from and the name of its people.

The Lady – This is the nickname of the Archgoddess of Eternal Light and Order.

The Twins – Isa and Bella are known as The Twins. They are great hackers and are from Barabal.

U

Uhna – The home world of Lilla's. It's oceanic, with lots of islands.

Umbrea Gauntlets – These worn leather gauntlets, four of them, were snuggled in by Xor. They are for short distance travel with a maximum capacity of two people. They open up a gateway that seems to consist of swirling shadows.

V

Valiant Effort – Is what it took to compose this long glossary . . .

W

War, Era – See under Era War.

X

Xor – The leader of the rebellion. He has three eyes but keeps the third closed for most of the time.

Y

A letter in the ABC. Also, short for why.

Z

Zillion Dark Servants – A lot of dark servants. Really.

AWARDS

2020 New York Book Festival
Winner: Romance
Honorable Mention: Science Fiction

2020 San Francisco Book Festival
Winner: Science Fiction

2020 Annual Best Book Awards
Winner: Best Cover-Fiction

2020 New England Book Festival
Winner: Science Fiction

@SGBlaiseAuthor

/thelastlumenian

sgblaiseofficial

www.thelastlumenian.com